# THE RETURN OF THE REBEL

**BY**
**JENNIFER FAYE**

In another life **Jennifer Faye** was a statistician. She still has a love for numbers, formulas and spreadsheets, but when she was presented with the opportunity to follow her lifelong passion and spend her days writing and pursuing her dream of becoming a Mills & Boon author, she couldn't pass it up. These days, when she's not writing, Jennifer enjoys reading, fine needlework, quilting, Tweeting and cheering on the Pittsburgh Penguins. She lives in Pennsylvania with her amazingly patient husband, two remarkably talented daughters and their two very spoiled fur babies, otherwise known as cats—but *shh…* don't tell them they're not human!

Jennifer loves to hear from readers—you can contact her via her website: www.jenniferfaye.com

In honor of my grandmother…

An amazing woman who had the patience to teach a very eager and curious little kid how to work a needle and thread. In the process she taught me that with perseverance you can achieve your dreams, whether they be big or small

# CHAPTER ONE

"You won't regret giving me this opportunity."

*And hopefully neither will I.*

Cleo Sinclair kept the worrisome thought to herself as she held her cheery smile in place. With the meeting at last over, she sailed out of the office of the vice president of player development, barely remembering to pull the door closed behind her. Away from Mr. Burns's cool demeanor and skeptical stare, she rotated her shoulders, easing the tension.

At the end of the hall, the elevator chimed and the door opened, allowing an employee to exit. Cleo stepped up her pace and slipped into the open car. Her pink manicured nail pressed the button for the main floor. Once the doors swished shut, the air whooshed out of her lungs and she leaned against the wall for support.

Step one was done. She had the job, albeit on a trial basis. Now on to step number two.

She had to prove to the ever-doubting Mr. Burns that she was up to his challenge. She could and would bring in wealthy clientele eager to gamble at one of Las Vegas's most luxurious establishments, the Glamour Hotel and Casino.

A glance at her image in the polished doors had her adjusting her cheery yellow dress, which dipped a little lower than she'd like. When she'd worked in the accounting department, her attire hadn't been so important. But now working the front-end of the casino, everything about her appearance mattered. She smoothed her hands over the skirt. It wasn't the fanciest outfit she'd ever stitched. In fact, she'd worried that she'd made a mistake by choosing to wear it, but with each compliment from her fellow employees, her nervousness had eased... That was, until her meeting.

She halted her rambling thoughts and inhaled a deep breath.

It was too late to second-guess herself. The train had left the station. The ship had sailed. Oh heck, it didn't matter what phrase she used. Her plan was in motion. And she would succeed.

After all, she'd just put her entire future on the line. There was no going back. No changing her mind. If this arrangement didn't work, she couldn't stay in Vegas nor would she be able to return home to Wyoming.

The elevator doors silently slid open, revealing lush carpeting leading to the casino area. The soft lighting added to the ambiance while the blinking lights on the slot machines lured guests to try their luck at winning a fortune. Without windows or clocks, minutes stretched into hours. In fact, she had found herself losing track of time on the numerous occasions she'd spent on the floor training for this promotion.

A cheer echoed through the room and she glanced around to see an excited crowd at the craps table. The palpable energy charged the room. Someone must be on a roll of luck. She hoped this would be her lucky day, too.

As of yet, her whale, the big client, hadn't checked in. The VP himself would be greeting the guest and then he'd phone her when her presence was required. Her boss had gone over the guest's preferences, including his favorite game—blackjack. Her job was to keep the whale happy by comping his meals and getting him tickets to whatever shows he preferred. But the utmost important thing was to maintain this guest's privacy, above and beyond their normal discretion. Even she didn't know his name yet.

With her family's ranch deep in debt, this was her only chance to chip in and prove to them that she was still a Sinclair. And she was doing what any Sinclair would do—taking a necessary calculated risk and making sure it paid off.

She wanted to be close by, so she headed for the China Cup, a little coffee shop just on the other side of the reception area. Her mouth watered in anticipation of her first sip of a mocha java latte. Her steps came faster and when her blue suede heels hit the marble floor by the front doors, they made a rapid staccato sound.

A line of guests waiting to check in trailed past the sculpted fountain, blocking her passage. She paused, finding the line almost reached the entrance. They must be here for the car convention that opened today. It was the biggest event along the strip. The hotel had sold out months in advance. This would be an ideal time for her to fish for new clients—if only Mr. Burns didn't have her on such a short leash, insisting she cater to this one whale only.

"Hey, buddy," grouched a man near the front of the line, "how about moving aside?"

"Yeah," chorused a screechy female voice. "The rest of us have reservations."

Shouts and complaints rippled through the lushly decorated lobby.

Cleo glanced at the front desk to find one employee on duty. What in the world? There were supposed to be three people helping with check-in, but the only person standing there was Lynn, their newest hire. The girl was so green that she made the grass on the eighteen-hole golf course look dull and grayish. Why would they leave her alone at the front desk, today of all days?

"There has to be a mistake." Rising frustration laced the voice of the man standing at the counter.

But it was more than the angry tone that drew Cleo's attention. A note of recognition chimed in the far recesses of her mind. She craned her neck for a better look. Only the back of his short brown hair and his blue-and-white-striped collared shirt were visible. She knew that voice, but from where?

She glanced around, hoping to find someone qualified to assist the now flustered desk clerk. When Cleo didn't see any hotel employees moving in to help, she stepped forward. The least she could do was maintain crowd control until someone showed up to help with registration.

"Check again." The man's posture was rigid. "It's under Joe Smith."

"I am, sir." Lynn studied the computer monitor. "I can't locate your name in our system."

"Call your supervisor."

"I—I can't. She's just left. She's ill."

"Then call her boss. Surely there's someone around here who knows what's going on."

While Lynn frantically stabbed at the phone pad trying to reach someone to straighten out things, Cleo stepped up behind the disgruntled man. He didn't notice her as he leaned both elbows on the counter, peering at the computer monitor. Her gaze slid over his broad shoulders to his tapered waist, where his jeans accentuated his finer assets. Realizing what she was doing, she jerked her attention upward.

"Excuse me, sir. Can I help?"

When the man straightened, he was much taller than

she'd anticipated. As he turned to her, she found herself straightening her spine and lifting her chin. His assessing glance sent a shiver of awareness down her arms. She shook off the sensation. Obviously she'd been concentrating on the problems with her family and her job a little too much. It had been years since a man had such an effect on her. Not since…

Jax Monroe!

His cool blue-gray gaze met and held hers. The chatter of excited voices and the jingle of the slot machines faded into the background. Her breath caught as she waited for a sign of recognition. But none came. No smile. No hug. Nothing. What was up with that?

She smiled at him. "Hey, Jax. Still making trouble, I see."

He made a point of checking out the ID badge pinned to her chest. Was it just her imagination or was he taking longer than necessary to verify her name?

"Jax, it hasn't been that many years. You've got to recognize me."

Sure she'd changed some, but so had he. His long brown hair had been cut off. Her fingers itched to brush over the supershort strands. And his face was now pale instead of the tanned complexion she recalled—back when they spent most of their time outdoors.

But not everything about him had changed. If you knew to look for it, there was still a little scar that threaded along his jaw. She clearly remembered the day he'd gotten it. They'd been fishing at the creek. He'd been goofing off when he'd slipped and fallen on rocks. He'd clambered back upright and laughed at himself until she'd pointed out he was bleeding.

They'd practically grown up together…even if he was five years her senior. Hope Springs, Wyoming, was a very small town and it was great seeing someone from home.

It'd been so long since she'd been there. And her last visit had been such a nightmare—

Her throat tightened. Could that be the answer? It might explain why he was acting as if he didn't know her. Even though he'd left Hope Springs years ago, it was possible he kept in contact with someone from there. Her stomach churned. Did he know about what she'd done?

"Jax, stop acting like you could forget the girl who used to follow you to our favorite watering hole."

"I think you must have me mistaken for someone else." He turned his back to her and waited while the clerk spoke in hushed tones on the phone.

Mistaken? Not a chance. She'd know those baby blues anywhere. They could still make her heart flutter with just a glance.

Even with the passage of time and some outward changes, it was impossible he'd forget her. She'd had a teenage crush on him of megaproportions. To say she thought the sun rose and set around him was putting it mildly. She'd have done anything for him. She *had* done anything for him, including lying. So whatever he had going on with this alias of his, she refused to lie for him again. Not here. Not when she could lose her job and so much more.

"Stop acting like you don't recognize me. We need to talk—"

He glanced over his shoulder at her. His eyes darkened and his voice lowered. "No, we don't."

"Your name is Jax Monroe. You're from Hope Springs, Wyoming—"

"Stop." He turned fully around. "You aren't going to let this drop, are you?"

She crossed her arms and shook her head. When his eyes flared, she realized she'd made the wrong move. Her arms pushed up on her chest, which was now peeking out from the diving neckline. She wanted to change positions but stubborn pride held her in place. Let him look. Maybe now he'd realize what he'd missed out on when he'd brushed off her inexperienced kiss and skipped town without a backward glance.

Jax Monroe couldn't help but stare at Cleo—all grown-up and filled out in the right places. Long wavy honey-gold locks just begged for him to run his fingers through them to see if they were as soft as they appeared. Wow! If he had known how hot she'd turn out, he might have reconsidered returning to Hope Springs. After all, she'd had a crush on him that was apparent to everyone in their hometown… But then he recalled how young she'd been back then—much too young for him.

And now, as much as her body had grown and changed from the gangly teenager he'd once known, there were other parts of her that were annoyingly the same. She still spoke her mind at the most inopportune time and without any thought of who might be listening.

What in the world had made him think that flying across the country to hide in plain sight was such a good idea? On second thought, maybe he should have stuck it out in New York until it was time for his courtroom testimony. But he'd already made his choice. And now that he was here, he was looking forward to seeing if Lady Luck was still on his side.

Now if only he could just get Cleo to quiet down before she revealed his identity to everyone in the hotel. Frustration bubbled in his veins as he considered clamping his hand over her pink glossy lips. Then a more tempting thought came to mind of how he might silence her—lip to lip.

One look at the agitation reflected in her eyes and he knew she'd slap him if he dared kiss her. Definitely not a viable option, even if Cleo wasn't his best friend's kid sister. Kurt had been the one guy who'd always accepted him as is—the same guy who'd saved his bacon more than once when he'd acted out after his old man had called him a good-for-nothing mooch. The only thing Kurt had ever asked of him was to keep his hands off his little sis.

Jax smiled as he recalled Cleo with knobby knees, freckles and a long ponytail. Boy had things changed. She was smooth and polished like a piece of fine art.

Cleo's green eyes narrowed. "Am I amusing you?"

"Um, no." He struggled to untangle his muddled thoughts. "I take it by your name tag that you work here."

Lines creased between her fine brows. "What's the matter with you? Have you been drinking?"

"What? Of course not." He'd watched his father live his life out of a scotch bottle and the way his mother tried to please him, with no luck. Jax refused to follow in his father's unhappy footsteps. "I don't drink."

"So why are you calling yourself Joe Smith?"

"Let's talk over there. Out of the way." He pointed to the edge of the counter, away from the incoming guests.

She turned to observe the long line before following him. "I don't know what game you're playing, but I won't let you cause trouble here."

"Lower your voice." Luckily no one appeared to notice them or their conversation. The guests were more interested in the arrival of an additional desk clerk than in what Cleo had to say. "I promise you I'm not here for any nefarious reason."

"Why should I believe you? I covered for you when you 'borrowed' the school mascot and when you pulled those numerous other pranks. I know the trouble you can cause."

"You've got to trust me."

She arched a disbelieving brow. "Says who?"

Little Cleo had certainly gained some spunk. Well, good for her. It was also a relief to know she wasn't still carrying that crazy torch for him. The last thing he needed at this critical juncture of his life was more complications.

Her finger poked his chest. "You're up to something and I want to know what it is." Her tone brooked no room for debate. He wouldn't be wiggling out of this confrontation with some flimsy story. "You can start by explaining your need for an alias."

"Just leave it be."

She shook her head. "I can't look the other way. We aren't kids anymore. This is where I work and I can't let you jeopardize my job." Cleo's voice rose with every word. "But if you turn around and leave now, we can forget we ever saw each other."

He doubted he'd ever be able to wipe her sexy image from his memory. Her polished persona stole his breath away. She may have been a cute kid, but she'd grown up to be a real knockout. And as for leaving here now, he wasn't about to do it. He had as much right to be here as anyone else.

Cleo leveled her shoulders and tapped her foot. He hated to tell her but if she was angling for an intimidating pose, she'd missed her mark. She was more alluring than scary.

"Don't make me call for security."

Heads were turning in their direction. The very last thing he wanted was to become a spectacle for the masses. "You wouldn't do that to an old friend, would you?"

"A few minutes ago you didn't even know me."

He raked his fingers through his hair. Back in New York when he'd started receiving phone calls where the person at the other end wouldn't speak, followed by notes warning him not to testify, this vacation had sounded like the perfect plan. What could be better than getting lost in a crowd while testing his luck at the blackjack table?

Ever since the assets of his investment firm had been frozen by the government until the trial was completed, he'd missed the rush of working the stock market—the flood of adrenaline. He'd hoped Vegas would give him a similar high—a chance to feel truly alive again instead of living his life from one medical test to the next.

When his doctor gave him the green light, he'd picked a spot on the map far from New York and booked a plane ticket. He'd requested an alias be used while he was at the Glamour just as a precaution. But he had no idea how much of that he should tell Cleo. If only she would trust him…for old times' sake.

"What's going on here?" A short, round man in a business suit approached them. He glanced at Cleo. "Do you intend to interrogate all of the casino's important guests in the middle of the lobby?"

Her expression morphed from frustration to one of shock. Her gaze moved back and forth between the two men as though waiting for an explanation.

When none came, she said, "But he is—"

"Your client. And you will treat him with respect." The man turned to Jax and held out his hand. "Hello, Mr. Smith. I'm Mr. Burns. We spoke on the phone. Let's talk someplace a little more private." He led them to a hallway just off the casino's main floor and into an empty office. "I think there must have been some sort of mix-up. I'll see about getting you a new casino host."

Jax's gaze moved to Cleo. Beneath the makeup her face had taken on a sickly pallor. And her eyes held a deer-in-headlights panic. His initial instinct was to ride to her rescue. She'd always been the one to offer him a helping hand all those years ago back in Hope Springs. There was a strange satisfaction in seeing the roles reversed. But that was then, and this was now.

And it only complicated matters that he couldn't keep his eyes off this grown-up version of her. She was no longer too young for him. In fact, the reasons he had to keep her at arm's length became more muddled the longer he was around her. It was best to end things right here. After all, it wasn't as if the man was going to fire her over this.

# CHAPTER TWO

THIS COULDN'T BE HAPPENING.

Jax was her whale?

How was she supposed to have anticipated that? The last time she'd seen him, he barely had two coins to rub together. And now he was an important player in Las Vegas. How exactly did that happen?

Cleo's gaze shifted between the men. Neither of them seemed to notice that she was in the room. Did they think they could decide her future without even so much as consulting her? She wasn't about to let that happen.

"No other host is needed." Both men turned. She leveled a determined stare at each man before continuing to make her point. "Mr. Burns, you misunderstood what you overheard. Jax and I are old friends."

Her boss turned a questioning gaze to Jax. "Is this true?"

Cleo begged Jax with her eyes to back her up. After all, he owed her.

As the quietness stretched on, Cleo shifted her weight from one foot to the other. What was Jax thinking? His silence was even worse than any words he could say. She had to do something, anything, to keep from being canned for arguing with a MVP. Jax? A whale? The world could certainly be a strange place at times.

Cleo turned to face her disapproving boss. "We both come from the same small town in Wyoming."

Mr. Burns crossed his arms. "And do you always treat people from your hometown with such hostility?"

"I wasn't—"

Her boss's bushy brows arched. "I know what I heard."

"But you misunderstood—"

"Enough." Mr. Burns's hand sliced through the air. "I will deal with you later. Go wait for me in my office."

She hated being dismissed as if she was a child. She hated the thought of walking away with things unresolved, but she didn't want to make things worse... But then again could they get any worse? It was almost a certainty that when Mr. Burns joined her it would be to dismiss her. Not even a full day in her new position and she was being fired.

As she started for the door, her thoughts turned to her family. Even before learning of her family's financial problems, she'd made plans to transfer to the casino floor. She was bored senseless working in the accounting department. To think she left the family ranch because the work was isolating and she'd ended up taking a position where she spent her days alone in an eight-by-eight cubicle where silence was the status quo.

But then one day out of the blue her brother had called. She'd been so happy to hear from a family member. She hadn't heard a word from them since the funeral.

However, Kurt hadn't phoned with the intent of mending fences. He had news—bad news. The ranch was in arrears on its mortgage. And considering her Ivy League tuition was in large part the reason the ranch had been mortgaged in the first place, he thought she might want to help save their heritage.

The news totally blindsided her. Never once in her life had she imagined that the family had money problems.

And to know that she was about to be condemned for yet another Sinclair tragedy was not something she could let happen. She could not change the past, but going forward, she hoped to bridge the gap with her family.

Her fingers gripped the cold metallic door handle. One thought rose above the others: Sinclairs do not give up. No matter what.

Her grandfather had taught her that the first time she'd gotten thrown from a horse. If you wanted to succeed, you had to get back in the saddle and ride. That's what Sinclairs did—roughed things out.

She leveled her shoulders, released the door handle and turned. "Mr. Burns, you're right." His eyes lit up as though he was shocked by her bold confession. But before he could utter a word she rushed on. "Jax and I were having a disagreement. However, at the time I had no idea he was your special guest. I merely thought he was—"

"Here to check up on her for her big brother." Jax stepped between them to gain Mr. Burns's full attention.

At last, Jax found his voice, but why now? What convinced him to finally come to her aid?

The answers would have to wait. His motives paled in comparison to her losing her job and letting her family down…again. At the moment, she didn't have much choice but to go along with his fabricated story.

"That's right," she chimed in, trying to sound as genuine as possible. "And I didn't want Jax reporting back to my family about what I've been up to since moving away."

Surprisingly Mr. Burns's lips lifted at the corners as amusement danced in his dark eyes. "Let me guess, your family doesn't know that you've been working in a casino and they wouldn't approve of it."

This time she didn't have to lie. "That pretty much sums it up. They are old-fashioned in their beliefs."

Mr. Burns's eyes narrowed. "Then unless you're planning to find another job, I suggest you treat all of Glamour's guests with a pleasant demeanor."

She forced a smile on her face. "Of course. It was just a mix-up."

Mr. Burns turned to Jax. "The question still remains… Would you like me to assign you another host?"

He rubbed the dark scruff on his jaw. "No. Cleo and I will be fine. And we have some catching up to do."

Mr. Burns's gaze shifted between them as though making up his mind. "If that is your wish, Cleo will remain as your host. I have you set up in our most exclusive residence." He handed Jax the key card. "The bungalow should provide you with the privacy you're seeking. Cleo can show you the way. Do you need anything else?"

"Not at this time. I'm sure if something comes up Cleo will be able to take care of it."

Mr. Burns nodded. "But remember, I'm just a phone call away."

"Thank you." Jax extended his hand to the man.

After they shook hands, Mr. Burns moved past her, pausing long enough to say softly, "One more slipup and you're done."

A cold chill ran down her spine. The man had it in for her ever since the episode that occurred shortly after she'd started working in the accounting department. She'd pointed out some irregularities in his expense account, which were subsequently rectified.

Still, rumors were circulating that the only reason Mr. Burns had agreed to the promotion was because it was an all-or-nothing proposition. Either she was successful at endearing the high rollers to gamble at the Glamour Hotel and Casino or she was out on the street. And without a good reference, no other business on the strip would touch her.

"Don't worry. I'll make sure Jax is well cared for." She pasted on a smile, hoping it would suffice.

"I would expect nothing less."

The irritating note of superiority in Mr. Burns's voice grated on her razor-thin nerves. If the man hadn't been so eager to please Jax, she would be out on the curb right now. The fact she felt indebted to Jax ate at her.

With the door firmly shut, Cleo turned to Jax. Her mouth moved but the words wouldn't come. At last, she ground out, "Thank you."

His brows rose in surprise. "You're welcome. But the part I don't understand is why your brother didn't mention that you are working here in Vegas—"

"You've been talking to Kurt?" The thought left her unsettled.

Jax nodded. "We've kept in touch since I left Hope Springs."

Why was this the first she'd heard of it? Kurt was five years her senior, but she'd been closest to him out of all four of her brothers. When she'd needed someone to talk to, he was the one she'd turned to. So how had she missed hearing about Jax?

She tilted her chin and met his gaze. "You know, it's funny he's never mentioned you since you skipped town."

"Maybe he thought it was for the best."

"Why would he think that?"

Jax gave her a do-you-really-need-to-ask-that-question look. "As I recall, his kid sister had a massive crush on me—the kid from the wrong side of the tracks. I'm guessing he wouldn't want you having anything further to do with me."

Heat flamed in her chest and licked at her cheeks. "That was a long time ago. You can't fault me for my lack of judgment. I was just a kid. I've grown up since then."

"Trust me, I've noticed."

The implication of his words only multiplied her discomfort. Why was she letting him get her worked up? Back then she'd been a teenager with raging hormones and a complete lack of sense. And the fact that her family disapproved of Jax had only made him all the more attractive. What girl didn't go through a stage of falling for a sexy bad boy?

But even now with this mature version of Jax, his sexiness had only escalated. And his dreamy smile still had the power to penetrate her defenses and turn her insides to mush.

"We aren't here to talk about the past." She cleared her throat and schooled her facial features into what she hoped was a serious expression. "Why don't I show you to your bungalow?"

"Listen, I don't want to get you in any more trouble with your boss, but this arrangement obviously isn't going to work. So I don't care how you want to explain it to him, but you can't be my casino host. Better yet, don't say anything to him and you'll officially be my host but from a distance. A long distance."

"What?" Her chest tightened. "I—I can't do that. You're one of the casino's most valuable players. Upper management would find out immediately and accuse me of neglecting my duties."

"I don't need a babysitter." His brows gathered. "I just want a quiet vacation."

"And you'll have one while I take care of you…er, manage your needs." She pressed her lips together, knowing that with each attempt to dig out of this uncomfortable hole, she was only making it deeper for herself.

A deep chuckle rumbled from his chest. "Cleo, you still have a way of making me smile."

She glanced up, noticing how his face lit up when he smiled, easing his worry lines. Maybe his new life of luxury wasn't all chocolate and roses. From the obvious size of his bank account, she couldn't imagine what problems might be plaguing him. For a second, she considered asking but resisted. It wasn't any of her business.

"Does that mean I can go ahead and do my job?"

"Still as persistent as ever." Jax shook his head. "All right. Maybe we can try it on a trial basis. But that's no guarantee it'll work."

It was so much better than a no and it would give her time to soften him up. Hope bloomed in her chest. She would make this work…one way or the other.

Before she could say anything else to amuse him and embarrass herself, she turned to exit the office. "I'll show you around. I'm sure you're anxious to get to the tables."

"Actually there's no rush."

Cleo glanced back. "Really? Because if you're concerned about unpacking, don't be. I can have the staff do that for you."

"Are you that eager for me to start losing my money?"

Her gaze narrowed at his snide comment. "I get paid based on how much you wager, win or lose. So if you'll follow me, I'll give you a quick tour of the casino on the way to your lodging."

"That won't be necessary. I'd just like to get there quickly and discreetly."

If he wasn't up to something, why was he acting so strange? And did this have anything to do with his new-found wealth? The questions buzzed through her mind.

He was no longer Jax Monroe, Hope Spring's rebel. The truth was she never believed that he was a bad boy, more likely misunderstood and living up to people's low expectations of him. Back in the day he'd been so sexy with his long hair and holey jeans. Every girl in town had her eye on him—including her.

Cleo couldn't wait to tell her mother about this amazing transformation. Suddenly her excitement dipped. The gaping hole in her heart throbbed. Sometimes when she got excited, she'd forget that her mother was no longer speaking to her.

"Was there something else?"

Cleo glanced up at him, unable to recall their discussion. "What?"

"You were about to show me to my room." Jax's penetrating gaze met hers, making her turn away before she said or did something stupid.

"Follow me." She started toward the players' area.

"Is there a back way to my room?"

She nodded and turned around, guiding him down a long nondescript maintenance hallway. Jax may be tall, handsome and mysterious, but she had to remember that he was her client—a stranger to her now.

She didn't even know if she should trust him, but a little voice in the back of her mind said that he was still the same good guy down deep where it counted. He was also the guy her family didn't approve of—at least not for her. It niggled her that he was good enough for her older brother to pal around with, but when it came to her, she'd been forbidden to hang out with him—not that it had stopped her.

The silence between them stretched on. She didn't do well with awkward moments. "We're having a vintage car show in our convention center, if you'd like to look around—"

"Maybe later."

So much for conversation. She didn't recall Jax being this quiet when he was a kid. In fact, there were times he hadn't known when to shut up. She couldn't believe she was missing that smart-mouthed kid—the same kid who would go out of his way to put a smile on her face. What in the world had changed him so drastically?

She stopped and pushed open a heavy steel door. The glare of the Nevada sun nearly blinded her. She blinked and her eyes soon adjusted. As she moved along the secluded footpath, the sound of laughter, the cacophony of voices and the splash of water filled the air.

Jax grabbed her arm, giving her pause. "I thought we were taking the back way to my room."

An army of goose bumps raced over her skin. She pulled away from his touch and ignored the fluttery feeling in her chest.

She lifted her chin to face him. "We are. Your bungalow is in a secluded area just beyond the pool. Don't worry, there's a path over here on the side that we can use."

As they passed the pool she found herself glancing over at the crowd of young people on summer break, enjoying themselves. Her family were ranchers—and ranchers didn't take holidays. Or so her parents told her every time she asked them if they could go on a trip like her friends did.

It was always expected that when she wasn't in class, she would be at home helping out. It's what her brothers did. No one ever seemed to understand she was different. Was it so wrong to want to hang out with her friends? Or take vacations?

It was always presumed she'd become a rancher's wife—just like her mother and grandmother. After all, she was a Sinclair and ranching was in their blood. Except somehow the love of ranching had skipped over her.

"This sure is different from Hope Springs," Jax said, as though he, too, were thinking about the old days.

"Is that good or bad?"

"Neither. Just an observation."

The desert air was dry and hot as it rushed past them. Even though the private walkway was ensconced with palms trees, large rocks and various types of greenery, she gazed longingly at the glimpses of the enormous pool that had a wall of granite with a beautiful waterfall on one side. A dip in the cool water was so tempting. But employees were forbidden to indulge. She wondered if that rule could be suspended if someone like Jax invited her for a swim. After all, her priority was to keep her clients happy.

"What has you smiling?"

She was smiling? She hadn't realized that her thoughts had transferred to her face. She'd have to be careful in the future. The last thing she needed was Jax getting any ideas about her meandering thoughts.

"I was just imagining how nice it'd be to take a dip in the pool."

"It is hot out."

"It's always hot in Vegas."

"So how is it that the only Sinclair girl ended up in Las Vegas? I'd have thought you'd be back in Hope Springs with a cowboy by your side and a baby in each arm."

Cleo stopped short on the narrow path. He almost ran into her. "Not you, too. You sound like my parents."

"Calm down. I can see I struck a chord. I just thought that with your close-knit family that you'd never want to leave."

"Well, you're wrong. Besides, you did the exact same thing. I don't see you rushing back." She eyed him accusingly.

"That's different—"

"How?"

"You know I couldn't stay there." His posture grew rigid. "After my mother died, my father only got meaner. I wouldn't wish that life on anyone."

The pieces of the past started to drop into place. "That's why you were always out and about. You were trying to avoid your father."

Jax nodded. "It was easier than having to deal with him."

"But why did you have to play into the negativity by being at the center of all of the trouble in Hope Springs? How was anyone supposed to give you the benefit of the doubt when you never gave them a chance to trust you?"

His blue eyes stared straight at her. "Why didn't you write me off like the rest of them?"

"Because I saw there was more to you than you were willing to let on." She wasn't going to say that she'd had a bad case of puppy love. Thankfully they arrived at his bungalow, putting an end to this awkward conversation. "This is where you'll be staying."

She swiped her master key card and pushed open the door. When she stepped back to let him pass, he shook his head and waved at her to go ahead. "Ladies first."

She smiled. "Thank you."

So the bad boy had transformed into a gentleman. She definitely approved of this change. But that didn't mean she'd let her guard down around him. In her experience, people only showed you the side of them that they wanted you to see.

She'd been so foolish in the past, always looking for the good in people. She'd been too trusting—too understanding. And what had that Pollyanna attitude gotten her? A broken heart and being disowned by her very own mother.

In the end, people always let you down.

"This is nice," Jax said, drawing her back to the here and now.

"Yes, it is. It's our most private and exclusive residence on the grounds."

This was actually the first time Cleo had been inside

the bungalow. Only the most valued players were invited to stay here. And it was hard to believe Jax was now one of the elite. A man like that would not need or want for much.

But that still left her wondering, what was up with him using an alias? And his request for privacy was so different from the Jax she knew back in Hope Springs. In those days, he seemed to open his mouth just to annoy someone who was hassling him. Now he put thought into what he said and, more important, what he didn't say.

So what twist of fate had put him in her path? And why did it have to be him who held her future in the palm of his hand? Her stomach dipped. How did she get him to agree to keep her on as his host—permanently?

# CHAPTER THREE

JAX KEPT HIS eyes on the room and not on Cleo. Did she have any idea how irresistible she looked? How in the world did she think that they were supposed to spend time together with her wearing a dress that accentuated her curves? But then again she'd look good in anything, including a paper bag.

"Do you like what you see?" Cleo glanced at him from the entryway.

Oh, he definitely liked the view. Way more than he should. He cleared his throat. "Yes… Yes, I do."

Forcing his attention back to his surroundings, he observed the oversize leather couches. They looked inviting. He could easily envision settling in and watching a baseball game on the big-screen television. In fact, the idea sounded like something he'd enjoy indulging in right now.

Not so long ago, he used to work nonstop. But then he'd gotten sick and everything had changed. He had yet to regain his stamina after his medical treatments. It frustrated him to have to slow down, but until this court case was resolved there really wasn't any work he could do. This was his first vacation. He was curious to see if it was as great as people let on. Or if he ended up as bored as he imagined.

"If there's anything you're missing, just let me know and I'll take care of it for you."

He was positive the one thing he wanted, she would not supply. Not that he should or would act on the desire to taste her sweet lips. Cleo was the very last person he'd have a fling with. She deserved so much more—more than he could offer anyone.

"Would you like me to get you anything? Extra towels? Some food?"

"I don't think so. You can go." He didn't miss the frown at his dismissive tone and total lack of manners. His weariness was messing with his mind. "Thank you for showing me here, but I'll be fine on my own."

He turned his back to her and eyed up the couch. After a little television and some shut-eye, he'd be good as new—he wished. But with each day that passed, he was feeling a bit more like his old self.

Cleo firmed her shoulders. "I'd like to finish our talk about me staying on as your casino host. Perhaps we can come up with some sort of compromise."

He was intrigued. "What sort of compromise?"

She shifted her weight from one blue suede stiletto to the other, deciding just how much information she had to impart. Considering that not only her job but also the possibility of mending fences with her family was riding on her bringing in a large influx of cash, she had no choice but to be totally honest.

"I'd better start at the beginning." She worried her bottom lip as she sorted out in her mind a good starting point. "The thing is I sort of went over Mr. Burns's head to get this position and now he's out to get me."

Jax's eyes lit up as a smile tugged at his lips. "What do you mean sort of went over his head? You either did or didn't do it."

She hated how he put her on the spot. "Fine. I went over his head. But I wouldn't have had to if he hadn't kept passing me over every time there was an opening. And I'd already impressed his boss with a special project I'd previously worked on."

"Some things don't change." Jax laughed, remembering how he'd envied the way her father catered to her. He'd never known anything close to that amount of love. His own father had been too caught up in his own needs to worry about his son. The sobering thought killed off his laughter. "Why should I care about this mess you've gotten yourself in? I'm not the one who decided to buck the chain of command."

"So beneath that designer jacket and short haircut, you're still the tough, 'don't care' Jax, aren't you?"

"You don't know a thing about me." The fact that she didn't think he'd changed stung more than he'd expected.

"Then why don't you tell me how you ended up in this exclusive bungalow?"

He let out a frustrated sigh as exhaustion coursed through his body. "This is exactly why I need another host. I shouldn't have to explain myself. A stranger wouldn't butt into my life."

A pained look crossed her face, making him regret his heated words.

"You're right. You don't owe me any explanations. I just need you to forget everything that happened up until this point and give me another chance to be the best casino host you've ever had." She twisted her hands together. "But there's one more thing you should know."

His patience was wearing thin and he was so tired. "What is it?"

"This job isn't just for me." Her voice was so low, he almost missed what she'd said.

"What are you talking about?" Then a thought struck him. His gaze sought out her left hand, finding her ring finger bare. But that didn't mean she wasn't a single mother. "Who's relying on you?"

She wrapped her long honey-gold hair around her finger in a similar manner to the way she used to twist her father and brothers around her pinkie. But they were a long way from Hope Springs and he wasn't so easily swayed. If only he could get past his fascination with this grown-up version of Cleo. It was just a lot to take in at once.

"It's the ranch—the Bar S." Her worried gaze met his. "It's in a serious bind."

The worry in her eyes ate at him. "Kurt never mentioned anything about problems with the ranch when we've talked."

"I'm sure it's a matter of Sinclair pride. That's what got us into this trouble in the first place. It seems my father had been juggling money to cover his bases for quite a while without telling anyone that the Sinclair fortune had dwindled to nothing."

The knowledge that the high-and-mighty Sinclairs had come down off their lofty spot in the community didn't give Jax the satisfaction he once thought it would. Maybe it was the distressed look on Cleo's face that drove home the reality of what she was telling him. People were about to lose their way of life—their home.

"But I don't understand. What does any of that have to do with you being my casino host?"

"I need money to send home to put toward the mortgage. It's in arrears."

The Bar S was mortgaged to the hilt? He'd always looked at that ranch in awe and dreamed of one day having a spread just like it. Why hadn't Kurt mentioned any of this to him?

Later he would have to call Kurt and see if there was something he could do to help. Just as quickly, he realized he couldn't do that without mentioning Cleo. This would take a lot more thought before he acted. And right now, he needed to straighten things out with Cleo.

In his exhausted state, his brain just wasn't making all of the necessary connections. "So you want to be a casino host to make money for the family?"

She nodded. "The position pays a lot more than being an accountant."

He leaned back on the banister at the bottom of the steps. "Oh, yes. You mentioned making a percentage of what I wager."

She cocked her head to the side and stared at him intently. "Are you okay?"

"Of course. Why?"

"It's just… Oh, never mind."

This wasn't good. The last thing he needed was for her to figure out that something truly was wrong with him. It was difficult for him to maintain a normal existence while waiting for his test results without having to deal with the pitying looks or the sympathy.

"Jax, you have to do this. You owe me."

This sparked his attention. He always made it a policy to pay his debts. The thought of owing Cleo didn't sit well with him. At all. "I do? Since when?"

"Remember when I saw you on the day you left town? You asked me not to tell anyone what you were up to and I kept that secret for you."

Getting away from Hope Springs had turned his life around. If his father had his way, Jax never would have made anything of himself. Only his father hadn't lived long enough to learn how he'd graduated from college at the top of his class and had made a killing in the stock market. Not that it mattered. All of that, including Cleo, was in his past. And he wasn't going to get caught up in looking back—he didn't when his biopsy came back positive and he refused to look back now.

Oblivious to his inner struggle, Cleo continued, "I knew what you were running from and I wanted to help. If your father had known where you went, he'd have tracked you down and dragged you back. He'd have made your life miserable."

"You knew where I went? How?"

"I didn't know for sure. But I had a pretty good guess. You didn't talk about your family much, but when you did, you mentioned your mother's sister in Virginia. I figured that's where you went."

He nodded. "It is. I spent the summer with her before I went on to college."

"Your mother would have been so proud of you."

He grew uncomfortable with all of this digging around in his past. His mother had been sick off and on most of his life until her frail body finally gave in and she passed away when he was a teenager. No one ever spoke of her because very few people knew her since she was usually housebound from one ailment or another. The doctors would have him believe that she had a weak body, but he never believed that was what did her in. He was convinced her spirit had been broken by his father, who bullied everyone and ruled the house with an iron fist.

"I'm sorry." Cleo stepped closer to him. "I shouldn't have brought it up."

"It's okay. It's nice having someone else around who remembers her. You were always kind to her and she liked you."

"I liked her, too."

He remembered how Cleo would stop by the house with school fund-raisers. She never rushed off. She'd sit down with his mother at the kitchen table and chat. At the time he hadn't liked Cleo wedging her way into his life, but now looking back he realized she'd recognized a loneliness in his mom and had tried her best to fill it.

"Your mother was a really nice lady. And she made the most delicious chocolate chip cookies."

Before he could say more, his phone buzzed. Adrenaline pumped through his veins. At last, he'd know his test results. He glanced over at Cleo. "I'll be right back."

He moved to the kitchen, seeking privacy. No one knew about his brush with death, and he intended to keep it that way. He didn't want people looking at him as if he was less of a man.

He went to answer the phone but the other party had already disconnected. Jax rushed to check the caller ID but it was blocked, leaving him no clue as to who was trying to contact him. If it was important, they'd call back.

He returned to the front room, where Cleo was studying what was bound to be an expensive painting. He could never tell a Rembrandt from a Picasso. He just knew what he liked.

Jax stuffed his hands into his pockets. His fingers brushed over the smooth metal of the old pocket watch that he kept with him as a good-luck charm. More times than he could count it had brought him peace of mind. Only today its magic hadn't worked.

Today it reminded him of the past and the fact that Cleo's grandfather had given him the watch. Jax's gut was telling him that her grandfather would want him to help Cleo, no matter how hard it would be for him.

Cleo could feel Jax's presence before she heard him. She turned and noticed the dark shadows beneath his eyes. She didn't know what the man had been up to lately, probably too much. He certainly needed some rest.

"I'll get out of your way. But before I go, I'd like to confirm our arrangement."

Jax's brows rose. "I didn't realize we'd come to any agreement."

"Seriously, you're going to make me plead with you?"

He looked as though he were weighing his options. "You really want to put up with me for the next few weeks?"

Was he talking about catering to his every whim and desire? Her mind filled with the vision of him pulling her close and pressing his lips to hers. Okay, so maybe she hadn't totally outgrown her childhood crush. But fantasies were one thing. Acting on them was quite a different subject.

She'd learned her lesson about love. Men were to be treated with caution. She may date now and then, but she never let those relationships get serious. By dating the same guy less than a handful of times, she never let herself get close enough to risk her heart.

With Jax, it'd be a temporary arrangement—no chance for either of them to get the wrong idea about their relationship. "If you agree, I'll do a good job for you."

He glanced down at his phone as though expecting it to ring again. "In exchange, you'll keep my identity a secret. As far as everyone is concerned I'm Mr. Smith."

"I will make your privacy my top priority. But what's up with all of the secrecy?"

"Let's just say I'm on a much-needed vacation and I don't want anyone to disturb it."

"If you're supposed to be here for some R and R, you might consider turning off your phone. There's nothing so important that it can't wait. Why don't you let me reserve you a blackjack table for later today?"

Jax smiled and shook his head. "With your determination, I think you'll do quite well in your new position."

She straightened her shoulders. "I plan to."

He moved toward the couch and picked up the television remote. It was almost as if he'd forgotten she was in the room.

"Mr. Smith." When he didn't respond, she added, "Jax, if you're going to go by a fake name, you should at least answer to it."

He looked over at her. "I'm sorry. I didn't hear you."

"I'll make sure your line of credit is established and your table is ready. I'll be back as soon as everything is in place."

"There's no need to rush. I'll be fine."

"The fridge is stocked. Help yourself." She started for the door. Curiosity was eating at her. Something was troubling him and she was starting to worry about him. "Jax, just tell me one thing, are you in trouble with the authorities?"

"Why would you ask that?" He expelled a weary sigh. "You're still puzzled by the alias. Did you ever just want to get away? Want to be someone else for a little bit?"

Sure she had, especially after growing up in a small town where everyone knew everybody else's business. She used to daydream about the day she'd get to leave. The funny thing was the farther she got from her hometown, the more she missed it. Not the ranching part but the people.

And now that her father was gone and the ranch was in trouble, she felt as though she should be there to help out. But she wasn't wanted. The backs of her eyes stung as she recalled how her mother had told her to leave at her father's funeral, accusing her of being responsible for his death.

Jax stepped closer. "Cleo, what is it?"

She blinked back the unshed tears. "Nothing."

"You sure don't look like it's nothing."

"Well, you would be wrong. So we'll keep each other's

secrets. Yours from the rest of the world and mine from my brother. Deal?"

He frowned but nodded.

She slipped out the door. It was only then that she could breathe easy. Jax was here for more than just a vacation. Of that she was certain. He had a problem and if she had to guess, it was what had him looking so run-down. It must be something big and troublesome. But what could it be?

And why was she letting herself get drawn in when she had enough of her own problems?

# CHAPTER FOUR

WHAT HAD MADE him think a trip to Las Vegas was a good idea?

Jax grabbed a bottle of water from the fully stocked fridge. In the past two days, Cleo seemed to be everywhere he turned. It was almost as if she had him under surveillance. He paused, considering the possibility. Then realizing he'd watched too many spy movies after his treatments, he dismissed the idea. Even that would be too much for her.

The stress of waiting for his latest test results combined with a restless night had his imagination on overdrive. He really did need this vacation more than he'd originally thought.

The afternoon sun filtered through the sheers on the windows, casting a golden glow over the room. The couch beckoned to him. If he just sat down here for a minute, he'd be fine. Putting his feet up on the coffee table, he leaned his head back against the smooth leather upholstery and closed his eyes. This felt so good…

*"Jax."*

*He turned down a dark alley. Rapid footsteps sounded behind him. A gunshot pierced the night. He flinched. His legs moved faster.*

*He glanced around. The alleyway was empty. His heart pounded harder. No place to hide. No place to rest.*

*His muscles ached. His lungs burned. Still, he couldn't stop. He had to keep going.*

*"Jax."*

*The female voice was growing closer. Where were they? He couldn't see them. He had to keep moving, keep one step ahead of the man in black.*

*A brick wall reared up in front of him. He stumbled. Fell. Before he could get to his feet a hand clutched his shoulder.*

*He jumped.*

*"Jax, you're safe."*

One second he was in the alleyway and the next he was staring into the most amazing forest-green eyes. He blinked, trying to make sense of what was real and what was a dream. He jerked himself away from her touch and sat upright.

Cleo knelt down in front of him with concern etched across her face. "You were having a nightmare. Are you okay?"

"Um, yeah." He ran a hand over his forehead. "It's a bit warm in here."

She grabbed the cold water bottle from the coffee table and handed it to him. "Have a drink. I'll adjust the thermostat." She moved across the room and adjusted the touch pad on the wall. "Sorry I'm late. I had to pick my cat up from the vet."

"No problem. I wasn't in any rush." He raked his fingers through his hair.

The nightmares had started when he'd been diagnosed with cancer. With both of his parents dead at an early age, he didn't hold out much hope for himself. He'd lost count of how many nights he'd woken up with his heart racing and drenched in sweat, but back then the dream had been a blur. As time went by he remembered more of the details. Thankfully he didn't have them every night, only those times when his illness was weighing heavily on his mind.

"Are you sure you're okay?" She sent him a questioning stare. "I could call a doctor."

"What? Why would you do that?"

It was impossible for her to know about his medical condition. There were no loose ends for her to pull. No stones for her to turn. He got to his feet, stretched and headed to the minibar for a fresh bottle of water. He unscrewed the cap and took a long drink.

"If you're sick—"

"Why do you keep insisting I'm sick?"

"Because you're pale and perspiring. And obviously exhausted if you didn't hear me knocking on the door."

"It's just jet lag."

"Jet lag? Three days after the fact? I don't think so."

She had a point, but he kept quiet. Let her think what she wanted. He wasn't about to tell her that he'd just finished up a round of chemo and was now awaiting test results to see if he was in the clear or if the dreaded disease was still lurking within him.

"Maybe you should sit back down and take it easy." She fluffed a throw pillow before returning it to the couch.

He'd been taking care of himself since he was a kid. He didn't need her mollycoddling him like…like his mother used to do when he was sick. And this illness was not something that you shared casually over coffee. He could barely admit to himself the changes that had taken place in his life over the past year.

Now he just needed to be treated as if he was normal. And maybe then he'd start to feel normal, too.

She turned a sympathetic gaze his way. "I can get you some aspirin."

"Stop fussing over me." The hurt expression on her face had him regretting his outburst. She was only trying to be nice. "Thank you, but I'm fine."

Her brow arched as she pressed her hands to her hips. "If you're so fine, prove it. Let's head over to the casino and see if you can win back some of that money you lost yesterday."

Actually that sounded like the best suggestion he'd heard in a while. Because there was no way he was going to fall asleep again anytime in the near future. "Lead the way."

Surprise lit up her eyes, but for once she didn't argue. She turned on her stilettos and headed straight for the door. His gaze drifted to her derriere, nicely displayed in a red skirt that showed off her curves. He had no idea where she bought her clothes, but it was as if they were tailored just for her.

His throat grew dry and he gulped down the rest of the water. She'd certainly grown up to be a knockout. He couldn't believe Kurt let her out of his sight. If she was his little sister, he'd definitely keep her under wraps—away from men like himself.

Then again he wasn't anyone that her brother should be worried about. He was far from being classified as a ladies' man these days. That was one of the reasons he'd decided to come to Vegas—to distance himself from the stark reality of his diagnosis. Here he could be Mr. Smith—Mr. No Worries.

He rushed to catch up with her on the footpath. For just a bit longer he could hang on to the illusion that he was the man he'd always been—a man with a promising future. Now that future was littered with uncertainties.

"Have you lived in New York long?"

"Ever since I finished college." He glanced her way. "Did you move here after you graduated?"

Sadness filled her eyes and she nodded. "My family wanted me to return home. They'd even made arrangements for me to work for Mr. Wetzel in town, processing taxes."

"I take it that wasn't what you had in mind for your future."

She shook her head. "I thought I knew everything when I finished college. At last, I was free to make my own choices—to forge my own direction wherever it led me."

"It looks like you did well with those choices."

Her shoulders drooped. "Looks can be deceiving."

He concurred wholeheartedly. Things were never quite what they seemed from the outside. He was just sorry that Cleo had to learn that lesson the hard way.

"Hang in there. I'm sure life has some amazing things in store for you."

"We'll see."

The fact that she felt comfortable enough to open up to him warmed a spot in his chest. But he couldn't let himself read too much into it. She was probably lonely being so far from her family. And it wouldn't do either of them any good if he tried to fill that empty spot. It'd only make it that much harder to walk away.

"You know, I can be on my own today. I don't want to take up all of your time. I'm sure by now you have other guests to look after."

"Actually you're my one and only guest. Mr. Burns has me on a very short leash." Her cherry-red lips lifted and her eyes sparkled. "So name your pleasure and I'll make sure it's provided."

The sweet lilt of her voice and the sight of her tempting lips sent his mind spiraling back in time. He clearly remembered the one and only kiss they'd shared. He hadn't even seen it coming and it was over before he could react. The strange thing was that after all of these years, he had never forgotten that innocent moment.

He'd been kissed countless times since then and by experienced women who knew how to turn a kiss into an adventure. So why had the memory of those other kisses faded while hers stood the test of time?

Every detail of that moment stood out in his mind. He recalled how the morning sun peeked over Cleo's shoulder. The golden rays made her hair glisten, giving it the illusion of a halo. Her cheeks were rosy with color and her eyes sparkled like fresh-cut emeralds.

He'd been so mesmerized by the stunning image that he hadn't expected her to lift up on her tiptoes. Her gaze met and held his as she leaned forward. Her puckered lips pressed to his mouth. In the next heartbeat, she pulled away. And then, as if horrified, her eyes grew round. She'd pressed a hand to her mouth and run off.

The buzz of his phone drew him back to the present. At last, it had to be his doctor with the confounded test results. He glanced at Cleo. There was no way he was having this conversation in front of her.

He never wanted her to know that he had…Hodgkin's lymphoma.

He swallowed hard, still not comfortable with the "C" word.

He held up a finger to Cleo. "You can go ahead. I've got to get this."

He took a step back toward the bungalow. In fact, he took numerous steps before he pressed the phone to his ear. "Hello?"

Nothing but silence greeted him. Not again.

"Hello? Who's there?"

Frustration bubbled through his veins. Was it possible the anonymous phone calls were starting again just like in New York? But how had they gotten this number? He'd just had it changed.

He checked the caller ID. It was blocked. But then he noticed the reception bars were down to just one. The knot of tension in his gut eased. Perhaps the calls hadn't started again. Perhaps it was just a case of spotty reception.

His gaze moved to Cleo. She was standing next to a large palm tree. In the background was a glimpse of the waterfall at the edge of the pool. Her striking beauty drew him in. A year or two ago, he'd have tossed caution to the wind and lived in the moment.

But the here and now was all he had these days. He couldn't forget that. And he noticed the more time they spent together, the more he had to remind himself that he was in no position to offer her anything. His life was a continual question mark. And that was no way for anyone to live.

Her gaze caught his and held it. He found himself smiling back. Maybe he was thinking about this all wrong. Would it be a crime to let down his defenses just a little and enjoy Cleo's company?

It had been so long since he'd let someone in, even if it was just to kick back and chat over a meal. He longed for a little companionship. But he'd have to be careful around Cleo. She had a way of sneaking past his defenses. And he couldn't afford to let her get too close. They'd both end up hurt.

These thoughts made him all the more determined to check out early. Once he spent a little more time at the tables and made it look good for her, he was leaving Vegas.

He didn't know where he'd go, but that didn't matter. Still, it'd sure be nice to take a few happy memories of Cleo's smile with him.

Cleo stood next to a palm tree, wishing Jax would hurry up.

It was a hot day even by Vegas standards. Perspiration trickled down her cleavage. If this was going to take a while, she'd wait for him inside.

She glanced over at him and noticed how his brows were drawn into a dark line. And his eyes were narrowed as though he were upset. Something was definitely wrong. Should she go to him?

She stepped forward. Then stopped. It wasn't her place to interfere. As long as she saw to his needs while he was here at the Glamour, her job was done. Maybe once he got a few winning hands, it'd cheer him up.

Yet when he joined her, she couldn't help but ask, "Is everything all right?"

He smiled but the expression didn't reach his eyes. "Things couldn't be better. I'm on vacation and being escorted by the most beautiful woman in Las Vegas."

Without warning, he held up his phone and snapped her picture.

"What'd you do that for?"

He shrugged. "Why not? This way I have a reminder of my trip."

"You already had one from the other day."

His smile warmed her insides. "I could never have too many pictures of you."

His compliment caused a fluttering sensation in her stomach and silenced any further objections. Instead she returned his smile and when he offered her his arm, she gladly accepted. In a peaceable silence, he escorted her into the casino.

Inside, colorful lights twinkled while the murmur of voices filled the room. A group cheered at the roulette table. There were plenty of things going on in here to distract both of them. While Jax played blackjack, Cleo checked in with the pit boss to see if there were any new high rollers she could introduce herself to.

After all, Jax wouldn't be here forever. When he was gone and she'd proven herself, she'd need other clients. She may only be on a trial period right now, but she didn't intend for it to stay that way for long. And for her to be successful, she needed to plan ahead.

Sadly today there weren't any new leads for her. So after making the rounds on the casino floor, she gravitated back to Jax's table.

"And how are we doing?" She flashed him her practiced smile.

He didn't smile back. "Seems Lady Luck is on holiday."

"I predict things will turn around."

He cocked a dark brow at her as though gauging her sincerity before playing another hand. And losing again. Cleo's anxiety rose. If he didn't start to win soon, he'd quit. Or worse, take his business to another casino on the strip. Vegas was full of choices.

She wondered if that held true for her, too. At first, being a casino host seemed like an exciting challenge, but even though she was new to the job, she was finding that it didn't give her a sense of fulfillment, either. Now the only reason she wanted this job was to help her family get the ranch out of arrears. Once that was achieved, she knew she'd be moving on to something else. Because one thing she knew for certain, being employed in a casino didn't make her any happier than working on her family's ranch.

The most fun she'd had since arriving in this town was buying a secondhand sewing machine and returning to a hobby she enjoyed immensely—creating fashions. Her family may think her passion was a waste of time, but it'd saved her a bundle of money by allowing her to dress in style for a fraction of the price.

After the last losing hand, Jax turned to her. "That's it! I'm done. And don't say a word. No platitude or hokey prediction is going to fix this. I just hope you don't ever try to make a living off being a fortune-teller," he teased. "Because you're lousy at it."

"I—I'm sorry."

"I know how you can make it up to me."

"How's that?" She'd do it as long as it wasn't too over-the-top.

"Have an early dinner with me."

He was asking her to dinner? Excitement bubbled up inside her. She just as quickly tamped it down. He was her client. She had to stay focused.

"Thank you. But I don't date clients."

This brought an unexpected smile to Jax's face. "That's good because I'm not interested in a date. I just thought if you're going to follow me around, you might as well eat, too. But if you're not hungry that's fine."

"Oh." Her stomach growled. Heat filled her cheeks. Strike that. She was a lot hungry. "I'll join you if you tell me how you ended up going from ragtag jeans to designer ones."

His brows lifted. "You really find it so surprising that a person can turn their life around?"

"From what I've witnessed, people say they're going to change, but they're usually lying."

Jax stopped walking and turned to her. "Since when

did Hope Springs's very own Pollyanna become such a pessimist?"

She glared at him. "I was not Pollyanna."

"Oh, yes, you were. There was hardly a time you weren't smiling, and you seemed to think it was your job to make everyone else in town smile, too."

She hated that he still thought of her as some foolish kid with unrealistic expectations. "I grew up and found out that life isn't like in the movies. It doesn't come with rainbows and happily-ever-afters."

She started to walk again, not caring now if he followed her or not. Of course she'd always been smiling when he was nearby, it was how he made her feel. He surely didn't think she was that happy around everyone. But then again maybe it was best she didn't squelch his misconception. It was for the best that he didn't know those smiles had been just for him.

"Hey, slow down." He grabbed for her arm but she pulled away and kept on moving. "I didn't mean to upset you. I just miss seeing you smile and laugh. You're always so serious these days."

"I smile." She lifted her chin and pasted on a smile.

"I meant a real one. Not one of those practiced smiles you use for guests."

Cleo paused at the restaurant entrance, waiting for the hostess to seat them. She didn't know why she still let him ruffle her feathers. She really needed to loosen up.

The hostess seated them in the corner where there was dim lighting and a candle burning in the middle of the table. She inwardly groaned at the romantic setting. She glanced around, finding the restaurant empty, except for one gentleman across the room.

Jax leaned back against the cushioned bench as though the atmosphere didn't faze him. "So tell me about him?"

"About who?"

"The guy who made you stop believing in happily-ever-afters."

Her initial instinct was to tell him to look in the mirror. He'd been the first guy to break her heart. But she didn't dare admit it to him. He'd think she was being ridiculous. After all, she'd just been a silly kid.

But to this day she could still remember how crushed she'd been when she'd acted on impulse. She'd stood up on her tiptoes and kissed him. He hadn't kissed her back. He hadn't said a word. Not even a smile. In fact, all he did was stare at her. She'd been mortified.

The next time she saw him, he'd been leaving her grandfather's house. She'd run to catch up to him. She didn't know what she'd been expecting him to say, but it sure wasn't goodbye. Nor had she anticipated him leaning forward, kissing her cheek and saying, "See you, kid."

She'd been so devastated by him leaving town that she hadn't eaten her dinner and had hidden in her room all night. Luckily being the only girl afforded her the luxury of having her own room, where no one could see the tears she cried.

Jax took a drink of ice water and studied her over the rim. "Aw, see, I was right. It was a man who turned you into such a jaded person."

Cleo was not about to confess her long-ago teenage crush on him nor mention her college boyfriend, who got her to trust him—to believe they might have a chance at a future—before he two-timed her with her roommate. Some things were better not discussed.

"Let's just say I grew up and learned that people always let you down." She had to remind herself of that hard-learned lesson when Jax was around. With him it was too easy to fall into old patterns and let down her guard.

Throughout the meal they compared notes about college life and who had it worse. When Jax claimed he lived a semester with not much more than a can of tuna for his supper, he won hands down.

Since he'd started asking questions, it was time he answered a few. "Now, tell me more about your life in New York. You've said very little about what you do there."

"What can I say, I like to be a man of mystery."

Now that she couldn't argue with. He'd been a mystery for as long as she'd known him. He'd give just so much of himself before a solid wall would come up and block everyone out. She always thought that it had something to do with the way his father mistreated him. She inwardly cringed remembering how that man would call Jax rude names in the middle of town.

"Well, I hate to tell you this, but you aren't as mysterious as you seem."

"Really?" Jax propped his elbows on the table and leaned forward. "And what is it you think you've uncovered about me?"

"I know you work in New York City for some investment firm."

"So far you're right. I run a hedge fund on Wall Street."

"That sounds very impressive." She couldn't hold back a big smile. "I'm so happy for you. I just wish your mother was still around to see what you've done with your life."

"I think she would have approved."

"I know she would have. She was always proud of you." Cleo's thoughts filled with memories of the people of Hope Springs. "Do you ever think about going home?"

"This from the girl who moved to Connecticut for college and then graduated and moved to Vegas. I don't see you rushing back to Wyoming."

She shrugged. "I'm not cut out to be a rancher, even

if I am a Sinclair. I just wish I could have convinced my family."

"Ah, so you're off in search of yourself."

After all of these years it was as if he could still read her thoughts. Before she could tell him more, shouting came from behind her followed by the sound of shattering glass.

# CHAPTER FIVE

WHY NOW?

For the first time in forever, Jax had been enjoying himself. Instead of worrying about his test results or the upcoming trial, he'd taken time to enjoy a good meal and an easy conversation. Cleo was perfect, from her sparkling smile to the way the candlelight made her blond curls shimmer. This was the closest he could ever envision himself getting with a woman and he hated that the moment had come to an abrupt end.

Stifling a groan of frustration, he turned his head. A man stumbled to his feet while berating a young waitress as she set a cup on the table. The woman's face was splotched with color while all around her on the floor were shards of broken glass.

"I'll get security," Cleo said, scrambling to her feet.

Jax wasn't about to stand by and watch the scene unfold. He strode across the empty dining room, hoping to reason with the man. "Is there a problem here?"

"What's it to you?" The man slurred his words.

"It looked like you might need some help." He'd had his share of experiences with men in this guy's condition and knew they could be unpredictable.

"Yeah, get her to bring me another drink." The man's

bloodshot eyes glared at him and then turn to the young waitress. "I don't want this coffee."

"I'm sorry. I can't serve you any more alcohol," the waitress stammered.

Before the man could move, Jax situated himself between the two of them. He'd seen enough of this thing when he was a kid, when he was too young to do anything about it. Now he wouldn't just stand by and let a man take his frustration out on this woman.

"Why don't you try the coffee?"

"Fine." The man glared at him before grabbing a large brown mug from the table behind him. "If you're so interested in the coffee, you have it."

The next thing Jax knew warm liquid hit him in the face. His hands balled at his sides and a growl started deep in his throat. With every muscle tensed, he stood there soaked as coffee continued to drip from his chin.

"Enjoy." The man staggered away.

Jax took a step in the man's direction then stopped. More than anything he wanted to go after him, but he knew better. Nothing good would come from exacerbating the situation.

He glanced over in time to see Cleo standing at the entrance to the restaurant with two burly security guards. "That's the guy."

While security dealt with the obnoxious man, Jax turned to the waitress. "Are you okay?"

She nodded and handed him a towel. "Thank you. I don't know what I'd have done if you hadn't been here."

He proceeded to dry his face. "Glad I could help."

"I tried to make him understand that I have to follow the rules. I—I wasn't sure what to do. I'm new and no one has ever acted like that before. I should have handled it better." The girl grew flustered and he felt bad for her.

"You did fine. He was just a difficult man. Here, let me give you a hand cleaning up." He knelt down and started placing the big pieces of glass on the tray.

"If there's ever anything I can do for you, just ask for Marylou."

"Thank you." He flashed her a reassuring smile. "I'll keep your offer in mind."

Cleo returned with a mop and bucket. She looked him over. "Are you okay? Did you get burned?"

"I'm fine. Luckily the coffee had time to cool down. I'm just a little wet."

She gave him one last look as though to determine whether he was telling the truth. Then she started mopping the floor. The three of them worked together until the mess was nothing more than a distant memory.

"Well, hero," Cleo said, smiling up at him, "let's get you back to the bungalow and into some dry clothes."

He shook his head. "I'm no hero."

"Yes, you are. Just like all those years ago when you stood between me and Billy Parsons when he insisted I hand over my lunch money. You're still playing the modest hero. That's one of the things that I always—" She clamped her lips together and glanced away.

His black mood started to lift. "That you always what?"

"That I...I always admired about you."

The way she stammered around, he couldn't help wondering if that was what she'd originally intended to say or if there was some other hidden truth that was making her look so uncomfortable. He knew she had a crush on him way back then. And in all honesty, he'd thought she was pretty great, too. But way too young for him.

"Come on. Let's get you out of these." She tugged at his damp, clingy T-shirt. "Then again your new cologne, eau de coffee, might be a big hit with the ladies."

"You think so? How's it working for you?"

Her petite nose curled up. "I don't think it's your scent."

Her soft laughter was the sweetest sound he'd ever heard. And her smile started a funny feeling in his chest. If only he could keep her smiling.

Her eyes twinkled. "Are you flirting with me?"

"If you have to ask, I must not be doing it right."

She laughed some more. "I'm glad not everything about you has changed. You were always a great guy in my book."

Her gaze lifted up to meet his. The tender look in her eyes touched something deep inside him—a part of him that he thought was long dead. In that moment, he felt more alive than he had in months.

Without thinking he reached out and caressed her cheek. "Thank you."

She leaned into his touch, short-circuiting the logical side of his brain. The only coherent thought in his head was to pull her close and kiss her. And this time he wouldn't be kissing her rosy cheek. This time he planned to find out if those cherry-red lips were as sweet and passionate as they were in his daydreams.

His head started to lower when he heard footsteps behind him. He pulled away. Frustration bound up in his gut. He'd been so close—a breath away from satisfying his desires.

His hands clenched at his sides as he worked to compose himself. A little voice in his head assured him that this was for the best, but it didn't stop the wave of disappointment. Only a moment or two more and he'd have had a tantalizing memory to take back to New York.

"What's going on here?" Mr. Burns demanded. "Security said there was some sort of incident."

Cleo stepped forward. "Mr. Smith played hero. Everything is fine now."

Mr. Burns frowned as he surveyed Jax's stained shirt. "I'm sorry about that. Please stop by the men's shop and pick out a replacement. Charge it to my account."

Cleo clasped her hands together. "I can explain—"

"Trust me, you'll get your chance in my office. I have something to take care of first, but I'll be there shortly."

"Yes, sir."

Cleo's worried gaze moved from Mr. Burns to Jax. He wanted to reassure her that everything would be all right. That if he had to he would go over this man's head because he was really starting to dislike her boss and the tone he used when speaking to her.

Not wanting to do anything to make her even more uncomfortable, he decided to wait until she was gone before he had a word with this man. Then he'd set him straight.

Talk about a long, miserable evening.

Not even the magnificent sunset with its brilliant orange-and-pink glow could lift Cleo's spirits. She strode along the path to Jax's bungalow, grateful for its privacy. Her steps picked up speed as she continued contemplating what had just happened.

What made everyone think they knew what was best for her? First her overbearing family. Then her two-timing boyfriend. And now Jax...

She'd been a fool to think Jax was different—that he respected her ability to take care of herself. Even if it was to learn from her mistakes. She could just add him to her ever-growing list of people who'd disappointed her.

Her lips firmed into a line, holding back a string of heated words. She only had herself to blame. When would she learn to be more cautious?

There had only been one other time when she'd been this worked up—the last day she'd argued with her father on the phone. Her stomach churned as the chilling memory surfaced. She recalled how her father had yelled and then the phone had gone dead. Not knowing what had happened to him, she'd practically climbed the walls waiting for him to call her back. Nothing could ever be that bad. And thankfully this day wouldn't end with someone dying.

But before she was done, Jax would get an earful.

She stopped outside the bungalow and took a deep breath, trying to calm her racing heart. Her tightly clenched fist knocked solidly on the door. She waited. No answer. She once again pounded on the solid wood door.

"I'm not leaving until you talk to me," she shouted.

The door yanked open just as she raised her clenched hand.

"I think the entire resort heard you." He glanced both ways. "I'm surprised no one has come running to find out what's wrong."

She lowered her hand and marched past him into the bungalow. "Do you know what I just spent the last hour or so doing?" Without even waiting for Jax to respond, she motored on. "I had to justify exactly why I should continue as a part of the player development team. And Mr. Burns wanted to know if there was something going on between the two of us. Otherwise he just couldn't understand why you'd be so adamant about keeping me on as your host."

Jax closed the door and turned. "And, gee, I thought you came here to thank me."

"Thank you? If it wasn't for you, I wouldn't be in this mess."

"Hey, this isn't my fault. And as I recall, in the beginning I suggested another casino host take over."

The fact he was making perfect sense was not helping

matters. "Still, did you have to threaten my boss? He already dislikes me. Now he outright hates me."

Jax crossed his arms, his biceps bulging. "I didn't exactly threaten him."

She pried her gaze from his muscles and looked into his blue eyes, which were just as disconcerting. "Are you saying you didn't mention something along the lines of if he fired me, you'd take your business elsewhere? As well as that of your friends?"

Jax shrugged. "Someone needed to put that man in his place. He couldn't keep treating you like that."

"But that wasn't your responsibility. I can take care of myself. Stop acting like one of my overprotective brothers." She started pacing through the spacious living area. "I know how to handle men like Mr. Burns."

"Fine. Maybe I did come on a little strong, but that man is annoying. I don't know how you can stand working for him." Jax strode out of the room and quickly returned with some water. "Drink this. It'll cool you off."

She placed her sunglasses and phone on the table in the entranceway and accepted the tall glass. After a long sip, she said, "I know I should be thanking you."

"That's not such a bad idea."

She drew in a deep breath and leveled her shoulders. "I'm sorry. I shouldn't have blown up at you."

"Apology accepted."

"But you don't understand. My entire life my brothers have interfered with everything I do, never letting me stand on my own two feet. And my mother was constantly overriding my decisions. I thought that it was all behind me when I left Wyoming."

"I remember how your brothers policed every guy who looked in your direction. Did you ever have a date in high school?"

She nodded. "Mama finally put her foot down and made them back off on the couple of boys she approved of."

"But not the guys you had your eye on."

She shook her head. "You know how old-fashioned my family can be, and Kurt is no better. He doesn't understand why I had to get away to try different things and find what makes me happy."

"I guess I hadn't thought of it that way." Jax placed his hand over his heart. "I promise in the future to let you fight your own battles."

"Thank you. But you do realize once you check out, Mr. Burns will find a way to get rid of me."

"Are you saying that I have to stay here indefinitely?" Jax smiled, causing her heart flutter.

"Yes. But in order to do that, you'll have to start winning."

He rubbed his jaw. "I suppose you're right. Maybe we should go give it another try. I'm feeling lucky now."

"Are you serious?" There was still a chance of turning things around if Jax continued to test his luck at the tables.

The light from his smile snuck between the cracks in her dark mood and lightened her spirits. She was drawn to him, but she steeled herself against the desire. There was still so much she didn't know about him.

She'd never met anyone who could affect her so deeply. She'd come in here ready to tell him what to do with the job he'd secured for her, but instead she was walking out the door with a smile on her face, anxious to prove Mr. Burns wrong.

In the warm evening, the lights along the pathway gave off a soft glow. Jax was just behind her and she could sense his gaze on her. What was going through his mind?

Was he remembering how he'd almost kissed her in the restaurant? Drat Mr. Burns for ruining the moment. After all, it wasn't as though they were starting something serious. It would have been a simple kiss.

"It's a beautiful evening," Jax said from behind her.

"Yes, it is." But it wasn't the darkening sky or warm breeze that held her interest.

When Jax made another comment, she couldn't quite catch his words. Afraid she missed something important, she stopped short. He bumped into her. His hands reached and wrapped around her waist. She automatically turned in his arms.

Her gaze met his and her heart skipped a beat. "I didn't hear you."

"I said the sunset wasn't nearly as beautiful as you."

He was so close. She could smell his male scent combined with a spicy aftershave. A much better fragrance for him than the coffee.

Her good intentions evaporated as his intense gaze held hers. In his eyes, she detected mounting interest. She reveled in the fact that she could evoke such a reaction in him. She moved a little closer and heard the swift intake of his breath. He might fight it, but he was as attracted to her as she was to him.

Then she did something spontaneous. She lifted up on her tiptoes and pressed her lips to his just the way she had all those years ago. But this time she didn't stop there. She was no longer young and inexperienced. And she fully intended to make an unforgettable point.

Her lips moved against his very still mouth. Surely he couldn't be that surprised. This had started long ago and tonight she wanted to turn her fantasy into reality. So that when they each went their separate ways, she would have this memory to hang on to during those sleepless nights.

Her hands slid up over his solid chest and his muscled shoulders and wrapped around his neck. Her fingertips slid through his hair. With a moan, he tightened his hold on her, drawing her closer. His lips moved beneath hers. And like a timeless dance their mouths opened and their tongues met. Was it possible that this kiss—that Jax himself—was even better than she ever imagined in her dreams?

His kiss became frenzied with need. She met him stroke for stroke. His excitement increased her pleasure. Time slipped away. The only thing that mattered now was the man holding her.

Then as quickly as the kiss had started, it ended. Jax released her and stepped back. His breathing was as rapid as hers but his gaze lowered. He refused to look at her. What was that all about?

"That shouldn't have happened." He raked his fingers through his hair, scattering the short strands.

This was not the reaction she'd expected. She inwardly groaned. Why should this time be any different? He didn't want her. The acknowledgment stung.

"You're right." What had she been thinking? "It was my fault. It won't happen again."

She went to turn away when he reached out to her. "Hey, this has nothing to do with you. You're beautiful. Any man would be crazy to turn you down."

"You're making too much of it."

When would she learn to think before acting? Every time she put herself out there, she'd been rejected, first by her ex and then by her very own mother. People couldn't love her as is. They always wanted her to be more outgoing, more compliant, more something. There was always an area where she fell short in their eyes. She didn't even know what Jax found lacking in her and she wasn't about to stick around to ask.

She sucked down the bruising ache in her chest. It wasn't as though she still carried a torch for him. The kiss had been nothing more than a passing fancy, not something serious.

Swallowing hard, she levelled her shoulders and met his gaze. "I have some stuff to do. You can go ahead without me. I'll call and make sure your blackjack table is ready." It was then that she realized she didn't have her phone. "I must have left my phone back at the bungalow."

Jax turned as though to walk with her.

She held up her hand to stop him. "Just go into the casino. I'll get it."

He looked as though he was going to argue but then thought better of it. "Are you sure?"

"Yes. Go ahead into the casino. You should be all set up at the same table as earlier."

"Cleo, I'm sorry. I didn't mean to hurt you—"

She waved away his platitude. "I'm fine. It was a mistake kissing you all those years ago and it was a mistake tonight."

His mouth opened but she didn't wait around to hear anything he had to say. She strode away, completely mortified by the way she'd thrown herself at him. What in the world had gotten into her? She'd like to blame it on a full moon, but there was none. This mortifying disaster was all her fault.

When she arrived at Jax's bungalow, she realized her pass card was with the phone locked inside. She expelled a sigh. Just what she needed now was to tell him that she had forgotten not only her phone but the hotel pass card, as well. Could she look any more incompetent this evening?

The sound of footsteps had her taking a calming breath. A shadow fell over her. She turned, expecting to find Jax, but instead a tall, muscular man dressed in a dark suit stood before her. The stranger was built like a linebacker and under different circumstances this might have intrigued her, but tonight she didn't want to be bothered.

Her gaze rose to his face. She was caught off guard by his dark, menacing eyes. "I'm sorry but this is a restricted area. Are you a guest of the hotel?"

The man's tanned face creased with an intimidating frown. "I'm looking for someone. A Jax Monroe."

She had no idea who this man was or who had pointed him in this direction, but the first rule about being a casino host was abiding by their client's wishes. And Jax had no wish for anyone to find him here.

"I can't help you. Did you try at the front desk?" She knew that they wouldn't release guest information, but she hoped this man didn't know that and would go away. "Maybe they can give you some information."

"Just tell me where I can find him."

An uneasy feeling inched down her spine. Was this the man Jax was avoiding? If so, she fully understood why Jax wouldn't want anything to do with him. Her mouth grew dry. The guy looked as though he could bench-press a car. And the menacing look in his eyes gave her the creeps.

Something definitely wasn't right here. Her palms grew moist. Standing alone with this man was not a good idea. It was time to get moving.

"I really need to be going. I have people waiting for me." She started walking, but instead of taking the private path back to the casino, she veered toward the pool, hoping there might still be some stragglers hanging out.

"Don't walk away from me. This is important. Just tell me where to find him and there won't be any trouble."

She didn't need to hear any more. She walked faster. The man easily kept pace.

The hairs on the back of her neck lifted. When she reached the pool area, luckily some young people were still milling about. Not that they were paying her any attention. Still, whatever this man meant by his threat, he wouldn't be foolish enough to try something with so many witnesses… Would he?

She got as far as the first line of lounge chairs when his meaty fingers reached out and clamped around her upper arm, halting her progress. She jerked her arm, but his grip was like a vice. Her heart jumped, lodging in her throat.

He pulled her to him. Her back pressed to his chest and he wrapped his hand over her mouth. "I want you to give Jax a message—"

Cleo bit down on the man's finger.

A curse thundered in her ears. He yanked his hand away. Never taking her eyes off him, she backed up. He lunged for her. In the ensuing struggle, her foot got caught in a lounge chair. She lost her balance and fell backward, hitting the concrete.

# CHAPTER SIX

"OPEN YOUR EYES."

Jax stared down at Cleo's pale, lifeless form on a stretcher in the back of an ambulance. His chest tightened as he said a silent prayer to the big guy upstairs. She just had to be all right. She had to be.

His thumb stroked the soft skin of her limp hand. He had no idea what had happened. When he'd heard there was a commotion out by the pool and Cleo hadn't returned, he'd gone looking for her. He never expected to find Cleo in a crumpled heap on the ground.

There hadn't been time to stop and ask questions. All he could think about was her opening her beautiful green eyes again. But one thing he knew in that moment was that the girl who'd given him a peck all those years ago still meant the world to him. He reached into his pocket. His fingers traced over the pocket watch—his good-luck charm. He was about to pull it out and press it into her limp hand when he noticed her fingers move.

"Jax? Where am I?"

Cleo's voice was weak but clear. He'd never heard anything so wonderful in his whole life. He longed to pull her into his arms and hold her close.

"You fell, but don't worry, you're going to be fine now." She tried to sit up, but the straps on the gurney held her down. "Not so fast, they still have to check you out. You got quite a bump on your head."

She glanced over, noticing the paramedic reading off her stats to the hospital.

"My leg hurts and I can't move it."

"They immobilized it. Looks like you banged it up pretty good."

She closed her eyes and he worried that she had slipped into unconsciousness, but she quickly opened them again. "I'm sorry to be such a bother."

He held her hand between both of his and gave it a reassuring squeeze. "You could never be a bother. Right now all you have to do is concentrate on getting better."

He wanted to ask her what happened, but now wasn't the time to get into it. Still, Cleo wasn't a clumsy person. When you lived on a ranch, you learned to be fast on your toes. So what exactly had happened to her?

He was still holding her hand as they backed up to the emergency room entrance. Her fingers were cold as she kept a firm grip on him. When he tried to pull away, she wouldn't let go.

"It's okay. They'll take good care of you." He stared straight into her eyes, noting the worry reflected in them. He lifted her hand and pressed his lips to her delicate skin. "You're safe now. I promise."

"Will…will you stay?"

"You bet. They couldn't drag me out of here if they tried."

"Thank you."

The fact that she wanted him with her, that he was able to provide some sort of comfort, stirred a strange sensation in his chest. It wasn't the protective feeling of a big brother watching over a little sister. No, this was something different—something much deeper. Much more powerful.

The scare had been of a magnitude that he'd never experienced before. He didn't know where the feelings came from or what to do with them—he just knew his place was right here by Cleo's side.

The ambulance doors swung open and they rushed her off. He wanted to go with her—to make sure that nothing happened to her. But as he started to follow Cleo's gurney, a nurse stepped in front of him and pointed the way to the waiting area, promising they would notify him when he could see her.

Frustration knotted his gut. The last time he'd let her out of his sight something bad had happened. But Cleo was safe now. She was in the hospital. Doctors and nurses would be seeing to her needs.

He entered the spacious waiting area lined with rows of black cushioned chairs. He took a deep breath as the reality of his location struck him. It wasn't so long ago he'd been the patient. Even though it had been a different hospital, the memory had him on edge. He didn't want to be here—not at all.

But he'd promised Cleo he'd stay. He wouldn't break his promise to her. It was the least he could do for her. He tried sitting but that lasted all of thirty seconds. He paced the length of the room. Back and forth. He wasn't the only one wearing a concerned expression. The waiting area was filled with young and old people all waiting for word on a loved one.

"Excuse me, Mr. Monroe."

He turned to find a police officer. "Yes."

"I'm here about the incident at the Glamour. Did you see anything?"

The police were involved. This wasn't good. "No, I didn't. I was inside and heard about the commotion by the pool. I went to investigate and that's when I found Cleo. Do you know what happened?"

"I'm still piecing things together. We have a report of a man getting into a scuffle with Ms. Sinclair and your name was mentioned."

"Have you talked with her?"

"Not yet. That's where I'm headed next."

Dread dug at Jax as he wondered if it had anything to do with his mysterious calls. "There's something you should know."

The officer turned his keen, observant eyes on him and listened intently as Jax revealed how he was a key witness in a federal money-laundering case. He also mentioned the strange phone calls that had started in New York.

The officer asked a few more questions, jotted out some notes and gave Jax his contact information. "If you think of anything at all that might be helpful, let me know."

"I will." And he meant it. He wasn't going to take unnecessary chances with the woman he…he…cared about.

Whether he liked it or not, she was definitely getting to him. She was making him feel things that he didn't have any right to feel. The only way to stop this growing attraction was to follow through with his plan to leave Vegas. He eyed up the exit. But he couldn't break his promise to her. He'd wait until he saw her and was certain she was going to be fine.

Almost a half hour later, a nurse stood at the security door that led into the examination area. "Mr. Monroe, you can come back now."

When he came to a stop next to Cleo's bed, he was stunned by what he saw. A white bandage was wrapped around her forehead. Her face was nearly as pale as the sheet. And her injured leg was elevated. He didn't know what he'd been expecting, but it wasn't her looking weak and helpless.

She studied him. "Do I really look that bad?"

He'd obviously let his poker face slip again. Still, the sight of her lying there injured had shaken him more than he'd anticipated. "Sorry. I wasn't expecting to find you all bandaged up."

"Jax, there's something I need to tell you—"

"And how's the patient?" A male voice came from behind him.

Jax turned to find a doctor in a white lab coat standing at the opening in the curtains surrounding the bed. He glanced back at Cleo. "We'll talk later. I'll just wait outside."

"It's okay." She grabbed his hand. "You can stay for this."

The doctor cleared his throat. "Ms. Sinclair has a mild concussion. We're still not certain about the extent of damage to her leg. I'm waiting on the films. However, I want to keep her in the hospital under observation. She was unconscious for a bit and I want to make sure there aren't any complications. But she's insisting that she's going home."

Jax turned to her. "You need to listen to the doctor. He knows what he's talking about."

"I'm not staying." A stubborn glint reflected in her eyes. "I can't sleep in hospitals. Besides, I feel fine now."

"She can go home as long as she isn't alone," the doctor said while looking directly at Jax. "Can you stay with her?"

"I don't need him." The sincerity in her pointed words poked at Jax. "I can take care of myself."

The doctor's brow drew together. "I'm sure you can in most cases, but you've got a serious bump on your head and you need to stay off your leg as much as possible. So either you stay here and let the nurses look after you or you can go home with…"

"Jax. Jax Monroe. And I'll see that she's taken care of."

Cleo worried her bottom lip. And in that hospital gown, she looked like a child again. All he wanted to do was take care of her any way possible…even if it meant getting closer to her instead of beating a trail into the sunset. That would have to wait for another day.

Cleo's worried gaze turned to him. "Are you sure about this?"

"I wouldn't have said it otherwise."

The doctor's gaze swung between the two of them, deciding if he could trust them. "Now that it's settled, I'll go check on things. If you wait in the lobby, we'll call you when she's ready to go."

Jax didn't mind a few minutes to himself to pull his scattered thoughts together. He started for the doorway when Cleo grabbed his hand.

"I need to talk to you. I just remembered something."

"Don't worry. We'll have plenty of time for that later."

"But this is important." Her distressed tone caught his attention.

He wondered if this had something to do with the police poking around. "I'm listening."

"There's a man after you."

"What?"

As though recalling her fingers were still gripping his hand, she let go and made a point of straightening her white sheet. "When I went back to the bungalow a man approached me. He wanted to know how to find you."

"And he attacked you?"

"Not really. When I tried to get away from him, he followed me. He grabbed my arm and put a hand over my mouth. He said he had a message for you."

Alarm arrowed through Jax's chest. "What is it?"

Cleo's gaze lowered. "I don't know. I bit his finger before he could relay the message. He let go of me and the rest is kind of a blur."

His gut was telling him trouble had followed him from New York. And Cleo had ended up paying the price. Guilt beat at his chest.

"Don't worry. He won't bother you anymore."

"How do you know? Who is this man? What does he want?"

Jax held up his hand, halting the flow of questions. "I don't know him, but I promise you won't have to deal with him again. Remember from here on out I'm in charge of your safety. Doctor's orders."

She started to sit up. "Jax, I need to know what's going on."

"Calm down." He placed a hand on her shoulder, pressing her back against the pillow. "When I learn something I'll tell you. Now I have a couple of phone calls to make."

Jax hated the thought that he'd dragged Cleo into his problems. He had no proof that this mystery man was tied into the money-laundering case, but he'd be willing to bet his fortune that he was right. His priority now had to be keeping Cleo safe. And since that hired thug knew her name, her face and where she worked, it wouldn't take long for him to track her down at home, either.

Just then the doctor returned. "We'll have you fixed up in no time."

That was Jax's cue to leave. He turned back to Cleo. "Don't worry. I'll take care of everything."

As he strode away, she called out, "What are you going to do?"

He didn't pause to answer because, at that moment, he didn't have a clue. It was obvious that he needed to get Cleo and himself out of Las Vegas. But how far could he take her with her injuries? If she needed further medical attention, he didn't want to be stuck out in the middle of nowhere. There had to be a compromise. A place where the thug hired to scare him into silence wouldn't think to look for either of them.

*Free at last.*

Cleo settled back against the leather seat of a large SUV. Even though her hospital stay had only lasted a matter of hours, for her it felt like days. And now Jax was playing the dutiful hero and riding to her rescue. She had no idea where he got this sweet ride, but she appreciated its spaciousness more than she could say.

"Thank you. But you really didn't have to go to such lengths. I could have called a taxi to take me back to my place."

"I don't think so. Remember I'm the one who promised the doctor I'd take care of you."

At the next traffic light, he turned left instead of right.

"You went the wrong way. Wait. How do you know where I live?"

"I don't."

"It's the other direction. I live at 331 Villa Drive, apartment C3. You can just turn left up here and loop around." When he kept going straight, she sat up a little straighter. "Where exactly are you taking me?"

"Do you always ask so many questions?"

She glared at him. "I demand to be taken back to my apartment."

"Not today. We're going someplace where you can rest and not worry about any unwanted guests."

"But I can't." She didn't like the sound of this. "I have a job…er, at least I hope I still have a job."

"Of course you do. You were injured on Glamour grounds while performing your duties. Therefore you're entitled to workers' compensation. Not even Mr. Burns would be foolish enough to let you go and face a lawsuit."

The medication they'd given her at the hospital was making her head woozy. "The doctor said it wouldn't be long until I could get around."

"And until then you need to rest as much as possible. Now just relax. I've got everything under control."

"How am I supposed to do that when you won't even tell me where we're going?"

"We aren't going far. Just north of the city. And I promise you'll like the accommodations."

He was trying to sound upbeat, but she knew he was worried. "You think that guy is going to come back, don't you?"

"He won't bother you where we're going."

She wanted to believe him, but she didn't even know what he was mixed up in. The adrenaline that had been driving her drained away, leaving her feeling wiped out. She was with Jax. Nothing would happen now because the one thing she did know was that she still trusted him. She instinctively knew that he'd protect her.

She leaned her head back, fighting to keep her eyes open. The image of her kitty came to mind. She'd called her neighbor Robyn McCreedy to check in on him. Still, it wasn't the same as being there, especially since he'd just been neutered.

"I can't stay here long. I have to get home."

"Don't worry. I'll get you home soon." Jax glanced over at her. "You can sleep. I'll let you know when we're there."

She really shouldn't trust him so easily, but her eyelids felt so very heavy. If she could just close her eyes for a minute, she'd be all right…

"Cleo, wake up. We're here."

Her eyes snapped open, not recognizing her surroundings. The bandage around her forehead was getting itchy so she rubbed at it, wanting to take it off. But the doctor had warned her to leave it on until the stitches on the back of her head had a chance to heal.

She gazed up at a large gate that was automatically opening for them. "Where are we?"

"Someplace safe."

Jax maneuvered the vehicle between the gates and down a road lined with jaw-dropping mansions. It was dark out, making it difficult to see the details of each impressive estate until they pulled into the driveway of a humongous home. She'd only ever seen something this extraordinary in glossy magazines.

Soft rays from the full moon bathed the white stucco home, giving it a magical glow. And it was two...no, wait, make that three stories high. With the lights on inside, it looked like a gem against the velvety night. Its sweeping length and elegance left her in awe.

"I hope you won't mind staying here."

She blinked, making sure that it was real. "Mind? It's amazing." Then she turned to him. "Is it yours?"

He shook his head. "I don't have any use for a place this big. It belongs to a friend of mine."

"That must be some friend. Is he famous?"

Jax chuckled. "You might say that. Remember the movie from last summer, *Shooting Stars?*"

"You mean the Western romance? I think everyone went to see it, including me. It was a great mix of action and passion."

"My friend will be glad to hear you're such a fan."

"He filmed it?"

"No, George starred in it."

Cleo's mouth gaped as she sat there trying to process

this information. "No way. Are you totally serious? He's drop-dead gorgeous."

Jax smiled and shook his head. "I do believe you're starstruck."

"Did you see the movie?" She fanned herself. "He's so hot. In the film he was the marshal and he was on the hunt for train robbers. He ended up rescuing the heroine from a train accident the robbers had caused. It was so romantic how he cared for her and kept her safe."

Jax cleared his throat. "I'll be sure to tell George when I talk to him. Now, is there any chance you want to go inside?"

"And see the rest of his house? You bet." She reached for the door.

"Wait! I'll help you. We don't need any more accidents tonight." He alighted from the vehicle and circled around to open her door.

"But how did you get George to lend you his house?"

Jax gave a nonchalant shrug. "It's not his primary residence. He spends most of his time in Hollywood."

"I still can't believe he's letting us stay here."

"Let's just say that he owed me a favor and I called it in. George is a really good guy. He was happy to do it."

"Did you tell your friend that we are on the run from some ape?"

"Ape, huh?" Jax smiled. "I'm glad to see your sense of humor hasn't been injured."

She thought back to her run-in with that man and a shiver ran down her spine. "I just refuse to give him power over me by calling him a big, mean, scary dude...even if he was one."

Refusing to dwell on what happened, she turned her attention to the long sweeping steps that led to the front door. And then she glanced down at her leg. This was going to be a challenge, especially when she wasn't used to getting around on one good leg.

But before she could ask Jax for the crutches, he scooped her into his arms. Her body landed against his solid chest. He'd definitely filled out in the years they'd been apart.

"What are you doing?"

"Taking you inside."

Her hand automatically slipped around his neck. "But I can manage—"

"Do you have to argue about everything?"

She pressed her lips shut. If he wanted to carry her up all of those steps, why should she complain? She wasn't feeling exactly steady on her feet. Tomorrow would be plenty early enough for her to prove her independence, even if she had to be aided by those confounded crutches.

Her head rested on his shoulder as he moved up the steps. Beneath the moonlight with the warm breeze swirling around them, it would be so easy to let her guard down. If she closed her eyes and inhaled his masculine scent, she could let herself get swept up in this very romantic scenario. Not that she had any intention of making a fool of herself again. If there was any more kissing, it would be Jax who made the first move.

One night here and then she'd return to her apartment to finish recuperating. Being situated in the middle unit of a young people's complex, tenants were coming and going at all hours of the day and night. She wouldn't have to worry about being alone. They'd be around if she called out for help. Yes, that would work. One night with Jax and then they'd go their separate ways.

Her thoughts turned back to Robyn, who was more than a neighbor—more like the sister Cleo never had. It was nice to have someone in her life now who cared. She'd told Robyn that she'd be home sometime that night. She really should let Robyn know that her plans had changed. She didn't want her to needlessly worry. Cleo reached for her phone but realized she didn't have it.

"Jax, I left my phone back at the bungalow."

"It's for the best."

"What? But I need my phone. How am I supposed to contact people and let them know that I'm okay?"

"They'll just have to wait. Phones have GPS tracking units in them. It's possible that thug could track us down that way. Don't worry. I got a disposable phone for emergencies."

The hairs on the back of her neck lifted. "Jax, how much trouble are you in?"

# CHAPTER SEVEN

ALONE AT LAST.

Jax gently lowered Cleo down onto a long white couch in the expansive living room. He regretted having to let her go. There was something so right about having her slight figure curled up next to him. It'd taken every bit of willpower to concentrate on climbing the stairs instead of turning his head and kissing her.

His gaze dipped down to her lips while remembering how sweet they'd tasted. This wasn't right. He should be worried about the man who'd run into Cleo at the hotel, not contemplating repeating their kiss because the one they'd shared earlier had been far too brief. And even worse, it had left him anxious for more of her touch.

He'd never had a woman distract him to this extent. What was so unique about Cleo? Could it be the fact she'd always been forbidden fruit? After all, she was one of Hope Springs's highly respected Sinclair clan whereas his own family had been barely tolerated.

The attraction appeared to be all one-sided as Cleo sat up and looked around the expansive room. "Did you see those posters in the hallway? This really is an honest-to-goodness movie star's house."

"Are you saying you doubted me?"

Her gaze darted around the room. "Look at the mantel. There's an award. Do you think he'd mind if I touched it?"

"I don't see why he would have to know." When she went to stand, Jax placed his hand on her shoulder. "I'll get it for you."

"Can you believe we're here? And look over there." She pointed to the wall to the left. "There's pictures of him with actresses and politicians. Look at that one of him with the president."

Jax chuckled at Cleo's awestruck face. He retrieved the gold figurine, surprised to find it was rather heavy, and handed it to her.

"I just can't believe you're friends with him. Can you get me his autograph?"

"I'm sure that can be arranged. Now sit there and don't move. I'll be back."

"Wait." She looked up. "You promised we'd talk."

"And we will right after I get our stuff. Just enjoy checking out that award."

The events of the day were catching up to him, and he couldn't wait until he got Cleo settled in bed. He inwardly groaned at the thought of her stretched out on some silky sheets. He gave himself a mental shake. That wouldn't and couldn't happen. Being a total gentleman tonight was going to be a feat all of its own.

Jax made a few trips to the car and deposited the final items next to the couch.

Cleo eyed up the stash. "What is all of that?"

"Things you'll need while we're here."

"But both of those bags look full. What did you buy?"

He handed over a shopping bag and she peered inside. Her lips formed an O and he realized too late that he'd given her the pink bag. Still, the color filling her cheeks matched the bag and made him smile.

"Don't worry. I didn't pick out the lingerie. Marylou helped me out."

Cleo's thin brows rose. "Marylou? You mean the woman from the restaurant? The one you rescued from that rude guy?"

He nodded. "She said that if I ever needed anything to ask. I couldn't risk going back into the Glamour and I didn't want to risk going to your place, so she discreetly picked up some of my things from the bungalow and bought you some essentials at the guest shops."

Cleo grimaced and adjusted her leg. "You're making this sound like we're going to be here for more than just tonight."

He glanced at his watch, realizing it was time for her pain medication. "We are. But don't worry. I have plenty of groceries."

She sat up straight. "I can't run off with you. I have responsibilities. People who will be worried about me."

"Listen," he replied as he got to his feet, "I'm not any happier about this than you are. But until the police track down this guy, we're staying put. Now it's time for your pain meds. I'll be right back."

"Jax, you're being ridiculous. I can get these things for myself."

He headed for the kitchen, ignoring her protest. Why did she have to be so stubborn? Couldn't she relax and let him take care of her? Did everything have to be a struggle?

He returned quickly, handing over the glass and the medication, which she took without so much as a comment. He sank down into the armchair across from her and folded his arms behind his head.

"You have to admit staying here won't be so bad." He was trying to convince himself as much as her. He leaned his head back. One by one the muscles in his body relaxed. "Even the furniture is comfortable."

He closed his eyes. This was the most relaxed he'd been in a long time. Was it the house? Or was it the company—Cleo's company—that had him thinking about the here and now instead of the uncertainty of his future?

"I'm still waiting."

Her voice startled him as he started to doze off. He lifted his head to look at her. "Waiting for what?"

"For you to explain why we're here. Who's the ape that's hunting you?"

Jax ran a hand over the evening stubble trailing down his jaw. "I honestly don't know who the man is. But the police are on it now. With the aid of the surveillance cameras at the casino, they'll be able to identify and locate him."

He hoped.

"But you do know why he's here and what he wants." Her eyes grew round. "Jax, what did you do?"

The fact she thought he might be on the wrong side of the law dug deep into his chest and pulled at the old scars on his heart. Years ago, when all of Hope Springs saw a delinquent kid, she'd looked at him as somebody worth befriending. Cleo always made him feel as though he mattered.

But for the first time, the look in her eyes had changed. Was she now looking at him as her mother had done and seeing him as the no-good Monroe kid who could never amount to anything but trouble. Anger and hurt churned in his gut. He thought he was far past these old feelings—yet being here with Cleo had rolled back time.

"I'm not a criminal," he ground out.

Color filled her cheeks. "I—I didn't mean it like that. This whole thing has me on edge."

"I guess once you're considered the bad boy, the reputation sticks." His jaw tightened, holding back old resentments.

"That's not true. You're forgetting all of the people who cared about you. People like Kurt and my grandfather."

"You're right." He sighed. "I shouldn't have gone off on you. It's just been a stressful day."

"And I deserve some answers."

"Yes, you do." Although he was certain his words would not give her the peace of mind she was seeking, he owed her the truth. "I'm a key witness in a federal court case."

"A witness." She leaned forward, resting her elbows on her knees. "I take it this isn't a simple murder case."

He couldn't help but smile at the way she classified murder as a simple case. "No, this isn't about murder. It's actually a white-collar crime."

The worry lines on her face smoothed. "Well, that doesn't sound so bad."

Would it be so wrong to let her cling to the idea that this case was no big deal? Then she wouldn't have to worry. But she also might decide to let down her guard, giving that thug a chance to get near her again. No, she definitely needed to know the whole truth.

"It's a money-laundering scam that involved my business partner. I blew the whistle on him before he could take us both down. I wore a wire and gave the government all the evidence they needed to make their case against him and his shady affiliates."

Cleo's face grew ashen. "That sounds dangerous."

"Let's just say these men aren't the friendliest people to cross."

"That...that man... Does he want to—"

"Scare me off? Yes, he does. But it won't work. I will finish what I started."

"Oh, Jax. What if—"

"There are no what-ifs. I just have a few more weeks until I return to New York for the trial and then this will all be over. Now it's time to call it a night. I don't know about you, but I'm exhausted. It's been a long day."

In truth, not only was he truly tired but he also needed some space. He was still smarting over the fact that Cleo thought he might be a criminal.

Her fine brows gathered. "You can't expect me to stay here with you until the trial."

"We'll have to see how things go. But for now you're staying where I can protect you."

He yawned. Maybe tonight he'd be able to fall asleep without the endless hours of staring into the dark. Or even worse, to drift off only to have that blasted recurring nightmare where he was chased down a dark alley. Stupid dream.

"Come on." He knelt down beside her and held out his arms. "Your chariot awaits."

Cleo's head felt fuzzy. She didn't know if it was the pain-killers or the information she'd just learned. Either way, it didn't matter. She was tired of being treated as if she was helpless. And she didn't need Jax making decisions for her.

When Jax reached out to her, she pushed aside his offer. "Thanks, but I can get to the bedroom on my own."

His face creased with frown lines, but he didn't argue. Instead he grabbed her crutches and held them out to her. "Are you sure?"

She nodded and placed the crutches under her arms. A bump on the head hadn't made her forget the way Jax had rejected her earlier that day. The memory still stung. Why should things change just because she got hurt?

They weren't a happy couple. They never would be.

She paused at the bottom of the long line of steps.

Suddenly, sleeping on the couch didn't sound like such a bad idea.

"Sure you haven't changed your mind?" Jax prodded in a persuasive voice.

"I can manage." All she had to do was focus. Soon she'd be upstairs and then she could lie down.

"You don't look so good."

"Thanks. You sure know how to give a girl a compliment."

"That isn't how I meant it and you know it. You're just being difficult."

He was right. But tonight she didn't care. Maybe it was the medicine or hitting her head, but she didn't feel like acting as if everything was all right when it clearly wasn't.

He followed her into a spacious bedroom with a king-size bed done up in peaches and cream. She sat down on the edge, very aware of Jax's presence. He knelt down in front of her to remove her shoe from her good leg. Why did he have to be so nice when she wanted to be angry with him?

"I can do it." She attempted to take over.

He brushed aside her hand. "You don't need to. That's what I'm here for."

His gentle tone smoothed her agitation. "I'm not even sure how I'll sleep tonight. Every time I close my eyes I see that ape man. You have to promise to be careful. He isn't a nice guy. He totally gave me the creeps."

"I'll be careful."

"You promise?"

"I do. I brought us here, didn't I? He won't know where to find us."

She lay back against the bed and closed her eyes, willing away the image of that man. Jax's warm fingers touched the bare skin of her calf, snapping her eyes open. What was he doing? Then she realized he was removing her sock. How could such a mundane task feel so amazing?

Dropping the sock, his fingers continued to work their magic, kneading and pressing on the sole of her foot. One by one her muscles relaxed and she turned to putty in his hands. The most amazing sensations coursed through her body. If he could do this massaging just one foot, she couldn't even imagine what other tricks he had up his sleeve.

"This will help you relax." His voice was soft and soothing.

She hadn't realized that she'd moaned out loud until he said, "I'm glad you're enjoying it."

"What can I say? I'm a sucker for a foot massage."

"Scoot back on the bed."

She did as he said, wondering what he was up to next. He grabbed a couple of pillows and propped up her injured leg. Then he sat down and put her other foot in his lap. The pad of his thumb rubbed up and down over the arch of her foot. She watched him as he used both hands to stretch her foot and then run both thumbs in circular patterns.

"Close your eyes," he said, still working his magic fingers.

She was in the midst of ecstasy and didn't want it to stop so she complied. Tomorrow she would stand her ground—yes, tomorrow. Tonight she would let him feel as though he were taking care of her... Just so long as his fingers kept moving.

Time slipped by and, at last, he stopped. She was lost somewhere between floating on a fluffy cloud and half-asleep. He got up and turned off the light.

"Don't go." She reached out to grab his hand. "Not yet."

"Cleo…"

All she knew was that she was in a happy place and she

didn't want it to end. Her body felt like mush. The darkness made her feel safe from his scrutinizing stare. She felt as though she could say anything to him. And in a sleepy haze she decided to throw caution to the wind.

"Why don't you find me attractive?"

She heard a swift intake of his breath. Then an awkward silence hung there.

The edge of the bed dipped as he sat down. The back of his hand glided over her cheek. "Who says I don't find you attractive?"

"When we kissed earlier, you pulled away. You didn't like it."

His voice was soft. "Did you ever think that I liked it too much?"

"Then kiss me now." He groaned but she wasn't giving up. "I've kissed you twice. You owe me."

Again there was an elongated silence. It had to be the medication because she'd never asked a man to kiss her. And it was so much easier to blame it on the painkillers than to admit how very much she wanted him. She'd never desired a man as she did Jax.

Then without warning he leaned over. His lips were just a breath away from hers. "Cleo, you don't know what you're asking of me."

"Yes, I do. I want you to kiss me. I want to know what it's like to be desired by Jax Monroe. Hope Springs's bad boy. Now a Wall Street tycoon. Kiss me, Jax. Please."

With a moan, his mouth pressed to hers. His kiss was hungry and needy. And her heart swelled. Somewhere in the haze of her mind there was a warning voice, but it was garbled and she didn't feel like heeding to caution. Here in the dark there was just the two of them.

His lips moved hungrily over hers like a starved man. And she met him kiss for kiss. Her fingers worked their way over his muscular shoulders to his neck and then her nails raked through his short hair.

The kiss went on and on and she never wanted it to end. She just floated along in the moment, enjoying having Jax so close. Because come the stark morning sun, she'd come to her senses. A relationship wasn't in the cards for her. But a fleeting moment of ecstasy was too tempting to pass up. Tomorrow would come all too quickly.

As though he could read her thoughts, he pulled back. His breathing was uneven and rapid. But as she reached out to him, he jumped to his feet.

"Cleo, you couldn't be more wrong. I want you more than I've ever wanted anyone. But this, you and me, it can't be."

"Of course it can't be," she spat out. No matter what he said, he didn't find her attractive enough. She blinked back the tears swarming in her eyes.

She'd miscalculated. Instead of the kiss making her feel better, she felt even worse knowing that he still thought that they were a mistake—that she was a mistake. She wanted to get as far away from him as she could, someplace where she could lick her wounds in private.

"I want to go home. Charlie needs me."

She rolled over onto her side, craving the company of her tabby cat. Anytime she was upset, he was right there with a loving rub and a cheerful purr. Her wounded body ached but it was nothing compared to the great big bruise on her heart.

# CHAPTER EIGHT

JAX YAWNED AGAIN. At this rate he'd need to brew another pot of coffee before lunch. He'd done nothing but toss and turn for hours last night. He'd finally dozed off sometime after three.

His mind had been crammed full with thoughts of the thug who had hurt Cleo. He'd even checked in with the police to see if the ape, as Cleo called him, had been arrested. So far, nothing. But the good news was they had his image from the resort's tapes and were working on identifying him.

Jax grabbed a spatula for the scrambled eggs. He wasn't used to cooking for anyone, but he didn't mind. What did bother him was having Cleo long for another man after he'd just got done kissing her. He snatched up a plate and placed it with a thunk on the counter.

The fact that she had Charlie in her life was for the best. A man in his position needed to keep clear of romantic entanglements. And even if his latest set of tests came back clear there was no guarantee they'd stay that way.

He drew his thoughts up short. None of it mattered because he had no intention of letting Cleo into his life—into his heart.

After the thug was arrested, Jax's plan was to return to his solitary life. With all of the money he'd made in the stock market, he could retire young. He didn't want to be one of those people who died at their desk. He wanted to get out and experience the world for as long as he had... And just as soon as this court case was over he'd get started.

No longer feeling so tired, he piled the scrambled eggs on the plate next to the buttered toast. When his friend said the housekeeper kept this place stocked, he hadn't been kidding. Jax really need not have bothered stopping at the store last night after he'd picked up the rental vehicle.

He placed the food and the orange juice on a tray, along with a red rose from the bouquet on the dining room table. Then on second thought, he returned the flower back to the vase. There was no reason to muddy the waters any further.

He carried the tray to the bedroom and tapped on the door. "Cleo, are you up?"

Silence greeted him.

He knocked louder. "Cleo, I've got your breakfast."

Still nothing.

Balancing the tray with one hand, he eased open the door and stepped inside. He came to a halt when he saw that the bed was already made up. His gaze flicked to the bathroom door. It was open and no sounds came from within.

Erring on the side of caution, he called out, "Cleo, are you decent?"

Again there was no response. He envisioned her passed out in the tub or worse. He set the tray on the end of the bed and rushed into the bathroom. The room was spacious, just like the rest of the house, but there was no sign of Cleo. He didn't understand. Where could she have gotten to?

The food long forgotten, he searched the other five bedrooms. She wasn't anywhere in the upstairs. He rushed to the sweeping staircase, which faced the wall of glass overlooking the front lawn and the drive. That was when he noticed the SUV was gone.

She'd run out on him!

But why?

Was she that upset about the kiss last night?

Did she feel guilty for cheating on Charlie?

His chest tightened. The doctor said she was supposed to be resting. What if she made her injuries worse? A knot formed in his gut. Or what if that thug caught up with her again?

He had to find her, but where did he start?

Cleo wished she hadn't been so spontaneous. Trying to get about with the aid of crutches was more work than she'd imagined. And now Jax had made her paranoid about the ape man staking out her place. She'd driven around the block three times looking for anyone or anything unusual, but nothing appeared to be out of place.

She pulled to a stop in a handicap parking space in front of her unit. She figured due to her unusual circumstances, she could park there for ten minutes—long enough to grab a few essentials and scoop up Charlie.

She'd just opened the driver's-side door when Robyn came up the walk, pushing a pink polka-dotted stroller. "Hey, girl, where have you been?"

Robyn was a good friend, but she was known for staying on top of the latest gossip in the complex. And this place was always rife with juicy stories. Cleo just hoped she wouldn't make a big deal over her injury.

Cleo reached over to the passenger seat and grabbed the crutches. With the crutches positioned outside the door, she carefully lowered herself to the ground. Her ankle pulsated with pain. It probably didn't help that she didn't take any of those pills the doctor prescribed for her. But she needed to be clearheaded for driving.

Cleo swung the door shut, almost losing her balance. She really did have to get the hang of the crutches since she was going to be on them for a while. "Sorry I didn't call again, but I didn't have my phone."

"I was hoping you were off with some hot guy, but by the looks of you, I guess that's wishful thinking. Unless you had a McSteamy doc taking care of you."

At the mention of a hot guy, her thoughts immediately went to Jax. He was definitely sexy in anyone's book. But she wasn't about to open that can of worms with Robyn, who was far too eager to help her find a "forever" guy. No matter how many times Cleo told her she wasn't interested, Robyn would still introduce her to any hot new tenants.

"Sorry. No hot doctors."

"When you called yesterday, you didn't say anything about it being this serious." Robyn frowned at her injured leg.

"I'm not that bad off." Cleo forced a smile, wanting to ease her friend's worry. "And the doctor said I was fine to go home."

It wasn't exactly a lie. She just left out the part about needing to be supervised for forty-eight hours. Come to think of it that probably meant she shouldn't be driving. But this was important.

"I don't know." Robyn gave her a hesitant stare. "You look about as appealing right now as Stephie's mashed peas. Definitely a bit green around the edges."

"Thanks. You really know how to cheer up a person," Cleo teased.

Robyn wasn't the type to mince words. And right about now, Cleo did feel pretty rotten. She hoped she never saw that ape man ever again. If it wasn't for him, she wouldn't be in this mess. The memory of him had her glancing around.

"You'll be back to normal after you get some rest." Robyn kept pace with her as they headed for their side-by-side apartments.

"You haven't seen any strangers lurking about, have you?"

"No." Robyn raised her brows. "Should I have?"

How much should she say? Probably as little as possible. Robyn had a good heart, but she had a habit of saying too much.

"There was just this creepy guy hitting on me at the casino. You know, the kind who won't take no for an answer."

Robyn's brunette bobbed hair swayed as she nodded. "Sometimes guys can be such jerks. And with you being so pretty, I'm surprised you don't get hit on more often."

"So if you see some tall guy with dark hair lurking about, call the cops."

"But what do I tell them?"

"Hmm…let's see." She stopped and thought for a moment. "I know, tell them that he's trespassing."

"Consider it done."

Luckily she lived on the first floor, saving her the task of going up and down more steps. They stopped at Cleo's door and it was then that she realized she didn't have her purse or her keys. Everything was back at the casino in her locker.

She turned to her friend. "I'm afraid I forgot my key. Would you mind letting me in?"

"Oh, sure. Let me grab the spare one. It's a good thing you gave it to me. I'll be right back."

Cleo hobbled around until she could lean against the wall. She wondered if Jax was awake yet. She'd considered telling him what she was up to, but when she'd gone to his room, the door was open and he was out cold. He was sprawled across the bed on his stomach while wearing nothing more than a pair of boxers.

He'd looked good—real good. She also remembered how he didn't want her—how he'd withdrawn from her. The memory dug at her heart.

Before turning away from his sleeping form, she'd noticed how the sheet had been pulled loose and kicked about. The pillows had been tossed off the bed as though he'd had a rough night. At least she had the satisfaction of knowing that he hadn't had a good sleep, either.

In no time, Robyn returned with the key in one hand and a baby monitor in the other. "If you lost your key during your accident, I can call the manager and have them change the lock. Of course, you know they're going to charge you for it. Like we don't already pay enough in rent."

"Thanks. But I know where it is. I just didn't have time to grab my things before they took me to the hospital." She wasn't about to add that she'd blacked out.

"Okay. But if you need anything, just phone me. By the way, Charlie wouldn't eat last night. I don't know if he's not feeling well or if he just missed you."

"I was worried about that. After his surgery, I want to keep a close eye on him. He didn't react well to the anesthesia." Cleo made her way over to the couch, where Charlie was curled up. He eyed her up but didn't make any movement. "Hey, buddy, it's okay. I'm here." She ran a hand down over his striped fur before scratching beneath his ear. Finally a faint purr started. "I'm sorry I wasn't here last night."

Instead of taking him with her, she was actually thinking of just staying home. According to Robyn there hadn't been any strangers lurking about. Apparently ape man had other people to push around.

The sound of the baby stirring came across the monitor. "I better go check on her," Robyn said, stepping out onto the walkway. "If you need anything else just let me know."

With her neighbor gone, Cleo turned to Charlie. "You do know that I'm going to be in trouble when Jax finds out I'm here with you."

Charlie blinked and licked his paw.

"I see you aren't the least bit worried. That makes one of us." She ruffled the fur on his head before locking the front door.

It was nice that Marylou had picked her out some new clothes, but they weren't really her taste and right now, she needed soft, stretchy shorts to get over her cast. And a comfy T-shirt. She may enjoy dressing up on most occasions, but this was different. Her body ached in places she didn't even think had been injured. Some loose-fitting clothes were definitely in order for today.

She hobbled toward the bedroom with Charlie leading the way. His tail hung low and he wasn't chatty like normal. The poor fellow. She felt really bad for him having surgery. At this point, she could kind of relate to not feeling so chipper. She'd have to remember to grab a bag of his favorite treats to take with them.

When her gaze landed on her bed, she thought that it never looked so inviting. So soft and snug. Maybe if she just lay down for a moment, she'd get her wind back. And she could give Charlie some much-needed attention as his love meter seemed to be low.

When Charlie eyed the bed hesitantly as though he wasn't so sure he could jump that high after his surgery, she scooped him up and deposited him in the middle of the bed. She could tell he was going to get as much babying out of this recovery as possible. And she didn't mind it a bit. She smiled as he circled once, then twice and finally sank down on the blue comforter.

After struggling to get changed into some comfy clothes, she lay down next to him, anxious to discard the crutches, which were as much a hindrance as a help. Her hand smoothed down over Charlie's back and his purr machine kicked into full gear.

"Sorry I wasn't here to take care of you last night. Some meanie sent me to the hospital."

Charlie yawned and then she yawned.

"I don't think he'll be back. Maybe we can both stay home."

She adjusted her pillow and closed her eyes for just a moment. After all, this guy was after Jax, not her. And Jax would be a lot safer if he didn't have to worry about caring for an injured woman. Especially after he made it perfectly clear that he wanted nothing to do with her. He felt an obligation toward her—nothing more.

Staying home was sounding ever-so-tempting. And with Robyn watching her back, she didn't have to worry.

"We'll be fine. Right, Charlie?"

# CHAPTER NINE

JAX KNOCKED ON the apartment door.

When there was no sound, he thought of trying the doorknob. But considering he might have mixed up Cleo's unit number, he wasn't going to risk it.

He rapped his knuckles again. Louder this time.

An adjacent door swung open and a young woman with straight brown hair, no makeup and stains on her blue shirt stuck her head out. She eyed him up suspiciously.

Maybe she'd know Cleo's whereabouts. He stepped toward her when she held up a cell phone. "Don't come any closer or I'll call the police."

"Hey, I don't want any trouble. I'm just here to see Cleo. This is her apartment, isn't it?"

"Don't play innocent with me. Cleo told me you'd be showing up and causing trouble. She's not interested in you. Time to move on, buddy."

Cleo told her neighbor about him? And what exactly had she been saying? It sure sounded bad.

Turning away from her kiss had been one of the hardest things he'd ever done. And if given another chance, he didn't know if he was strong enough to resist her.

Just then the door to Cleo's apartment opened. "Jax, how'd you get here?"

For the first time since he found her missing, he

breathed easy. His initial instinct was to pull her into his arms, but one glimpse of the wounded look in her eyes had him frozen in place. It was for the best, even if it didn't feel like it at the moment.

Giving in to his desires was what kept getting them into trouble. First they kissed and she took off only to run into ape man. And then there was last night's kiss, where she got upset and left without a word. This time he wasn't giving her another reason to walk away.

"Do you want me to get the police?" The young woman looked far too eager to place the call.

Jax rolled his eyes. "Please tell her that I'm not here to hurt you."

Cleo smiled as though she was enjoying this. He didn't find it the least bit amusing. He hadn't thought about anything besides her safety on the ride here. A tension headache spanned his forehead. He didn't know what he'd have done if she hadn't been here.

"It's okay, Robyn." Cleo smiled at her neighbor. "Jax is an old friend of mine. He's been looking after me since my accident."

The woman's whole demeanor changed and a smile pulled at her lips. "No wonder you didn't come home last night. I wouldn't have, either."

Cleo sighed. "Robyn, it's not what you're thinking."

"Then you must be blind, girl. Otherwise how could you pass him up?" Robyn flashed Jax a bright smile before backing into her apartment and closing the door.

Color flooded Cleo's cheeks, giving them a rosy glow. "I'm sorry about her. Robyn means well but is a bit misguided at times."

He nodded, understanding why Cleo wasn't eager to hook up with him the way her neighbor thought she should be. And that reason was named Charlie. Jax's jaw tightened. He at least wanted to get a look at this guy.

Cleo adjusted her crutches. "How did you get here?"

"I didn't have much choice. I took a taxi."

"Oh. Sorry. I was only borrowing the SUV. I would have brought it back."

From the looks of her in a rumpled T-shirt and mussed-up hair, he'd just awoken her from a nap. "I take it you weren't in any hurry to come back." He pressed his hands to his waist and frowned at Cleo. "Mind telling me what's so urgent that you had to go and run off without saying anything to me?"

"Charlie needed me. And…and you were sleeping. I didn't want to bother you since I figured you'd try to stop me."

"You're right. I would have." Jax's body tensed. "This Charlie, is he that important to you?"

She nodded. Just then there was a meow and Jax looked down to find a tabby cat rubbing against Cleo's ankles before stepping outside.

"Charlie, come back."

That was Charlie? Her cat? The knot in his gut eased. Then in spite of himself, he laughed. He'd been jealous over a cat.

"Don't just stand there laughing," she said. "Grab him."

Charlie appeared to be enjoying himself, exploring the great outdoors. When Jax set off in pursuit, the cat picked up speed.

"Here kitty, kitty."

"His name is Charlie."

Of course it was. He felt like such an idiot for getting bent out of shape over a cat. Not that he had any right to be jealous of anyone. On second thought, it would have been better if Charlie had turned out to be her boyfriend.

He could put her safety in another man's hands and walk away. At least he wanted to believe he could have turned his back and forgotten her.

The cat stopped to investigate a potted plant and Jax made his move, wrapping his hands around the cat's rib cage.

"Be careful," Cleo called out. "Support his back feet."

Jax adjusted his hold and the cat seemed to relax. That was good because he didn't know one thing about felines. His family didn't have cats or dogs. Not even goldfish. His father thought that they were a waste of money. That was what he'd loved about the Sinclair's ranch. They had lots of animals, from cats to steers. He'd always dreamed of living on a spread like theirs. So when the senior Sinclair took him under his wing and showed him how to work on a ranch, he was thrilled. He'd done something he enjoyed while making some pocket money.

"What are you smiling about?" Cleo eyed him. "Did Charlie find your ticklish spot?"

"Not hardly." He wasn't ticklish.

Cleo sighed. "Well, bring him inside and be gentle. He just had surgery."

Jax stared down at the furball. It didn't look as if anything was wrong with him. But Jax would take Cleo's word for it and as carefully as possible placed the cat on the couch.

"Enough about the cat. What I want to know is why you took off. Don't you realize that the thug who hurt you is still out there?"

"I was careful."

"I talked to the police on my way here." He waited to see if the reminder of their situation would gain her attention.

She didn't raise her head to look at him. Instead she

fussed over the cat. "What did they say? Has he been arrested?"

"No. And he was spotted in this area last night, but he eluded the police in the darkness."

She glanced up. The light in her eyes dimmed. "Oh. I didn't think—"

"Exactly. Now let's get you out of here."

He strode over and reached for the door.

"Wait. I'm not ready. I want to grab a few things. And you'll need to load the litter box in the car while I put Charlie in his carrier."

"I don't think so. I'm not hauling some howling cat around in the car."

Cleo frowned at him. "Charlie doesn't howl. He's not a dog."

"Howl. Meow. It's all the same." He wasn't a cat person.

"And don't forget to scoop the litter before loading it."

"No way. I'm not hauling around a litter box and a cat."

A few minutes later, Cleo settled on the passenger seat of the SUV. "Did you remember to grab extra kitty litter?"

"Yes." Jax's grumpy tone made her smile. "I don't know how something so small can require so much stuff."

He'd grow to like Charlie. She was sure of it because beneath all of that gruff, Jax had a big heart, even if he refused to acknowledge it.

"It's okay, Charlie. He's not normally this grouchy. He just woke up on the wrong side of the bed."

"I did not," Jax grumbled from the hatch as he stowed away her crutches.

In no time at all, they were on the road. She noticed how Jax kept checking the mirrors. She supposed she hadn't made the wisest choice this morning. Her gaze moved back to Charlie—but he needed her.

She glanced at Jax as he focused on traffic. "How long are you planning to keep us hidden away?"

Jax's fingers tightened on the wheel. "As long as it takes to make sure you're safe."

"I'm not your responsibility. I moved to Las Vegas to get away from my family and their overbearing expectations and overprotectiveness. Now you're trying to do the same thing."

"Well, if you don't like staying with me, I can get you an airline ticket. I'm sure your mother would enjoy the visit—"

"No!"

Jax glanced her way. She pressed her lips together, feeling stupid for reacting so strongly. If she wasn't careful Jax would start asking questions—questions she didn't want to answer. Once he knew what she'd done—the irreparable damage she was responsible for—it'd only confirm his decision that she was not worthy of his attention. She couldn't bear to have him look at her the way her mother had done.

"I can't go back there. Hope Springs is in my past."

"And does that include your family?"

She shrugged. A mix of feelings churned in her stomach, making her nauseous.

"What's going on, Cleo? Your family used to mean everything to you. Now you'll do anything to send them money, but you balk at the mention of visiting them."

His voice was soft and soothing, inviting her confidence. Still, she worried about what he'd think of her once he knew.

"Cleo, I'm concerned about you. Something serious is going on. And if you won't give me the answers then I'll have to go to Kurt for the truth—"

"No!" Her fingers twisted together. "Don't do that. I— I'll tell you."

He had her between a rock and a hard place and she hated it. Dredging up these painful memories would be torture. And for the first time to speak them out loud would just make what happened so fresh in her mind.

While living in Las Vegas, she'd been able to pretend that things were okay. To colleagues, she'd act as though she had a loving family missing her back in Wyoming. She was able to bluff her way through most days, but not today.

Maybe it would do her some good. Getting it off her chest might help. For so long now she'd been choking down the anger and hurt. She drew in a deep breath to steady her nerves.

"Things haven't been the same since my father died."

Jax cleared his throat. "Your brother mentioned that there'd been some drama at your father's funeral, but he didn't go into details and I didn't push. I figured he'd tell me if he wanted me to know."

"It was all about me." The weight of guilt settled on her chest. "The funeral was…was my fault…"

"What?" Jax pulled off the side of the deserted roadway and put the vehicle in Park. "Cleo, you aren't making any sense."

His face started to blur behind a wall of unshed tears. She blinked repeatedly. "It's my fault that my father died."

"How? Weren't you living here in Las Vegas at the time?"

"I'd just moved here." She inhaled a steadying breath. "I was on the phone with him and we were arguing. I didn't know at the time that he was in the pickup, transporting a mare he'd bought in hopes of luring me home. I might not like working around the ranch, but I still have a big soft spot for horses and he knew it."

Jax didn't say anything. He just reached out and squeezed her hand, allowing her to proceed at her own pace. This was something she'd never shared with anyone...ever.

Somehow it seemed fitting that she turned to Jax. He wasn't as close to the situation as her family and yet he wasn't so distant, either.

Cleo inhaled a steadying breath. "He kept telling me to come home. He was always going on about how much my mother missed me, but I didn't want to hear it. I was so stubborn. So determined that everything had to be my way. I was finally away from that suppressive atmosphere and making decisions for myself. I didn't want to go back and marry one of the locals. It might be the right life for some people...but not me."

The backs of her eyes smarted as a tear spilled onto her cheek. She dashed it away. This wasn't the time to fall apart. She needed to get through this. After all, Jax deserved to know what sort of woman he was putting his neck on the line to protect.

"No one can blame you—"

"But they do. And they should. If only I hadn't fought with him...he wouldn't have died."

"You don't know that." He placed a finger beneath her chin and lifted her face to meet his gaze. "And you can't live your life according to someone else's wishes. At some point you have to stand your ground."

She shook her head. "Sometimes the price is just too steep."

He gave her hand a squeeze. She drew strength from his touch.

"I—I told him—" her throat grew thick as she pushed through "—that there wasn't anything that he could say or do to get me to come home."

Another tear splashed onto her cheek. She sniffled and

ran the back of her hand over her cheeks. Why had she been so stubborn? So determined that she was right?

She pulled her hand from Jax's, no longer feeling worthy of his understanding. And he'd have no choice but to agree once she told him the price of her independence.

Her voice cracked with emotion. "Those were the last words I spoke to him."

She stared straight ahead at the desert, not wanting to see the look of disgust in Jax's eyes. She wouldn't be able to finish if she looked at him.

"The line… It went dead. I thought he'd hung up on me. I thought… Oh, it doesn't matter." She sniffled, trying to maintain a bit of composure. "I found out later…that he'd blown through a stop sign. He…he was broadsided."

Jax leaned forward, squeezing her shoulder. "It was an accident. It could have happened to anyone."

"But it didn't." She turned to Jax. "If I hadn't been arguing with him, he wouldn't have been distracted. He always obeyed stop signs. This is all on me."

"How do you know that he wasn't tired? Or he hadn't been distracted by something falling off the dashboard or the seat. Maybe he reached over to pick it up."

She shook her head, taking a second to collect herself. "I know what happened because there was an investigation. The police determined he was talking to me at the time of the accident."

"I'm sorry, Cleo. But this isn't your fault."

"My mother would disagree. She totally flipped out on me. She ordered me out of the funeral home. She said as far as she was concerned, she…she had no daughter."

"She didn't mean it—"

By now the tears were running unleashed. "Yes, she did. I was banished from Hope Springs. I tried to call a couple of times after that, but she hung up."

"She was in shock and mourning the loss of your father. I'm sure she didn't mean it."

"Even my brothers have changed. They speak to me, but it's not the same. Nothing is the same. Everyone blames me and they're right. This is my punishment."

Jax placed a finger beneath her chin and turned her head until she was facing him. "None of them had any right to lay this at your feet. You didn't know he was on the phone while driving. Not to speak ill of the dead, but the decision to talk on the phone while driving is all on him. And second, he didn't have a right to demand you come home."

Had she heard Jax correctly? Wait. This wasn't the way she thought this conversation would go.

"You don't blame me?"

"Of course not. And if your mother had been thinking clearly, she wouldn't have blamed you, either. It was an accident. And no one person was to blame. It was a culmination of events."

She wanted to believe him—wanted to shed the weight of guilt that had kept her isolated in Las Vegas through the lonely holidays, missing how her brothers would gather around the tree on Christmas Eve passing out gifts. And later how they'd argue over who got to carve the turkey.

Cleo blinked repeatedly. She might not have wanted to be a rancher, but that didn't mean she wanted to walk away from her family. She just wanted them to respect that she was grown-up now and fully capable of making her own choices on where she lived and how she lived her life. In her worst nightmare, she never dreamed she'd be labeled a black sheep and banished from her home.

"Remember when you were a kid, you always had your head in the clouds." Jax looked her in the eye. "You dreamed about those fancy fashion shows and how you wanted to travel to Milan and Paris. I never saw anyone who liked clothes as much as you."

She lifted her head to look him in the eye. "You remember that?"

"Those days that you'd sit and talk about places you'd learned about in one of your magazines taught me something important. You made me realize I could dream bigger than Hope Springs."

"I thought you were bored stiff listening to me."

"Not at all. You were like a breath of fresh air after hearing my father rant on and on about all of the injustices in this world." Jax leaned toward her. "You don't know how much I enjoyed our talks down by the creek."

"You mean when you were supposed to be fishing. And I was supposed to be quiet so as not to scare off the fish." They shared a smile.

"But you were so much more interesting." He leaned closer. "I had a hard time keeping my attention on my fishing pole. I'm lucky a big fish didn't swim off with it because you were all I could think about."

He'd noticed her? How had she missed the signs?

His fingers stroked her cheek. "But you were far too young and most definitely off-limits back then."

"And now?" Where had that question come from?

"And now I can do this..."

His hand slipped down to cup her neck. Could he feel the way he made her pulse jump? Did he know in that moment she couldn't think of anything but him?

With mere inches between them, she wondered if he'd put her out of her misery and kiss her. Her gaze moved from his tempting lips to his eyes. They were dark with a definite glint of interest in them.

Her heart pounded so loud that it was the only sound

she could hear. Logic fled her. Instead she mentally willed him closer. Her eyelids slid shut as her anticipation grew.

And then he was there. His lips tentatively pressed to hers.

Butterflies fluttered in her stomach. This was like an out-of-body experience where her body did what it desired and she sat back luxuriating in the most exquisite sensations. She didn't think it was possible but with each kiss, they got better. She wasn't sure how he could improve on perfection, but somehow he did.

She leaned into his kiss, meeting his hunger with her own. Her head spun and she didn't want this moment to end. She reached out to him, wanting to pull him closer, but the darn seat belts did their jobs and restrained them, as did the cat carrier in her lap.

Charlie meowed his protest at being jostled around. They pulled apart. But Jax's gaze held hers and she wanted to know what he was thinking—what he was feeling. But a louder protest from the cat carrier drew her attention.

She squeezed her fingers past the metal bars, trying to soothe Charlie. "It's okay, boy. I didn't mean to bounce you around."

Jax shifted the SUV into gear. "You know if it wasn't for you and your dreams, I never would have dared to imagine another life for myself. I'd have most likely given up on school and ended up just as disillusioned about life as my father. It's hard to tell where I'd be now."

She smiled through her tears. "You probably wouldn't be sitting on the side of the road with a crying woman who's holding a cat on her lap."

"Probably not. But right now, I can't think of anyplace I'd rather be."

Jax eased back onto the roadway and they headed north

to their five-star getaway. Her stomach quivered as she
wondered where they went from here. Was this all some
sort of sympathy? Or was there a deeper meaning to that
kiss?

# CHAPTER TEN

TREAD CAREFULLY.

After a week of sharing the mansion, Jax found himself susceptible to Cleo's enchanting spell. He'd found her fascinating as a kid, and as a woman, she was near irresistible. But no matter how sweet and enticing she may be, he couldn't keep finding excuses to touch her—to kiss her. The best thing he could do was find a way to reunite her with her family.

But first, he had something he had to do. He was tired of waiting for the doctor's office to call. He could only figure they'd lost his new number and that was why they hadn't called with his test results.

He glanced around for Cleo. Not finding any signs of her, he grabbed the cell phone from the kitchen counter and dialed the familiar number. After two rings, it switched to a prerecorded message announcing the doctor was out of the office for the next week.

Jax cursed under his breath and resisted the urge to throw the phone across the room. Of all the times for the doctor to have a personal life, why did it have to be now?

The distinct sound of Cleo's crutches echoed down the hall. He cleared the number and placed the phone back on the counter. He'd just turned around when she entered the room.

She stopped in front of him with a frown marring her beautiful face. "Have you seen Charlie?"

"I wasn't exactly looking for him. Why?"

"I don't know. He's just usually wherever I am, and I haven't seen him since first thing this morning."

"In a house this size it wouldn't be hard for him to find a hiding spot."

A frown settled on her face. "I know, but I just worry."

She fussed over that cat like a mother caring for a young child. The image of her holding a baby in her arms came to mind. That was yet another reason why they shouldn't be playing house.

Jax shifted his weight from one foot to the other. "I'll... um, go look around for him. Why don't you sit down? You know what the doctor said about resting."

"How could I forget? You remind me every day." She started toward the family room before calling over her shoulder, "While you're upstairs would you mind grabbing the blue tote bag from my bedroom?"

"Your wish is my command."

He took the steps two at a time. His gaze scanned the hallway for any sign of the feline. How in the world was he going to find a little cat in this big house? He'd probably found a nice dark corner to take a catnap.

But first Jax needed to get the bag for Cleo. He worried that she was overdoing it and he didn't want her to reinjure herself. He told himself that it was no more care than he'd give to a coworker or neighbor... But then again he wouldn't be kissing them. And with each passing day it was getting harder to keep Cleo at arm's length.

Not only was he painfully attracted to her, but her passion for life made him want to set out on a new adventure. He found himself daydreaming about having a full life— no longer spending his days chained to a desk and computer. His thoughts trailed back to Hope Springs with its wide-open spaces and its endless possibilities. But most of all, he envisioned Cleo by his side.

However, for that to happen, he'd have to sentence her to an eventual life of caring for an ill man with a tenuous future—only to wind up a young widow. Cold fingers of apprehension gripped his throat, cutting off his breath. He refused to do that to Cleo. He banished the unsettling thoughts to the back of his mind. No matter how tempting a life with her might seem, he couldn't put her in that horrendous situation.

With the blue bag in hand, he returned to the family room, where Cleo had turned on the big-screen TV. A fashion design competition was on. "I take it you still enjoy clothes."

She nodded while rummaging through the oversize bag and pulling out a sketch pad and a pack of pencils.

"Some things don't change."

"Did you find Charlie?" She glanced at him expectantly.

He'd forgotten about the furball. Where in the world did he even begin to look for the cat?

As though reading his mind, Cleo said, "You'll have to get down on all fours. He likes to nap in cozy, dark spots."

Jax expelled a sigh. He might as well start in here. "Here kitty, kitty."

He crawled around on the floor looking under every piece of furniture in the room. There was no cat to be found.

Jax sat up on his knees next to Cleo. "He isn't in here." His gaze moved to the sketch pad in her hands. "What are you doing?"

She jerked the pad against her chest. "Why?"

"I'm curious."

"You'll just laugh."

"Why would I laugh? Obviously you're drawing something that's important to you. I'm just curious what it is."

Her shoulders drooped and the lines in her face eased. "It's just that when I was growing up my brothers would always poke fun at my drawings. I guess I didn't realize, until now, how touchy I've become."

"Can I see? I promise to be on my best behavior."

Her mouth pulled to the side as she thought it over before she nodded. When she turned the pad around, he sat up straighter, truly interested. There was the outline of a woman with no face, but the details were in the soft pink dress with a long skirt and a halter-style top.

"That's impressive." He meant it. "Instead of going to college to become an accountant, you should have considered pursuing art."

"You really think it's that good."

He nodded. "If I had to draw it, there'd be a stick figure on the page. It wouldn't be that good of one, either. And as for the clothes, um…do rectangles and squares count?"

"I don't think so. They'd be awfully uncomfortable."

The rays from Cleo's smile filled his chest with warmth. Until that moment he hadn't realized how empty his life had been, even before the cancer. Sure, he had his work, and his amazing success at such a young age was very rewarding. But when he returned to his apartment in the evenings, it was dark and empty. There wasn't so much as a fish or a Charlie waiting for him.

He didn't know how he'd ever go back to that solitary life after sharing this place with Cleo…and her furball. The cat really wasn't so bad after all. In fact, he rather liked the little guy, which was probably a good thing since the cat had taken to snuggling up on his chest when he was sleeping. He'd surprisingly grown used to Charlie's nightly visits.

Jax knew he was setting himself up for a fall because this arrangement was not permanent—no matter how much he might like it to be otherwise. But he had resolved not to fight it. There was no harm in enjoying Cleo's company—as long as he kept his hands to himself.

"So what do you do with your drawings?"

"Actually they are sketches of clothes I plan to make." Her eyes never left his, as though she was anxious to gauge his reaction. "Aren't you going to say anything?"

"I don't know what to say except…wow! You're a lady of many talents."

"You're really impressed?"

"Of course I am. Did you make what you're wearing now?"

His gaze moved to the pink-and-white tiny T-shirt and gray sweat shorts. It didn't matter what she wore, she always looked beautiful.

Cleo shook her head. "I only make dress clothes like the ones you saw me in at the Glamour Hotel."

"Have you been doing this for long?"

She nodded. "My grandmother taught me how to sew at an early age. She was a very patient woman. More so than I could ever hope to be."

He glanced through her sketchbook. Each drawing was more impressive than the last. "Have you sent these out to professionals?"

Color infused her cheeks. "I couldn't do that."

He caught the uncertainty in her eyes. "I'm no expert, but I think you should follow your dream. If you want I can make some calls."

"No!" She grabbed the sketch pad from him. "I already

know my clothes aren't good enough. I've been told they're too frivolous. It'd be a waste of time."

Anger warmed his veins. "And who told you that?"

"My parents. They said that if I insisted on going to college that I must take up a skill that was practical and would eventually provide me with a substantial income when I finished."

He wanted to argue with her and those misconceptions that her parents drilled into her head. They had stolen her dreams. And now he was determined to find a way to give them back to her.

Jax sat down on the carpet and leaned an elbow on the couch near Cleo's pink-painted toes. "Boy, your parents were more set in their ways than I ever imagined."

"Now you're seeing why I moved across the country for college and why I was arguing with my father..."

Not wanting her to return to that dark, quiet place where she locked him out, he said, "So this sketch, is it an outfit for yourself?"

Her gaze snapped back from that faraway look. "Um... no. It's actually for Robyn. She's always going on about my clothes and how pretty they are, which is so sweet. Anyway she wanted me to make an outfit for her. It's nice to have someone appreciate my efforts."

If Cleo ever hoped to make peace with her mother, she had to lighten up on her. Maybe he could try to help bridge that gap. He hated the thought of Cleo with no family. He wouldn't wish a solitary existence on anyone, especially when he knew as sure as he was sitting there that deep down where it counted, her mother loved her.

"Cleo, did you ever think that maybe your parents saw your fashion magazines and your high-class creations as a rejection of the life they chose to lead? Or maybe they were afraid that if they encouraged you to follow your dreams that you'd up and leave Hope Springs—leave them."

A light shone in her eyes. "But I never looked down on them or the ranch. It's my...was my home."

"But every time you complained about having to ride the fence line or feed the herd, maybe they took it as a strike against their lifestyle. I'm not saying it was right what they said or how they made you feel, but maybe they thought if you lost interest in fashion that you would realize the ranch was the right place for you."

Cleo's fine brows arched. "You really think that's what it was about?"

Jax raked his fingers through his hair. "I don't have all of the answers. I just know that a mother's love runs deep. You've both made mistakes. How long has it been since you tried to talk to her?"

"Almost two years. The last time I called was a month after the funeral. She told me never to call again." Cleo's eyes shimmered and she blinked repeatedly.

"Try to forget what she said in a moment of grief and follow your heart. When you talk to her be honest about who you are and what you want in life. Maybe she'll surprise you. What do you have to lose?"

Cleo shook her head. "I—I can't do that. I can't have her say those hurtful things again. I'm fine with the way things are now."

"Then you're lying to me and yourself. This distance isn't making you happy. You may have all of the independence in the world, but it'll never replace the love of your family. And don't doubt that they love you just as much as you love them." He got to his feet. "Now I have a cat to track down."

He didn't want to push Cleo too far too fast, but before they went their separate ways, he hoped she'd work up the courage to call home. The sooner, the better. Otherwise he wasn't sure if he could just walk away from her and leave her alone.

A few days later, Cleo was still thinking over Jax's words. The fact that he'd come to her mother's defense she found confusing. Why was he pushing this? There had never been any love between him and her mother. In fact, as a kid, Jax used to revel in egging her mother on by doing things to irritate her. So why was he suddenly coming to her mother's aid?

It didn't make any sense. But more than that, Cleo didn't feel worthy to be part of the Sinclair clan any longer. Not when her actions contributed to her father's death—the man who gave her the dream of an Ivy League school even though he'd had to put the family's heritage at risk to do it. And how did she repay him? By her last words to him being ones of anger.

Cleo gave herself a mental jerk. She wasn't going down that painful road again. She'd thought she'd tucked all of these memories into a locked box in the back of her mind. Now the memories had broken the padlock and were spilling out faster than she could push the lid closed.

What she needed to do was quit thinking. She'd done enough of that all afternoon and right about now, the most delightful aroma was coming from the kitchen.

Tired of sketching, she closed the pad and placed it on the glass coffee table alongside her colored pencils. She grabbed the crutches that she was now more adept at using and made her way to the kitchen.

From the hallway, she could hear Jax talking but she couldn't make out what he was saying until she got closer. "Don't look so down. Us guys have to stick together. I'm sure that surgery wasn't easy."

*Surgery? Oh, having Charlie neutered.* She smiled as she listened to Jax sympathizing with the cat. He continued to talk as if Charlie understood every word he said.

"Here. Maybe this will cheer you up."

Cleo turned the corner in time to find Jax doling out some treats before turning his attention back to the stove.

"So you and Charlie are buddies now?"

Jax jerked around from where he'd been stirring a steaming pot. With the spoon still in his hand, the tomato sauce dripped all over the black-and-white floor tiles. The sheepish look reminded her of the expression her brothers would get when caught stealing one of her mother's cookies fresh from the oven.

"You heard that?"

"I did." She worked her way over to the island and pulled out a stool. "I told you Charlie would grow on you."

Jax turned away and busied himself cleaning up the mess. "There. All cleaned up." He tossed the paper towels in the trash and washed his hands. "I hope you like pasta."

"Smells delicious to me. What is it?"

"My version of Sicilian pasta." He broke up some capellini and dunked it in a pot of boiling water. "It'll be ready shortly if you want to go back to the family room. I can bring it in there."

"I'm bored with my own company. Mind if I stay and watch?"

He cocked a smile. "Is that your way of saying that I'm interesting? Or am I just the best of the worst?"

She laughed. "Hmm…I'm not going to answer on the grounds that it might incriminate me."

"I see how you are," he said teasingly as he moved to the fridge.

She wouldn't have missed this for anything in the world. As he bent over to retrieve some salad makings, she couldn't help but take in the way his faded jeans accentuated his backside. There wasn't an ounce of flab on the guy. Between his good looks and wealth, why was he still single?

"So do you do this often?"

He turned around with a head of iceberg lettuce in one hand and a large tomato in the other. "No. I rarely cook."

Then an unhappy thought came to mind. "Is that because there's a woman around to do the cooking for you?"

His gaze caught hers. "And what would you say if I told you that she cooks, cleans and folds my underwear, too?"

The thought that he'd be involved with someone hadn't even crossed her mind. An uneasy feeling stirred within her. She didn't know why she'd just assumed he was available. He was sexy and rich. He could have his choice of women.

"Before you go jumping to the wrong conclusion," Jax said, "you should know that she's my cleaning lady. She's old enough to be my mother and she's happily married."

Cleo breathed easier. "That's good because I'm never going to be the other woman. Especially when I know firsthand how much it hurts everyone involved." Then realizing she'd said too much, heat licked at her cheeks.

She glanced up, catching the slack-jawed look on Jax's face.

"I would never want you to be the other woman. If you were mine, there wouldn't be anyone else in my life but you. You'd be all I'd need."

Her gaze met his. Her heart thump-thumped in her chest. She'd only ever dreamed of someone speaking such endearing words to her.

The kitchen timer buzzed. In a blink the fairy-tale moment ended.

Jax moved around the counter. "I have to take care of

the pasta, but don't go anywhere. We aren't through with this conversation."

She watched as he drained the pasta, dribbled some olive oil on it, gave it a toss and put the lid on the pan. She thought of sneaking off while he stirred the sauce, but she was certain that he'd track her down. She might as well get this over with. Her stomach growled its agreement. Her only road to dinner was a detour through her past.

After turning down the heat and giving the sauce one final stir, Jax joined her at the counter. He settled down on the stool and faced her, "Now, what is this about you being hurt by another woman?"

"It's not worth getting into the details. Let's just say the moral of the story is I let myself fall for the wrong guy. And now I know better. So let's have dinner and forget all of this."

"Not so fast. I want to know the parts you're skipping over."

She exhaled an exasperated sigh. She hated to think about how naive she'd been. She'd never be that trusting again because putting your heart on the line was just asking to be hurt—even from those that you'd least expect.

"It was my last year in college and I'd fallen hard for this guy from my public speaking class. He was charming and charismatic. Let's just say he aced the class without breaking a sweat."

"And you fell for his charms, not knowing that he had a darker side?"

She nodded. "He was perfect. Good-looking. Talkative. Funny. Or so I thought at the time."

"What kind of things did he like to talk about?"

She shrugged. "His classes. His future plans. Football. Nothing specific."

"Did he ever care about what was important to you?"

"Not really." She stopped, not realizing until that moment that most of their conversations had revolved around him. "When I had news, he'd quickly change the subject back to him. I guess I should have seen the warning signs earlier."

"It's not your fault. You tried. He obviously didn't. So what made you see him as the jerk that he is?"

"We'd been dating for a little more than six months when I didn't feel well and came back to my dorm room early from a class to find him in bed with my roommate."

Jax clenched his hands. "If I'd been around, he wouldn't have gotten away with that."

She took comfort in hearing the protective tones in Jax's voice. "Well, I'm glad you weren't there."

Jax's brows rose in a question.

"He wasn't worth you getting into trouble. Besides, I've lived and learned, even if it was the hard way. The important part is I won't be making those same mistakes again."

"But you have to know that all men aren't like him." Jax's voice grew deep. "If you were mine, I'd never look at another woman as long as I lived."

Her gaze met his. Her heart once again went thump-thump. "Seriously? You'd really only have eyes for me?"

"You're the most beautiful woman in the world." His thumb stroked her cheek, followed her jawline and rubbed over her bottom lip. His gaze never left hers.

His touch sent her insides quivering with excitement. She was drawn to him like a butterfly to a field of poppies. Not waiting for him to make the first move, she pressed her lips to his thumb. His eyes lit up with excitement. She was enjoying this new side of herself and she didn't want this moment to end.

The tip of her tongue darted out, stroking the length of his finger. She immediately heard the swift intake of his breath. He wanted her. And she wanted him. There were no strings. No promises. Just the intrigue of finding out where this moment might lead.

Jax pulled away. "I have to get the sauce... It's getting too hot. It's bubbling over. I don't want it to...uh, burn."

He moved away and Cleo smiled to herself knowing that she'd gotten to him. This thing between them, whatever it was, was not over. Not by a long shot.

Jax kept his attention focused on the food. "You know there are good guys in this world."

"I know. You're one of them."

He shook his head. "I don't mean me. I'm not right for you. But there's someone better waiting to find you."

"I doubt it." The smiled faded from her face. "Besides, the people that you're supposed to be able to trust the most are the first ones to let you down when you really need them."

"We're not talking about jerk face anymore, are we?"

She shook her head and lowered her gaze to the floor. She couldn't help but think of her family. They were the ones she always thought she could count on—no matter what.

"I honestly think you should call you mother."

He was really pushing for a mother-daughter reunion. Buy why? Was he that anxious to get rid of her and he just couldn't bring himself to say it?

Dread filled her heart. She'd been down this road before. Her instinct was to leave and not look back. She could return to the casino and he could fly back to New York. But as much as she wanted that to happen, some ape man out there was looking for them. For now, they were stuck here together.

# CHAPTER ELEVEN

BY THE END of the week, Cleo had promised she'd call her mother if he'd just quit pestering her.

Now the moment of truth had arrived. She stared at the disposable cell phone the same way she would a rattler—one false move and she'd be in a world of regret. Whatever made her think calling home was a good idea? Oh, yes, Jax. He seemed to be full of all sorts of advice these days.

And the part she hated most was knowing he was right. She missed her family. After fighting to follow her own path in life and to be able to make her own choices, she still didn't feel complete. There was a gap in her life—her mother and brothers.

Jax's voice echoed in her mind. *Deep down she still loves you. What do you have to lose?*

Inhaling a steadying breath, Cleo picked up the phone. She didn't know if she was strong enough to do as Jax suggested, but she could do the next best thing. She dialed an old, familiar number. Her stomach quivered like a dried leaf on a blustery fall day. What if—

"Hello?"

She knew the deep timbre of the male voice. "Kurt, it's Cleo."

"Cleo?" Her oldest brother said her name as if he was

talking to a ghost. "What are you doing calling? Is something wrong?"

It was not exactly the greeting she'd been hoping for. This was nothing like the cheerful calls she'd used to make from college. But then again that was another lifetime. Things had changed irrevocably since then.

"I—I— How are things there?"

"Not so good. I've been putting off telling Mom about the mess with the bank, but I need to do it soon."

"You know Mom has no head for business. That's why Dad left you in charge. If you tell her, she'll just worry." And have one more thing to hold against Cleo.

"And if we don't come up with some money soon, there won't be a business for any of us to worry about."

Cleo worried the inside of her lip, wondering if she should mention her promotion. After her accident and now with her missing work, she didn't know if she'd still have a job when she returned. Although Jax seemed certain that her job was protected. Maybe he was right.

"I got a big promotion at work." Then in her excitement, she forgot that she hadn't told her family about her job at the casino.

"That's nice, sis. But we need more than a bump in your paycheck to cover the arrears on this loan." He sighed. "I should tell you that I've had to sell off some of the stock, including Buttercup."

Cleo gasped. She loved and missed the even-tempered mare. The backs of her eyes started to burn. It was the last gift her father had given her—no, it wasn't. There was the horse her father had bought for her as a bribe to move home. But the horse had died in the same accident that snuffed out her father's life. With that sobering thought in mind, she knew she had no right to complain about her brother's actions.

"I'm sorry, Cleo. I've had to drastically reduce the overhead."

She swiped at her eyes and sniffled. "I—I understand."

Maybe Jax was right. Maybe now was the time to be up front with her family about her choices. It was time to quit sneaking around and pretending to be the person they wanted her to be instead of showing them the real Cleo.

Taking a calming breath, she gripped the phone tightly. "Kurt, this promotion is a lot more than a bump in my check. I'm now working as a casino host."

"What?" There was a pause as though he were letting the news sink in. "You mean you wear slinky outfits and flirt with men to get them to gamble more?"

"No. I wear really nice clothes. In fact, I design and make my own clothes."

She considered mentioning that Jax was one of her clients so her brother wouldn't worry so much, but under the circumstances, she realized that it was best to keep Jax and this mess with ape man to herself. It would be safest for everyone—especially Jax. And she didn't want to jeopardize Jax's friendship with her brother, if Kurt decided to act all protective of his little sister.

Without giving her brother an opportunity to hassle her about her career choice, she hurried on. "I'll forward you some money as soon as I get paid." And now for the real reason she'd called. "How are Joe, Stephen and Cassidy?"

"They're fine. Cleo, what is it you really want to know?"

Kurt always knew when she was hedging around something. "And how's Mom doing?"

"You know, same as always. Busy with this and that. But the arthritis in her fingers is getting worse. If you're really curious to know how she's doing, you should call her."

Her chest tightened at the thought of being rejected by

her mother again. She didn't know if she could open herself up to the potential for that kind of pain.

"I—I don't think that's a good idea. I tried calling her after the funeral. She told me not to call back and hung up."

"I'm sorry, sis." He expelled a weary sigh. "Mom wasn't herself after Dad died. She was angry with everyone for a long time. Most of all I think she was angry with Dad for leaving her. She's been lost without him."

"I remember how in love they were after so many years. I always dreamed of having a marriage like theirs."

"You can still have that, if you want it."

"Listen to who's talking. You're older than me and you have yet to settle down and start a family."

"I have a lot of responsibilities. I don't have time for that stuff."

Another pang of guilt assaulted her. If she hadn't been arguing with her father that day, he wouldn't have died. Her mother wouldn't have melted down. And her brother wouldn't be devoting his every waking hour to keeping the ranch afloat. Kurt might be happily married by now with a baby on the way.

"I should go." She didn't know what else to say. There were no words to repair the damage that had been done.

"Cleo, call Mom. Enough time has passed. I think she'd want to hear from you."

After promising to think it over, Cleo disconnected the call. She still wasn't sure about calling her mother. After all, her mother was right. The tragedy of her father's death was her fault—no matter what Jax said. Why should her mother forgive her? If the roles were reversed, she didn't honestly know how she'd deal with such a profound loss.

The phone buzzed, startling her. She glanced at the screen, but didn't recognize the number.

"Jax! Jax! Phone."

She didn't know where he'd been but he entered the family room at a dead run, grabbed the phone and punched the talk button. "Yes." A pause. "Yes, it is."

He strolled out of the room.

That was strange. She thought that it was dangerous to let people have their phone number because of the GPS tracking system. So who did Jax trust enough with their location? The police? And why was his face creased with worry lines?

Jax's entire body tensed as he waited for the doctor to come on the line. He paced back and forth on the veranda. The afternoon sun was hot, but his need for privacy trumped being comfortable. He didn't normally pray, but in this instance if he had any points with God, he could use some help now.

"Jax, this is Dr. Collins. How are you doing?"

Did he mean besides the stress of knowing that his clients were up in arms because the funds in his investment accounts had been seized as evidence until this trial was over? Apart from the fact some thug attacked the woman that he…that he considered a close friend? Or aside from the fact that he was secluded in a ritzy home with a woman who could make him want her with just a look?

"I'm doing good," he lied.

"That's what I like to hear from my patients. But something tells me even if you weren't feeling like your old self yet, you wouldn't say anything. Don't push yourself too hard, too fast. And if you won't listen to me, at least listen to your body. It'll tell you what it needs."

Enough of this, he needed to know where he stood. "Doc, what did the tests reveal?"

"Nothing. That is to say there's nothing wrong with you. At this point, you are fit and healthy."

"Really?" His legs felt like jelly. He sank down on a chair. "You're absolutely positive?"

"I am. You can relax now. There's no reason you can't continue with a normal, healthy life."

Immediately Cleo's face came to mind. "But the cancer, it can come back, can't it?"

There was a distinct pause. "I won't lie to you. It can. For the next couple of years we'll keep a close eye on you. If anything develops, we'll catch it early. But I would think positive."

"Thanks, Doc."

They talked a few more minutes and Jax promised to schedule a follow-up appointment in six months. By the time he got off the phone, he was so relieved, he pumped his fists and yelled, "Yes!" like a pro football player after scoring the winning touchdown in the final seconds of the game.

This was the game of his life. After months of tests and treatments, the endless wonder and worry, he could at last relax. For the moment, he was healthy.

He let himself back in the house, eager to seek out Cleo. She was curled up again with her pencils and sketch pad. She glanced up when he entered the room.

"Is everything okay?"

"Um, yes." Had she heard him cheering? He doubted it. The house was far too big for voices to carry that far. "I actually got some good news."

"You did? That's great." She smiled and patted the spot on the couch next to her. "Come sit down. You can tell me your good news, and I need your opinion on something."

For the first time since he had found the lump under his arm, he had energy and felt as if he could run a marathon. Okay, maybe not a marathon but at least around the block.

The invitation to sit next to the most gorgeous woman

in the world was just too tempting to resist. However, he forced himself to leave a comfortable distance between them.

Charlie lifted his head from where he was sleeping on the opposite side of Cleo, eyed him up and then promptly went back to sleep. He was going to miss Charlie. Every time he opened the fridge and grabbed for the bag of lunch meat, the cat knew it and made a beeline for the kitchen so he could have some, too.

Needing a moment or two to sort out what to say to her, Jax said, "First, tell me how the conversation with your mother went."

"It didn't."

He turned to look directly at her. "What do you mean, it didn't?"

"I didn't call her."

"But I thought that's why you borrowed the phone."

She went on to tell him how she called her brother instead. Jax's body tensed as he wondered if this thing between Cleo and himself could ruin a lifetime friendship with Kurt. He hated the thought of losing yet another person from his life.

"Did you mention anything about us?" He braced himself for the answer.

"No, I didn't." Cleo's eyes filled with compassion. "I didn't feel it was my place. I know how protective Kurt can be, and I know he made you promise to stay away from me."

"You do?"

She smiled at him. "Let's just say that a little sister can have big ears when the need arises. I figure if there's ever anything to tell him about us, you'll find a way to tell him. After all, it isn't like I'm a teenager any longer."

"Maybe you're right." He desperately wanted to believe

her. But he knew he was jumping too far ahead. It wasn't as if they had a future. "And right now Kurt has enough on his mind."

Two V-shaped lines formed between her brows. "Do you think I'll get paid much for the time I was your casino host? You know, before ape man ruined things?"

"You don't have anything to worry about. I wagered a sizable fortune while I was at the Glamour. And lost quite a bit. All in all you should get a generous paycheck."

"Oh, good!" Color immediately rushed to her cheeks and she glanced away. "Sorry. I didn't mean I was excited about your loss...just that I'd have some money to send home to Kurt. He sounded defeated on the phone."

"I understand." Jax wanted to ease the worry on her face, but he still wasn't sure how to go about it without overstepping. "I'd like to help."

"You would?"

"Yes. I've been doing some thinking about this even before I heard that the Bar S was in trouble."

"We could definitely use the help." She looked up at him with a hopeful gleam. "What did you have in mind?"

He wasn't so sure how Cleo would feel about his idea. In fact, he was hesitant to bring it up. Maybe he should just go directly to Kurt with it. But then again if he couldn't get it past Cleo, he'd never get her brother to agree.

"I want to buy your grandfather's ranch."

Cleo sat back. Her eyes opened wide. "But why?"

"I'm tired of New York. I accomplished what I went there to do."

"Make yourself into a business success?"

He nodded. "Now I want to try something different."

"But I would have thought you'd be settled in New York. Won't you miss it?"

He shrugged. "Some. Certainly the coffee shop down

the street from my apartment building. They have the best bagels. But I need something more."

"What did you have in mind?"

"I thought of returning to Hope Springs. I miss the wide-open space."

"You mean to move there permanently?"

"It's one possibility. I was planning to explore the idea when the strange phone calls started. I didn't want to travel to Hope Springs and have trouble follow me there. That would just reinforce some folks' opinions that I'm still bad news."

"No one would say that."

He eyed her, knowing she was lying just to make him feel better. "Your mother might disagree."

She reached out and squeezed his arm, sending a sensation zinging through his veins and settling in his chest. He stared deep into her eyes, wanting to pull her into his arms. Since he'd talked to the doctor, he felt as though he had a new lease on life.

But before he could move, Cleo's smile morphed into a frown.

"What is it?" He'd fix it if he could. Right about now, he'd do anything for her.

"I'm just worried about my job at the casino. I can't lose it."

At least he could reassure her. "You don't have to worry. Your job will be there waiting for you as soon as you're ready."

"I don't know. I didn't complete the one task Mr. Burns gave me."

"What was that?"

"Keeping you happy."

"Oh, trust me. You've made me very happy."

"Really?"

He nodded and her eyes twinkled with mischief.

She leaned forward and in a breathy voice said, "Maybe I could make you happier."

In an instant, her lips pressed to his. His heart slammed into his ribs. Now wasn't the time for overthinking things. It was a time for decisive action. His hands slipped around her waist, pulling her closer. Every nerve ending sprang to life. He hadn't felt this free, this alive, in forever.

Cleo smelled like a field of wildflowers. He didn't know if it was her perfume or shampoo, but there was something about her that had an intoxicating effect on him.

Who'd ever think that the girl who gave him that inexperienced peck all those years ago would grow up to give such passionate kisses? Her lips moved over his in a fervent hunger. And when she moaned, it was his undoing. In that moment, it didn't matter what she'd ask of him, he'd be helpless to deny her.

Her fingers trailed up his neck. Her nails scraped against his scalp. It was the most stimulating sensation. He couldn't believe the girl whose ponytails he used to pull and who would flash him a smile lined with braces was now this red-hot siren in his arms setting his whole body on fire.

She pulled back just far enough to murmur, "Let's move this to the bedroom, where my cast won't be in the way."

It was as if she'd dumped a bucket of icy cold mountain water over his head. He…he couldn't do that, no matter how much he wanted her. He turned his head away, trying to get a grip.

"We can't." He couldn't look her in the face.

She placed her fingers under his chin and attempted to turn his head, but he resisted. He felt like a wild animal that had been caught in a trap. There was no getting away.

No pretending that he was the same Jax that he'd been all those years ago.

"You can kiss me, but you can't even look at me now." Irritation threaded through her voice. "What's the matter? Don't my kisses stack up to the other women you've known?"

He swung around and looked at her point-blank. "They aren't even in the same ballpark. Yours are so much sweeter. You're amazing."

"Then I don't understand. What's the problem? Why do you keep pulling me close only to shove me away?"

For the lack of anything better, he fell back on a cliché. "It's not you, it's me."

Cleo rolled her eyes. "You've got to do better than that. I want to know the truth."

"Can't we just forget this happened?"

"No, we can't. I want you. And you obviously want me. You owe me the truth. What's holding you back?"

There was no way out of this. He supposed he did owe her the truth, but somehow that didn't make it any easier to say.

# CHAPTER TWELVE

JAX COULDN'T BELIEVE he was about to bare his soul to Cleo.

His gut knotted as he pictured her withdrawing from him—of her looking at him differently. He didn't want to make this confession. But what choice did he have? She needed to realize here and now that they could never be more than friends.

He lifted his head to meet her questioning gaze. "I'm not the same man you used to know."

She squeezed his hand. "And I'm not a kid anymore. But I think you figured that out."

He pulled away, needing to think straight. "This isn't easy for me to say."

She reached out and gripped his thigh. "You've listened and understood my problems. Trust me to understand yours."

Realizing he needed more distance between them if he was ever going to say this, he got to his feet. If she kept touching him, he'd never get these words out.

He strode over to the wall of windows and wished he could just keep walking off into the desert—where no one knew him and no one cared about his story. He honestly never planned to have this conversation with anyone. Yet somehow when he wasn't looking, Cleo had snuck past his defenses. She'd gotten closer to him than anyone ever had in his life. And now he had to give them both a strong dose of reality.

He leveled his shoulders and turned. "I have cancer."

She fell back against the couch as though his words had physically knocked the breath out of her. "Are…are you dying?"

He shook his head. "I have Hodgkin's lymphoma. Luckily I found the lump early on. And I've since been through the treatments."

"Are you cured?"

He shook his head. "But I just found out that I'm in remission."

The fright in her eyes eased to a look of concern. He wished she would say something. Do something. Even if it was to walk away. At least then he'd know where they stood.

As the silence stretched on, his patience snapped. "Cleo, did you hear me? I have cancer."

"I heard you. I'm just wondering, with both of your parents gone, did you go through this all by yourself?"

He didn't see why any of that mattered now. "Yes, I did."

"You know if you'd called me or even Kurt, we'd have been there for you."

Her words stirred a spot in his chest. The thought that she'd even offer to stand by him through such a tough time said so much about her sweet nature. Cleo may have grown up and changed on the outside, but inside, where it counted, she was still the caring and thoughtful person he'd known all those years ago.

He drew his thoughts up short. He was letting himself get distracted. He had to be sure she understood what he was trying to tell her—that he couldn't be with her the way she wanted. That this thing between them had gone as far as he could let it go.

"I'm so sorry you felt you had to go through that all alone."

"Cleo, you aren't understanding what I'm trying to tell you."

"Yes, I am. You told me that you were very sick and you had no one there to stand by your side. But now you don't have to face the future alone. You have me. I'll be there to hold your hand. Or read you silly stories from magazines. Whatever you need."

She wanted to be there for him? Really be there. Not just with words but with action, too. His gaze blurred and he blinked rapidly. No one since his mother had ever put his needs first. He glanced away and rubbed at his eyes. Someday Cleo would make some man amazingly happy. He envied that person.

Jax cleared the lump in his throat. "You won't need to do that. My treatments are done for now. But that's no guarantee there won't be a recurrence."

There. He'd said it all. She knew now she'd be wasting her time on him. He turned his back, unable to watch her walk away.

He waited. Listening. Longing for this agonizing moment to be over. Just like when he was a kid and got caught stealing a locket for his dying mother. She always wanted one to hold pictures of the two men in her life, but his father told her it was a waste of money. Some people had looked at Jax with pity and a certain amount of resignation. Others had turned their backs on him. He hadn't cared. It was the only thing he'd been able to do for her on her deathbed and it had been worth every cruel look. Why should he think that now would be any different?

But in the next moment, he remembered how Cleo paid for the necklace. He'd been so embarrassed, he'd run off. Afterward she'd never mentioned it. And it had taken him time, but eventually he'd paid her back every single penny he owed her.

The next thing he knew Cleo's arms wrapped around him—hugging him. Her cheek pressed to his back. And he could feel the dampness through his T-shirt of what must surely be her tears. Just like all those years ago, she was there for him.

He carefully turned, trying not to knock her off-balance and reinjure her leg. He wrapped his arms around her, taking comfort in her warmth. He braced himself as she hesitantly raised her gaze until she met his.

In her eyes he found understanding. How could he have ever doubted her?

He held her to his chest and lowered his cheek to the top of her head. He stayed there in her embrace, absorbing the peace that came with her acceptance of what had happened to him. He didn't know until that moment just how much he needed her to understand—to make him feel normal.

"Thank you," he whispered into her hair.

She squeezed him tighter.

He breathed in her strength and let it settle his nerves. He didn't know that it was possible to feel even better than when he got the test results from the doctor. But right now, he felt as though he could take on the world...and win.

Jax eased back from Cleo just far enough to look into her eyes. He needed to hear it with his own ears. "You're really not put off by my cancer?"

"I think you are the most wonderful man both inside and out. No disease can change that." She followed her words with a kiss that left no doubt about what she had in mind.

Believing in her words, he gave in to his long-withheld desires. He scooped her up into his arms and carried her upstairs, leaving Charlie to finish his catnap alone.

* * *

Cleo woke up and ran her hand over an empty bed.

Her eyes sprang open. The golden rays of the setting sun mocked the fact that she was alone.

"Jax?" She glanced toward the bathroom, finding it dark and empty.

Old insecurities plagued her. Her stomach roiled. What had she done opening herself up to him? When would she ever learn?

She threw on her clothes and worked her way downstairs, unsure what reaction she'd receive. Did he regret their time together? Did he consider what they'd shared a mistake?

It was better to get this over right away than to let it drag out, no matter how much it hurt. It was as her grandfather told her as a kid. The bandage hurt less when it came off fast.

She found Jax in the kitchen—a room in which he'd spent a lot of time creating such amazing meals. Not that she had any appetite right now.

He turned to her. "Hey, sleepyhead. I wasn't sure when you were going to wake up." He put down the dish towel in his hands as his brows gathered. "What's the matter?"

"I woke up and you were gone."

He approached her. "Is that all that's bothering you? I mean, if I did something wrong—"

"No. You were amazing." Her stomach shivered as she continued to open herself up to him. "It's just that when I woke up and found you gone, I thought... Well, I didn't know what I thought."

He wrapped his arms around her waist. "I didn't mean to worry you. I couldn't sleep so I thought I'd make you something to eat."

"Really?"

"Honest. I thought you needed some rest. Otherwise I would have stayed and done more of this…"

He nuzzled her neck. Shivers cascaded down her arms as his lips moved over the sensitive part of her neck. Maybe she was crazy for letting down her guard with him, but she wanted so badly to believe that he was different from the others in her life.

She lifted his chin until her lips could claim his. She'd never ever tire of his kisses. She finally understood the age-old adage that the best things in life are worth fighting for. She'd known for years that Jax was special, but it wasn't until now that she knew exactly how special.

He pulled back and looked at her. "You know if you keep this up, I'm going to burn dinner."

"Would that be so bad?" she teased.

"Aren't you turning into a little temptress."

He moved to the stove and her gaze followed him, drinking in his good looks. There was just something so sexy about having a man cook for her. She noticed his off-white T-shirt and the way it clung to his muscular shoulders and broad chest. She smiled when she spied a few drops of his culinary creation dribbled down the front of his shirt. Still, he was the hottest cook she'd ever laid eyes on.

He paused from adding some spices to the pot on the stove. "See something that you like?"

"Most definitely." And she wasn't talking about the food.

She wanted to share her happiness with someone— she thought of her mother. She'd been so eager for Cleo to fall in love with someone from Hope Springs and now her wish would come true. Cleo reached out for the phone resting on the counter. Then paused. She clenched her fist and pulled back.

Her hand returned to her side. Even if she and her mother were speaking again, she'd never approve of this match. Not that this was anything permanent, maybe it never would be. She and Jax still had so much to figure out.

"What are you thinking about?" Jax stood next to the stove with a spoon in his hand.

"What?" It took her a moment to process what he'd said. "Oh, nothing important."

"It sure looked like it was important. One second you're smiling like the Cheshire cat and the next you're frowning. What gives?"

"Is that soup?" She inhaled the gentle tomato aroma and forced her thoughts away from her mother. "I smell bacon, don't I?"

"You're changing the subject. If this is about us making love, I want to know."

She shook her head, anxious to assure him that his lovemaking had rocked her world. "You definitely don't have a thing to worry about in that department."

"I don't?" He put down the spoon and approached her. "Are you sure?"

She pulled on his arms, lowering his face to her level. She kissed him thoroughly just to be sure not to leave any lingering doubts in his mind.

She pulled back and flashed him a big smile. "Now do you believe me?"

He smiled back and nodded. "Now I better get back to the stove before the tortellini soup burns."

"It smells delicious."

He gave the pot a stir before adding the pasta. "So have you thought any more about calling your mother?"

Well, that question had certainly come out of left field. What had he been doing, reading her thoughts? She sure hoped not.

"Um…some. But I don't know."

"I do." He sent her a reassuring look. "Time has passed since the funeral. I'm sure that she's thinking much clearer now. This is your mother. You need to give her a chance. The phone's on the counter."

"I don't know. Maybe I'll call tomorrow."

"There isn't always a tomorrow. I can tell you that I would do anything to hear my mother's voice again."

Her gaze strayed to the phone. Was he right? Should she seize the moment?

A movement out of the corner of her eye caught her attention. She jerked around to glance out the French doors leading to the veranda. The sun was setting, sending splashes of purples and pinks streaking across the sky. The breeze over the desert rushed past the palm trees, rustling the fronds. But she didn't see anything out of place.

Figuring it was probably just a bird or something, she turned back to Jax. "I promise, I will call her."

"Soon?"

"Yes, soon."

"How about tomorrow?"

"You aren't going to give up until you have an exact time, are you?"

"Maybe just the hour. It doesn't have to include the very second," he teased.

"Fine, tomorrow after lunch, I'll call. But I don't want to ruin tonight. It's a new beginning for us."

"Cleo, about that. We need to talk this over. We have to be realistic about things between us. Your life is in Las Vegas and mine is in New York—" His head snapped around to the French doors.

She knew where he was going with the conversation and she didn't like it. It was inevitable that sooner or later he'd want out of this relationship. "Jax, I think we should—"

"Shh…"

She followed his gaze to the doors. "Did you see something?"

His hands balled up and his arms tensed. "More like someone."

A shiver raced over her skin. "Do you think it's ape man?"

"I don't know. But I'm not waiting around to find out. Call the police. I'm going to investigate."

"But you can't. It's not safe."

"Close the blinds. Turn off the lights. And stay inside."

The thought of losing someone else she loved had her bottom lip quivering. She grabbed for the phone and panicked. She stared at the electronic device, willing her jumbled thoughts to settle. Her finger trembled as she punched out 911. Her heart echoed in her ears. Taking deep breaths, she forced herself to calm down long enough to answer all of the operator's questions.

Nausea rolled through her stomach, one wave after the other. She grabbed for the crutches, fumbling and knocking one to the ground. She cursed under her breath. With jerky movements, she struggled to reach it.

Should she hide? Yes, that was a good idea. Her head swung around the kitchen, looking for a hiding spot. She moved to the living room, but it was an open floor plan. But in the entranceway was a coat closet. She'd just opened the door when she heard the distant wail of a siren. Thank God they were close by.

Minutes later, Jax returned and she was never so glad to see someone as she was him. He rushed over and held her in his strong arms.

"Everything's okay now," he murmured.

After a reassuring hug, she pulled back. "Was it ape man?"

Jax nodded. "I was able to give the police a description and they're tracking him down. Hopefully this will be over soon."

"I'm not holding my breath. That guy seems to slip away at every turn."

"Everyone's luck runs out eventually. He's bound to make a mistake and they'll be waiting for him."

Her gaze met his. "I was so worried about you. You shouldn't have gone after him."

Jax shot her a reassuring smile that lit up his eyes. "You're talking to a man who fought cancer and won the first round. Chasing down a thug is nothing compared to that."

She hugged him close, knowing they still had to talk but this wasn't the time. Right now, she just wanted to appreciate what they had at this moment. The future would be here soon enough.

# CHAPTER THIRTEEN

THE TIME HAD come to keep her promise.

The following day, Cleo sat down in the family room. The cell phone sat atop the sketch pad. She reached out but then pulled back. She was making too big a deal of this. If Jax was brave enough to chase after ape man, surely she could find the courage to call her mother. After all, what was the worst that could happen?

Her mother could simply hang up. Tell her that she didn't love her. Tell her that—

Cleo halted her rambling thoughts. If she was going to fill her mind with doom and gloom, she might as well experience the reality. It couldn't be as horrible as she was imagining. Right?

After all, Jax and Kurt both thought that it was for the best. They wouldn't intentionally set her up to get hurt. But she worried that they based their opinions on wishful thinking. Drawing in a deep breath, she dialed the number. Her hands grew damp and her fingers were ice-cold. Maybe her mother wouldn't be home. Maybe she'd be out visiting—

"Hello?" The warm, easy strains of her mother's voice sounded the same as ever.

Suddenly the words Cleo had planned to say balled up in the back of her throat.

"Hello, is anyone there?"

Drawing together her scattered thoughts, Cleo swallowed hard. "Mom, it's Cleo."

She waited for the phone to be slammed down, but there was no click. In fact, there were no sounds at all. Had the connection dropped?

"Mom, are you there?"

"I'm here." Her mother's voice took on a weary tone. "I've been praying that I hadn't run you off for good. You don't know how many times I've wanted to call you."

Cleo's chest swelled with hope. Did this mean that they could bury the past and move forward? She wanted to ask but didn't want to jump ahead. Slow and steady wins the race, her grandfather used to say.

After a deep breath, Cleo asked, "Why didn't you call?"

A noticeable pause ensued.

"Because I…I wasn't sure you'd want to talk to me after what happened. I knew you were right. I'd overstepped in your life too many times. I had to give you this chance to decide if you still wanted to return to this family that isn't always perfect."

"I do," Cleo choked out past the ginormous lump lodged in her throat. "I miss you."

There was a big sigh on the other end of the phone as if her mother had been holding her breath. "You don't know how grateful I am to hear those words. I'm so ashamed of how I've treated you…of how I talked to you."

"It's okay, Mom. I understand. I deserved your anger."

"No, you didn't. Don't ever believe that. I've had a lot of time to think this over. I realize now that when you lived here, I tried to make all of your choices for you. I'm the reason you went so far away to school."

Cleo couldn't deny the truth of her mother's words. "There were other reasons for choosing the college that

I did. Like their amazing reputation. And the fact I got a partial scholarship."

"I know you're trying to make me feel better, but you don't have to. I understand what happened."

"The main thing is I miss my family and I've realized how important you all are to me."

Her mother's voice grew soft as though she was crying. "The day you were arguing with your father, it was because you didn't want to come home because I would be here." Her mother's sob ripped through the scar on Cleo's heart. "I'm the reason the family was torn apart. It was me! Not you."

"Mom, that's not true. It was me, too. I needed a chance to find out what makes me happy."

Her mother sniffled. "And did you? Find out what makes you happy?"

"I'm working on it."

"Cleo, I know that I don't have any right to ask this but could you forgive me for the way I treated you at the funeral and afterward? I can't even believe the things that came out of my mouth. I'm so ashamed that I spoke to one of my children in that manner. I'm a terrible mother."

"No, you're not. Everyone makes mistakes. Especially me. This whole nightmare is of my making. If I hadn't been so stubborn when Dad called—so certain I knew everything—"

"The accident was not your fault. And I'm so sorry that I said it was. I don't know if I'll ever forgive myself for turning my pain and anguish on you like I did." Her voice cracked and Cleo knew that her mother was crying, which brought tears to her own eyes. "I don't have any excuses except that I was out of my mind with grief. I had to be to speak to you like that."

"Mom, I love you. And I understand. A friend of mine explained it to me."

"Tell your friend that I'm deeply indebted to them."

That touched upon another sensitive subject—Jax. Maybe it would be best to wait—to put it off until things were more stable between them. But if this was to be a new beginning for them, she wanted to get things out in the open. There was no way that she could go back to pretending to be the complacent daughter.

"Mom, the friend who talked me into calling you, it was… It was Jax."

"No. Not him."

The palpable disapproval in her mother's voice caused dread to churn in Cleo's stomach. She recognized her mother's tone and whatever followed was never good news.

"Mom, he's changed—"

"Cleo, are you trying to tell me that you're involved with that man?"

Anger warmed her blood. Jax deserved a lot more respect than being call "that man." She may not have stood up for him back in Hope Springs, but she wasn't about to let him down now.

"His name is Jax. And…and yes, we're involved."

"But, Cleo, you could do so much better for yourself. The Riley boy is just down the lane. He's still single and he's taking over his father's ranch—"

"Mom, I thought you just got done saying that you regretted trying to make my decisions for me. Listen to me. I'm interested in Jax. I've been crazy about him since I was a kid."

"I know." Her mother groaned. "The whole world knew."

A smile pulled at Cleo's face, easing some of the tension. "I wasn't very good at hiding my feelings, was I?"

"Not at all. But why you had to choose him over the other boys in Hope Springs is beyond me."

Cleo accepted that her mother would never approve of her choices. There was nothing she could do to change her mother's attitude, but Cleo promised that she'd stay true to herself. Going forward, her choices would be made based on what was best for herself and not just to please someone else.

"But I don't understand," her mother continued, pulling Cleo from her thoughts. "When Jax left Hope Springs all those years ago, no one knew where he went. How did you find him?"

Obviously Kurt excelled at keeping secrets. It seemed she wasn't the only one not to know of his ongoing friendship with Jax. Instead of being upset with her brother, she was grateful to him for being such a good friend to Jax.

"It was fate, Mom. He walked into my life one day and we've been playing catch-up ever since."

Her mother let out an unimpressed "hmprf" sound.

"Mom, he's changed—"

"People don't change that much. Look where he came from. The nut doesn't fall far from the tree."

"You're wrong about Jax. He's nothing like his father. He takes after his mother. He's kind and thoughtful. I wish you'd give him a chance."

"To watch him break your heart? I don't think so."

"He won't do that."

Her mother rushed the conversation on to other subjects and since they hadn't talked in close to two years, a lot had happened in and around Hope Springs. In the end, Cleo grew quiet and listened. She wasn't going to convince her mother that Jax was a good guy and the knowledge ate at her.

Was it possible to reconcile with her mother when she was so outspoken in her objection to Jax?

"How did the conversation go?"

Cleo jerked around to see Jax entering the room. "Where did you come from?"

"I was out talking with the security guys. Now that we know that the thug is in the area, I've hired extra protection. I want him caught and I want this over."

"But will it ever be over? If you stop him, won't someone else fill his place?"

"It isn't likely. Remember the court case isn't far off now. Soon I'll be stepping on a plane to testify. Once that's done there won't be a reason for them to try to intimidate me or anyone I care about."

She looked him in the eyes. "You really believe that?"

"I do."

She relaxed. "Then let's hope he's caught soon."

"And now back to my question. How did the conversation with your mother go?"

"Not like I'd hoped." Cleo slouched against the couch and crossed her arms.

"You didn't expect miracles, did you?"

"She said that she'd made a mistake by trying to make my decisions for me. And then she turned around and tried to do the exact same thing. It was like she hadn't really heard me."

Jax pulled up a barstool next to her. "How exactly did she do this?"

"You don't want to know." And she didn't want to hurt him by repeating her mother's unkind words.

The frustration churned inside Cleo. If only she didn't have this cast, she'd go for a walk. But then again she couldn't do that, either, because crazy ape man was out there somewhere. Her body tensed.

Jax placed a reassuring hand on her leg. "Something tells me that you mentioned my name to her and that it didn't go over so well—"

"No, it didn't. Then she tried hooking me up with the guy down the road who's taking over his father's ranch. And she thinks that you can't change. She's the one who hasn't changed."

"Slow down. Take a breath." He reached for her hand and held it. "I think she's trying, but she's still your mom. And she'll always want what's best for her little girl."

"But that's just it. I'm an adult now. And she has to start trusting me to know what I want—right or wrong. I've got to learn these things for myself."

"Maybe it's best if you avoid talking about me. I won't come between you and your family."

"Speaking of which, Mom might tell Kurt about us. I didn't even think to tell her to keep it to herself."

"Don't worry about it." But by the frown lines framing Jax's face, he was worried. "I told you that I'm not going to come between you and your family and I meant it."

"Why?" She wasn't going to let him off the hook until he answered her. "This thing between us is special. It's worth fighting for."

He raked his fingers through his hair. "It isn't that easy. There's still so much we don't know about each other."

"I'm willing to learn."

"And what if you don't like everything you learn?"

"Why are you making this so difficult?" She crossed her arms and stared at him. "Are you trying to tell me you're having second thoughts about us?"

"I just want you to slow down. Don't rush things, Cleo. There's a lot to take into consideration."

"I'm not rushing. But obviously we see things differently."

"Maybe. I don't know." His face was creased with frown lines. "I came in here to tell you that I have to go to the police station. They might have a lead. I'll be back later."

This wasn't the end. It was just the beginning. With time Jax would come to terms with that. She wasn't about to let him walk out of her life again.

Cleo felt like a canary in a gilded cage. Only the saying didn't quite fit. Though she loved to sing, her voice was best not heard.

She was tired of being confined, even if it was in this luxurious mansion. She would do anything to get out. Today's follow-up appointment with the doctor sounded like a vacation. She couldn't wait to kick back and feel the sun on her face while the breeze rustled through the open car window.

During the past few days, Jax had withdrawn from her. He was hiding behind a wall of indifference and acting as though they were nothing more than friends. When he said he didn't want to rush into anything, he hadn't been kidding. So how did she get through to him? How did she convince him to take a chance on them?

Not even her drawings could hold her attention—they had no flash or flair. They were flat and boring. She tossed the pad aside. It didn't help that she had no fabric to work with or sewing machine to stitch together her ideas. She missed bringing her art to life. And as luxurious as this house was, it didn't come with the one place she liked to unwind and lose herself—her sewing room.

The simple truth was she missed her life, even as mundane as it was compared to living here like royalty.

The buzzer on the dryer went off. She glanced down at Charlie, who was curled up on her lap. His eyes opened but his head didn't move. She ran her hand over his silky smooth coat. With Jax holed up in the office at the back of the house, working on the computer, she'd decided to do some laundry.

"You've got to move, kitty." She picked up Charlie and placed him on the couch cushion. "I might as well make myself useful since I don't seem to be inspired to draw at the moment."

With the laundry room on the second floor, she headed up the steps. In no time, she had a load of Jax's clothes folded and placed neatly in a basket. The next task was figuring how to get the clothes to the bedroom. She couldn't imagine juggling a full basket while using her crutches, so she got creative. She shoved the basket along the floor with her foot. Granted it wasn't exactly the fastest approach but it did the trick.

She opened the dresser drawer to put away Jax's T-shirts when she noticed the glint of a gold chain. She'd never seen Jax wear jewelry beyond a watch, not even as a teenager. She lifted a couple of T-shirts and froze.

She blinked, but the pocket watch was still there.

*What in the world?*

Her fingers trembled as she picked it up. She moved to the bed and dropped down on it. When her grandfather had suddenly died, no one could figure out what had happened to the watch—her grandfather's pride and joy.

What did it mean that Jax had it?

She clutched the watch as the past unfolded itself in her mind. Like an old projector, the scenes of yesteryear started to come into focus. Her thoughts swept back to the last time she was with Jax in Hope Springs.

She'd been walking home from her best friend's house after doing homework. She saw Jax hightailing it from her grandfather's house. She'd rushed to catch up to him, wanting to show off her new outfit. It was the latest rage at the mall and she'd even put on some of her friend's makeup, hoping to convince him that she was not just a little kid anymore… After all, she was going to be fourteen the following week. Looking back now, she realized how foolish she'd been. But at the time, no one could tell her that an eighteen-year-old was too old for her.

So she'd stopped on the road and waited for him to catch up, but he just kept walking. No greeting. No teasing her. No nothing. She'd rushed to keep up to his longlegged pace.

When he noticed that she was going to follow him wherever he went, he stopped and looked at her. "Hey, kid, can you keep a secret?"

She'd nodded, reveling in the fact that he was going to take her into his confidence. She'd thought that it meant something special—that she was special. She hadn't been expecting the next part.

"Okay. But first pinkie swear you won't tell anyone, not even Kurt."

Once she'd given her heartfelt pledge to keep his secret, he surprised her.

"I'm leaving Hope Springs."

"When are you coming back?"

"I'm not. That's the point."

She remembered how she'd struggled to hold back the tears and failed miserably. Maybe that was why he'd broken down and kissed her…right on the cheek.

And that was the last time anyone from Hope Springs had laid eyes on him…except for her brother. She stared at the pocket watch, wondering what it meant that Jax possessed it. She knew that he did errands for her grandfather, but was there more to their relationship than mucking stalls and fixing fence lines?

She had to be sure to phrase her questions just so. She

didn't know want transpired between Jax and her grandfather so she didn't want to accuse him of anything. But then again, she needed to know the truth.

"Cleo, we've got to leave for the doctor's or we'll be late," Jax called up the steps.

She hastily put the watch back where she'd found it. They'd have plenty of time to discuss this later. Right now, she needed the doctor to assure Jax that he didn't have to watch over her any longer—that she was perfectly fine to take care of herself.

She didn't need him.

The bold lie settled front and center in her thoughts, weighing her down. The truth was she wanted him in her life so much it scared her.

When had Jax come to mean so much to her? Her thoughts rolled back in time, unable to nail down a specific moment when things had dramatically changed between them. Her feelings for him had grown and changed gradually as they spent day after day together.

And this was nothing like the schoolgirl crush she'd had on him all those years ago in Hope Springs. These feelings went far deeper and had a sharp edge when she thought of Jax leaving—and he would soon. He'd said more than once that his life wasn't here in Las Vegas.

This appointment was the beginning of the end for them. Her shoulders drooped. Once they got the all clear from the doctor, it'd be one less reason for Jax to stick around. And from the sounds of it the police were closing in on ape man. In no time at all, Jax would be on a plane for New York. And their time together would be nothing but another memory.

# CHAPTER FOURTEEN

JAX GLANCED OVER at Cleo, noticing that she'd had something on her mind during their trip into the city.

"Is everything okay?" he asked.

She smiled, but it didn't quite reach her eyes. "You heard the doctor. I'm healing up nicely."

"This isn't about the doctor's visit. Something has been bothering you since we left the house. I thought you'd be happy getting out of there for a while."

"I am." Her tone was flat.

She was lying, but why? He sure didn't understand women. Give them what they want and they are still unhappy. Maybe she was hungry. He could whip them up an early dinner and perhaps that would lighten her spirits. She always liked his cooking.

He eased the SUV onto the highway. "What sounds good for dinner?"

"Didn't you hear the doctor? I can take care of myself. You don't have to keep hovering and doing things for me."

"But why should you have to cook when I'm around and I don't mind?"

"But that's the thing, you aren't always going to be around. As you keep reminding me, your life is in New York. Not here."

He glanced in her direction, noticing her crossed arms

and the frown on her face. She'd been in an unusual mood ever since he told her that it was time to leave for her appointment. He sure wished he knew what had triggered it.

But before he could probe further, he spotted a much larger problem. A big black pickup truck was quickly gaining ground on them. Jax picked up speed as he kept glancing in the mirror at the vehicle's reinforced front bumper and the exhaust pipes trailing up each side of the cab.

The truck had been tailing them since they'd pulled out of the parking lot at the doctor's office. He did not have a good feeling about this. Not at all.

"Maybe now is the time to talk," Cleo said tentatively. "I found something earlier—"

"Can this wait?" His gaze strayed to the rearview mirror. The pickup was closing in fast.

"I think it's waited long enough."

"Hold on!"

He swerved over into the fast lane and accelerated. The pickup did the same. Definitely not a good sign.

"What are you doing?" Cleo screeched. "Have you lost your mind?"

"I think we're being followed. Our exit is just ahead."

He didn't bother with his turn signal. Instead he waited until the last moment then swerved over through the slow lane and onto the exit ramp. Horns blared. Jax kept going.

The pickup followed.

He just had to keep Cleo safe. He'd do anything for her. And in this particular moment, he didn't have time to contemplate exactly how deep that feeling went.

"Grab the phone from my pocket and call Detective Jones."

Any other time he might have gotten a cheap thrill out of Cleo fishing around in his pants pocket, but his attention was on more important matters. He had no idea what the thug behind him had in mind and he didn't want to find out.

Cleo quickly found the saved number on the phone and spoke with the detective. She disconnected the call. "He said to head for the house. He already has units in the area."

"Good."

A loud thump and they lunged forward, restrained by the safety belts. The SUV shuddered. The pickup had hit them from behind and Jax wasn't giving the creep a chance to do it again. Jax tramped on the accelerator. The SUV rapidly gained speed, putting distance between them. He sure hoped Detective Jones was right about the nearby units.

Cleo reached out and squeezed his leg. In that moment he acknowledged something that he'd been fighting for so long—he loved her. And he would do anything to keep her safe and happy.

More determined than ever to get them to safety, he turned right toward their gated community. And that was when he spotted the nail strips on the road and was able to cut the wheel and avoid them. Fortunately the truck behind them didn't have the luxury of time and hit the strips, blowing out the tires.

Jax slowed to a stop and threw the SUV in Park. He glanced out the side window in time to see the police arrest the thug.

Cleo took off her seat belt and shimmied over next to him to peer out the side window. "Is it really over?"

"Let's hope so."

Instead of throwing her arms around him and kissing him, she settled back in her seat. "It's about time."

What a strange reaction. Ever since they left for the doctor's office it was as if a wall had gone up between them. And he didn't like it. Not one little bit. But until he knew what the problem was, he couldn't fix it.

Jax entered the house smiling. It had certainly been a day for good news. First Cleo's doctor's appointment and now the police had made an arrest. At last, their problems were truly over.

"Cleo." He glanced around the living room. No sign of her.

He moved to the family room. She wasn't there, either, but he noticed her sketch pad on the coffee table and Charlie curled up on the couch. Something told him that she hadn't been gone long, because where Cleo was, Charlie wasn't far behind.

Next he checked the kitchen. It was empty, too.

"Cleo!"

When she didn't answer, he started to worry. Maybe she'd fallen. She'd been getting around with ease, but she did have a habit of pushing her limits. He took the steps two at a time.

"Cleo, where are you?"

He scanned her bedroom. Then he glanced in his room. She was sitting on the bed with her back to him.

"Hey, didn't you hear me calling you?"

She shrugged but didn't say a word.

He stepped farther into the room. "Are you okay?"

She shook her head this time. He sure wished she'd speak, it would make this so much easier. At least then he'd know what was wrong. He started around the bed and stopped in front of her. She was gazing down at something in her hands. It took him a second to recognize the familiar object in her hand.

"Cleo, listen. I can explain this."

"I always wondered what happened to this watch. It

was one of my grandfather's most treasured possessions. I just never would have guessed that he'd given it to you."

Jax sat down on the bed next to her. "Your grandfather was a very special man. I've never known anyone with a bigger heart."

She smiled. "I'm so glad you got to know that part of him."

"He took me under his wing and showed me that a man could make his own happiness. He showed me how to work hard for my money. And he taught me respect. In all of the ways that count, your grandfather was more a father to me than my biological one."

"I'm glad he was able to be there for you, especially after your mom passed on. He liked you, too. But that doesn't explain why he gave you this." She dangled the pocket watch.

Jax reached for it, but she jerked it out of his reach. He sighed. "It isn't what you're thinking."

"Really? And now you're a mind reader—"

"Obviously you think I came to have it by some under-handed way. But I didn't." He knelt down in front of her. "You've got to believe me. I wouldn't have done anything to hurt your grandfather. If it wasn't for him, I wouldn't be here today. I'd probably still be in Hope Springs, following in my father's unhappy steps."

Her brow crinkled as her lips pursed together in thought. "For him to give you this, it had to be for some really important reason because this is a family heirloom. Did you know that it belonged to my great-grandfather? It was supposed to be passed down to my father. And then to my oldest brother, Kurt. So you'll see why I'm confused about how you ended up with it."

"Your grandfather gave it to me the day I left Hope

Springs." Jax got to his feet and started to pace. "He told me to sell it when I got to where I was going."

She shook her head. "But why this? And what do you know about the money missing from his bank accounts?"

"I don't know anything about his bank accounts, but…" Jax wasn't so sure how she would take this and he hated the thought of letting her down. "He took care of my college tuition as well as my room and board. I didn't know how he arranged it and he wouldn't say. But when you were dirt-poor like I was and someone drops you a rope to pull you out of poverty, you act first and think later. Can you understand that?"

She continued to look at him. He could see the wheels in her mind spinning. But he hoped he was getting through to her. Finally she nodded. But he didn't give her a chance to say anything, he kept going. He had to make sure she believed he wouldn't hurt her family in any way. In secret, he'd always dreamed about what it would be like to be a Sinclair—to be a part of a loving, close-knit family.

"By the time my brain caught up with everything, your grandfather had passed on and all I could do was make the most of the generous gift he'd given me."

"And that explains the withdrawals from his bank accounts that no one could account for."

"I'm sorry." He felt really bad for upsetting the family. "I never meant to take away your inheritance. I was young and I hadn't thought through his generous offer. All I could envision was an escape from an unhappy life."

"Don't be." Her words shocked him. "If anyone should understand about rushing off to chase your dreams without thinking about what it took to get you there—it's me."

"Does this mean you believe me about the money and the pocket watch?" He held his breath waiting for her confirmation.

"You know, it's almost like my grandfather knew something all those years ago that we didn't have a clue about. It's like he knew someday we'd find our way together." She held up the watch. "And this is like his blessing for us."

She was being a bit dramatic, but he had to admit that he liked the idea. "You really think your grandfather would approve of you being in my arms?"

She nodded and smiled up at him.

Jax stood and drew her up into his embrace. He never ever wanted to let her go. She fit so perfectly against him. It was as though she'd been made just for him.

She pulled back and looked into his eyes. "What did you come in here to tell me?"

"That's right. I have good news." He paused, thinking about kissing her now and saving the talking for later. "But it can wait."

He leaned forward, but she pressed a hand to his chest. "It can't wait. I need to know what's happening."

Jax tightened his hold on her, not wanting the moment to end, but realized he might as well get this out of the way. "Okay. Apparently ape man wasn't a hired thug. He's actually the brother of my former partner. He was a one-man team out to protect the goose that laid his golden egg. Now that he's been arrested, we don't have to worry."

"Are you certain?"

"Positive. He confessed."

Cleo threw her arms around Jax and hugged him tight. But instead of following it up with the kiss he'd been anticipating, she pulled back and gave him a serious look.

"What does this mean?"

He brushed a strand of hair from her cheek. "As tempting as it is to stay, we can't go on living here forever. Eventually my friend will want his house back."

"I suppose you're right. Even if it's the fanciest house I've ever been in. Do we have to leave now?"

Jax shook his head. There was absolutely no other place he wanted to be. "I think we can stay another night."

"Good." She snuggled closer to him. "I'm just so glad you're safe."

"How glad?" He smiled and glanced at her very kiss-able lips.

In the next moment, her mouth pressed to his. She was bold and persuasive, leaving no doubt of what she had on her mind. And he liked it. He liked it a whole lot.

He met her move for move, needing to feel their close-ness once more. As she opened up to him, she tasted of chocolate. It had never tasted so good. A moan grew deep in his throat.

Things were about to change for them. They could move forward—think about the future. And the past could fall away behind them. They could make their own memories starting with today.

Because with Cleo, he was alive. She cared about him as no one else ever had. The knowledge sealed the hole in his heart—the empty spot where the love of a family was supposed to be. Cleo was all of the family he'd ever need.

# CHAPTER FIFTEEN

"Jax, you missed my street."

He glanced in the rearview mirror as the street sign faded into the distance. He'd been distracted by the way her hand rested on his leg. "Sorry. I'll turn around."

"No need. You can just circle the block." There was a slight pause. "It's great to be going home. Don't get me wrong. Staying in a movie star's mansion was an experience I'll never forget. It sure is a long way from Hope Springs, Wyoming."

"Is that good or bad?"

"Part of me misses Hope Springs, but another part doesn't want to be stuck in that small town for the rest of my life. There are so many places to see and things to do."

"You know, your fashion designs could be the key to having the best of both worlds."

"You think so?" He nodded and she continued, "But I haven't even shown anyone my drawings."

This was his moment to confess what he'd been up to while she'd been drawing. He just hoped she approved. If not, this might very well be the last time she talked to him and that thought knotted his gut.

"Actually I've been told by an expert that you have amazing talent and a bright future, if you pursue it."

"What? But how?" There was a pause as though she was trying to make sense of things. "Jax, what did you do?"

He pulled into a parking spot, put the SUV in Park and turned off the engine. He rubbed his head, suddenly in doubt of his actions, which was so unlike him. He was a man of decision—split-second decisions. That was how he'd been able to amass a fortune.

But when it came to Cleo, he felt constantly off-kilter. But surely she'd be happy about this, right? No point in delaying the inevitable.

"I sent some of your sketches to a friend of a friend. And I included a picture of you in that yellow outfit you had on at the casino."

"You didn't?" She looked at him as though she was waiting for him to say he was joking.

"Cleo, I'm serious. I sent your stuff to an industry professional. He is interested in meeting with you."

"Why didn't you ask me first?"

"I thought about it, but I didn't know how it'd work out. I mean, I'm no judge of fashion. I just know what I like—"

"So if this expert didn't like what they saw, you didn't want to hurt me."

He nodded, relieved that she understood his motive. "Exactly. I have his name and number written down." Jax reached into his pocket and withdrew the slip of paper. "He's expecting your call."

"I should be upset with you for going behind my back, but I'm grateful. Thank you. You're the first person since my grandmother to believe I could make my dreams come true without just settling for what is expected of me."

He reached out for her hand and took it in his own. "You can do whatever you set your mind to. And I'm going to enjoy watching you succeed."

She leaned over and hugged him. His heart pounded

beneath her cheek. What had he ever done to be lucky enough to have someone so special in his life?

Cleo lifted her head and looked at him. "But next time you have a brilliant idea, talk to me first. Agreed?"

He expelled a pent-up breath. "Agreed."

"Now let's get inside. Charlie is anxious to get out of this carrier."

Jax dashed out the door and strode around the front of the vehicle to assist her. "Would you mind taking Charlie while I grab my crutches? We can come back out later for the rest of our stuff. Not that there's a lot of it."

He did as she asked and escorted her up the walk. Cleo smiled and greeted the other people coming and going. This place was crawling with young people, from college students to young mothers with strollers. He could imagine Cleo fitting in well here.

"I've never had a houseguest before." Cleo sent him a hesitant glance. "You'll be my first. I wish I'd known you were staying. I'd have cleaned up some."

Staying? Here? With her? Like an honest-to-goodness couple? The reality of the situation was setting in and all of the uncertainties in the back of his mind came rushing forth—from the potential for his cancer to return to her mother's dislike of him. Jax shoved the doubts away. After all, this was what he wanted—Cleo in his life.

"I'm sure you don't have to worry." He sent her a reassuring smile even though he was feeling anything but assured. "Remember I was already here and the place looked great."

Before they could say much else, Robyn exited her apartment. She was pushing a pink baby stroller in their direction.

"Oh, look! Robyn has her daughter all dressed up in an outfit I made her." Cleo picked up her pace on the crutches.

"Welcome home." The young woman's face lit up with a broad smile. "Stephie is wide-awake and anxious for Auntie Cleo to visit with her."

Cleo stopped and leaned over the stroller. "Hey, cutie, aren't you adorable."

Jax had never seen Cleo with a baby. Her whole demeanor changed. She almost glowed as she oohed and ahhed over the child. What was it about babies that could affect women of all ages so deeply?

Jax stood back as the women went on and on about the baby. He tried his best to act as if nothing was bothering him, but inside their words were shattering the dreams he'd had about his future—a future with Cleo. With each laugh and smile, his hopes were splintering into shards that cut deep.

What made him think Cleo would fit into his predetermined world?

She was still so young and full of possibilities. His life choices had been drastically narrowed when he'd received his cancer diagnosis. Having a family of his own was not an option for him.

Aside from the question of the lifesaving treatments causing fertility issues, he wouldn't subject his child to the uncertainty of his cancer making a recurrence. He knew the agony of being a child and losing a parent. He didn't want to pass on that unhappy legacy.

Cleo had him thinking about all sorts of things he'd never thought about before. Like moving to Las Vegas instead of Hope Springs. He'd let himself get caught up in the moment. First the doctor called with the news that his test results were good and then he'd given in to his desires. It'd been like the fall of dominoes—one thing leading to another. And now Cleo was expecting him to make her happy and as much as he wanted to do just that, he couldn't.

The truth of the matter was he lived a life of uncertainty. It was bad enough that he had to live every day with a big question mark over his head. It wasn't fair to ask Cleo to give up her chance to be a mother to live with a man who could become sick again.

The best thing he could do for Cleo was walk away. Forget his dreams of making a future with her. He'd never felt so awful about a decision as he did now. How was he supposed to walk away from the woman whose smile could light up his whole world? He couldn't even imagine his life without her in it. But it wasn't as if he had a choice. He had to do what was best for her.

And that wasn't him.

He carried her belongings into the apartment and Cleo followed him. When she closed the front door, the walls seemed to close in on him. He didn't belong here. He didn't belong with her.

She proceeded to give him the grand tour of her two-bedroom apartment. "And this is my sewing room. Don't mind the mess. I've been working on an order for Robyn. Her older sister is pregnant and she wanted me to make some clothes and stitch up a comforter like I'd done for Stephie."

His gaze took in the array of baby blue, yellow and green fabrics. The knife of guilt stabbed at him for even considering asking Cleo to spend her life with him. And when she held up little bib overalls and her face scrunched up into a huge smile as if she was imagining her own baby someday in the outfit, he couldn't breathe.

He needed to leave. He needed space. Someplace where the pain wasn't so severe. Where there weren't reminders of everything he'd never have.

"I've got to go." He started for the door.

"Leave? Where are you going? I thought you'd stay here until your flight to New York."

"I—I can't."

"What's wrong? You've been acting strange ever since we got here."

He wanted to walk away without her hating him. The thought of her looking at him with loathing in her eyes made his stomach roil. There had to be a way to part on good terms. After all, soon he'd return to New York.

Maybe that was the answer. He could remind her that they led separate lives miles from each other. In no time, she'd get on with her life. She'd forget him. With her beauty, she could have any guy she set her heart on.

"I'm just tired." He could feel her staring at him, trying to guess if he was telling the whole truth or not. "I thought I'd go back to the casino and make sure things are squared away there."

"The casino?" A frown pulled at her face. "Are you tired of me?"

The sadness in her eyes cracked his resolve. "Of course not. I just... We can't pretend that my life is here. I belong in New York. I have the court case coming up. I can't back out now. Too much is at stake."

Her eyes shimmered. "This thing that happened between us. Are you saying it was all a lie?"

He shook his head. "It was a beautiful dream. One I will always treasure."

"Then why?" Her voice cracked with emotion. "Why are you doing this?"

"Because it isn't fair to you." The truth came tumbling out. "I can't tie you down to a life with a cancer patient."

"But you're cured. You said your tests were clear."

"But if it spread once there's no reason to think that it

might not recur. And I can't put you through that. Living with this uncertainty is horrible."

"But we can lean on each other. We can get through it together."

She had an answer for everything. But he had something she couldn't fix.

"And I can't give you children."

"I don't want kids." She said it way too fast—like a needy child desperate to say anything to get what they wanted without thinking of the ramification of their words.

"Your lips say one thing but your body says something else. I watched you just moments ago with that baby. I never saw that peaceful look on your face before. You were in your element. You practically glowed."

"But...but—"

"There's no but for this. I've tried to do this as nice as I could but you won't let go. Cleo, your mother was right. I'm not the man for you. I take what I want and I wanted you."

"Because you love me."

He stilled himself, holding back the rush of emotions. He'd never lied to her, ever—until now. But it was necessary. It was for her own good. But when he searched for the words to deny his love for her, his voice failed him.

She stepped up to him and stabbed him in the chest. "You can't deny it because it's true. We've shared so much. We're building something. We...we're falling in love."

"This is all my fault. I'm selfish and an uncaring jerk."

"That's not true."

"Yes, it is, or I wouldn't be putting you through this."

In that particular moment, he hated himself for hurting her. He wasn't deserving of her love.

He dipped his head and planted a quick kiss to her cheek. "Have a good life. You deserve the best."

He turned and started walking. He had to get away before she wore through the last of his resistance. She had no idea how hard it was to act as if he didn't care about her when his heart thumped out her name with every beat.

It was only after he was headed down the sidewalk to the SUV that he realized they'd done this scene once before…long ago when he left Hope Springs. Back then he was walking away from one of his dearest friends. This time he was walking away from the woman who held his heart in her hands.

# CHAPTER SIXTEEN

UNABLE TO SLEEP since Jax walked out the door, Cleo found herself spending all of her time in her sewing room. It was where she lost herself when the world turned dark and gray. And thanks to her sketch pad, she had plenty of creations to keep her hands busy. But her mind kept stumbling back to Jax.

She wanted to yell at him and tell him that he didn't know what she was thinking, but the truth was he had been pretty accurate. She'd blurted out that she didn't want kids in desperation to keep him from leaving.

It pained her to admit it, but she was doing exactly what she promised herself she wouldn't do. She was making a monumental decision based on what Jax wanted—not what she wanted. And that was a recipe for disaster.

Jax had been right to turn down her plea. She didn't know how she felt about kids. In all honesty, she hadn't given the subject much thought. At this point in her life, she still had lots of time to start a family—if she chose to.

She found herself in Robyn's living room to drop off the baby items Robyn had ordered for her sister's upcoming baby shower and yet somehow Cleo had ended up staying for a chat. While she waited for her friend to return with the coffee, she pulled her grandfather's pocket watch from her pocket. Her thumb rubbed over the engraved design.

She'd found the watch in her duffel bag she'd brought back from the mansion. She knew for certain she hadn't placed it in there because she'd given it back to Jax. Obviously her grandfather had loved Jax and wanted him to have the watch. The fact that Jax still had it and hadn't sold it as her grandfather had given him liberty to do was a tribute to Jax's feelings for him.

No man who was selfish and uncaring would carry around a memento and then hand it over to her because he saw how much it meant to her. Only a man with a heart of gold would be that thoughtful and generous.

"What's that in your hand?" Robyn asked as she placed a cup of steaming coffee in front of her.

"It belongs to Jax. He forgot it."

"He'll be missing it. You should catch up to him before he heads to the airport."

"Maybe." But she still had something to get straight in her mind before she faced Jax. "How did you know if you wanted kids?"

"That's easy. I always enjoyed them. And Mike comes from a big family. So we agreed to have at least two babies. Why?"

She could feel her friend's intent stare while Cleo concentrated on stirring the sweetener into her coffee. "The strange thing is I've never really thought about kids... until now."

"Are you pregnant?"

Cleo's head jerked up so she could gauge the look on her friend's face. She was serious. Cleo inwardly groaned. Maybe agreeing to stay and talk wasn't the best choice. She already had enough problems on her mind.

"No. I'm not pregnant. And don't even think of wishing it on me. You've got the mommy genes. The jury is still out for me."

Robyn held up her hands all innocentlike. "Sorry, I jumped to the wrong conclusion."

"Stephie's adorable, but I'm not ready for that kind of commitment. Is that bad? I mean, I'm only twenty-five. If I don't want kids now, do you think I'll never want them?"

Robyn shrugged and sat back in her chair. "I pretty much knew what I wanted early in life, but everyone is different. Do you have to know now? Does this have something to do with Mr. Tall, Dark and Dreamy?"

"He has reason to think he can't have kids and he doesn't think it's fair to tie me down. He thinks that eventually I'll want them."

"He could be right."

"Or he could be wrong." Cleo sent her friend a pointed stare.

She didn't want Robyn siding with Jax. She wanted her friend to say his logic was flawed. Because deep inside, her gut was screaming that they belonged together…no matter how her mother felt. And she certainly wasn't going to let the worry of cancer dictate her future. Life didn't come with guarantees. If only she could convince Jax of that.

Robyn shrugged and sipped at her coffee. "You said he couldn't have children. You know that's different than him not wanting children. Does he want children?"

"I—I don't know. We never really discussed it."

"If it's a matter of him not being able to father a baby, you must realize that in this day and age you have so many options to choose from."

"You're right." Hope bloomed in her chest. "I wish I'd thought of that before."

Cleo honestly didn't know if he was interested in having children or not. She'd been so caught off guard by his abrupt turnaround regarding their relationship that her mind hadn't been able to string two thoughts together much less ask intelligent questions. But Robyn had brought up a valid point and Cleo wasn't about to let him off the hook until he gave her an honest answer.

She refused to stand by and let him make a unilateral decision about their relationship. He needed to hear her thoughts on the matter. And there was no time to waste. If she had to follow him all the way to New York, she'd do it. This was too important to let the moment slip by. If there was even the slightest possibility they could make this relationship work, she wanted that chance   they deserved it. And she wouldn't be dissuaded by a truckload of what-ifs.

"I've got to go. I have a pocket watch to return." With the aid of her crutches, she stood. "Thanks for the coffee."

"I wish I could see this." Robyn let out an exaggerated sigh. "I miss all of the good parts. Just promise me you'll fill me in on the details later."

"Maybe."

While Robyn sputtered and spurted over her noncommittal answer, Cleo rushed out the door. There were some things that didn't need to be shared even with her closest friend. She just hoped there would be some special memories created today.

With a quick change into a red-and-white-flowered sundress, she felt more feminine and confident. Nothing like a beautiful outfit to bolster one's nerves. She tramped the gas as she zipped across town to the Glamour Hotel and Casino. She just hoped she was in time. She knew that Jax had booked his flight for home today, but she had no idea when it would depart. If she had to, she'd track him down at the airport and buy a plane ticket if that's what it took. They weren't finished talking. Not by a long shot.

She hustled up to his bungalow. Ignoring the Do Not Disturb sign, she knocked. When he didn't answer right away, she pounded harder on the door.

The door swung open. "What's all the racket about?"

Jax stood in the doorway. His hair was rumpled. His torso was bare, revealing his rock-solid abs. And his khaki shorts were wrinkled and hung low as if he hadn't been eating. She didn't have to ask. She could see he wasn't any happier with this separation than she was.

She drew her gaze back to his unshaven face. "You've had your say, now I'm going to have mine."

"Don't, Cleo. Everything has been said." He started to shut the door in her face.

She moved quickly, angling her crutch in the way. "What gives you the right to speak for me? And to make up my mind for me?"

She pushed him aside and entered the bungalow, which looked as if it hadn't been visited by housekeeping in days. Clothes were strewn about. Pillows and blankets littered the couch. And through all of the mess, she didn't see any signs of food. This whole mess was so unlike the clean-up-after-himself Jax who she'd been living with for the past month.

She turned to him, finding that he'd closed the door, giving them some privacy. "I've had time to think things over and you're wrong."

His brows drew together into a dark line. "I'm not wrong. You just want to believe the impossible."

"What's impossible? Us being together?" When he nodded, she rushed on, "I disagree."

He sighed and rubbed the back of his neck. "Cleo, you're just making this harder on both of us."

"Good. It should be hard to walk away from someone you care about, especially when you're doing it for all of the wrong reasons."

"I'm doing what is best for you."

"But see, I don't want you deciding what's best for me.

I already went through that back in Hope Springs. It was why I left. And now you're trying to do the same thing. It's time people listen to me and respect my feelings."

"I've always respected you and your feelings."

At last, she felt as though she was making some progress. "Then it's time you stop talking and listen to what I have to say."

"Can I at least put on a shirt?"

She nodded. But that was all she was going to wait around for. This needed to be said before she burst. Because she wasn't going anywhere until he heard her out about everything. Including the part she'd been too afraid to come straight out and say before now—she loved him.

Jax needed a moment to gather his thoughts.

In reality, he needed to back away before he pulled Cleo into his arms and kissed her into silence. Secretly he'd been wishing she'd show up, but logic told him that this talk would not end happily—for either of them. Why couldn't she have just left things alone?

He walked over to the couch and grabbed his discarded T-shirt. He'd spent the past couple of days doing nothing but trying to forget the fun and the laughter when he was around Cleo. She was his sunshine and without her, life was like a blustery gray day. But he couldn't be greedy. Her happiness was more important to him. He'd forgotten that for a moment, but he wouldn't forget it again. He just had to make her understand that she was setting her sights on the wrong man...no matter how touched he was that she chose him.

Taking a deep breath in and slowly blowing it out, he turned. "Okay, I'm listening. But I don't have long. I have some packing to do before I head to the airport."

Cleo's gaze slowly surveyed the room before cocking an eyebrow at him.

"Like I said, I have things to do before heading to the airport." He wasn't about to admit to her that he'd been so miserable since he walked away from her that he hadn't wanted to be disturbed by anyone, including housekeeping.

"Then you won't want to forget to pack this." She withdrew the pocket watch from her purse and placed it in his hand, wrapping his fingers around it.

"I can't take this. It belonged to your grandfather."

"And he wanted you to have it. He wouldn't have gone out of his way to help you if you hadn't come to mean a great deal to him. His son was busy with his own family. And my grandmother was gone. I was too young then to understand how lonely he must have been. So you filled in that gaping hole and I'm sure he took great pleasure in being able to help you."

Jax's throat tightened as his hand lowered. He couldn't believe how Cleo was able to be so positive when it would be so easy for her to hate him for taking what would have been her inheritance money and the pocket watch.

He wasn't going to continue to argue about it. "I'll keep it until you or Kurt have children of your own and then you can have it for them."

"Speaking of children, since when do you get to dictate whether I'll have any or not?"

He inwardly groaned. She had a stubborn glint in her eyes. She wasn't going to leave until he convinced her that walking away was the best option. Why did Cleo always have to do things the hard way?

"I saw you the other day with that baby. It was obvious that you're a natural mother. And don't even try to tell me again that you don't want children just because you know that I can't give you any."

She pressed her hands to her hips. "You're right, that was wrong of me."

At last, he was getting through to her. He wanted to be happy for her that she was seeing reason and was no longer willing to throw her life away on him, but it only made him sadder.

She tilted her chin. "The thing is I don't know if I want to have children. As of today, I don't. But tomorrow, who knows. When my biological clock starts to tick, I might totally change my mind."

"Then you accept that we can't be together."

"The thing is I've heard you say that you can't have children, but you've never said whether you want them or not."

"What does that matter?"

She smiled as though she knew something he didn't. "I had to be reminded that being a parent isn't a matter of DNA. And there are so many options open to people wanting to give love to a child, from adoption to foster parenting. And if we want a baby, there are sperm banks."

He was surprised by how much thought she'd put into this after her emotional response the other night. This time he was persuaded to believe she'd really thought this over. She deserved an honest answer.

"Until I spent time with you, I hadn't given kids any thought. My childhood wasn't the happiest so I wasn't inclined to be a family man, but being around you has me rethinking my stance."

"So then kids are a possibility for you, too." She smiled up at him as if she'd bested him.

"You're forgetting one big thing. The cancer. My life is lived one test result to the next."

"Then maybe you should broaden your horizons and quit living test to test. No one says you have to."

"But you don't understand, it could come back."

"And it might not. It's kinda like looking at a glass of water. You can either view it as a glass half-full or half-empty. I choose to look at it as half-full."

He raked his fingers through his hair. "It isn't fair to put a wife and child through the uncertainty."

"So you're saying that my father shouldn't have married my mother and that my brothers and I were a big mistake."

"Of course not. That's not the same thing."

"Why isn't it? My father died young. My younger brothers were still in school. We all still needed him." She stepped up to Jax and looked him in the eyes. "Life doesn't come with guarantees."

"But—"

She pressed her fingers to his lips. "I'd rather live a month or a year with you in my life than fifty years alone. You've been in my heart since I was a teenager."

He took her hand in his. "But your mother…"

"Will have to get used to the idea that you and I belong together."

"And you're absolutely certain that you want me, flaws and all."

Her eyes lit up and she nodded vigorously. "I'm absolutely certain. But I do have one question."

His chest tightened. He wasn't sure he was ready for any more proclamations. His mind was still trying to process everything she'd said. "What is it?"

"I love you. And I need to know if you feel the same for me."

Now this part was easy.

He'd been so busy trying to hide his feelings from both of them that he just now realized he'd never spoken the words of his heart.

He wrapped one arm around her waist and pulled her close. With his other hand, he brushed back her hair and looked into her mesmerizing green eyes—eyes he could see his whole future in.

"I can't honestly tell you when I first started to fall in love with you. There are too many moments to choose from. But I've been having a heck of a time trying to figure out how to go on without you."

"And now you won't have to."

"You're certain this is what you want—that I am what you want?"

"Most definitely."

He lifted her into his arms and pressed his lips to hers. He couldn't imagine how he'd ever gotten lucky enough to have this ray of sunshine in his life, but he planned to do everything he could so she never ever regretted her decision.

# EPILOGUE

*One year later...*

JAX WAS CERTAIN he'd never tire of staring at his beautiful wife. He was so glad that she hadn't given up on him and had made him see things her way—the way they should be. Together.

Cleo sent him a hesitant look. "Are you sure about this?"

He nodded and smiled, hoping to ease her worries. Over the past year they'd learned to rely on each other during moments of uncertainty. And in return, she'd gotten him to appreciate each day and to stop fretting about tomorrow. Whatever came their way, they'd face together.

"Don't worry. Everything will be fine." He pulled on a blue T-shirt. "Your mother loves you and she'll want whatever will make you the happiest. After all, Kurt finally came around to the idea of us as a couple."

She smiled at him, filling his chest with a warm, familiar sensation. "I can't believe you convinced him to be your best man."

"You do know I had to swear on my life to keep you happy, don't you?"

She leaned over to him, her lips almost touching his. The breath in his throat hitched. It didn't matter how many times she kissed him, it would never lose its excitement.

Her mouth pressed to his and he pulled her close, but all too soon she was backing away.

"Now, was making that promise to my brother such a hardship?"

"Um…not when you put it that way." He grinned at her. "Now why don't you come back over here?"

"I have to get ready." Cleo struggled to fasten her necklace. "I just don't understand why we have to tell my mother about our plans. Can't we just tell her we're going on vacation?"

"Because we're all working on building a strong, open relationship." He stepped up and helped her with the clasp. "After all, she loves you enough to give me a chance, right?"

With a shrug, Cleo said, "I guess."

"Then you need to give her a chance and be honest with her."

Cleo rushed into the walk-in closet of their newly built house in Hope Springs. She returned with a pair of blue stilettos.

He eyed them up suspiciously. Obviously his wife was far more nervous about this talk with her mother than he'd originally thought. "Um, are you sure you want to wear those to the Jubilee?"

She frowned at him before rushing back into the closet. He smiled to himself. Life with Cleo was never boring.

After he'd testified in the money-laundering case, he was hailed as a star by both the press and her family. He'd finished up his work in New York City and returned to Cleo in Las Vegas just as he promised. But after a while they agreed that Vegas didn't feel like home to either of them. So Cleo tendered her resignation at the Glamour and they bought her grandfather's ranch from the family, and in the process, they'd put the Sinclair ranch back on solid financial ground.

Cleo slipped on a pair of colorful cowboy boots. "I just don't think Mom's going to be happy with our decision. She's been hinting about grandkids since you and I said 'I do' on Valentine's Day."

"And she's just going to have to understand that my wife has dreams to fulfill. By the way, I have our tickets to New York in my jacket pocket. We take off tonight after the festivities."

"You mean after we tell my mother that we're going to put off adoption and launch a fashion line instead."

"Exactly."

Just then Charlie strolled into the room and rubbed over Jax's legs. "Hey, boy, where have you been all morning?"

Charlie meowed in response and Jax couldn't resist kneeling down to scratch behind the cat's ear. "And don't worry. While we're gone, you're going to the ranch house to visit with your other feline friends."

"Mom really has become quite the cat lady." Cleo ran her fingers over her hair, trying to improve on perfection. At least that's how she looked in his book.

"It's good for her. Now she has furbabies to fuss over instead of you and your brothers."

"If only it was that easy. I still don't think she's going to take the news well."

Jax approached his wife and wrapped his arms around her waist, pulling her close. "I insist you quit worrying. Where's that fiery woman who told me what was up when I was foolish enough to try to walk away from the best thing that ever happened to me?"

"She's still here." Cleo smiled up at him before planting a stirring kiss on his lips. "And look how wonderful that has turned out."

"And if you keep kissing me like that we are going to be quite late for the Jubilee."

"You shouldn't tease me," she taunted.

"Who's teasing?" He tumbled her onto the bed.

She gazed up at him with happiness reflected in her eyes. "I love you, Mr. Monroe."

"And I will always love you."

* * * * *

# HER IRRESISTIBLE
# PROTECTOR

BY
MICHELLE DOUGLAS

At the age of eight **Michelle Douglas** was asked what she wanted to be when she grew up. She answered, 'A writer.' Years later she read an article about romance writing and thought, *Ooh, that'll be fun*. She was right. When she's not writing she can usually be found with her nose buried in a book. She is currently enrolled in an English Masters programme for the sole purpose of indulging her reading and writing habits further. She lives in a leafy suburb of Newcastle, on Australia's east coast, with her own romantic hero—husband Greg, who is the inspiration behind all her happy endings.

Michelle would love you to visit her at her website: www.michelle-douglas.com

To my irresistible little sister, Jess.

# CHAPTER ONE

'YES!' TASH FLUNG up the lid of the washing machine, bunched up a T-shirt and lobbed it into the dryer. A pair of shorts followed and then another T-shirt and a pair of tracksuit pants. 'Oh, yes, and she's going for the record...' A rolled-up sweatshirt sailed through the air and into the dryer without touching the sides. She grinned. As soon as she switched that baby on, her holiday officially started.

One glorious week.

Just to herself.

She did a little dance. A week! A whole week.

A knock on the front door pulled her up mid-shimmy and the next T-shirt sailed past the dryer to land in the laundry tub. She turned to glare.

*No, no, don't glare. Holiday, remember?*

She let out a breath, reaching for her customary languor and shrugged it on. As soon as she was out of Sydney she could carry on with as much uncool excitement as she pleased, but until then she had no intention of ruining her tough-customer image.

Chin tilted?

Check.

Swagger?

Check.

Bored facial expression?

Check.

At seventeen it had taken her weeks—months!—to perfect that particular attitude. Now she could slip it on at will.

She strode down the hallway, determined to get rid of whoever was on the other side as quickly as she could. Throwing open the door, she glanced at the figure outlined on the other side of the screen and everything slammed to a halt—her feet, her mind, her holiday mood. Screaming started up inside her head. Air pressed hard against her lungs—hot, dry and choking.

She swallowed to mute the screaming and folded her arms to hide the way her hands had started to shake from the surge of adrenaline that flooded her. Every stomach muscle she possessed—and her weekly Judo class ensured they were all well-honed—clenched up hard and tight until they hurt.

Mitch King.

*Officer* Mitchell King stared back at her like some upright holy warrior. From the top of his close-cut blond hair to the tips of his scrubbed-to-within-an-inch-of-their-lives boots. Even out of uniform he looked as if he should be wearing one. Everything about him shouted clean-cut hero—the strong square jaw, the not quite even teeth and the direct blue of his eyes. A man on a mission. A man who knew right from wrong. No shades of grey here, thank you very much.

Tash didn't reach out to unlatch the screen. She didn't break the silence.

'May I come in?' he finally asked.

She let her attitude prickle up around her like razor wire. Kinking an eyebrow, she leant one shoulder against the wall. 'Are you here to arrest me?'

His eyes narrowed. She knew their exact shade of blue, though the screen guarded her against their potency. Sort of. Her stomach clenched so hard she thought it might cramp.

'Of course not.'

'Then no, I don't think so.'

She started to close the door. He kept his voice even. 'It wasn't really a question, Tash. If you close the door in my face I'll break it down.'

She didn't doubt that for a single moment. As far as *Officer* Mitchell King was concerned, the ends always justified the means. For sheer cold-blooded ruthlessness, nobody else came close.

Without a word, she unclasped the door and then turned and hip-swayed down the corridor into the kitchen. She added the provocative sway to her hips because it was more dignified than thumbing her nose. And because without her usual uniform of jeans and work boots she felt vulnerable. A hip-sway distracted most men

Not that Mitch King was *most men*.

She turned, hands on hips, when she reached the kitchen, but the sun flooding in at the windows reminded her it was summer and that she had big plans for this week.

Just as soon as she got rid of her unwelcome visitor.

'How can I help you?'

The twist of his lips told her he'd read her animosity. As she'd meant him to. She'd lived in the same suburb as Mitch for most of her twenty-five years, but they hadn't spoken once in the last eight.

And if it'd been another eight it would've been too soon.

He didn't bother with pleasantries. 'We have a problem and I'm afraid you're not going to like the solution.' He planted his feet, but his eyes gentled. 'I can't tell you how sorry I am about that.'

He might look like an angel, but the man could probably deceive the devil himself.

She shook the thought off, refusing to allow soft summer eyes or firm lips that promised heaven to sway her. She wasn't seventeen years old anymore. 'I'm not interested in your sentiments.'

His mouth hardened.

'What's this problem? If it's anything to do with the pub then you'll have to speak to Clarke.'

'It's not about the pub.'

For the last three years Tash had managed the Royal Oak, a local establishment that serviced the factory workers in the area. It wasn't a genteel or trendy establishment by any means, but it was clean and generally free of trouble and Tash had every intention of making sure it stayed that way. She folded her arms and stuck out a hip. 'Well, if it isn't about the pub...?'

Mitch didn't even glance at her hip and she couldn't have said why, but it irked her. A tic did start up at the side of his jaw, though. He wasn't as calm as he'd like her to think.

'Have you spoken to Rick Bradford recently?'

It took every muscle she possessed to not let her jaw drop. When she was sure she had that under control she let rip with a short savage laugh. 'You have to be joking, right? The last time you and I spoke about Rick, you arrested him. Unfairly, I might add. If you think I'm going to chew the fat with you about Rick then you are an unmitigated idiot.' She put all the feeling she could into that *unmitigated*. It was a nice big word for a girl like her to know.

One of Mitch's hands clenched—a strong brown hand. He leaned in towards her, his eyes chips of ice, all warmth gone. 'So nothing's changed? You still see him through rose-coloured glasses?' His lip curled. 'What is it with women and bad boys?'

She lifted her chin. 'From memory, it wasn't the bad boy I fell for.'

He froze. He glanced away. So did she, wishing she could take the words back. It grew so silent the only sounds she was aware of were the low hum of the refrigerator and one of her neighbours starting up a lawnmower.

Mitch cleared his throat and from the corner of her eye she saw him reach into his pocket. He pulled out a packet of photographs and held them out towards her. 'We believe Rick is responsible for this.'

She didn't want to take the photographs. She wanted to slap his hand away, herd him back down the hallway and shove him out of her door. Mitch had always considered Rick a troublemaker. When she and Rick had been in school, if anyone had been caught shoplifting then, according to Mitch, Rick must've been behind it. If there'd been a fight in the playground then Rick must've instigated it. If there was graffiti on the train station walls Rick must've put it there. She snorted. Crazy! And yet it had always been Rick's grandmother's door the police had come knocking on first.

And when kids in the area had been caught smoking pot, Mitch had been convinced that Rick was the supplier.

Mitch had been wrong. Oh, so, wrong. But that hadn't stopped her best friend from going down for it all the same. He'd served fifteen months in prison. And she'd unwittingly helped put him there.

But not again. She'd learned some smarts in the last eight years. She knew better than to trust any man. Especially the one standing in front of her.

She reached out and took the photographs. The first one showed a house gutted by fire. She tossed it onto the counter. 'Rick is not, nor has he ever been, an arsonist.'

The second showed a crashed car. She glanced up and raised an eyebrow.

'The brake lines on the car were deliberately severed. The woman was lucky to get out of it with nothing but a broken collarbone and a concussion.'

She threw it to the bench to join its partner. 'Rick would never hurt a woman.' Rick protected women. She didn't bother saying that out loud, though. Mitch would never believe her.

The third and fourth photos made her stomach churn. 'And he certainly wouldn't senselessly slaughter animals. That's…' The photographs showed a field of sheep with their throats cut. One of them was a close-up. She slammed it face down to the bench. Acid burned her stomach. This was just another of Mitch's witch-hunts.

'That's what's happened to Rick's last three girlfriends.'

'I'm sorry, Officer King, but I'm afraid I can't help you with your enquiries.'

'Have you spoken to Rick recently?'

He'd rung her two nights ago to tell her he was coming to town.

'No.' She kept her face bland and unreadable. She'd practised and practised that skill until she had it down pat. 'I haven't spoken to Rick in months.'

His eyes narrowed. 'I'm not sure I believe you.'

She lifted a shoulder and let it drop. 'I don't care what you believe.' She paused and forced herself to complete an insolent survey of all six feet two inches of honed male flesh. Mitch still had a great body. She kinked an eyebrow when she met his gaze again, keeping her face bland. 'But it has to be said, you used a smoother approach last time.'

And, just like that, the air shimmered with unspoken tension. As if it hadn't been shimmering enough before!

'You're never going to forgive me, are you?'

'Nope.'

'I was trying to protect you.'

'Liar.'

She spoke so softly it almost sounded like an endearment. He took a step back, shrugged his official demeanour back on like a second skin. 'We have it on fairly good authority that Rick is headed for Sydney.'

She kept her mouth shut.

'And we think you're next on his hit list.'

It took an effort of will not to roll her eyes. 'Besides the fact that I know Rick would never hurt a woman—*any* woman—I've never been his girlfriend. I think that rules me out, don't you?'

'No.'

It was the way he said it. It made her blood run cold. Mitch might not make the law, but he sure as heck ensured it was enforced to the letter. Regardless of the cost—to himself or to others. 'What makes you so sure I'm next on the hit list?'

'A crumpled-up piece of paper with your address on it.'

She went cold all over. 'Found where?'

'In that field of slaughtered sheep.'

She folded her arms, resisting the urge to chafe them instead.

'Two undercover officers from Central Sydney are on their way here now. One of them fits your description.'

*We have a problem...you won't like the solution.*

'And the bit I'm not going to like?'

'They're going to stake out your house to wait for Rick, and we have to get you out of here.'

She went to shake her head.

'For your own protection.'

It should've sounded ludicrously melodramatic, but it didn't. She stared at him for a long tension-fraught moment, taking in the way his mouth tightened and his shoulders tensed. '*We* meaning you?'

He nodded.

'This is a bit beneath you these days, isn't it?' He'd progressed through the ranks of the force with a speed that was apparently a credit to him and his family. She might call him Officer, but he was a detective now. She couldn't believe he hadn't moved to a flashier suburb and wiped the dust of this working-class neighbourhood from the soles of his polished boots. She couldn't believe he was standing in her kitchen asking her about Rick Bradford *again.*

She pointed to the suitcase on the sofa, open but neatly packed. 'Look, I'm about to head off on holiday for a week. Up the coast. I won't be around to spoil your stakeout or whatever it is you have planned.'

'You don't understand, Tash. We need to get you somewhere safe. We don't want to risk you ending up in hospital…or worse.'

'Why you?' The question burst from her, but she couldn't help it. She didn't want anything to do with this man. Ever. Again.

His nostrils flared. 'My history with Bradford is well known.' The words came out clipped and short. 'The powers that be want me out of the way.'

'So even your superiors think your judgement is clouded on the issue?'

He didn't say anything. He simply reached across and turned the photograph of the sheep over; spread each photograph out so she could experience their full impact.

She cut short a shudder. *Show no weakness.* Rick wasn't responsible for those dreadful things, but someone was. Someone who wanted to frame him or hurt him in some way. Someone who didn't care who they hurt in the process. She couldn't stop her gaze from flicking to the other photos—the burned-out house. How dreadful to lose all you owned in the world in one fell swoop. She glanced around her open-plan kitchen and living room. She didn't have much, but…

She glanced at the photo of the crumpled car and swallowed. Some of the questions Rick had asked her the other night made sudden and sinister sense—*Have any new people come to the area? Has anything unusual happened lately?* He'd asked them all in such a way that he hadn't raised her suspicions, but now…

She knew her rights. She could say no. For heaven's sake, she hadn't had a holiday *ever*. But she owed Rick. If she could help bring this situation to a swift conclusion—help clear him —the sacrifice of a holiday would be a small price to pay.

'Where do you mean to take me?' She didn't doubt for a moment that Mitch had an ironclad plan.

He met her gaze and just shrugged.

Obviously it was a *secret* ironclad plan. 'How long do you think this operation is going to take?'

'No more than a few days.'

She glanced at the photographs again. Who on earth would want to hurt those women? And what did it all have to do with Rick?

A burned-out house. Severed brake lines. Slaughtered sheep. She suppressed a shiver. She might've learned some street smarts in the last few years, she might be known as someone not to mess with, but she had no desire to come face to face with whoever was responsible for all of that. She knew self-defence and she had a smart mouth, but this… It was out of her league.

Self-preservation battled with pride. Common sense eventually won out. She might hate Mitch, but not enough to endanger her own life. She could put up with him escorting her to wherever it was she needed to go. 'When do we have to leave?'

'Within the hour would be good.'

She bit back a sigh. 'You said there were two officers coming? I'll make up the bed in the spare room.'

'Just leave the linen out. They can make up their own beds.'

Typical male.

Her hand clenched. There was nothing typical about Mitch King, and she'd do well not to forget it. 'Then I guess I'll just throw the rest of the wet things in the dryer, pack a bag and get changed.'

'Tash, thank you.' She must've looked blank because he added, 'For being so reasonable about this.'

His gaze lowered to her fist. She unclenched it and pasted a fake smile to her face. 'I'm no longer an over-wrought teenager, *Officer* King. I have absolutely no desire to meet the person responsible for those awful things.' She gestured to the photos. 'But I can tell you now, you're on the wrong trail if you think it's Rick.' And the sooner the police found that out the better.

He didn't say anything for a long moment. 'I suppose it's too much to hope that you'll call me Mitch?'

'You suppose right.'

She stalked off, heart thumping.

'You already have a suitcase packed. You won't need to pack a separate bag.'

'They're holiday things.' Swimsuits and shorts and bright T-shirts. If she was lucky she still might get away for a couple of days.

'Which will all be fine,' he called after her.

That sounded promising. She wondered if the NSW Police Force budget extended to putting her up in a nice resort somewhere on the North Coast. It'd mean her week wouldn't be a complete loss.

She focused on that rather than the thought of spending the next few hours in Mitch's company.

She wasn't a teenager, she thought, lifting her chin. She was an adult woman with clear vision and hard-won wisdom. And she had Mitch's measure now.

*Fool me once, shame on you. Fool me twice...*

She shook her head. It wasn't going to happen.

After switching the dryer on she shot into her bedroom and pulled her mobile phone from her pocket, flicked through her list of stored numbers until she came to Rick's. She had to warn him of the welcome he could expect when he arrived in Sydney.

Mitch suddenly loomed in the doorway. Damn it! She hit delete and Rick's number disappeared.

His eyes could knife a lesser person. 'Were you trying to ring Bradford?'

'I'm ringing Mandy next door and leaving a message on her answer machine to tell her I'm letting some out of town friends stay. You know what this place is like. If strangers suddenly show up without explanation there'll be all sorts of alarms raised.'

He loomed in the doorway while she made the call. When she was done he held out his hand for the phone.

She lifted her chin and went to put it in her pocket instead.

'Don't test me on this, Tash.'

One glance at his face told her he'd take it by force if necessary. Steeling herself, she slapped it into his palm. 'I can see the next few hours are going to be a whole barrel-load of laughs. Now, I'd like some privacy while I get dressed. Unless you mean to force your company on that head too.'

Without a word, he turned and stalked off. Tash had to sit down on the edge of her bed and breathe in for several long moments. She pushed herself upright again to pull on her usual armour of jeans, work boots and a black T-shirt.

It wasn't until they were driving over the Sydney Harbour Bridge with its comprehensive view of the Opera House and harbour that Tash realised how completely she drew Mitch's scent into her lungs. She stared out of the passenger window, barely noticing the colourful yachts below or the way the light glinted on the harbour in perfect summer exuberance.

Mitch's scent hadn't changed. Not one little bit. He still smelled of oranges and the tiniest hint of mint. Her lungs swelled to drink it in as if starved. With an abrupt movement she lowered the window, blasting her sinuses with warm summer air.

Mitch glanced at her briefly and she met his gaze just to prove she could. What she saw in their depths, though, shook her to her core. She understood the concern. She was a citizen at risk and he was the officer charged with protecting her. Her lips twisted. And she knew how seriously he took that duty.

But…regret?

Like him, she turned her gaze back to the front and tried to ignore the pounding of her heart.

'You will be safe, Tash, I promise. This will all be over before you know it.'

She believed him. Still, the sooner he dropped her off at the 'secret' location and went on his merry way the better.

Another ten minutes of bone-stretching tension crawled by.

'How is Rick doing?'

He spoke so softly she almost didn't hear him. She wished she hadn't.

Her fingers curved into talons. It took an effort of will not to bare her teeth at him like some wild thing. Eight years ago he'd taken from her not only her best friend, but also her self-esteem and her conviction that good trumped evil. She pushed a laugh out of her throat, but it was harsh and guttural. 'Do you really think I'm naïve enough to discuss him with you again? Or perhaps you think him stupid enough to discuss his comings and goings with me?'

His knuckles whitened about the steering wheel. She dragged her gaze back to the front. She remembered those hands more than she remembered his eyes or his smile. She remembered how he'd held her hand in his and the way his thumb had rubbed back and forth across her wrist, making her blood quicken, making her wish he'd do so much more with those hands. She remembered how one of his fingers had trailed down her cheek, and how it had made her feel like the most beautiful girl in the world. She remembered how his hands had curved about her face the couple of times he'd kissed her, as if she were precious.

Precious? She'd been nothing more than a means to an end.

She could almost forgive him for arresting Rick. He was a police officer and it was his duty to uphold the law. And once he'd seen what was happening, Rick had made sure all the evidence had pointed to him. Rick had taken the blame and had sworn her to silence. She couldn't blame Mitch for any of that. But she would never forgive him for using her to bring about that arrest, for lying to her, for betraying her so completely. For making her think he loved her. All in the line of duty.

'I only meant that I'd heard he'd been doing some good

work with troubled youths down in Melbourne. That's a tough gig. I admire him for taking it on.'

Back then she'd been utterly clueless.

But not anymore. Seemingly innocuous questions or nicely worded flatteries would never draw her again. 'Well, maybe you'd like to make a donation to that cause the next time you have your chequebook open, *Officer* King.'

They didn't speak again. They drove along in a silence that itched and burned and bristled for another hour. Tash didn't say a word when he turned onto the freeway and headed north. He didn't volunteer any information either. Now there was a surprise.

Eventually he turned onto a small sealed road that wound effortlessly through bushland with only the odd farm dotted here and there to show any signs of habitation. Before they reached the road's end Mitch swung the car onto an obscured bush track.

'This isn't the way to a nice resort,' she growled.

'What on earth gave you the idea I was taking you to a resort?'

Her nose curled. 'Wishful thinking.'

He grinned and her heart sped up. Just like that. Idiot heart.

'Then where on earth are you taking me?' She made her voice tart. 'Or do we have to wait for a Cone of Silence to descend before that's to be revealed?'

'I'm taking you to a cabin.'

Her lip and nose curled this time. 'Please tell me it has running water and electricity.'

'It has both.'

How gullible did he think she was? 'I don't see any powerlines.'

'There's a generator.'

'Is there a flushing toilet?'

He flashed her a grimace pregnant with apology.

She huffed back in her seat and folded her arms. 'Why can't I go to a resort under an assumed name or something? I'll pay out of my own pocket.'

'It's not a question of money, Tash. It's a question of keeping you safe. The best way of doing that is to make you disappear, take you out of circulation.'

'You can't keep me here against my will.' Though they both knew that, if he chose to, he could.

'Do you really want to risk leaving?'

She glared out at the ghost gums and banksia trees.

He parked the car beneath a makeshift shelter that blended into the native Australian landscape. 'We have to walk the rest of the way.'

Oh, this was getting better and better.

He held his hands up at her glare. 'I swear it's only three minutes of easy walking.'

It would've been easy if it hadn't been for the bull ants. She yelped the moment she saw the first one.

Mitch spun around. 'What's wrong?'

She pointed.

'For heaven's sake, you're wearing work boots. They're not going to hurt you.'

'I hate them.' She'd sat on a nest of them once when she'd been small and she'd never forgotten it. They'd injected so much venom she'd developed a fever that night and had ended up in the emergency room of the local hospital. Her father had clouted her at the time for being so stupid as to sit on an ant nest. Then he'd clouted her when they'd got home from hospital for the additional inconvenience.

The memory made her stomach churn. She pushed a hand into the small of Mitch's back. 'Go faster.' He felt lean and hard beneath her fingertips. 'In fact, run.'

'Tash!' Exasperation laced his voice. He swung around to her, but whatever he saw in her face cut off the rest of his words. He knew she had demons. And she really hated him for that.

Thankfully, he didn't say a word. With a shake of his head he started to jog, her suitcase tucked easily under one of his arms as if it weighed nothing. She stayed close at his heels, her handbag bumping at her hip and her feet tingling in abhorrence at the thought of ants.

Mitch slowed to a walk when they emerged into a clearing. Tash checked the ground for signs of bull ants before lifting her head. The clearing of lush grass opened up to a view so unexpectedly elemental and beautiful, so unspoilt, it momentarily robbed her of the ability to speak. She stumbled forward, her jaw sagging.

The curve of land they stood on caught an ocean breeze and below stretched a small beach. What the beach lacked in size it made up for in perfect golden glamour—the sand glittering in the sun and the waves whooshing up on the shore in perfect curls, the water stunningly clear and the whitecaps gloriously white. Beyond the bay the sea glimmered blue and green without a whitecap in sight.

To the left of them lounged a largish cabin, screened on its seaward side by wattle trees. The flowers were long gone, but the delicate green tracery moved in the breeze as if dancing to something slow and dreamy. Behind it stood a forest of ghost gums and banksia trees.

'Where…where are we?'

Mitch turned from unlocking the cabin's door. His mouth hooked up when he saw where she'd stopped. 'Pretty, isn't it?'

'Beautiful.' It might just make up for the rustic amenities. Suddenly, spending a few days in a secret cabin with a private beach didn't seem such a hardship after all.

She followed Mitch inside. She didn't bother trying to hide her relief.

He grinned. 'Not as bad as you were expecting?'

The main room, complete with a rug on the floor and a comfy-looking sofa against one wall, was warm and welcoming. To the left was a fully equipped kitchenette, with a microwave oven and bar fridge. A table with three mismatched chairs stood nearby and a solid wooden bookcase full of books and knick-knacks acted as a kind of divider between kitchen and living areas. There were even pictures on the wall.

He gestured to a doorway and Tash moved aside the blanket tacked to its frame to glance inside. It held a big double bed with a blue-and-white patchwork quilt. A white blanket box sat beneath the window. She shook her head, turning on the spot to take it all in. 'It's lovely. Truly lovely.' If she'd owned a cabin, this was exactly what she'd want it to look like. 'Who owns it?'

He glanced away. 'I do.'

Her jaw dropped. 'This is yours?'

'I bought the land five years ago.' He shrugged. 'I've spent my holidays and free weekends building this cabin.'

He'd what? For one outrageous moment she wanted to run away. Instead, she swallowed. 'Thank you for letting me use it.'

He didn't say anything.

She moistened suddenly parched lips. 'I guess you'd better show me the lavatory, and how the generator works. And then you can get back to cleaning up the streets and keeping the peace.'

Would he have to face whoever had hurt those women? Her heart surged against her ribs. She took a step back. She wouldn't want anyone to have to deal with someone that angry and unbalanced. Not even Mitch.

He frowned and cleared his throat. 'Tash, I think you've misunderstood the situation.'

She straightened from surveying the titles in the bookcase. Not that she'd taken in a single one of them. 'Oh?'

'I'm not leaving you here alone. I'm your bodyguard for the duration of the operation.'

She dropped down onto the sofa. It really was very comfortable.

# CHAPTER TWO

TASH'S EXPRESSION TOLD Mitch more than words could that she'd rather face whoever was responsible for hurting those women than spend any more time in his company.

He swung away, biting back a curse. They both knew the person responsible was Rick, and no doubt she still thought she could save him. Just as she'd thought eight years ago. He wasn't going to let that happen. He wasn't giving Rick the chance to hurt Tash again.

He waited for hysterics.

And kept right on waiting.

He should've known better. Tash didn't do hysterics. Not anymore.

Eventually he rolled his shoulders. She might never forgive him for putting Rick behind bars, but she was right—she wasn't the sweet, easily-rocked young girl she'd once been either. His heart bled a little at that, knowing he'd been partly responsible for that hardening, for her toughening up. He'd tried to apologise back then, but she hadn't wanted to listen. A part of him hadn't really blamed her.

He rubbed the back of his neck. Ancient history—that was all it was, and that was how it should stay. He pulled his hand back down to his side and bit back a sigh. It'd help if he didn't remember the events of eight years ago as if they'd only happened last week. His lips twisted. And how those events had changed his life forever.

*For the better.*

And for the worse.

'Is that really necessary—a bodyguard?'

He turned back and aimed for neutral and professional. He'd found that difficult eight years ago and he didn't find it any easier now. 'I don't make the rules, Tash. I just follow orders.'

'To the letter.'

He ignored her sarcasm. 'Naturally, you'll have the bedroom.' He gestured. 'I'll be on the couch.'

One quirk of her eyebrow told him that had never been in doubt.

A reluctant grin tugged at his lips. He had to admire her spunk. 'Let's get a couple of things out of the way and then we can relax.'

'Relax? You really think that's going to happen?'

Her hazel eyes, a bit too large for her face, mocked him. They wielded the same power, the same kick of awareness now as they had eight years ago. When she'd been a slip of a girl and he'd been a hungry young constable eager for promotion. Seventeen. He'd had to keep reminding himself of that fact at the time.

*She's not seventeen any more.*

His chin shot up. He had no intention of letting his guard down while they were out here in the wild. None! He wouldn't relax until Bradford was in custody. There might be history between him and Tash, but he refused to be distracted by it. Or by her.

Besides, his lips twisted, she'd rather drink poison than become involved with him again.

It didn't mean he wasn't going to try and make this as easy on her as possible, though.

'What do we need to get out of the way?'

Her question hauled him back. 'First I'll show you the amenities.' The sooner she'd had a chance to rant about those the better.

She sighed when she saw the small outbuilding with its pan toilet and the bucketful of dirt and small spade beside it. 'At least it has a door.' She glanced in. 'And seems to be relatively spider-free.'

He remembered her reaction to the bull ants and made a mental note to make sure it remained spider-free. 'And this is the shower.' He gestured to the canvas hut nearby. A camp shower he'd only erected yesterday.

'Hot water?'

He shook his head. Her shoulders drooped a little and he had to fight the urge to swear. Tash might act tough—as if she could take on anything the world wanted to throw at her—but beneath it all he knew how vulnerable she was… and how gentle. If he found Rick first…

His hands clenched again. He would keep her safe. He swore that much.

No one would find them out here.

And the undercover detectives would deal with Rick with their usual efficiency. It suddenly occurred to him that he didn't envy them their job. Arresting Rick again would give him no satisfaction. Other than to know Tash was safe, that was.

Instead of a stake-out he got to spend the next few days in paradise with a beautiful woman. *Who hates your guts.* He planted his hands on his hips and glared up at the sky. *Professional, keep it professional.* It was all he had. In his bones he knew that as long as they stayed out here they'd be safe. All he had to do in the meantime was maintain his professionalism.

He turned back to find her surveying him with narrowed eyes. She pointed to the shower. 'When did you put that up?'

'Yesterday.'

'So you knew—' She broke off and folded her arms. 'No, you didn't.'

'I was spending a few days on leave out here.'

The brown flecks within the brilliant green of her irises gleamed like amber. He'd never seen eyes like them before.

'So I'm interrupting your leave.'

'It's no big deal.'

'Well, it only seems fair as you're interrupting my holiday,' she drawled. But the way she gripped her hands in front of her was at odds with the tone of her voice. The space between them filled with an edgy silence.

He cleared his throat. 'I'm impressed,' he managed, suddenly thirsting for an ice-cold beer and it wasn't even lunchtime. But her hair gleamed a dark rich brown and the sun bore down on his uncovered head. 'You don't seem too horrified by the amenities.'

She smiled. It was sudden and unconsciously sweet and it jammed his breath in his throat. 'I'm just thankful I don't have to relieve myself behind a bush. Rick and I would sometimes take off to the National Park for a couple of days and that was usually the case there.'

The moment the words left her mouth she looked as if she'd like to call them back.

He should change the subject, try and put her at her ease. But… 'You want to talk about it? Clear the air?'

She turned to face him fully. 'About Rick?' she said, obviously deciding not to misunderstand him.

'I know you hate me for arresting him.'

'I stopped hating you for that years ago, *Officer* King.'

That *Officer* set his teeth on edge. She wanted to bait him, wanted to prick and needle him. Normally he could shrug that kind of thing off. He tried to focus on the content of the conversation rather than the tone. 'If that's the case, then what's the problem?'

'The problem is I haven't forgiven you for using me to do it. I haven't forgiven you for pretending to be in love with me, for making me trust you, and then betraying me the way you did.'

The accusation in her eyes cut at him. His mouth filled with acid. She'd given her friendship to him freely and he'd abused it. 'Would it make a difference if I told you how sorry I am about that?'

'No. And frankly, Mitch, I don't want to talk about it. Let's just focus on getting through the next few days as easily and quickly as possible, all right?'

So that was what he could do with his olive branch, huh? Right. He nodded once and rolled his shoulders to try and ease the burn between them.

Tash tossed her head and tried to ignore the darkness in Mitch's eyes. She reached up behind to scratch between her shoulder blades. 'Is there anything else I need to know?'

He didn't smile. The shadows in his eyes didn't retreat. 'Don't go off on your own.' He gestured to the coastal forest that surrounded them.

She tried to get the expression in his eyes out of her mind. He wasn't some cute, roly-poly Labrador puppy she'd just kicked, but a grown man who'd screwed her over.

She puffed out a breath. She wanted—needed—him to keep his distance.

She scowled and glanced up into the never-ending blue of the sky. 'We're safe here, right?'

'Yes.'

'Some semi-deranged criminals aren't going to come crashing through the undergrowth, are they?'

He widened his stance. 'Practically guaranteed not to happen. Next to nobody knows about this place.'

'Right, then.' She dusted off her hands. 'I don't see why we can't carry on as we planned to before all of this nonsense.'

Three frown lines marred his forehead. 'I'm not catching your drift.'

'You'd planned on a few days R & R out here, right?'

'Right.' He drew the word out.

'Me, too. Well, not *here*, obviously, but I'd planned on spending a significant amount of this coming week on a beach.' She'd planned to travel five or six hours further up the coast, but…whatever. 'And for the rest of it I was planning to read a big fat novel or two, order takeaway pizza, eat too much chocolate and not do a scrap of work.'

After three years of working without a break, she deserved a holiday.

'You're suggesting we holiday together?'

'Not together!'

His lips twisted. 'Of course not. My mistake.'

'But…' If she wasn't going to worry herself into an early grave…'Yes, to the holiday bit.'

He shifted his weight again and it drew her attention to the long, clean lines of his legs. Her mouth dried. 'Except—' she suddenly pointed at him '—you're not to go strutting around without a stitch of clothing on like you probably do when you're here on your own. Skinny-dipping is prohibited.'

She shouldn't have thought of Mitch naked. A whole host of illicit images pounded at her. Her cheeks started to burn. Very slowly a grin spread across his face. Eyes as warm as Mediterranean nights urged her to drop the attitude. Hands that, apparently, hadn't lost their allure for her over the past eight years tempted her to let down her guard. And the combined scent of mint and citrus curled around her, making her mouth water and an ache start up low in her belly.

Her chest cramped. Her pulse pounded. Her hands clenched.

His grin hooked up the right side of his mouth in the most intriguing way and her heart started to hammer. He leant in closer, swamping her with heat and mint and citrus. 'It'd be almost worth it just to see the look on your face. You might have a smart mouth and attitude to burn, Tash Buckley, but I have a feeling it'd be as easy as ever to unsettle you.'

It couldn't be possible! She fell back a step. She couldn't still want Mitch after all this time.

'Do it and I leave.' Fear made her voice tart.

He eased back and the tropical blue of his eyes hardened to chips of ice. 'Then you'd be a fool.'

Maybe, but at least she'd be a fool with her heart intact.

'We carry on exactly as we'd planned...*separately*.'

She turned and stalked back towards the cabin.

It was only for a couple of days, three at most, she told herself, storming into the bedroom where Mitch had deposited her suitcase. She flung it open and with as much speed as possible slipped into her swimming costume. All she had to do was keep things polite and pleasant. She might have to work at it, but...

Pleasant? She grimaced and pulled a shirtdress on over her head. Okay, pleasant might not be possible, but polite—distantly polite...very distantly—that should be manageable. For heaven's sake. The man was only doing his job. She owed him some measure of gratitude whether she liked it or not.

Okay, well, obviously she didn't like it, but she could

be adult about this. She gritted her teeth. She would be adult about this.

She practised a smile. There wasn't a mirror in the bedroom to tell her how well she'd pulled it off. It felt plastic, but it had to be better than a snarl, right? She slipped her feet into flip-flops and sauntered back into the main room. Mitch sat at the table, just…

She swallowed. He just sat there.

She recalled his attempt to apologise.

She recalled the way she'd spurned it, threw it back in his face and her smile started to slip. With a Herculean effort she slotted it back into place. 'Mitch?'

He glanced up. He took in her bare legs and something flashed in his eyes. An answering tightness clenched her stomach.

She shook herself. 'I, um…' She frowned and leaned towards him. 'If I weren't here, what would you be doing?'

He shrugged. It seemed casual but something told her it wasn't. She swallowed and suspected her smile had become a grimace. 'Well, if I were you, I'd get on with it.'

*Unless it was walking around naked or skinny-dipping.*

'I suspect my being on the beach might cramp your style,' he drawled, his eyes hard in a way that didn't fit her memory of him.

He could be right. 'There's room enough for the both of us on your beach.'

'That's not the impression I got.'

She knew she'd been churlish, but… She tossed her head. Given their history, the least he deserved was churlish. He sure as heck couldn't imagine she'd be doing cartwheels about any of this.

She backed up a step. 'I'm going to go for that swim.' She didn't wait for him to answer, but shot straight out of the door and down the track that led to the beach.

The headlands on either side pushed straight out to sea, the weathered rocks grey and smooth. In a storm or high seas it would probably be dangerous to swim here, but on a clear easy day like today curling waves rolled up to shore, set after perfect set. It was the ideal surf for body boarding. Not that she had a body board. She'd have to content herself with body surfing instead.

She dropped her towel to the fine white-gold sand and, refusing to turn around and glance back behind her, set straight off for the water.

She paddled for a couple of moments, the shock of cold water tightening her skin. Lifting her face to the sun, she relished the contrast between the cold and the heat.

And then she surveyed the surf. She'd never swum at a deserted beach before. Even though she was a strong swimmer she preferred the safety of a patrolled beach. Today, though, knowing Mitch would undoubtedly be watching from some hidey-hole, she moved forwards into the water, greeting the waves and finally diving beneath one. She caught a couple of waves and in less than five minutes she gave herself up to the joy of being in the water.

And every time thoughts of Mitch or Rick and the threat to her wellbeing intruded, she pushed them right back out again.

She practised handstands until waves knocked her over. She caught waves until she was worn out. She floated, relishing the sense of weightlessness and the cool water enveloping her.

'Tash!'

The shout came from the shoreline. She started and gulped a mouthful of water, remembering in a rush that someone wished her ill. She turned to find Mitch waving her in.

Why?

Could this whole nightmare be over already?

With a queer twist in her abdomen, she headed for the shore. She took the towel he handed her. 'What's up?'

'You've been out there for an hour and a half. Don't you think it's time for a break?'

An hour and a half? She blotted moisture from her skin and tried to appear unfazed and unflustered.

She had nothing to be flustered about.

Except for the way Mitch's eyes kept flicking to her legs…and her hips.

He jerked away. 'And beyond time to top up the sunscreen.'

She squeezed water from her hair, towelled off as best she could and then pulled her dress back over her head. She did her absolute best to ignore him, but it wasn't easy when he paced a few short metres away, back and forth, back and forth, on those strong tanned legs of his.

She tore her gaze away to slap a sunhat to her head and spread her towel out. She collapsed on it and then pulled a tube of sunscreen from her bag. She reapplied it to her face, and then her arms and legs. She finally donned a pair of sunglasses.

He didn't say a word.

His silence irked her. 'Any news?'

He stopped pacing and shook his head. 'No news.' His face softened slightly. 'But I thought you might be hungry so I made lunch. Only sandwiches and fruit.'

She didn't want his face to soften when he looked at her! She didn't want her belly softening when she looked at him! She didn't want him looking out for her, bossing her around or telling her what to do!

'I don't need you doing things for me or telling me what to do. I'm capable of deciding when I need to put on sunscreen and I can make my own lunch!' The words rocked out of her with too much force.

He stiffened and his eyes flashed. 'I think you meant to say, "Thank you, Mitch, for going to the trouble".'

Ha! 'You, at least, are being paid to be here, being paid to make lunch, being paid to keep an eagle eye on me, while I'm supposed to just submit and say "Thank you, Mitch"?' She let fly with a loose laugh. 'As if that's going to happen.'

He threw the picnic basket to the sand. 'You want to quibble about money when your life is in danger?'

She hated the way her pulse leapt at his wide-legged stance and flashing eyes.

He wheeled away. 'If you think I'm going to keep taking this crap from you, Tash, you're sorely mistaken.'

He wheeled back and she leapt to her feet. 'What are you going to do about it,' she shot at him, slamming her hands to her hips. 'Throw me in a police cell?'

'The NSW Police Force is doing everything it can to keep you safe! Would it seriously hurt you to show some gratitude?'

'If it were any other officer here then there'd be no problem on that head. Get another officer down here today and I'll show all the gratitude you want!'

His face twisted and his voice rose. 'It's school holidays. Summer. There isn't another damn person available unless I call Peters in from her holiday *with her kids.* Is *that* what you want?'

She almost said yes, but in all conscience couldn't.

He slashed a hand through the air. 'Rick has timed this perfectly!'

It was as if he'd hurtled her back eight years—back to the confusion, the pain and the rage. The helplessness. The realisation of what she'd done. The realisation of what he'd done. 'Rick is innocent you block-headed idiot!' she screamed as loud as she could.

His eyes blazed like blue fire. 'You're the idiot—the *blind* idiot—where Rick is concerned.'

Every muscle bunched and tensed until she shook with it, frustration a murderous black bile in her blood. She not only knew how to disable, but how to make a person scream with pain while she did it. And she wanted to make Mitch howl. Her hands clenched and her temples pounded with such force she thought her head would explode.

She clenched a fist…raised it…

And then her father's image rose up in her mind and she went cold all over. She took a step back, her hand falling to her side, her chest rising and falling and burning. 'I have never loathed anyone in all my life with the intensity I hate you, Officer Mitchell King.'

He paled.

'I do not want to be here with you.' *She'd almost struck him!* 'What are my other options?'

'There's a safe house in Hornsby. You'd need to remain inside at all times, hidden.' He swung away, raked a hand back through his hair. 'I remembered how active you were—how much you hated being cooped up—and figured you'd prefer being out here.'

She swore and sat, rested her head in her hands for a bit. They couldn't go on like this. *She'd almost hit him!* The thought of being cooped up in a hot sweaty suburb didn't appeal one bit, though, either.

What on earth had happened to polite distance?

She lifted her head. She dragged in a breath. 'What kind of sandwiches did you make?'

'Ham and tomato.'

Her favourite. She reached into the basket and took one. 'Thank you.' But it came out stilted.

He sat then too, but he kept the basket between them. Wise. Very wise.

'I'm sorry.'

She didn't want an apology. She wanted him gone. *You can't have that. Get over it.*

'If I have this wrong and you'd prefer the safe house just say the word.'

She considered it. Seriously considered it. She stared at the beach, the surf, the sky. Eventually she shook her head. 'This,' she gestured to the beach, 'is better.'

A heavy silence descended.

*Would you like to clear the air?*

She set down her sandwich. Would it help?

Her chest cramped as she looked at him. 'Do you know I never trusted another man after what you did?'

He bowed as if buffeted by a sudden breeze. 'Tash.'

Her name groaned out of him and she didn't answer the incredulity in his voice. She couldn't.

He raked both hands back through his hair. 'Jesus, Tash, you were just a kid!'

She stiffened at that. 'What? You don't think a seventeen-year-old can truly love?' She'd loved him with her whole heart. She'd never felt as intensely, as passionately, as deeply about any man. Not before. Not since.

She never wanted to feel that way again. When she thought he'd returned her feelings she'd been on top of the world. When she'd found out he'd used her to gain information that had led to Rick's arrest...

Betrayed didn't begin to describe it. No amount of jubilation, not the highest of highs, was worth that kind of devastation.

He turned to her, his face grey. 'I'm sorry, truly sorry. I thought...I thought you'd get over it. I thought you'd treat it as a light flirtation. It wasn't until afterwards I realised how much I'd hurt you.'

'Light flirtation?' She stared at him in disbelief. 'Mitch, seventeen-year-old girls don't treat anything as light except, perhaps, parental rules.'

Which was why she'd sneaked out to meet Mitch that night. It was why she'd taken him to Cheryl's party. A party that had been raided as soon as Mitch's suspicions that cannabis was present were confirmed. Until that night she'd kept her 'romance' with Mitch a secret from everyone. Because he'd asked her to. Because it was the one bright thing she could hold onto when everything else around her was shabby and tacky. She hadn't wanted to let reality intrude.

In hindsight, what he'd been doing had become obvious, only she'd been too besotted at the time to see it, too distracted by the presents he'd brought her—chocolates, books and knick-knacks that she'd treasured. She'd been too awed by the attention he'd paid her, too thrilled by the desire in his eyes. Too consumed by the physical mayhem he'd created in her.

She'd been altogether too stupid, too gullible and too naïve. But she'd learned her lesson—trust no one.

'I was twenty-two and I thought I knew everything.' He gave a laugh that scraped her nerve-endings raw.

Twenty-two? He'd seemed like a god to her back then. She'd forgotten how young he'd been too.

'But I got a lot of things wrong, Tash.'

She wouldn't argue with that, but something in his tone had her swinging to him. 'Like?' The question was out before she knew it.

He stared down at his hands and then out at the water. He didn't wear sunglasses to shade his eyes and she could see the lines fanning out from their corners. He must be what—thirty, now? He was too young for so many lines.

And just like that her heart started to burn for him.

She stiffened and took another bite of her sandwich. She wasn't forgiving him.

'When I first started in the police force I was hungry to save the world.' His lips twisted. 'You can translate that into hungry for promotion if you like.'

'Which is why nailing Rick on drug charges was such a coup for you.'

He nodded.

*Hungry to save the world?* She scowled at the water. He hadn't saved. He'd only destroyed. The sad thing was, he didn't know just how much he'd destroyed. And even now she couldn't tell him. Wouldn't tell him.

'So you must be pleased with yourself these days.' She rested back on one hand as if she didn't have a care in the world. As if they were talking about nothing more innocuous than the weather. 'Moving up through the ranks as you have with such commendable speed.'

'You'd think so.'

She frowned and moistened her lips.

'But I got *you* wrong, Tash. I misjudged what I'd need to do, what I'd need to sacrifice, to rise up through the ranks and make a difference. I don't know if you remember this, but the day Rick was found guilty and was sentenced you turned to me with such a look in your eyes.'

The look had been heartbreak. Her eyes burned. 'It didn't stop you then and it hasn't stopped you now.' And she'd best not forget that.

He was quiet for a long moment. 'Some things are worth fighting for. I happen to think the law and justice are two of those things.'

'And if someone gets hurt in the crossfire?'

'In the interests of the greater good then...' He hesitated. 'I won't pretend that I don't regret it.'

The innate ruthlessness chilled her.

A seagull landed nearby. It squawked at them, obviously hoping they'd throw some scraps. She went to toss it her crust but Mitch's hand on her arm stopped her. She froze beneath his touch.

'It's cruel to feed them. Their digestive systems aren't designed to eat bread...or chips,' he added, referring to the tourist habit of tossing gulls hot salted chips.

She nodded and he removed his hand and she found she could breathe again, although her heart pounded harder than the occasion demanded. 'Why on earth did you want to be a policeman anyway?'

His face darkened. He stared out to sea. 'I haven't told anyone this before. But if anyone deserves to know it's you.'

He turned and she may as well have not been wearing sunglasses at all. Her breath became trapped by the lump in her throat. The lump stretched into a painful burn that made her eyes sting. And all she could remember was the way his hands had cupped her face eight years ago and how utterly she'd given her heart to him.

'No,' she croaked.

He frowned. 'No?'

*Clear the air?* She gave a harsh laugh that made his nostrils flare. Clearing the air wasn't helping at all. This wasn't clearing anything, only clouding it.

'No,' she repeated, clearing her throat so the word emerged stronger. 'I don't want to know anything more about you, Officer King. You can keep your secrets to yourself.'

With that she rose, shook out her towel and strode off towards the cabin. She entered it only to find him two paces behind. She whirled on him. 'Are you going to dog my every footstep?'

He stepped around her, seized a bottle of water from the fridge and grabbed the backpack from the table. 'Help yourself to whatever you want, Ms Buckley.' He waved a hand around the kitchen. 'I'll be down on the beach if you need anything.'

The 'Ms Buckley' stung, but she had no one to blame but herself.

She hitched up her chin. 'Thank you.' Her voice came out cold, polite and distant. If she'd had any energy to spare she'd have applauded her poise.

Without another word, he left.

She clenched her eyes shut. Letting her guard down around Mitch would be fatal. He might come across all caring and solicitous, but he didn't trust her any more now than he had back then. That backpack being a case in point. He'd been *very* careful to take it with him. She'd bet her life it contained her cell phone. And his. Along with the car keys. He wasn't giving her a chance to get her hands on any of them.

'Regret? Yeah, right,' she muttered. Mitch would say anything and do anything to get what he wanted. All in the line of duty, of course.

Well, one thing was for certain. He wasn't getting her.

Tash had a shower.

She fully explored the inside of the cabin. It was well-stocked. She had to give Mitch credit for that. She didn't find her cell phone. Not that she expected to.

She lay on the bed and stared up at the ceiling. Despite all the sun and surf earlier, a nap eluded her. Her mind circled with questions and fears instead. What kind of trouble was Rick in? Was he safe? Who was behind the

violence against those women? Did someone really want
to hurt her? If so, why?

She leapt off the bed to browse the bookcase. She selected a book at random. Fifteen minutes later she threw it
down with a growl. The one thing she didn't need to read
was a graphic police procedural.

Not that she was scared. Not out here.

*Not with Mitch so close.*

The thought whispered through her. She shook it away.

She made tea and drank it without tasting a single drop.

Finally she pulled on her tennis shoes, grabbed an apple
and headed back down to the beach. Activity—that was
what she needed. She wasn't used to lazing around with
nothing to do.

The minute Mitch saw her he snapped his cell phone
shut with a curt, 'I've got to go.' He shoved it into the
backpack.

He didn't tell her who he'd been talking to.

She didn't ask.

'If it's *legal*,' she drawled, channelling icy politeness
that bordered on incivility, 'I was planning to go for a
walk…just along the shoreline.' She wanted to add 'Alone'
but figured that'd be overkill.

'Sure.' He lay back on the sand and adjusted his cap
over his eyes. 'Beyond those rocks there—' he waved to
the left '—is a broad rock shelf. The rock pools are pretty
at low tide.'

Right. Was it low tide now? 'Thanks.' Again—icy and
uncivil. It had to be better than shouting at him, though,
surely? With a shake of her head, she turned and stalked
off.

For the next hour Tash lost herself in the strange wonder
of the rock pools. She discovered brightly coloured anem-
ones, tiny starfish, small crabs and little silver fish. She

found brightly coloured pebbles, and bright green clumps of seaweed. She found fully contained worlds that seemed to be in perfect harmony.

She grimaced as a hermit crab pounced and devoured a tiny fish. It was a beautiful world, but a savage one too.

Still, with the sounds of the waves breaking on the reef, the cries of the seagulls and the tang of salt on the air mixing with the scents of the eucalypts and casuarinas onshore, it worked to ease some of the tension from her muscles.

Until the image of Mitch's shuttered face rose up in her mind.

Had she really cut him off so pitilessly and walked away when he'd been about to reveal something that obviously meant a lot to him, some secret he'd never shared before? She slammed her hands to her hips. She glanced first one way then another before crouching back down.

'What a cow!' she murmured, scratching her hands back through her hair and knocking off her hat. She snatched it back up, settled it more firmly on her head. She was better off not knowing his secrets and he'd be better off not sharing them with her.

She thumped down to sit on hard rock. How were they going to get through three more days of this? Her mouth went dry. For heaven's sake she'd nearly hit him. They couldn't go on like this.

She forced steel to her legs and pushed back to her feet, startling the tiny fish in the rock pool. They flashed silver as they scattered to hide in the weed and overhangs. *For heaven's sake, it was eight years ago. Get over it!*

She passed a hand over her eyes. She hadn't spent the last eight years nursing her wound. But…seeing him when she'd least expected to had brought it all rushing back—the pain, the disillusion, the anger. Nothing good had come from any of it. All she'd been able to do was lash out in an effort to protect herself. *Very adult of you, Tash.*

She closed her eyes and lifted her face to the sun. She stayed like that, motionless, for several long moments. Swallowing, she turned and headed back the way she'd come.

Mitch still lay on his back with his cap over his eyes. She set her shoulders and went to nudge him with a foot and then thought the better of it. 'Are you asleep?' she murmured instead. She said it quietly so he could ignore her if he wanted.

'Nope.'

But he didn't sit up.

She sat, but not too close. 'I have a proposition for you.'

He still didn't sit up. In fact, he didn't say anything at all. She refused to get passive aggressive. She refused to get up and stalk off. 'The police want to question Rick, right?'

He hadn't been moving before, but he stilled completely at her words. She stared at him and pursed her lips. *Act like an adult.* 'I'd rather have this conversation face to face.'

Very slowly Mitch pushed up into a sitting position. What was she up to now? He settled his cap back onto his head. 'You know we do.'

'But you don't have enough evidence to arrest him, do you? All of your so-called evidence is merely circumstantial.'

'What are you getting at, Tash?' He reached across and removed her sunglasses, dropping them to her lap. He wanted to see her eyes. He wanted to know if she was lying to him, if she was planning something stupid. Not that she was the easy-to-read girl she'd once been, but he'd become adept at reading people. You had to in this job.

Her face, however, gave nothing away. She merely blinked a couple of times while her eyes adjusted to the light.

'If you think for one moment I'll believe you mean to grass Rick up or set him up, then you can think again.'

She leaned back and stared down her nose at him. 'I might consider you a treacherous snake in the grass but I never thought of you as stupid. Of course I'm not going to grass Rick up.'

She said it all so matter-of-factly and without rancour that it surprised a laugh out of him.

'I know Rick isn't responsible for these crimes you're fingering him for.'

All of his mirth fled. She was so blind where Bradford was concerned.

'Let me ring him. Let me speak to him.'

He stiffened. Every muscle screamed *no*. If he said no outright, though, she'd get up and walk away. He didn't want her to walk away. He was tired of that cold shoulder of hers.

His lips twisted. So much for professionalism.

Her hazel eyes with their bright points of gold surveyed him steadily. He bit back a curse. 'Why would I let you do that? Why would I give you the opportunity to warn him we're on his tail?'

She leaned towards him and the shape of her lips held him momentarily spellbound. 'Whatever happened to innocent until proven guilty?'

'I know Bradford.'

'You always had it in for him—why?'

'He was a drug runner!'

'You had it in for him well before that. For what? Shoplifting a couple of chocolate bars and a bit of petty vandalism? For heaven's sake, Mitch, those things were a rite of passage where we grew up. You know that as well as I do. I'm guilty of exactly the same things!'

He clenched his teeth so hard he could feel the pulse at the base of his jaw start to thump. Eventually he managed to unclench them. 'He was the ringleader who led kids like you and Cheryl O'Hara astray.'

'Cheryl?' She closed her eyes. When she opened them again her eyes had turned dark and murky. 'You're wrong. You don't know how wrong.'

Her certainty made something inside him snap. 'I know he hit you all right!' The words burst from him like bullets—hard, sharp and lethal. His hands clenched. His gut clenched. Bradford had hit her and the knowledge still made him want to tear the guy apart with his bare hands. How could she still defend him after all this time? 'I know that mongrel beat you up!'

Her back stiffened. 'He most certainly did not!'

Her hauteur gave him pause, but not for long. He stabbed a finger at her. 'The first time I saw you after my basic training, you had a bruise on your cheek. A couple of months later, you had a black eye.' One incident could be shrugged off as an accident. But two? Not a chance.

Tash folded her arms.

'You had a black eye and Rick had two black eyes, a broken nose and a cut lip.'

She lifted her chin.

'I asked your father about it. He told me Rick had hit you and that he'd, um…taken Rick to task for it.'

'And you believed him?'

He sensed the scorn deep inside her. It burned brighter and fiercer until her eyes almost turned green. 'Of course I believed him!'

The scorn flared with greater intent. 'Of course you did.'

She went to rise, but he caught hold of her wrist, keeping her in place. 'Are you telling me Rick didn't hit you?'

With surprising agility she twisted out of his grip and it suddenly occurred to him that she only remained where she was because she chose to. 'Of course he never hit me!'

'Then who...?'

She raised an eyebrow, not even trying to hide her derision. 'You're the detective, you work it out!'

Mitch watched her stalk back up to the cabin. When she was out of earshot, he let loose with a whole litany of curses. What on earth had possessed him to bring her here? What had made him think it a good idea? Why had he thought this would work?

He fell back to the sand to stare at the sky. All he wanted to do was keep her safe!

*Of course he never hit me!*

He sat back up with a frown. Her voice, her face, her eyes, they'd all conveyed too much authenticity. He wiped his palms down his board shorts. If Rick hadn't hit her then who the hell had?

His skin turned clammy. His mouth dried. A sheen of ice froze his scalp. No. Please God. He couldn't have gotten it so wrong!

He launched himself upright and sped towards the cabin. He flung the door open and didn't bother closing it. Tash spun around from washing her hands in the sink.

'Your father,' he croaked. 'Was it your father who hit you?'

She folded her arms and glared. 'Well you saw how handy he was with his fists.'

Not a direct answer, but he saw the truth in her eyes. His stomach pitched and he had to swallow to battle nausea. How could he have gotten it so wrong? All this time...

'Why didn't you tell me?'

Her lips twisted as if he were the most pathetic thing she'd ever seen. 'You never asked.'

Every word found its mark, knifing through him in accusation.

'My father was a big man. You saw the results of his handiwork.'

He had. He dragged a hand down his face. 'Rick tried to stop him?' From hitting her?

Again she didn't answer, but something bitter and broken stretched through her eyes. 'And you decided to do nothing about it.'

A fist tightened vice-like about his chest. Tash was right. He'd chosen to do nothing, believing Rick had come by his just deserts. Oh, he'd taken Mr Buckley to task and told him to never take the law into his own hands again, but...

He'd gotten it wrong. So wrong.

She twisted the knife in deeper. 'If you'd tried to befriend Rick instead of hassling him at every turn, you might've been able to help. He had enough misery in his life without you adding to it.'

She stalked past him and into the bedroom, and this time he didn't try to stop her.

# CHAPTER THREE

MITCH STUMBLED BACK OUTSIDE. The bright light half-blinded him, but it was the light of new knowledge that made him reel.

How had he read her situation so wrong back then?

He wove his way back down to the beach—to where he'd left the backpack and his beach towel. He'd been twenty-two and so sure he knew everything. He'd known nothing!

He raked both hands back through his hair and let forth a curse that turned the air blue. How much had he contributed to Rick's spiral into crime? If he'd taken the youth under his wing could he have…?

A growl burst from the back of his throat. Rick would've resisted any overture of friendship from him. Rick hadn't trusted anyone in a position of authority. One of the few delights Rick had enjoyed, as far as Mitch had been able to tell, was flouting authority with a casual insolence designed to set teeth on edge, breaking rules wherever possible and laughing in the face of the consequences.

Given the boy's home life, Mitch could hardly blame him for his anger and lack of trust. Even when that anger had found a voice in petty crime. But as soon as Rick had progressed to drugs he'd stepped over an invisible line.

Mitch glared out at the horizon. He refused to take responsibility for that.

But it didn't change the fact that he and Rick had more in common than he'd thought—they both loathed violence against women. At least, Rick had before he'd gone to jail.

Mitch rested his hands on his knees, pulled in a breath and let it out slowly before straightening. It might not be the case anymore. Prison changed a man, and from all he'd heard Bradford hadn't been a model prisoner.

He thought back to those photographs and his stomach hardened. Prison could send men who were on the brink right over it. The Central Sydney detectives in charge of the case thought him *guilty as sin.* Those were Detective Glastonbury's exact words. Mitch had no reason to doubt them. Rick mightn't have been responsible for hurting Tash eight years ago, but he was responsible for this latest spate of violence. Mitch was sure of it, even if Tash couldn't see it.

*Just like you were sure he'd hit Tash eight years ago?*

He swung away. It wasn't just Rick's connection to the three women. There was compelling physical evidence too. The evidence *wasn't* just circumstantial. Ice tiptoed down each of his vertebrae. He would not give Rick the chance to hurt a fourth victim. His lips thinned. Bradford must have a heck of a grudge against Tash—might even hold her responsible for his going to jail. That would make him dangerous. Savage.

He pushed his shoulders back, his nostrils flaring. Tash's protector had become a predator.

*Teenage girls don't take anything lightly.*

Rick had stood up to her father, had tried to take him on. Mitch's heart pounded against the walls of his chest. No wonder she had him up on a pedestal. No wonder she refused to listen to reason now. This would all eventually lead to more disillusionment on her part and she didn't deserve that.

He bit back a curse, swept up his towel, backpack and sunglasses and marched back towards the cabin.

Tash wasn't in the main room, which meant she must be in the bedroom. He stared at the blanket he'd tacked to the doorframe in an attempt to give her a measure of privacy. 'Tash?'

No answer.

He threw his towel on the back of a chair, lowered the backpack onto it and tossed his glasses to the table with so much force they slid off the other side. Biting back a curse, he picked them up and slammed them back to the table.

'Tash, I want to talk to you!'

His words emerged at a bellow. He grimaced. Wrong tack. Totally wrong tack. He closed his eyes and counted to five. He opened them, counselling himself to moderate his tone. 'I want you to tell me about this proposition of yours. Why should I let you ring Rick?'

Finally the blanket was pushed aside as if she'd been standing on the other side the entire time, waiting for the right moment to make an entrance. 'Do you mean to give my idea a fair hearing?'

Her scepticism stung. 'I'm not making any promises. The ultimate decision rests with the detective in charge, not me. But if your idea has merit then I'll put it forward.'

He waited for some crack about him always following the rules or something, but she remained silent. 'Why?' she eventually asked, not moving from the doorway.

She acted as if he were the predator rather than Rick. He tried to relax.

'I mean I could tell down at the beach that you didn't like the idea.'

He'd grown better at reading people, but so had she. It'd be wise not to forget that.

She folded her arms. 'Well?'

His chin rose. 'I'm sorry I got things wrong eight years ago. I'm sorry I jumped to conclusions and didn't ask the right questions.'

She glanced away.

Mitch hardened his heart. 'You might not want to hear my apology, but that's not going to stop me from uttering it. I *am* sorry. You might not want to accept that, but that's your problem.'

'Problem?' she spluttered, her eyes glaring back into his.

'What else would you call that chip on your shoulder?'

Her eyes narrowed.

'But I'm through with apologising now. I'm sorry I got some things wrong back then. I'm sorry I hurt you. Now, you've made it abundantly clear that you don't want to be friends. Fine. So let's dispense with the pretence and keep everything on a professional footing.'

She blinked.

'Eight years ago I made a mistake. If I can in some measure rectify that now then I will.'

She finally moved further into the room, letting the blanket drop behind her. 'Are you saying you believe Rick is innocent?'

'That's not what I'm saying.'

Her lips tightened, but she didn't turn and stalk back into the bedroom. Instead, she strode to the fridge, pulled out a jug of iced water and snagged a couple of glasses from the kitchen bench. She sat at the table—in the seat nearest the backpack, as if to deliberately taunt him. He had to bite back a grin. They both knew she hadn't a hope of getting more than three steps away with it if she tried.

She poured them both a glass of water. 'The police want to question Rick, right?'

He sat too and curled a hand around his glass, relishing its coolness. 'That's right.'

'Do you actually want to arrest him?'

He wasn't telling her that but, man, she could keep her face smooth and unreadable these days. 'We'll want to hold him for questioning.'

'So, in the interest of achieving that, you're staking out my house whilst providing me with a bodyguard for what—three days? Does that seem like a reasonable use of police time and resources?'

'We take violence against women very seriously.'

She went on as if he hadn't spoken. 'When I believe that with a single phone call I could convince Rick to walk into the nearest police station.'

He leaned across the table. 'To give himself up?'

She glared. 'To *assist* with your enquiries,' she snapped. 'I hope whoever *questions* Rick is more open-minded than you are, Officer King.'

He gulped water down to drown the immediate response that surged to his lips. 'Why would Rick do that?'

She ran a finger through the condensation forming on her glass. 'Because, against all the odds, Rick still trusts me.'

That was just what Bradford wanted her to think while he lulled her into a false sense of security. 'And you expect me to believe you'll just hand him in?' What was her game?

Her eyes flashed fire and he waited for her to start yelling at him all over again. She didn't, but the fire didn't dim. He had an unbidden image of her naked with that kind of fire glowing in her eyes. Would they—?

He tried to wipe his mind clear of the images that flung themselves at him in vivid succession.

'We're working on two different premises here.'

He hauled himself back to the present and this moment.

'You're operating under the mistaken illusion that Rick is guilty. I'm operating under the correct assumption that he's innocent.'

'If he's so innocent, Tash, why hasn't he already contacted the police?'

'What if he's not even aware of these crimes yet?'

He hated to shatter her illusions but the sooner she faced up to the reality the safer she'd be. 'Physical evidence linking him with the crime scenes has been found. We know he's recently been in the houses of each of the victims.'

She sucked her bottom lip into her mouth.

'He knows, Tash.' He resisted adding *he's guilty as sin*, even as he thought it. Her eyes flashed again anyway.

'Were his fingerprints found on a can of kerosene that could've been used to start the fire, or on a knife that might've been used to slit those sheep's throats or on the car that crashed?'

'No, but—'

'But nothing!' She dismissed his words with a slash of her hand.

'Despite what I've just said, you still believe he knows nothing about these crimes?' It took all of his strength to remain at the table like a civilised person, instead of overturning it like a mad man.

'No.'

The air was punched out of him.

'If he's been to see these women recently then he's bound to know about the crimes.' Her lips tightened. 'But Rick has no reason to trust the police. Maybe he's trying to find some hard and fast evidence first. Maybe he's trying to solve the crime himself.'

He could see how she could make that leap into her own mind, but he wasn't buying into it. 'Who do you think is responsible then?'

The fire in her eyes dimmed. 'I don't know. My best bet would be someone he was in jail with. Someone he made an enemy of. Someone who wants to get back at him.'

He clamped down on his tongue for three seconds before releasing it. 'Why would talking to you change his mind about going to the police?'

'Like I said, he trusts me. If he's innocent, as I believe he is, then he doesn't really have anything to fear. Other than how long it will take you lot to find out who's really responsible.'

He mulled that over for a moment.

'And if it brings a quick resolution to this mess then surely it's worth it.'

She had a point, but… He caught her gaze and held it. 'How do I know that you won't simply warn him about the stake-out?'

Her gaze didn't waver but a certain satisfaction spread across her face. 'You don't. You'll simply have to trust me, Officer King.'

She practically purred his name. It was all he could do not to reach across and kiss her.

Tash held her breath and waited to see what decision Mitch would come to. The sooner this farce was over—the sooner she was away from Mitch—the better.

*But it's not a farce*, a tiny voice whispered through her.

No, not a farce. Someone really was out there hurting women. And she was next on this madman's list. Her skin iced over.

She planted her hands on the table. 'Mitch?'

He glanced up, his eyes widening at her use of his name instead of the sarcastic *Officer King*. 'You seem to forget that I have a personal stake in making sure the correct criminal is caught.'

She had absolutely no desire whatsoever to meet this person—whoever he was—face to face. She thought of those sheep, of that crumpled car and that burned-out shell of a house and had to suppress a shiver.

He reached out as if to take her hand, but his hand fell short. The blood pounded through her. 'I haven't forgotten that for a single moment.'

She believed him. Despite their history—or maybe even because of it—he would do everything in his power to keep her safe.

'Then surely my suggestion is worth considering?'

Eventually he nodded. 'You're right.'

She sat up straighter. 'Really?'

'Can you pass the backpack over?'

She did.

Her heart dipped, though, when he pulled his phone from the bag rather than hers. Of course he'd run this by his superiors first. In fact, this whole show of openness could just be a front to win her over.

Not going to happen.

What guarantee did she have that he'd argue her case sufficiently?

None.

*You'll have to trust him.*

That wasn't going to happen either.

'Detective Glastonbury, it's Detective King here.'

She snapped to attention.

'No, no trouble and no sightings from our end either.'

She listened as he outlined her proposition. Some of the

tension trickled out of her when she realised he was arguing her case with creditable conviction.

'I believe she's trustworthy.'

She blinked. Did he mean her?

'But—'

She glanced up but, other than recognising that he listened intently, she couldn't make out anything else from his expression. Eventually he nodded and said, 'I understand.'

Her heart dipped. He rang off and her nose curled. 'They didn't go for it. I'm sorry.'

Was he? She shrugged. 'What was their beef?'

'Besides the fact that they believe they're tightening the net about him and will have him soon anyway?'

She heaved back a sigh. 'They didn't want to take the risk that I might tip him off.'

He hesitated.

'Out with it.'

'They seized his phone records.'

She gazed back at him blankly.

'Tash, they know you spoke to him on Thursday night for over ten minutes.'

*Oh.*

'You lied about that.'

Yeah, she had. There didn't seem to be much to say after that. Except… 'If they have his phone records then surely they can trace where he is by his mobile phone signal?'

'They did. His phone had been dumped in a garbage can in a shopping centre.'

*Right.*

'You want to tell me what you and Rick spoke about?'

'Nope.'

'You're not doing yourself any favours.'

'If he doesn't have his phone my plan wouldn't have worked anyway.'

His gaze never left her face and it took all of her will-power to not fidget under it. She shrugged again. 'Besides, I can tell you that we just shot the breeze together until I'm blue in the face, but you still won't believe me.'

His lips twisted into a sort of half-grimace, half-rueful smile. She stared at that mouth and remembered how it had felt against hers. So long ago. Would it feel the same now?

'I guess the point is moot. In a couple of days Rick will be in custody and enquiries will be underway.'

His voice dragged her back. She tried to shake herself free from the fascination gripping her. She and Mitch were obviously stuck out here for the duration and she'd have to learn to deal with it. But...

She sank back in her chair. What were they going to do for the next three days? Swim, soak up some rays, read a book or two?

She was honest enough to admit she might find some distraction in the swimming, but she wouldn't be able to relax enough to savour anything sedentary.

She bit back a sigh. 'Well, thank you for at least running my idea past the powers-that-be.' She sipped her water, circling a finger through the watermark it had left on the table. 'And thank you for arguing my case. You didn't have to do that.'

He rose and stowed the mobile phone into the backpack and then dropped the bag to the floor near the wall. He didn't sit again. 'You didn't think I would?'

She moistened her lips and shook her head. He hadn't thought her idea a good one in the first place.

'Careful, Tash; you're letting your resentment cloud

your perception. It would probably be wiser to judge me on who I am now rather than who I was eight years ago.'

That had an uncanny ring of truth to it and it almost raised her hackles. She forced them back down. She was tired of sniping at him. She needed to deal with this situation like an adult.

He glanced at his wristwatch. 'Time to get dinner on.'

She blinked. She opened her mouth. She closed it again.

He kinked an eyebrow. 'What?'

'You can cook?'

'Of course I can cook,' he said incredulously. 'It's not rocket science.' He went to the fridge and removed a tray of minced meat. 'Just because I'm male doesn't mean I'm useless in the kitchen.'

She kept her mouth firmly zipped.

'So I'd appreciate it if you'd keep your sexist views to yourself.'

That was almost enough to make her unzip it.

He stilled and then turned to her, a couple of fresh tomatoes and a jar of tomato paste in his hands. 'You were being sexist, right?'

She considered drawling, *Absolutely*, and leaving it at that, but the word wouldn't come.

'You weren't?' His shoulders relaxed. 'Sorry; I thought…' He shrugged. 'I'm not a gourmet or anything, but I can get by. I find cooking relaxing, don't you?'

Oh, um… She swallowed. 'It just seems like another chore to me.'

He stilled and then he swung around, his eyes narrowing in on her face and at the way she worried at the water ring. One corner of his mouth lifted and her blood chugged. 'Can't cook, huh?'

Sprung. She refused to show any regret on that front, though. 'Can't say I've had much use for cooking.'

He placed a chopping board on the table and proceeded to dice an onion. 'What do you eat, then?'

His fingers were deft and while he was nowhere near as speedy as the celebrity chefs she sometimes watched on the television, he was quick enough and relaxed into the bargain.

'Tash?'

She suddenly realised she'd been staring at him slicing and dicing, completely caught up in the rhythm of it. She forced her gaze from his hands. She didn't want to think about his hands.

Of course, all she could then think about was Mitch's hands. Doing things they had no right doing and things she had no right thinking about.

*Don't go there.*

She cleared her throat. 'On the days I go into work I usually get a hot meal at the pub. The bistro does your average pub grub—schnitzel and salad, bangers and mash, calamari and chips.'

'What do you do for your other meals of the day?'

She shrugged. 'Cereal.'

He stopped chopping—tomatoes this time—to stare at her. 'You mean breakfast cereal?'

Her shoulders started to inch up towards her ears. She forced them back down. 'I like cereal. I get the healthy stuff.' Most of the time.

'You eat cereal for dinner?'

'Sometimes. So what? Can't you chop and talk at the same time?'

'Can you cook anything?'

'I can fry an egg.' Though she hardly ever did. 'Do beans on toast count?'

'I...' He shrugged. 'Sure, why not.' He sent her a quick glance. 'What about salad?'

'I buy that pre-packaged stuff from the supermarket. I don't see why you'd go to the trouble of chopping all that stuff up if you can buy it already made.'

'Because it's fresher and might taste better?'

'Or if you were counting your pennies,' she added as an afterthought. 'Luckily, these days I don't have to worry about that.'

She, Rick and Mitch had all grown up in a solidly working class neighbourhood. Money had been an issue for a lot of people.

Had it for Mitch and his parents? He'd been too far ahead of her in school for her to know much about him. It occurred to her then that he hadn't offered up much information about himself when he'd first befriended her either.

Her lips twisted. Unlike her. Had he played her or what?

*You're in his cabin. He's keeping you safe. He just argued your case to his superiors. Cut the guy some slack. For heaven's sake, he's cooking you dinner!*

Eight years ago he'd only been twenty-two. So young. She hadn't factored that in. Maybe because she'd slammed a lid on those memories and hadn't let them see the light of day since.

'You like your job at the Royal Oak?'

There was a hint of that *you shouldn't be working in a pub* disapproval that she so often got, a hint of disbelief that a barmaid might, in fact, enjoy her job.

'Yeah, I do.' She rested her elbows on the table as if his disapproval didn't bother her in the slightest. 'I'm good at what I do. I like our regulars and get on well with them. They treat me with respect.'

A smile played around the corners of his mouth. 'What?' she demanded. 'You're not going to tell me nice girls don't work in pubs, are you? Because I have news for you—I'm not a nice girl.'

He threw his head back and laughed. The sound filled the cabin with warmth. It filled her with warmth. She stared at him. She couldn't help it.

'I was going to say that I hear you run a tight ship. The regulars show you respect because they know if they step out of line they'll be out on their ear.'

She grinned down at her hands. 'Saves a lot of time in the long run.'

'I keep waiting to hear that you've bought the place.'

'The pub?' She gaped at him. 'Me?'

'Why not?'

'Oh, I don't know,' she drawled. 'But maybe the fact I don't have any business qualifications or accountancy skills might do for a start.'

'You could get them,' he challenged. 'Rumour has it that you've singlehandedly turned that hotel around.'

'Rumour exaggerates. I merely had some ideas that Clarke let me put into practice. I had support. The staff at the pub are great. We're a good team.' She frowned. 'Have you heard rumours that Clarke is selling?'

'No.'

She shook her head. She didn't want to own a pub. She was happy with things just the way they were. She pulled herself back into the here and now and nodded towards the chopping board. 'What are you making?'

'A big batch of savoury mince.' He stilled before setting his knife down. 'I didn't ask if there's anything you don't eat.'

'I'm not fussy.' She couldn't have afforded to be, growing up with her father.

'What's your favourite meal?'

'Fish and chips.' The days her father had brought fish

and chips home for dinner had been good days—days she'd been able to relax her guard and breathe a bit easier. 'What about you?' she found herself asking. Given her reaction to him this morning, it seemed amazing to her that they could be talking like this.

'Beef Wellington.'

She knew what it was but she'd never tried it.

'The beauty of savoury mince is that we can use it to make shepherd's pie tonight, cottage pie tomorrow and have it with rice the night after.'

'If one has to cook then I can see the attraction in that,' she said. 'As long as you like savoury mince.' She had to choke back a laugh at the look he sent her. 'Relax. Savoury mince is fine by me.'

'It could get monotonous.'

She kept her face deadpan. 'Do you have cereal?'

'Yes.'

She knew he did. She'd checked earlier. 'Then I'll be fine.'

One side of his mouth hooked up. 'Glad that's sorted.'

She flashed back to the moment on the beach earlier when he'd been about to tell her why he'd joined the police force and her far from civil response. The memory of that other moment when she'd almost physically lashed out at him still made her stomach churn. She had to find a way to get through the next few days without doing something she'd regret forever...and without losing her marbles. She poured herself another glass of water. 'Uh, Mitch, I've been less than gracious today.'

He'd brought too many memories hurtling back.

'I want to apologise. We're never going to agree about Rick so I propose we postpone any further discussion about him until we leave here.'

He stilled from where he'd started browning mince in the frying pan. 'You mean that?'

'I can't see that it'll help us achieve anything.'

'And what do you want to achieve?'

'I'd like us to get through the next couple of days as peacefully as we can.' And with her self-respect intact. It wasn't just memories that Mitch had brought rushing back but those same feelings of desire and need too. Back then, she hadn't known how to deal with them but she was a grown woman now. Lashing out at every opportunity was not the mature thing to do. It was time to get a grip on herself.

'You won't get an argument from me on that head, Tash.'

She counted up the number of times he'd apologised to her today. It had to have been at least five. She swallowed. 'So you accept my apology?'

'Yes.

She let out a breath she hadn't known she'd been holding. 'Thank you.'

He didn't say anything else. He added ingredients to the mince and continued stirring. She moistened her lips again, her throat so dry she wasn't sure she could form coherent words. 'So—' she gulped more water '—why was it you decided to become a police officer?'

He didn't turn around again immediately. He measured out a glass of water and poured it over the mince, added some stuff in jars. Eventually he put the lid on the frying pan and lowered the heat. 'You know what, Tash? I think you were right earlier. I don't think it's any of your business after all.'

Her head rocked back. It took all of her strength to school the shock from her face, though nothing could alleviate the sting from her soul.

'That needs to simmer for half an hour. I'm going to take a quick shower.'

He took the backpack and left the cabin.

She drained the glass of water. 'Right,' she murmured to the silence.

With eyes that were too hot she rose and walked down to the beach, praying the evening cool would find a way to soothe the tempest raging inside her.

# CHAPTER FOUR

MITCH CLOCKED THE exact moment Tash peeped around the blanket and into the main room of the cabin. He didn't need to check his watch. He'd done that five minutes ago—one forty-five a.m. The release of sleep obviously eluded her, as it did him. Given the scenario he'd presented her with this morning, it was hardly surprising.

The extent of her anger and resentment towards him throughout the day *had* surprised him, though, which was why her suggestion of a truce had blown him completely out of the water.

He sat up. Some inner voice warned him it'd be wiser to feign sleep, but he ignored it. 'Can't sleep?'

She moved more fully into the room. 'Sorry, I didn't mean to disturb you.'

'You didn't.' It hadn't been her restless tossing and turning in the next room, but an unfamiliar heat that prickled his skin and scorched his thoughts that had kept him awake. His lips twisted. And an all too familiar heat balled in his groin. He didn't know why Tash affected him like this. He knew prettier women. He sure as heck knew more welcoming women. It was useless denying it, though. Something in her called to something in him.

He blew out a breath. 'I can't sleep either.'

'Is the sofa uncomfortable?'

'Not at all.' It was a big old blousy thing that let him stretch out his full length. He couldn't blame the sofa.

He'd left a night lamp burning in the kitchen and in the faint glow it cast out he saw the way she bit her lip, the way one foot rubbed back and forth over the other. 'Are you worried you're not safe out here?'

She wore a pair of soft cotton shorts in an indeterminate grey that came down to her knees and a faded red T-shirt. Her hair was tousled—testament to her tossing and turning—and she didn't wear a scrap of make-up.

The burn in his groin intensified. He gritted his teeth and tried to ignore it. *Professionalism.*

Another glance at her—at those turned down lips—and he wanted to pat the sofa beside him, wrap an arm around those slim shoulders and give her all the reassurance she needed.

Ha! If he tried that she'd deck him. He forced himself to focus on her needs rather than the insistent ache of his body. 'I'm confident danger won't follow us here. That said, I'll feel better when this is all over.' When he knew that she was safe.

She lifted a foot and rubbed it against the back of her calf. 'Me too.'

She had nicely toned calves. In fact, she had nice legs all round. Spectacular, in fact and—

*Stop staring!*

She smoothed her hair down. 'I know that sitting up all night thinking about it isn't going to prove particularly productive.'

'No.' Unfortunately, the only idea that came to him to take her mind off the situation was illicit, forbidden and would rightfully earn him a black eye and a knee to the groin. It'd have her tearing out of here and putting herself in the way of danger too. He fisted his hands in the blanket and dragged in a deep breath.

'What I need is a generous glass of red.' That foot made another journey up her calf. 'That'd make me drowsy enough to sleep.'

It travelled back down to rest on the floor. He jerked back. Did he have any wine in the place? He didn't drink much wine.

'Mind you, it'd only give me nightmares in the end so it'd probably be a false economy anyway.'

He hauled himself off the sofa. She took a step back as if the movement had startled her and he made himself slow and gentle his strides. 'I might have just the thing.'

Brandy. He opened a kitchen cupboard and reached right to the back. Yep—as he'd hoped—a new bottle. It was a nice bottle too.

He poured them both generous snifters. Carrying the glasses in one hand and with the bottle tucked under his arm, he opened the cabin door and stepped outside. All the time he was careful not to move too close to her. He didn't want to spook her any more than she already was. In fact, he didn't even speak again, but after a brief hesitation she followed him.

He sat to one side of the front step and set the glasses down. She settled on the other side of the step a good arm's length away. The cool night air and the scent of the sea eased the tightness inside him.

She picked up one of the glasses and sniffed. 'I don't like Scotch.'

'It's brandy.'

She wrinkled her nose. 'They smell the same to me.'

'Heathen!' He feigned outrage, picking up his glass. 'What kind of barmaid are you?'

It was lighter out here in the moon and starlight than

inside and he watched as one side of her mouth kinked upwards. She stuck her nose in the air. 'I'll have you know that I'm a hotel manager not a barmaid.'

'Same difference.'

A sound left her that was almost a laugh and more of that tightness eased out of him.

'Try it. Just a sip. You might be pleasantly surprised.' He swirled the brandy in his glass, brought it to his nose before taking a generous sip. He held the liquid in his mouth for a moment, savouring its warmth before swallowing and sharing the smoky heat with his throat and stomach.

She watched him. Closely. Just how closely made his stomach clench. And then she copied his actions. Her nose wrinkled as if waiting for a bad taste, but after a moment her face cleared. 'Okay, that's not so bad. Maybe I could get used to this stuff after all.'

On the surface she was remarkably cool, but as he stared at her hands—at the way they cupped the glass—the tension wound up tight inside him again. 'Tash, I've never had a premeditated threat of violence directed at me.' The violence he'd experienced had been immediate—violence he'd been ready for, violence he'd been trained to counter and deal with.

She didn't say anything.

'I imagine it's pretty frightening.'

She stared down into her glass with a frown. 'There's a part of me that just can't seem to take it seriously.' She lifted an eyebrow—at the glass, not at him. 'I'm no stranger to anger and fighting. I've seen more pub brawls than I can count on both hands, and I've broken a lot of them up. Before that there was my father. With all of that, though, I knew where the threat was coming from, but this...' She lifted her head and met his gaze. 'It's alien to me.'

There was nothing to say to that. He just nodded and tried to swallow the bile that rose in his throat.

'That flash of temper which makes someone strike out—I understand that. I don't condone it, but I understand it. And I know how to read the signs. What I don't understand is cold-bloodedly plotting to hurt someone.'

'People do it.' He kept his voice even. He didn't want to frighten her, but he wanted her to remain on her guard.

'Yes.' The word was nothing but a sigh.

Talking about this threat, worrying about it and picking at it wouldn't help her relax. 'Tell me something.'

'What?'

'What made you offer a truce this afternoon?'

She stilled for a long moment and then seemed to mentally shake herself. 'Oh, that.' She turned from staring into her glass.

Yes, that. He wanted to trust her, but he didn't.

For a fraction of a second her nostrils flared. 'That flash of violence we just spoke about… I found myself in the grip of it earlier. I nearly hit you.'

His head rocked back and it felt as if a giant fist tightened about his chest squeezing until he could hardly breathe.

'I've never hit someone in temper before. I've not even come close to it.' She stared into the night and he sensed her revulsion simmering just below the surface. Revulsion aimed at herself this time, not him. 'I never want to be pushed to those limits again.'

He'd done a job on this woman, no doubt about it. He hadn't meant to, but that was no excuse. 'I had landed you with a corker this morning, Tash. That kind of shock can emerge in any number of confronting ways, including bursts of temper. Don't be too hard on yourself.'

'Perhaps.' She stared back down into her glass. 'But it

wasn't just that. Being forced to spend time in your company along with the whole Rick déjà vu thing hurtled me back into the past and to how I felt back then. Today's events ripped the lid off all of that. The result was…well, you saw.'

Bile burned his throat. He couldn't take a sip of brandy now if his life depended on it.

'I know you apologised, and I believe you meant it, but…'

She didn't go on. He didn't know whether to be sorry or relieved. 'You shouldn't have bottled that stuff up. Why didn't you talk to someone?'

She gave a laugh devoid of mirth and raised a snarky eyebrow. 'Who? Who could I have talked to, Mitch? My father?'

He closed his eyes.

'You'd taken my best friend away.'

Rick. He cracked his eyes back open. 'You must've had girlfriends.'

'All who blamed me for Rick's arrest.'

For a moment he thought he might throw up.

'Just as I'd have blamed them if the situation had been reversed. Because the sad fact of the matter is if I hadn't taken you to the party that night you'd never have discovered the drugs. Therefore, Rick would never have been arrested.'

'Not then, maybe.'

She merely shrugged.

He tried to swallow but couldn't. The world Tash had grown up in had been harsh and inflexible, the people unyielding to outsiders and unforgiving of their own. Mitch had effectively ostracised her from her community.

*You put a drug supplier behind bars.* Rick had possessed a lot of influence over Tash. By arresting Rick he might, in fact, have saved her from a drug overdose. He might have saved her life.

'Besides, trusting you hadn't turned out all that well for me so it wasn't an exercise I was eager to repeat.'

*Do you know I never trusted another man after what you did?* Her earlier words haunted him.

'Given all that, why aren't you still actively hating me?'

'Maybe I do.' She squinted out into the darkness. 'Or maybe it's finally run its course.' She lifted her head. 'Yes, that's what it feels like—as if today was some kind of catharsis. I no longer hate you for the same reason I no longer hate my father.'

She put him in the same category as her father? A wave of tiredness so black swept over him, blotting out the light from the moon and the stars.

'I don't know if you remember what it's like to be a kid, Mitch.' He stiffened. His arms broke out in goose flesh. 'But it's something I can never forget. One has so little power as a minor. You're always at the mercy of other people's whims and impulses.'

He remembered. Bile burned his throat. Oh, yes, how well he remembered.

She turned to him. 'But I'm no longer a child. I'm the one who calls the shots in my life now. My father can no longer hurt me. Neither can you.'

Her words opened up an abyss inside him. 'Tash,' he croaked. 'I—'

'I'm not saying this to make you feel guilty. You were only twenty-two. I forgot how young you were.'

'If I could go back and change how I dealt with it all, I would.'

'So you say.' There was a surprising lack of bitterness in her voice. 'But that's no longer here nor there to me. If you need to square something with your conscience then that's your affair. What I think shouldn't matter.'

It did if he wanted her friendship.

He reared back. What was he thinking? She would *never* trust him again.

'You didn't move to the Western suburbs of Sydney until you were twelve, right?'

She had a good memory.

'And your family was what—middle class…white-collar?'

'I lived with my grandparents. My grandfather was an accountant.' He was careful to keep all inflection from his voice.

'So money was never an issue?'

'No, I was lucky.' He forced those words out. 'I had opportunities.' Opportunities kids like Tash and Rick had never had.

She nodded. 'You were never one of us and that helps too. You didn't really know what you were doing.'

He'd been getting a criminal off the street!

But he knew that wasn't what she meant, and he didn't want to start fighting with her again so he kept his mouth shut.

'You see, if you'd been through what me and Rick and Cheryl and the rest of us had experienced I do think you might've acted differently.'

He stilled.

'It doesn't change what happened, but it means I can look on you with a kinder eye than I might otherwise.'

He stared out into the night and raked a hand through his hair.

'You asked,' she finally said.

And she'd given him one heck of an answer.

And he didn't want to talk about this anymore. 'Where were you going to go for your holiday?'

She didn't even blink at the change in subject. 'North. I'd have liked to have made it as far as Byron Bay. I've never been there, but I've heard lots about it. It's supposed to be very beautiful, but it's a long way—at least a ten-hour drive. I was going to drive as far as Coffs Harbour today and then see how I felt. Five nights in Coffs sounded awfully nice too.'

Coffs Harbour was probably the midway point between Sydney and Byron Bay. It was a nice-sized town with plenty to do.

'What did you have planned for those five nights?'

'Besides swimming, reading a novel or two and eating takeaway every night?'

'Besides that.' He could provide her with the beach for swimming. He had a bookcase full of books. They couldn't do takeaway but he could cook a burger on the barbecue. He could also do a mean steak and salad. The cabin might be rustic but he always ate well when he was here. He mentally stowed the leftover savoury mince in the freezer.

She rested her arms on her knees, her brandy clasped lightly in her fingers. The moon wove silver streaks through her hair and eyelashes until she looked almost ethereal. An ache started up deep inside him. He'd hurt this woman badly. He'd like to make it up to her if he could. He'd do everything to keep her safe, and if he could help her forget for a few hours here and there about Rick and the violence he had planned for her, then he'd do that too.

He topped up her brandy, careful not to get too close. 'Well?' he prompted.

'I wanted to try my hand at something I hadn't done before, like surfboarding or something. I thought I could get some lessons. And maybe I'd have ridden around on one of those paddleboats for a bit.'

'Sounds like fun.'

Her lips twisted in a rueful smile. 'Yeah, it does. And I haven't had any real time off in over three years.'

'Three years!' He gaped at her. She'd been in permanent full-time employment all of that time. 'That's illegal!'

She snorted. 'What? Going to arrest me?'

'Someone needs to have a word with Clarke,' he growled. Tash deserved something better than working in a pub, being a *slave* in a pub.

'Staff turnover, Clarke's mother got sick et cetera et cetera. Time got away. None of it was planned. Clarke and I came to a financial arrangement that suited us both.'

She'd wanted to build a nest egg, to have a financial security blanket. He understood that, but—

'So butt out.'

He raised his hands. 'Butting out.' They both sipped their brandy.

'So what else were you going to do on this holiday of yours?'

'I wanted to do something different, out of the ordinary like...'

He leaned towards her, intrigued at the way she broke off. 'Like?'

'You'll think it's dumb...'

Now she really had his attention. 'Try me.'

She lifted one shoulder and rubbed her chin against it before reaching up to scratch her shoulder. 'There's a native wildlife sanctuary just outside of Coffs. They rescue injured wildlife plus they have a koala-breeding programme. There's all sorts of wildlife there—echidnas, possums and emus. You can even feed the kangaroos.' She shook out her hair, not looking at him. 'I was going to spend a day there, take a picnic and make a donation. I thought it sounded…fun.'

A smile lit his insides. 'Beneath that smart-mouth tough-cookie exterior you're nothing but a big softie.'

The eyes she turned to him, though, had seen too much hard experience and he sobered.

He pulled a breath into cramped lungs and tried not to focus on the tempting allure of her lips. 'I don't think that's dumb. I think it sounds kind of nice. It sounds like a good place to support.' He'd bet her father had never taken her to the zoo. At least his father—

He cut the thought off.

She looked at him then. Really looked at him and it made his gut clench. Her gaze lowered to his lips and more than just his stomach tightened. He swore he could see the flare of gold in her eyes, but it was abruptly cut off. She moved away from him, even though there was a significant distance between them already.

Was she worried he'd try and close that gap?

In one fluid motion she rose to her feet. 'I believe the brandy did the trick. Thanks, Mitch.'

He could've sworn, though, that she'd have preferred to call him Officer King. He called a goodnight after her. He did what he could to make his mind blank, but Tash filled it.

She hadn't had a holiday in three years? He gave a low whistle. Bradford couldn't have timed his vendetta at a worse time if he'd tried. He…

Mitch stiffened. A grim black seam of something hard and unyielding solidified inside him. If Bradford had been in contact with Tash, maybe he'd timed it exactly as he'd wanted to? Maybe he'd meant to attack at the precise moment Tash would least likely be missed?

In the dark his hand clenched. She wasn't a stupid

woman. She couldn't know the kind of man Rick had become.

He meant to make sure she didn't find out first-hand. In the meanwhile, sitting around and brooding on it would send her stir-crazy. He had to come up with something, and fast.

Tash glanced up from washing her breakfast bowl to find Mitch staring at her. His regard made her pulse leap. 'What?' She grabbed a tea towel and started wiping vigorously.

'I had a thought last night.'

Her hands stilled. 'About how to bring this situation to a quick conclusion?'

He shifted his weight. 'That's out of my jurisdiction, I'm afraid.'

If it had been left up to him would he have let her ring Rick? She shook the thought off. What did it matter now anyhow? He continued to survey her and the expression on his face kept shifting so she couldn't get a proper handle on him. One moment he looked as if he expected her to yell at him—the kicked-puppy expression. The next he looked as if he'd like to gobble her up—starting at her toes and slowly moving upwards until he'd explored every inch of her. Her toes curled. 'A thought?' she choked out.

He nodded at the bowl she still rubbed. 'Are you done there?'

'Uh, sure.'

She set it on the shelf. In the next moment she found her hand enclosed in his as he hauled her out of the door. 'Ta-da!' He dropped her hand with a flourish and gestured to a kayak.

Her jaw fell open. She glanced at him out of the corner of her eyes. 'Okay.' She drew the word out.

He rolled his shoulders. 'Look, I know it's not a surf-board or a paddleboat, but I thought this might be fun.'

She swung to him as their conversation from the previous evening came back to her. *I wanted to try my hand at something I hadn't done before.* She'd never kayaked before. She walked around it. 'Where did you manage to dig this up from?'

'I've had it leaning against the back of the cabin beneath some canvas.'

That'd explain all of the banging and thumping earlier.

'And I've made sure it's completely spider-free.'

She appreciated that.

'So...' He rubbed the back of his neck and glanced at her from disconcertingly blue eyes. 'What do you think?'

For some reason his uncertainty touched her. And she had to give him credit—he really was trying to make this ordeal as easy for her as he could. She glanced at the kayak and then at the blue glitter of the beach below. Excitement shifted through her. 'You're going to teach me how to drive this thing?'

'That's the plan.'

'And we're allowed to go outside this little bay here to explore?'

'Yep.'

'Then I think it sounds perfect!'

He grinned. It made her blink. She made herself look back at the kayak. *He's an attractive man, but you can't go there again.*

Ha! Tell that to her pulse!

She pulled in a breath. She was tired. This was a strange situation. Everything was bound to feel topsy-turvy.

'Okay, how's this for a plan? We make up a picnic—we can stow it here in the front.' He slapped a hand down on the...bow? Was that what it was called? 'And then we

head up along the coast until we feel we've had enough,
stop to eat and then head back?'

That sounded great, but… 'Are you allowed to do that?'

He shrugged. 'Sure.'

He didn't say anything more and she didn't press him
for details. She lifted a paddle. 'I'm used to carrying trays
of drinks and hefting the odd keg into place, but I don't
know how long I could paddle for.'

'That won't matter. If you get tired you can take it easy.
I'm used to it.'

She eyed him uncertainly. 'You sure you won't mind
picking up my slack?'

'Tash, this is supposed to be an exercise in fun and fri-
volity—a bit of R & R—not something to stress about.'

'Oh, okay.' She nibbled her lip. 'I'm a bit out of practice with that.' And she wasn't used to not pulling her own
weight. She shook herself. 'Something I can do, however,
is make sandwiches.'

He whistled in mock admiration and she was tempted
to give him a playful push…but that would mean touching him. It'd mean pressing her hand against that tanned
firm flesh and—

*Stop it!*

'So how about I pack a picnic?' Her voice came out at
a squeak. 'While you do whatever needs doing with the
kayak?'

'Sounds good to me.'

She raced back inside. She stood in the kitchen for several long moments before remembering what she was about
and kicking herself into action.

When Tash had finished making sandwiches and had
put them into an airtight plastic container, Mitch stowed
them into a waterproof sack with bottles of water. She

handed him a couple of apples. He raised an eyebrow. 'That's not holiday food.'

She shrugged. 'They fill you up when you're hungry, though.'

He added them to the sack and then reached for a packet of shortbread cream biscuits and waggled them at her before adding them to the bounty too. 'That's holiday food. C'mon.'

He hoisted the sack onto his shoulder and she followed him down to the beach, where he'd already taken the kayak. He shot her a grin. 'Excited?'

Right on cue, her stomach started to flutter and she found herself smiling back. She shrugged, though, struggling for casual. It wouldn't do to jump up and down like a little kid. 'Sure.'

She had a feeling, though, that he saw through her pretence of unconcern.

She shrugged the thought off. She had a feeling she wasn't as perturbed by that as she should be, but she was determined to enjoy the sun and sea and the novelty of learning something new.

'Right, you sit in the front.'

He held the kayak steady while she settled herself where he indicated. He pushed them off and slid in behind her in one smooth motion. It made her mouth dry when she realised how fit he must be to do that all so effortlessly.

She shook herself and settled her cap on her head more securely. It was early—neither of them had slept late—and the air was still cool. She relished the feel of it against the bare skin of her arms…and the contrast to all of the latent strength and heat at her back. She swallowed and tried to dismiss that thought. 'I, uh…the motion is so smooth.'

'We're lucky. It's very calm today.'

There was something in his voice… No, there was

something no longer in his voice—a tension, a strain—and its absence made him sound younger, freer. She wanted to turn to look.

And then she was glad she couldn't.

Mitch gave her a few instructions and soon they were working in sync without needing to exchange a word. They turned right out of Mitch's tiny bay and headed north along the coast. They were only about a hundred metres offshore, but the swell was gentle and the four solid weeks of recent fine weather ensured the water was clear. She gave herself up to the buoyancy of the kayak and the freshness of the morning.

'Look.' Mitch tapped her shoulder and pointed downwards. Below them swam a large stingray, flapping along as easily and lightly as they did.

A sigh eased out of her. 'Beautiful,' she breathed, drawing the scent of the ocean into her lungs. 'It's so quiet out here.'

The only sounds were the soft splashing of their paddles, the lapping of water against the kayak and the sound of birdsong onshore.

'It's why I prefer a kayak to a speedboat. I'm sure waterskiing and all of that speed is fun, but…'

She could almost feel the way he lifted a shoulder in a shrug. 'But nothing could beat the tranquillity of this,' she finished for him.

'The quiet doesn't scare you?'

Not when he had her back. She shook her head.

'No?'

She realised he'd misinterpreted the action. 'I…' She moistened her lips. 'I can see why the quiet and solitude might intimidate some people, but…' She remembered the bliss of the silence when she and Rick had taken off camping as teenagers. 'But I like it. The city is never quiet. This is…'

She stiffened.

'What?' he demanded.

'Relaxing,' she finally said. 'This is relaxing.' Surely she'd relaxed at some stage during the last three or four years? One didn't need a holiday to relax.

She bit her lip. Sure she had.

But not like this.

# CHAPTER FIVE

TASH SHRUGGED THE unsettling thought aside—something she'd been doing a lot since being landed with Mitch's company. She'd revisit it later. Who knew? It might be a good thing, all of this revisiting issues from the past. Maybe she could lay them to rest and...

And what?

She waved a hand in front of her face. 'How far along the coastline have you explored?'

'I've been miles and miles in both directions. Sometimes I pack a picnic and make a day of it—stop somewhere for a swim and lunch. Sometimes I only take the kayak out for an hour.'

A sigh whispered out of her. If she stayed here longer maybe she'd get a chance to—

She blinked. What on earth...? That was a crazy thought and one definitely not worth revisiting! She couldn't wait to get home and for things to return to normal.

They manoeuvred around a rocky outcrop. A flash of movement caught her eye. She leaned forward so quickly the kayak rocked. 'A seal!'

Behind her, Mitch chuckled and did something to steady them. 'He suns himself there pretty regularly.'

A seal! She'd seen a seal! She sat dazed for a moment before remembering to paddle again.

They continued at a leisurely pace until Tash lost all sense of time. She saw seagulls diving for fish, pelicans gliding along the surface of the water, another stingray and a school of silver fish. The peace of the day and the warmth of the sun and the feeling of being at one with nature filtered into her soul until she felt light and warm and right.

Mitch touched her shoulder and his finger seemed to linger there a couple of beats too long. A pulse started beating in her throat. 'Can you see that there?' He pointed.

She blinked and did her best to follow the direction of his finger rather than on the warmth that lingered at her shoulder. She shaded her eyes and ordered them to focus. 'Um…' She cleared her throat. 'What is it?'

'A sea cave.'

She almost swung to look at him, more sure of herself now in the kayak, but then she remembered the heat in his eyes last night that had rivalled the burn of the brandy in her stomach, and she resisted the urge. 'A sea cave? Have you ever been in there?'

'Uh huh.' He moved them towards it. 'You want to see?'

She stared at the opening that emerged in the rock…at the darkness beyond. 'I, uh…take it it's safe?'

'It is at low tide, which it is now.'

It was? She glanced around, feeling like an ignorant landlubber.

'Are you claustrophobic?'

She shook her head.

'Shall I take us inside?'

A shiver—part fear, part anticipation as if she were about to embark on a roller coaster ride—shook her. 'Yes, please.' This sea cave reminded her of the Aladdin's Cave picture books she'd borrowed from the school library once.

She rested her paddle across her knees and Mitch swung the kayak into the narrow opening. The tunnel lasted for maybe five or six metres before opening out into a shallow pool with a tiny shell-encrusted beach at its far end. Fissures in the rock above let in long shafts of light. Salt crystals lining the interior sparkled silver all around them, turning the cave into a glittering fairyland.

Her mouth formed a perfect O. 'I've never seen anything like this in my life,' she whispered. 'This is like something from *Arabian Nights*.' On impulse she turned to him. He did something with his paddle so the kayak barely moved in response to her movement. 'May I take a shell as a souvenir?'

The half-light softened his face, turning him into a sort of soft focus angel. The longer she stared at him the more he came into focus. And then he smiled. She blinked and forced her eyes back to the front. Her heart pounded. 'I, um…' Darn it! Work, brain! Work, mouth! 'That is if you don't mind.'

Her voice croaked out of her, but he didn't say anything, just moved them towards the tiny beach and she wondered if he'd noticed her reaction—her momentary fascination with him.

*Fascination, huh? Is that what you call it?*

She clenched her eyes shut.

Her breathing grew more erratic rather than less. She tried telling herself it was the exertion of paddling, but it wasn't. Mitch had a smile that could make a woman forget which way was up. A flicker of heat licked low in her belly. She swallowed and clenched her thighs together. Mitch had a kind of face that could make a woman forget vows she'd made to herself—vows to never fall for him again, to not expose herself to his treachery.

Only he wasn't being treacherous at the moment, was he? He was trying to give her a holiday.

*He wants Rick behind bars. Again.*

But that didn't really have anything to do with her. He hadn't asked her anything about Rick so far today, hadn't tried to find out if she knew Rick's whereabouts or how the police could find him.

They landed against the beach with a tiny bump and scrape. Mitch vaulted lightly out and she barely noticed the gentle rock from side to side he steadied it again so quickly. He reached out to take her hand. 'Keep your shoes on. The shells are sharp.'

She put her hand in his, all of his latent power pressed against her palm, and curled around her fingers in undiscovered promise as he pulled her upright and helped her step out of the kayak. Her heart fluttered up into her throat, nearly smothering her. 'Thank you.' Her voice came out breathy, thready.

He let go of her and she had to lock her knees to stay upright. She glanced around, forced herself to feign interest in her surroundings rather than the man beside her. At the very back of the cave where it was darkest a couple of straggly plants clung to the rock—obviously a place where the tide rarely reached. 'It'd be possible to hide away from the world in here.'

She had a sudden vision of a thick blanket spread on the smoother ground beyond the shells, a bottle of champagne, strawberries...and a naked man.

The vision of her and Mitch making love here hit her hard and hot. Heat pooled between her legs, her breasts grew heavy and her lips parted. She shot a look at him from beneath heavy eyelids—took in his wide shoulders, the depth of his chest and those rippling biceps.

He'd be sheer heaven to touch.

She lifted her gaze to find him staring down at her. Her tongue inched out to touch her lips, moisten them... sensitize them.

He backed up, his face suddenly tight. 'Pick your shell, Tash.'

The warning in his voice slapped her like a dash of icy water. She snapped away and crouched down, scrabbling wildly. This...this desire was just a carry-over from eight years ago when she'd been a crazy stupid teenager.

Except...

She'd never wanted him with this kind of carnal heat back then.

And there were more reasons than she could count why she should resist the pull now.

Her hand closed about a shell—a fan, grey on the outside and pink on the inside. She rose to her feet. 'Thank you.'

Thank you for the adventure.

Thank you for the reminder.

Without another word they climbed back into the kayak and paddled away.

They emerged back into the sunlight and Mitch had to fight the urge to swear. His head pounded, his groin pounded and his knuckles had turned a sickly white around the paddle. With a superhuman effort he pulled air into his lungs and loosened his grip.

He ached with every atom of his being to turn the boat towards the shore and make for it with all the speed his body possessed, to spread the towels on the beach and lay Tash down on them and—

*Real professional!*

'I think it might be time to head home.'

His words emerged wooden, forbidding and non-negotiable. Not what he'd intended. Tash's back stiffened and he grimaced and silently cursed. Why couldn't he find a speck of moderation around this woman?

She tossed her head. 'I feel as if I could keep kayaking all day.'

Her attempt to drag this tension-filled, gut-wrenching moment back within the realms of normality didn't stop him from wanting her either.

Yesterday she might've acted like a brat but today she was all woman. In more ways than one. His knuckles turned white again. 'Believe me, your back and shoulders will be sore enough tomorrow as it is.'

An hour later, when they turned back into the cove leading up to the cabin, he'd formulated a plan. First, though, he had to get them safely back onto the beach.

The surf had started to build so he brought the kayak in on an angle, straightening when they caught a wave that they rode all the way into shore without incident. Tash let out a cry of delight that she cut off too quickly. The grin that had built inside him at the exhilaration slid off his face.

He pulled the kayak up onto the beach. Tash scrambled out without waiting for him to offer his hand. He seized her towel and spread it out on the sand. He set the cooler bag with their lunch beside it. 'You wanted some sun and surf.' He bowed, doing his utmost to keep this low-key. 'It all awaits.'

She bit her lip and glanced at the kayak. 'You don't need any help with…anything?'

'Nope.'

He wanted her down here, enjoying herself and in holiday mode. He needed to get up to the cabin and away from her as fast as he could. He needed a chance to get his head screwed on straight again. He needed to remember why they were here.

She pulled her sunglasses from her shorts pocket and settled them high on her nose and pulled the brim of her cap down low. She sat on her towel without another word.

He hovered uncertainly. Eventually she deigned to glance at him. 'No doubt you have phone calls to make.' And just like that she extinguished the holiday mood. Her cool politeness, however, didn't dampen the fire that still raged within him.

He seized the sack with the phones and settled it on one shoulder. He lifted the kayak onto his other shoulder and set off for the cabin.

The minute he was inside he poured himself a glass of iced water and chugged it down. He collapsed to the sofa, head in hands. 'Damn it!' His job was to protect her, to keep her safe. She was vulnerable right now and seducing her would be unforgivable.

*There mightn't be much seduction involved.*

The expression on her face in the cave burned itself afresh on his brain and he groaned. He could not take advantage of her vulnerability. It'd be...

Divine? Amazing? The best?

It'd be despicable.

He rose and gulped down more iced water. He *wasn't* going to sleep with his reluctant house guest, and he *would* make her time here as pleasant as he could. It wouldn't erase the past, it wouldn't change the fact he'd hurt her, but it might mitigate it a little.

His lips twisted. Who on earth was he trying to help feel better—Tash or himself?

Perhaps both of them.

He shoved that thought aside and sat at the table. He needed to come up with a practical plan to get them through the rest of today and tomorrow and, if he needed to, the day after that. Detective Glastonbury would inform him as soon as Bradford was taken into custody, but until then they remained here. Stranded alone together.

He dragged a hand down his face. *Take it a day at a*

*time.* All he had to figure out at the moment was how to get them through the rest of this afternoon and this evening *safely.* He thought hard. Eventually the tension in his shoulders eased and his breathing grew more regular. He could do this. *He could.*

Mitch glanced up from his spot on the sofa where he flicked through a computer magazine when Tash emerged from the bedroom. She'd come up from the beach mid-afternoon, had a shower and had then holed up in the bedroom for… He glanced at his watch. It was five o'clock. That made it two hours.

'I had a nap. Went out like a light.'

He wished she'd smile.

He closed the magazine. 'Holidays are hard work.' Her lips twisted but it was less of a smile than a grimace. He rushed on before she could remind him this was no holiday. 'You didn't get much sleep last night and it's amazing how much all of that swimming and kayaking can take out of you.'

'It was good tired,' she admitted. 'But now I need a coffee. Want one?'

'No, thanks.'

She made instant. He rolled his eyes. 'There's a coffee machine there, Tash.'

She shrugged. 'Takes too long. Too much fuss. I'm happy with instant.'

'Some things are worth taking their time over.'

His voice slid out like silk—smooth and suggestive. Her eyes flew to his, her cup halted halfway to her mouth. His gut tightened. *Crap!* He cleared his throat and battled to make his voice crisp, to banish any suggestiveness from it completely.

'You said you wanted to do new things on your holiday, right? To learn new things?' He couldn't let his guard down for a moment. As it was it took a Herculean effort to battle the urge to tease her further.

Her eyes narrowed. She finally took a sip of her coffee. 'Uh huh.'

'This afternoon I'm going to teach you to cook.'

She stared at him and lowered her mug. 'Mitch, I wanted to learn *fun* new things.'

'I'm going to teach you how to make a cake.'

She pursed her lips. She set her mug on the table and reached up behind to scratch between her shoulder blades. 'What kind?' she finally asked.

He let out a breath. 'Chocolate.'

'Won't it take me longer than an afternoon to learn how to do that?'

A rush of tenderness swept through him at her wide eyes. 'You'll be amazed how easy it is.'

'If that's the case, then…then can we make frosting too?'

'Chocolate butter frosting okay with you?'

Finally a smile touched her lips and he wanted to high-five someone. 'I'm not convinced the making will be fun, but the eating will be.' She rolled her eyes. 'Not that my hips need it.'

She slapped a hand to her rump. He followed the action. He went to say there was absolutely nothing wrong with her figure, that it was, in fact, spectacular, but she froze as if realising she'd just invited his view on the matter. They both looked away at the same time.

'Have a seat and finish your coffee,' he murmured, stumbling to his feet. 'I'll get the equipment and ingredients ready.'

He taught Tash how to make a cake. He barked out instructions and she followed them to the letter—measuring, mixing and beating.

Correction—he tried to bark his instructions. He tried to keep his voice level and impersonal. But he found it almost impossible to keep the warmth out of his voice.

They laughed. Not a lot, but they laughed all the same and he couldn't remember the last time he'd felt so good.

As long as he remembered to keep his thoughts focused on the task at hand instead of the way her hair fell over her shoulders or how deft and clever her fingers were. Those fingers evoked images of—

He snapped to. 'I said beat the mixture. Put some back into it.'

She did as he said. She stopped a minute later, breathing hard. Would she breathe like that when she was making vigorous uninhibited love?

'This is harder work than paddling.'

He laughed. 'Baking as a workout? I hadn't thought of that before.'

'You could make a DVD combining an exercise workout with cooking. You could use your police credentials—Master Police Chef.'

'Cooking Bootcamp.'

And then they were both laughing.

She was a different woman from yesterday. Yesterday she'd radiated anger and resentment and badass attitude. But this afternoon... He swallowed. She wasn't just attractive—on every level—she was the most attractive woman he'd ever met.

Ever. His mouth dried.

Everything inside him gravitated towards her. It thrilled him to make her laugh, to bring a sparkle to her eyes. He thirsted to learn everything about her. And every atom of his body fired with a longing to make love with her. His heart hammered against his ribs. So much for professionalism.

He pulled in a breath. It'd only be unprofessional if he acted on it. He had to keep his head. Yesterday she'd hated him. He was jaded enough to know that today's turnaround might not be motivated by maturity but a need to get back at him, to revenge herself on him. She could be setting him up just to reject him. Payback.

He didn't want to believe it. It didn't square with what he'd known about her eight years ago. Eight years was a long time, though, and people changed. And he truly didn't want to travel that path with her.

He regretted hurting her with every fibre that made him who he was, but her hurting him in return wouldn't do either of them any credit. And whether she knew it or not, it wouldn't make her feel better.

'How long do we cook it for?'

He snapped to and found she'd poured the mixture into the prepared cake tin. *Keep your head.* 'Forty minutes.'

She put the tin in the oven and then glanced at her watch and counted off forty minutes. 'How come you know how to make a cake from scratch without needing to follow a recipe?'

'My grandmother liked to bake.' It had brought her a measure of comfort on the bad days. And on those bad days he'd liked to keep her company so he'd feigned an interest. It had taken their minds off other things.

'What about your mum? Does she like to bake or is she like me?'

His gut screwed up, but he feigned outrage. 'What do you mean—like you? Are you telling me you didn't enjoy that?'

She stared back. Her hands went to her hips and he waited for her to challenge him, to delve further into areas where he didn't want to go. He clocked the moment she decided to bite her questions back. Whether she was after payback or not, he could see she was fighting to maintain her own distance.

Smart girl. But it made his heart sink all the same.

'I think the most pressing question, Tash, is how come you never learned to cook?'

She collected up the bowls and measuring jugs and other assorted paraphernalia they'd used and took them to the sink. 'There's no mystery there. My mother left when I was eight. My father didn't cook. So I had no one to teach me.' She said it without self-pity. 'I learned to heat up tinned food and make toast. That seemed sufficient at the time.'

He wanted to curse on her behalf. Instead he took her by the shoulders and led her from the sink and to a chair at the table. 'You made the cake so I clean up.'

She looked as if she might argue. In the end she just shrugged. 'Should I make the frosting now?'

'We don't want it to set yet, so no. We can't ice the cake,' he explained, 'until it's cooled or the icing melts and runs everywhere.'

'Oh, okay. That makes sense.'

'Have you ever seen her again? Your mother,' he clarified. 'Have you ever tried to find her?'

'Nope. She left me with a man who was too ready with his fists. I don't blame her for leaving, but I do blame her for leaving me in that situation. I'm not interested in knowing a person like that.'

Her words chilled him.

'Do you see your father any more?'

'Nope.'

She didn't expand. Questions chafed at him. Questions he had no right to ask—especially if he had no intention of answering her questions in return. Damn it! Why hadn't he dug deeper eight years ago and found out what had been really happening?

When he glanced at her there was a glint of laughter in her eyes. 'I'll tell you about me and my father if you tell me what happened to your parents. Did they abandon you with your grandparents?'

Bile filled his mouth. 'They died when I was ten.'

Her head reared back. Her lips parted as her eyes widened. 'Oh, Mitch, that was truly clumsy of me. I'm sorry.'

He nodded.

'I mean I'm sorry I asked the way I did…and I'm sorry for your loss too, of course.'

Her face radiated sincerity. He nodded again. 'Thank you.'

Silence stretched between them. Eventually Tash cleared her throat. 'I, um…stood up to my father.'

He turned from the sink. 'You what?'

'I was eighteen and he came at me and I…um…decked him.'

He stared at her. Her father had been a big man.

'I didn't do it in anger. In fact I was quite clinical about it. I just wanted to stop him.'

This slip of a girl had stopped that six feet two inches and two hundred pounds worth of hard muscle?

'I've been doing judo since I was fifteen.'

'You have?'

'Rick talked me into it.'

He swallowed. In a lot of ways Rick had been a better friend to her than he'd ever been.

'It helped me to avoid the worst of my father's violence, to dodge it, but I'd always been too afraid to retaliate. One day, though, I was just tired of being frightened all the time.'

'Jeez, Tash!'

'I didn't break his ribs. I didn't break his nose or his arm.'

Had all those things happened to her?

'But I did set him on his backside and disabled him completely. And then I told him I would break each and every one of those things if he ever tried hitting me again.'

'What happened?'

'I moved out and we haven't spoken since.'

He saw it then. She refused to allow herself to ever be vulnerable to the people who'd hurt her, and who could blame her? They were supposed to have looked after her and taken care of her. Instead they'd betrayed her.

Just as he'd done.

Tash jumped when Mitch clapped his hands. 'Enough of that! This is a holiday, remember?'

That was an out-and-out lie, but she appreciated his efforts all the same.

'C'mon.'

He gestured for her to get up and she had to stifle a groan. 'Mitch, there was relaxation down on my list too, you know.'

'Oh, ye of little faith.'

He led her outside and she came up short when she saw a camp table and chair set up on the grass. The chair faced seaward. With his hands on her shoulders, he propelled her into that chair. 'Don't move.'

He disappeared, only to return a couple of minutes later. He set a glass of beer on the table in front of her, a bowl of mixed nuts and her fat novel. 'Happy hour.'

She stared at it all, her mouth agape.

'Relax, Tash. Enjoy my special homebrew, enjoy the view and relish just being.'

'What about you?' The minute the words left her mouth she could've bitten her tongue out. He'd made it plain that their relationship was strictly business, even if she did catch him looking at her with so much heat in his eyes at times she was afraid she'd spontaneously combust. She shifted on the chair. 'I mean I'm sure you've earned a chance to take the weight off too.'

'I'm all good.'

Now that was an understatement. *Stop it!* She seized the glass and took a gulp.

'What do you think?'

She took another sip. 'I'm not usually a fan of home-brew, but this isn't half bad.'

He laughed down at her. 'High praise indeed.'

'I'm a hotel manager.' She lifted her nose into the air. 'I know my beer.'

His grin lifted the right side of his mouth higher than his left. She couldn't look away. 'Enjoy it all while I go take care of dinner.'

She blinked. 'Thank you.' But she doubted he'd heard. By the time she'd managed to untangle her tongue he'd already vaulted onto the cabin's tiny veranda and was practically through the door.

Nobody had ever pampered her like this. Nobody had ever taken such pains to ensure she enjoyed herself. She stared at the view, but more often than not her eyes drifted back to the cabin.

Why was he being so nice to her? Especially when she'd been so awful to him yesterday?

*Because he's a nice man.*

She forced her gaze to the front and that glorious ocean view. She sipped the homebrew. She crunched a couple of nuts. He regretted hurting her eight years ago. She didn't want to acknowledge it—her resentment had provided her with a convenient shield—but it was the truth. She no longer doubted it. She scowled and selected a brazil nut, crunched it with extra ferocity. It didn't mean she had to forgive him, though.

She traced the pattern on the cover of her novel, glared at it. Okay, she could forgive him, but she didn't have to trust him. Yesterday where there'd been a roar and burn of resentment, today there was only a whisper and an ache.

She rolled her shoulders. She didn't hate Mitch any more. It was good to know.

She took another sip and then very carefully set her glass down. None of that changed the fact that Mitch believed Rick guilty of terrible crimes or that he would use her to bring about an arrest if he could.

Yeah, well, he could do it without her help. She wasn't risking her heart like that a second time. Nor was she risking Rick's freedom again. She knew what Rick had done and what he hadn't done. Even if she wasn't at liberty to talk about it. A promise was a promise.

All the beauty in the view and the surroundings lost their appeal. If only...

'Bon appétit!'

Mitch appeared with a flourish. 'I'm sorry I can't manage takeaway pizza out here, but I thought homemade hamburgers might make a reasonable substitute. After all, they're nearly takeaway.'

For a crazy moment she had to fight back tears.

'Tash?'

She didn't know what to say. Surely she could trust him with the truth. They could keep it all unofficial and off the record, couldn't they?

'You don't like hamburgers?'

'I love hamburgers.' Her voice came out strangled.

He crouched down beside her. 'I swear I'm going to keep you safe. You don't need to worry.'

She shook her head. She couldn't tell him anything. Mitch and his job couldn't be separated.

Besides, he meant *his* idea of safe. But who was going to keep her heart safe from him?

'I know you will, Mitch.' She fought for a smile. 'This looks great.' Without another word she pulled her hamburger towards her and started to eat.

# CHAPTER SIX

THE NEXT DAY Mitch took Tash fishing—another new experience. They sat on the rocks at one end of the bay and dangled fishing rods into the water for two hours.

The air barely moved and the sun warmed her skin with a customary benevolence she'd started to relish. Occasionally a swell of water would hit the rocks beneath them in a way that would lift it and send a fine spray of droplets over them. She could almost feel herself breathing in time to the swell of the sea, dragging in the mingled scents of salt, sea and eucalyptus into her lungs.

She and Mitch barely spoke. She operated under the premise that talking would scare away the fish. Rather than making her squirm, she relaxed into the silence. And the more she relaxed the more air it seemed she could draw into her lungs.

She caught two fish. Mitch identified them, but one of them was too small so they tossed it back. Mitch caught three fish—a tailor and two mullet. He turned to her with a grin that cracked her chest open wide. 'Guess what we're having for lunch?'

She stared, and then her throat thickened. She had to swallow before she could speak. 'Fish and chips?'

'The very one.'

Her favourite.

She'd never have fish and chips again without thinking of this day. And him.

'Why are you being so nice to me?' she blurted out. She didn't mean to break the summer-holiday spell, but she couldn't hold the question back.

He gazed at her and she couldn't read a single thought in his face.

'I mean you could've just left me to my own devices, stayed out of my way as much as you could while still keeping an eye on me. But you haven't. You've tried to take my mind off the fact that someone wants to hurt me. You've tried to give me the holiday I'm missing out on. You didn't have to do any of that.'

He looked away. 'I'm enjoying it too.'

'I know, but it's not what I asked.'

He turned back and, while she couldn't make out his thoughts, she recognised the turbulence in his eyes. She could let the matter drop. She could say it didn't matter and that she wouldn't look a gift horse in the mouth, but she didn't want to. She wanted to know why.

*And why do you want to know that?*

Without warning, the blood started to thunder in her ears. Mitch lifted one broad shoulder. 'On Saturday it was because I felt bad that you were in this situation.'

Pity. She tried to keep her face unreadable.

'And you can add guilt to the mix when I found out about your father…about how I'd read that situation so wrong.'

She bit back a sigh.

His gaze speared to hers.

'I like you, Tash.'

Her heart threatened to pummel its way out of her chest.

'I liked you eight years ago. I wish I'd—'

He broke off and stared out to sea.

'You used me eight years ago.'

'Yes, I did. And I'm sorry.'

She lifted a shoulder; let it drop. 'I believe you. I'm not looking for another apology, but what's to say you're not using me again now?' And that, just like eight years ago, he wasn't doing his best to make her fall for him, hook, line and sinker?

Hook, line and sinker? And here they were, fishing. That'd almost be funny except she'd lost her funny bone.

They'd both set their rods to one side. With nothing to encumber him, Mitch leaned in close, trapping her against warm rock. She stared at a tanned forearm and her gaze made a slow salacious survey along it, taking in the strong wrist, the dusting of light hairs along a lean contoured muscle and further up to biceps that flexed with calculated accommodation. Her stomach fluttered. It threatened to dissolve when she studied shoulders so broad they'd withstand storms and gales and other catastrophes. 'Do you know how revealing your question is, Tash?'

She made herself frown. *Keep breathing. Don't forget to keep breathing.*

'It sounds as if you want to trust me, but are afraid I'll take advantage of you again.'

His words wove around her, pregnant with promise and charged with a sensuality she wanted to fall into. She did want to trust him. It might make her an idiot, but...

He leaned in even closer and she could smell the warmth of the sun on his skin. He removed his sunglasses and the lick of his desire flicked along her veins as she gazed into eyes too blue surely to contain lies. The urge to drag his lips down to hers swelled inside her until she could barely think of anything else. She ached to kiss him as a fully-grown woman. She craved to touch him, to taste him, to push him beyond the couple of fleeting kisses they'd shared eight years ago.

When he reached out to remove her sunglasses she snapped back to herself. Very gently she shook her head and pushed him away.

She'd had a lot of practice at pushing men away—it was her default position—but it had never been this hard before.

A sigh eased out of him, but he moved out of her personal space and back to his piece of rock. It was all she could do not to heave out a sigh too.

'I don't know how to answer your question, Tash. At least, not in a way that could convince you I'm not trying to use you to gain inside information on Rick.'

They were both silent.

'I'm not part of the team currently investigating him. My boss knew I had this place and knew we all had a history. I suspect he wanted me out of the way.'

*Interesting.*

'But, other than the preliminary questions I asked you about Rick on Monday, I haven't mentioned him again. Maybe that'll speak more loudly in my favour than any other assurances I can give you.'

She moistened her lips. 'But you're giving me those assurances as well?'

He held her gaze. 'Yes.'

'There is something you ought to know about Rick.' The blood thundered in her ears. 'He wasn't the drug supplier eight years ago. He took the rap for someone else. And, before you ask, I'm not at liberty to tell you who that someone is.'

His head snapped back. His eyes narrowed, instantly alert. 'Are you being threatened or blackmailed by this person?'

'No, but I made a promise.'

'Do you think this has a bearing on the current case?'

She shook her head. 'I just think it's something you ought to know, that's all.'

His gaze sharpened. 'Why? Especially if you won't tell me the truth so amends can be made to Rick.'

'Why?' She flung out a hand. 'Because, Mitch, you keep getting Rick wrong and it seems to me that it's in my best interests if this time you get him right.'

'Oh, my God!' Tash groaned her pleasure. 'These are the best fish and chips I have ever eaten in my life!'

That sparked the beginning of a smile from Mitch, but she'd hoped for more. Since their conversation about Rick, he'd been quiet. Too quiet.

He was probably mulling everything over and trying to determine whether she could possibly be telling him the truth. And, if so, who on earth could be responsible instead.

Mitch was a good cop, but she and Rick had protected Cheryl well. She doubted his suspicion would fall there. And she was glad about that. She and Rick might've had things hard, but Cheryl had had them so much harder.

'Mitch?'

He barely glanced up.

She waved a hand in front of his face. 'Can you stop working and enjoy the day and this place the way you've been trying to get me to?'

'But—'

'No buts. Let sleeping dogs lie. Believe me, it's for the best.'

Cheryl had gone on to make something of herself. She'd always been smart and she'd worked hard. That shouldn't all become forfeit now because of one stupid youthful mistake.

'Who are you to decide that?'

He glared. She blinked, and then she swallowed. 'So... so you believe me then?'

He swiped a hand through the air. 'I don't know.'

They sat outside at the camp table and the conversation seemed at odds with the beauty of their surroundings. 'I shouldn't have mentioned it.' She should've kept her mouth firmly shut.

'You should've *mentioned it* eight years ago.' His words emerged low and savage.

She responded as if bitten. 'What do you care, huh? You got to close the case! You got the kudos and the promotion and the satisfaction of being considered the brightest new spark on the force. *You* got everything you wanted.'

He shot to his feet. 'I happen to believe in the law and justice!' His chair crashed to the ground. 'I want the right people charged with the crimes they're responsible for! I'm not after quick fixes. I'm after the truth. What right did you or Rick or any of the others that you ran around with back then have to pervert the course of justice?'

His anger sparked hers and she shot to her feet too. 'What right?' she spat. 'What right? Truth and justice were myths where I came from. Where was this Utopian ideal when my father was laying into me with his fists? Where was it when Rick's mother was selling her body on the street?'

'You never told me about your situation! You never told anyone.'

But the evidence had been there if he or any of the authorities had looked harder.

'As for Rick's mother...' He rubbed the back of his neck. 'It's why social services placed him with his grandmother.'

'Oh, for heaven's sake, Mitch! His grandmother was turning tricks too.'

His jaw slackened and all of the fight drained out of her. 'We had no faith in a system that had done us no favours.'

The anger seemed to bleed out of him then too. 'Did you ever really trust me, Tash?'

'I trusted you, just not what you stood for.'

'And what if that's one and the same thing?'

She righted her chair and sat heavily. 'That's what I'm afraid of.'

Mitch righted his chair and sat too. Their half-finished lunch seemed to mock her. She suspected his appetite had gone the way of hers.

'I don't expect you to understand us or our motives back then. Unless you've grown up that way…' She trailed off. She was glad Mitch hadn't grown up like she had. She wished she believed in truth and justice the way he did.

'You think my life has been a bed of roses?'

He gave a laugh she didn't understand and her chin came up. 'I wouldn't have a clue. How could I? You never talked about your childhood. So you can lose the tone and the attitude, buster.'

Amazingly, he almost smiled and she found an answering tug deep down inside her. She did her best to resist it.

'I moved to the Western suburbs of Sydney with my grandparents when I was twelve.'

She held her breath to see if he would continue.

'And you're right, I didn't experience the poverty or the poor education or lack of health benefits or any of the other things that were rife throughout the area and made your life so difficult.'

She hadn't known Mitch until he'd returned from his police training, when all the girls in her year at high school had declared him the hottest thing on two legs.

'Where had you lived before that?'

'A small rural town in northern New South Wales. King

is my mother's maiden name. My grandparents changed my name by deed poll when I came to live with them.'

She sat back, a chill chasing its way down her back. 'Why?'

'To protect my privacy. To give me a chance to start over.'

She stared at him. Her skin tightened at the grim set of his face. 'To start over from what?'

His face froze into an unfamiliar immobility. 'When I was twelve my father murdered my mother.'

The words were weighted all wrong and it took a moment for their meaning to hit her. When they did she swayed and braced one hand against the table to prevent herself from falling. The table tipped dangerously and for a moment everything on it was in danger of sliding into her lap.

*What?*

*What!*

She slammed her other hand down to the table to steady it, to steady herself, to counter the painful pounding of her heart. She wanted to ask him to repeat what he'd just said. Had he really said...? A gaping hole billowed in her stomach. She opened her mouth... But what could she say? There were no words adequate to sweep away the horror of his revelation and what he'd been forced to live with.

*I was hungry to save the world.*

He shrugged and a vice tightened about her ribs. Mitch hadn't wanted to save the world. He'd just wanted to save his mum. Twelve years old! Her hands clenched. She bit back tears. 'Mitch, I'm so sorry. That's...it's...I'm so sorry.'

How did someone overcome such a thing? The grudge she'd held against him for the last eight years suddenly seemed petty and trivial. The remnants of it disappeared without so much as a *poof*!

She adjusted her cap and tried to rein in the racing of her heart. 'I think it's amazing—everything you've achieved—after that kind of trauma.' It was the kind of thing that could ruin a person's life forever.

'It's a testament to my grandparents' love and care.'

His face had shuttered against her. 'Do you hate him?' she whispered. 'Your father?'

'I did for a long time, but not any more.' He lifted his chin and his gaze was almost a physical brush against her skin, like the soft breeze that danced between them. She breathed in the scent of salt and sun-warmed grasses. Listened to the rhythmic whoosh of the waves on the beach. Very slowly it eased the pounding of her pulse.

They stared at each other for what seemed like a very long time. 'I feel as if I'm finally starting to understand you,' she said.

'Is that a good thing?'

It wasn't necessarily comfortable, but… 'I think so. I can see now why becoming—being—a policeman is so important to you, why it's a vocation and not just a job.' He wanted to protect people like his mother. 'I can see why truth and justice are concepts you want to believe in and uphold.'

Her thoughts started to swirl every which way like a beer pulled too hard that became all froth. One thought eventually detached itself and demanded her attention. She sat on her hands and ground her toes against the rubber of her flip-flops. 'I owe you an apology.'

His lips flattened against his teeth. 'I don't want your pity, Tash. It's not why I told you my story.'

'Pity isn't my primary emotion at the moment.' She shifted on her chair. 'Shame is.' She held up a hand to stall him when he leaned towards her. 'I know that's not what you intended either so cool down. Your story has helped me put what happened between us into perspective. It's obvious I've held onto my grudge and sense of injury for far too long. I thought you were some black-hearted, double-crossing, holier-than-thou hypocrite who'd do anything for a promotion. It was easier to blame you than... than to take a long hard look at myself.'

'I did deceive you,' he said quietly. 'I led you on, gained your trust, let you think I was interested in you.'

'Yes, but you were motivated by much purer motives than I've ever attributed to you before. You weren't a cold-hearted traitor hell-bent on being fast-tracked through the force for your own glory. You were just like me—trying to do the best you could with the resources you had available.'

She couldn't say the realisation left her feeling lighter, but it did leave her feeling cleaner.

He was silent for a moment. 'Are you trying to tell me you've forgiven me?'

She smiled then. 'I'm trying to say that, if you're amenable, I'd like to be friends.'

Really? Had she really just offered Mitch friendship? She waited for panic and regrets to rip through her, to bathe her in a cold sweat, for a retraction to form on her lips. But none of that happened.

Those blue eyes surveyed her steadily. 'You sure about that?'

She moistened her lips and nodded. 'I'm sure.'

Mitch's gazed snagged on her lips and his eyes darkened. An answering heat swam through her, threatening to drown her, and *that* thickened her throat with panic. 'Friendship is all I'm offering, Mitch.'

He snapped back to himself. 'Of course.'

She shrugged. 'I mean...'

'What?' he barked.

'You might not want that.' He might have enough friends.

'I want.'

The way he said that made her swallow. 'It might not work.'

He folded his arms. 'Why not?'

She couldn't think of a single reason. She glared at him. 'Fine. We're friends then.'

He grinned and her blood leapt. 'Have you ever snorkelled, Tash?'

She shook her head.

'Then you're in for a treat this afternoon.'

The snorkelling was fun.

Once Tash managed to drag her attention from Mitch's powerfully muscled body, that was.

After the snorkelling he left her alone to swim and loaf on the beach with a book. Eventually, though, he called her up to the cabin.

'What's this?' she asked, surveying the sandwiches cut into small triangles and arranged on plates, the cheese and crackers, and the two generous slices of the cake they'd baked and iced yesterday. 'Are we having a campers' version of high tea?'

'Neither of us finished our lunch and I want you to keep your strength up for this evening's entertainment.'

*This evening's entertainment!* If he'd said that to her while they'd been snorkelling she'd have gulped water and sunk.

He glanced around at her and a laugh snorted out of him. 'I could only wish!'

Heat stampeded into her face. His words should've put her mind at rest, only… Actually, her mind was fine; it was her body that wanted to squirm and scratch and find some outlet to soothe the restlessness coursing through it.

'Have something to eat, Tash. You must be hungry after all of that exercise.'

She reached for a sandwich and devoured it. Mitch matched her sandwich for sandwich, bite for bite, and she couldn't help wondering if he'd make love with the same enthusiasm. He caught her gaze and, to her horror, she suspected her conjecture was plain for him to read. Her heart flattened and then pounded so hard it almost winded her. 'I, uh…this is the best cake that was ever baked, you know?'

'That was never in question.'

'What are we doing this evening? What are these entertainments you're talking about?'

'Never you mind. I expect you'll want a shower first, but all will be revealed soon enough.'

Right. 'So it doesn't involve swimming or water sports?'

'Nope. There'll be a bit of walking involved, but not a lot. You might want to cover your legs and wear sneakers.'

'Okay.'

She sliced off a piece of cheese and ate it before declaring she couldn't eat another thing. She drained her bottle of water and then headed for the shower.

When she finally joined Mitch again in the main living area, the salt washed from her hair and body, she wore a pair of cargo pants and a T-shirt. The only covered shoes she had with her were her work boots so she tugged those on. They probably looked incongruous with the rest of her outfit, but the warmth in Mitch's eyes informed her she looked just fine.

Better than fine, in fact.

She swallowed and tried not to dwell on that.

Oh, dear Lord, she needed a cold shower.

*You just had one!*

Mitch wore a pair of shorts, a sand-coloured polo shirt

that somehow made the blue of his eyes all the more vivid, and tennis shoes without socks. He looked just as tempting now as he had on the beach in his board shorts. Her heart thumped. Her mouth dried. There was no point denying it. A big part of her wished this evening's entertainments involved staying in, lighting candles and—

'Ready for another adventure?'

She snapped to, straightened and nodded. 'Sure am.'

He ushered her outside, settling the backpack on his shoulder. She tried to not let her gaze linger on those shoulders.

'So what are we doing? Where are we going?' She desperately needed to move her mind to safer channels.

'We're going for a walk.'

The rest of her questions dried on her tongue when he reached across and took her hand and led her along a track into the eucalypt forest. She stared at their linked hands and something started to burn low in her belly.

'You uh…worried I'm going to trip over?'

He sent her a grin. 'Nah, I just want to hold your hand, Tash. Is that a problem?'

She was sure it should be, but she found herself shaking her head and mouthing a silent, 'No.'

'Good.'

*So, you going to let him kiss you next? Make love with you because you sure as heck don't have a problem with those things either, do you?*

She waved a hand in front of her face. *Quiet!*

Mitch squeezed her hand and then released it. 'We'll have to go in single file from here for a bit, and we'll need to be as quiet as we can.'

She opened her mouth, but after a second closed it again and just nodded. He wanted to surprise her and she found she didn't want to spoil his fun. When he set off she followed, curling her fingers into her palm and holding it against her chest.

Late afternoon light filtered down from the heights of the trees. Birdsong rang in the treetops. She identified the laughter of a kookaburra and the warbling of three magpies, recognised the noisy miners as they darted among the branches and caught a flash of a blue wren in amongst the dense scrub. The sound of cicadas stop-started in their strange musical round.

She loved this time of day and she allowed the sounds and scents of the forest to filter through and relax her. They walked for somewhere close to ten minutes, she guessed, before Mitch stopped. He held a finger up to his lips and then pointed to the clearing ahead. He eased forward and she crept along after him. He stopped again and motioned for her to ease up beside him. And that was when she saw it. Them.

Kangaroos.

Actually, they were wallabies—the kangaroo's smaller cousin—but she wasn't all that concerned with semantics as she crouched beside Mitch, mouth agape, and watched them.

There had to be at least a dozen of them grazing in contented clusters in the clearing. Gripping Mitch's arm, she grinned at him and pointed to a joey in its mother's pouch. He pointed to another one.

She couldn't remember the last time she'd seen kangaroos—or wallabies—in the wild. She stared, drinking in their oddness—their long ears and tiny front paws, the way they balanced on strong tails and the cute pointed faces of the joeys. Sometimes it wasn't a face but a flash of a hind leg stretching from the pouch.

At the same time and on a more primitive level, she relished the muscled strength of Mitch as she leaned into him, his shoulder and arm warm and reassuring where it pressed against hers.

A tiny breeze danced up then and the largest buck stretched up, sniffing the air. Without warning, as one they all leapt off into the deeper gloom of the forest.

She stood and stretched. She couldn't wipe the grin from her face. 'That was really something!'

He grinned back. 'Thought you'd enjoy it. I know it's not the same as visiting a wildlife park where you'd get a chance to feed and pet them, but—'

'It's better,' she said, and she meant it.

The sun had started to set and the shadows in the forest started to deepen. Mitch swung the backpack off his shoulder. Was her phone still in there? She shrugged, not much caring if it was or wasn't. He rummaged in its depths before handing her a bottle of water and producing a torch. He swung its light into the trees surrounding them. He moved around from tree to tree for probably two or three minutes before he found what he was looking for.

'There.' He drew her in closer to his side so she could follow the line of his arm and the beam of light.

'Oh!' she gasped. She took the torch from him and moved closer to the tree. 'A koala!' She stared and stared. It didn't move. It rested in the fork of the tree, obviously asleep. Apparently, koalas slept for around twenty hours a day. She refused to take her eyes from it, afraid it'd disappear. 'I've never seen a koala in the wild before.'

'It's something, isn't it?'

He'd moved up behind her and his heat surrounded her, his breath disturbing the hair at her temple. Pinpricks of awareness tiptoed up her spine, one vertebra at a time. She swallowed. She should say something to try and dispel the awareness before it sunk its claws into her any deeper. 'Is there a cuter animal on the planet?'

'I don't know if you think they're cuter...' she heard the smile in his voice '...but if you're happy to sit on that log over there for a while the possums will show themselves soon.'

She didn't move towards the log. She turned to him instead. He mightn't have been able to give her surfboarding lessons, but he had given her the surf. Paddleboats had been out of the question, but he'd taken her kayaking. Takeaway pizza might've been off the menu but he'd found a way to give her fish and chips. And now he'd shared the magic of the local wildlife with her.

He'd tried to give her everything she'd wanted from a holiday. What was more, he'd made her forget the malice awaiting her at home. 'You've given me the most perfect couple of days, Mitch.'

'I'm glad.'

This man had been through so much pain and suffering himself and all he wanted to do was ease it in others. How could she have misjudged him so badly? She couldn't tell if his eyes had darkened or if that was the night deepening. 'You've made me forget the bad stuff.'

'That was the plan.'

She moved closer and she suddenly felt more alive than she ever had before. 'I don't think I will ever be able to thank you properly for that.' The torch slipped from her fingers to the ground at her feet. She lifted her hands, flattened them against his chest. She couldn't mistake the way his breath hitched or the way his heart pounded against her palm.

'Tash.'

Her name growled from him and she had a feeling he'd meant it as a warning, but it came out as a caress. When she stood on tiptoe to touch her lips to his, his hands shot to her shoulders as if to put her away from him, but his lips opened to hers and their tongues danced. He tasted of the sea and summer and shady glades and she forgot who was kissing who as their bodies crashed together, needing the contact and seeking more.

Eventually he held her away from him, breathing hard as if he'd been sprinting. 'That's not the way to thank me, Tash.'

She gripped his forearms to try and find her balance. 'It stopped being a thank you after the first kiss.'

'You said this was a bad idea.'

'When?'

'This afternoon you said friendship was all that was on offer. This morning you backed away from a kiss.'

The words emerged through gritted teeth and she could see how tightly he held himself in check. She sympathised. She hadn't wanted him with this kind of physical ferocity eight years ago. She could see now how careful he'd been with her back then. If he'd chosen to, he could've created this kind of heat in her. She wouldn't have been ready for it. She wouldn't have known how to deal with it. But there wasn't a doubt in her mind that she'd have succumbed to it.

He hadn't let that happen then, but she was more than ready for it to happen now. 'I must've had rocks in my head.' Her fingers curled into the material of his shirt. 'Besides, I understand it's a woman's prerogative to change her mind.'

He groaned.

She frowned. 'You think it's a bad idea?'

'I'm supposed to be guarding you, protecting you.'

'Correction—you're making sure I'm out of harm's way. You said the danger wouldn't follow us here.'

'It won't, but—'

'Then the idea that you need to be hyper-vigilant is nonsense and you know it.'

He didn't say anything.

'You know there is something that could make my holiday truly unforgettable.'

'What's that?'

'A holiday fling.'

He swore. It came out sounding like an endearment.

'I know most people consider me a tough customer with attitude to burn. That translates in some circles as me being considered something of a...*bad* girl.'

His eyes widened. His nostrils flared.

'The fact of the matter is the opposite is true.' The very opposite, in fact, but she had no intention of sharing that.

His body was beautiful and utterly beguiling and everything inside her arched towards it, aching to explore it.

His eyes gleamed in the light of the rising moon. 'Are you telling me, Tash, that you want to do something wild and reckless?'

She smiled back at him. 'I'm glad to see you've finally got with the programme, Officer King.'

# CHAPTER SEVEN

THEY MADE IT back to the cabin in record time.

No sooner had they slammed the door behind them than Mitch backed her up against it, his lips hot and hungry on hers. A faint circle of yellow light pooled around the lamp on the kitchen bench, and moonlight filtered through the windows to wink off the framed prints on the walls and a couple of glittery book spines in the bookcase.

The rough wood of the door jabbed into her back. Slipping her arms from around his neck, she leant them against his chest and walked him backwards into the room, not breaking the lip lock, enjoying the feel and taste of him too much.

One of his hands snaked around her backside, pulling her hard against him. She gasped as the heat in her spread further, the need…and the thrill. Her knees started to buckle and he lowered them to the ground with more speed than grace so that she straddled him. Their noses collided, her elbow hit the ground with a crack and Mitch swore as something of his—an ankle or shin—connected with the hard leg of the coffee table.

She ignored it all. She wanted skin on skin contact. Now!

With a growl she bunched up his T-shirt and ran her hands over his stomach and chest. Mitch moaned, his muscles clenching beneath her fingertips. In the dim light his muscled flesh gleamed. She ran her hands over him again. He jerked beneath her touch, his eyes glittering.

She did that? Created that need, that fever in him? Her?

She ran her hands lower, dipping them beneath the waistband—the tantalisingly low waistband—of his shorts and his body bucked beneath her touch. She grinned. She sat up straighter and tossed her hair.

'Tash,' he warned.

'I want you to take your shirt off,' she commanded.

He rose up on his elbows to survey her. It pushed the bulge in his shorts more firmly against the juncture of her thighs.

'Oh!' She swayed. She had to swallow, twice, to clear her head.

He grinned that slow crooked grin and her pulse rate ratcheted up another notch. 'So that's how you want to play it, huh?'

With another man she suspected self-consciousness would've crippled her by now, but not with Mitch. The fire in his eyes didn't leave any room for that kind of nonsense.

Should she tell him…?

She hitched up her chin. 'You have a problem with that?'

In one swift motion he pulled his shirt over his head and tossed it to one side. She didn't bother watching to see where it fell. She was too busy taking in the broad sweep of his shoulders and the depth of his chest, the way the muscles in his upper arms bulged and the lean tapering of his stomach that had more definition than a dictionary. And then she let her hands follow her gaze—slowly and comprehensively. She wanted to know every inch of this man.

His hands snaked under her shirt, playing havoc with her concentration, and she batted them away. 'No touching!'

He grinned and her blood heated up so fast it almost

bubbled. 'At least take your shirt off too.' His voice came out like warm honey, flowing over her in promised sweetness. 'It's only fair.'

She considered that. She didn't care about fair. All she wanted to do was drive Mitch crazy in the same way he'd driven her crazy since they'd first met. That was why she pulled her shirt over her head and tossed it one way. It was why she unclasped her bra and tossed it the other. And it was why she squirmed in what she hoped was a seductive way, thrusting her breasts forward, nipples peaking as the grin dropped away from his face and he moistened his lips. 'You're beautiful,' he said, his voice a hoarse groan in the semi-darkness.

Astride him like this, she felt beautiful.

He reached for her again, but she wrapped her fingers around his wrists and pushed them down to the ground beside his head. 'All my life I've been a good girl.'

She didn't expect him to believe her. She didn't expect anyone to believe her. She'd always acted as if she'd been around the block a few times, but it simply wasn't the truth. Would Mitch run for the hills if he knew she was a virgin? She wasn't taking that chance. Maybe he wouldn't even notice.

She stared into his eyes. 'Just once I want to act out and be the bad girl, be…depraved.'

Pushing his hands down had brought her face close to his. Those mesmerising blue eyes locked to hers. 'Have you been reading *Fifty Shades*, Tash?'

Just the way he said it made her feel deliciously racy. 'What if I have?'

'Would you like me to spank you?' He lifted his head and his lips brushed her ear as he spoke, his breath stirred the hair at her temple and her nipples started to ache. 'Should I get my handcuffs?'

'If you do I'll brain you with them.' But her voice came out on nothing more than a whisper of breath. The low rumble in his throat told her he didn't believe her.

He lifted his head again and slid a warm moist tongue across one of her nipples. She stiffened as if electrified, every nerve in her body springing to life. The knot in her stomach grew.

'I said no touch—'

He took the nipple all the way into his mouth and suckled. She arched against him with a gasp that was half moan. Nothing had ever felt so good, so urgent!

In one fluid motion he sat up, his mouth never leaving her breast, one hand between her shoulder blades to pull her more firmly against him while his free hand cupped her other breast, the thumb moving back and forth until she thought she might drown in sensation.

Her breath came in short sharp pants. She arched against his mouth. She arched against his groin. Both of them had grown slick with perspiration.

'You know what I think?' He pressed hot moist kisses to her neck, his finger flipping open the fly button of her cargo pants as if he'd done so a thousand times before.

'What's that?' she panted.

'What you really need...'

He didn't really mean to spank her, did he? It might get her hot to talk about it but she'd run a mile if he tried it. She pushed away from him to stare into his eyes. He brushed the hair off her face. 'What you really need, Natasha Buckley...'

His use of her full name in his desire-thickened murmur made her shiver. He ran his fingers down the side of her breasts and she had to catch her lip between her teeth to stop from crying out.

'...is to lose control.'

She did?

'You repress too much, little Miss Wound-Too-Tight, but not tonight.'

'I am not—'

His mouth captured a nipple again.

She moaned when deft, knowing fingers did things that had never been done to her before.

'You were saying?' he said lazily against her mouth, before rolling them both over.

Her knee hit the coffee table and his elbow cracked on something. 'When I was seventeen and fantasizing about making love with you, it wasn't like this.'

'No?' He stared down at her as she tried to unpin her hair from beneath her.

'Everything was smooth and cool and graceful. There was no sweat, no bumping of noses and...'

He cupped her breast and ran a thumb back and forth over her nipple. 'Was there any of this?'

She swallowed. 'Of course.' But back then there'd been nothing so raw and elemental as the sensations crowding her now. She hadn't even dreamt of such a thing. 'But please, Mitch, I'm going to be black and blue tomorrow.'

'You're going to be very, *very* satisfied tomorrow,' he promised, a glint in his eye.

Hauling himself to his feet, he picked her up and strode towards the bedroom.

Mitch stared up at the ceiling, his fingers idly running up and down Tash's back. He loved the feel of her bare skin against him, her warm breath on his chest.

They hadn't spoken.

Yet.

He hadn't opened his mouth because making love with Tash had been so intense it'd rocked the very fabric of his world. He wasn't sure how she felt. He knew he'd given her pleasure, but...

He glanced down at her. 'You okay?'

He could feel her smile against him. She snuggled closer. 'I'm better than okay.'

He let out a careful breath and closed his eyes for a moment. 'Why didn't you tell me?' he asked quietly.

She stilled. He tightened an arm about her so she wouldn't move away. 'You could tell, then?'

'Uh huh.'

She'd given him her virginity. Why? Did that mean something? If she'd been holding onto it for this long then it had to mean something, didn't it?

He frowned at the ceiling. 'You should've told me.'

'Why?'

He moved away a little to stare down into her face. 'Because I'd have been gentler, more careful.'

'I don't have any complaints.'

That didn't answer the question.

'And I didn't want to give you an excuse to stop.'

'I'm not sure I could've stopped,' he was honest enough to admit.

She'd given him her virginity and, while he couldn't explain it, she was now burned onto his soul. He had a feeling that should frighten him, but it didn't. What worried him was the way he wanted to beat his chest and shout out a Tarzan cry like some primitive being.

'Would you have believed me?'

He stiffened until he recognised there was no accusation in her voice. 'It's a surprise,' he admitted. 'But I'd have believed you.'

She lifted up on one elbow to stare down into his face. 'Did it affect your pleasure? Was it not—'

'You rocked, Tash. We rocked. I can't remember the last

time I...' He trailed off. He couldn't remember the last time making love had touched him so deeply. 'It was amazing.'

Her smile squeezed something tight in his chest.

'Rest now.' He pressed her head back to his shoulder, wrapped an arm securely about her. She'd given him her virginity. It *had* to mean something.

When Mitch woke the next morning, he knew exactly what the previous night meant. It meant that he and Tash belonged together. He knew that with every fibre that made him who he was. And he needed to make sure they were on the same page about that.

Tash wasn't in bed with him, but the scent of coffee told him she wasn't far.

He grinned, suddenly flooded with more energy than he could ever remember—it coursed through every atom until he zinged with it, floated with it and felt as if he could conquer the world. He swooped out into the main room of the cabin, pulled on a pair of tracksuit pants, and a quick glance out of the door told him Tash was down on the beach. He made a flask of tea, grabbed a packet of biscuits and headed down to the beach.

She turned before his feet hit the sand, a smile lifting her lips. As he made his way across to where she sat, her eyes made a slow—and comprehensive—appraisal of his body, and the gleam that lit them nearly made him stumble. Then he had to fight the urge to run to her, sticking his chest out and beating it caveman-style. And he was glad—*very* glad—he hadn't bothered with a shirt. He wished she hadn't bothered with a shirt either. No matter. He meant to divest her of it as soon as possible.

'Good morning.' Her voice held a breathy edge that made him hard in an instant.

He dropped a kiss to her lips—quick, light, playful—and then fell down beside her. 'I come bearing breakfast.'

She glanced at the biscuits and then arched an eyebrow. 'I'm going to need more than that to keep me going today.'

He nearly tossed the flask and biscuits to one side to take her then and there on the sand under the sun. He pulled back at the last moment. She was probably sore after last night. And they had plenty of time. They had the rest of their lives. 'I'll cook up something more substantial in a bit,' he promised. 'I wanted to talk.'

She trailed a finger along his inner thigh. 'It's not what I had in mind.'

He captured her hand, kissed her fingers. The hunger in her eyes, the laughter and warmth in her face, told him she was in as deep as he was. His heart soared. 'Last night was incredible.'

'You won't get any arguments from me on that head.'

'It might sound like a cliché, Tash, but last night meant something to me. Something big.'

The amber in her eyes turned gold.

'We've only been out here three days—four counting today—but I feel as if my whole life has been turned on its head.'

She stared at him and then finally nodded. 'Me too.'

He kissed her fingers again and then released her to pour them mugs of tea. He tore open the biscuits, ravenous.

She took one and nibbled the edge. 'I can't help feeling things have been moving a whole lot faster than they should be.'

'Or perhaps they're moving at exactly the right pace.'

She'd given him her virginity. And he knew what that meant—she was his and he was going to love and protect her for the rest of their lives. He'd let her down once. He wasn't letting her down again.

'I lay awake for a long time last night, thinking.' He'd felt alive and contented—whole in a way he hadn't thought possible. When his father had killed his mother it had fractured something inside him. Last night Tash had put him back together. He turned to her. 'We belong together, you and me.' Nothing had ever made more sense to him than that.

Her hand froze halfway to her mouth with her biscuit. She stared at him, her jaw slack. He didn't blame her for her surprise. The realisation had shocked him too.

'Look, I thought about it long and hard. You want to hear my plan?'

She moistened her lips. 'Okay.'

He pulled in a breath. 'This is what I think we should do. When we get back to Sydney, you should move in with me.' His house was in a nicer suburb than Tash's. 'You can give up your job.'

He hated the thought of her slaving away behind the bar of the Royal Oak. 'That pub is in a rough neighbourhood and I hate the thought of you being subjected to any kind of violence or threat.' He pulled in a breath. 'You can go back to school if you want.' She could train for a better job, a safer job. Eventually they'd marry and have a couple of kids. It'd be perfect. But that could wait. He didn't want to rush her.

'Have you completely lost your mind?'

Tash struggled to her feet, spraying sand all over the biscuits. The only reason the tea didn't go flying was that Mitch put a hand out to steady the flask.

'I'm not going back to school! What on earth would I want to do that for?'

He spread his hands. 'It was just a suggestion and—'

'I'm not giving up my job!'

'It puts you in danger!' He shot upright too.

'Garbage! I can handle myself at work.' She poked him in the chest. 'I like my job. I'm good at it. That means something to me.'

His face twisted in frustration. 'But—'

'And it's not as dangerous as your job!'

'That's different!'

'How?' she shot back. 'You like it, don't you? You're good at it, aren't you?' She folded her arms. 'Are you going to volunteer to give it up in this cosy little scenario of yours?'

He scowled. 'Of course not.'

'I'm *not* moving in with you, Mitch.'

She had a feeling she was ticking each of these points off in the wrong order. 'We've known each other for all of three days!' Things never worked out as rosily as Mitch was picturing. He knew that!

'It's not about how long you know someone. It's about how well you know them.' He thumped his chest. '*In here.* It's having the courage to follow through on your convictions.'

He was calling her a coward? She clenched her hands so hard she shook. 'I'll give you convictions! What you want to do is set me up in a pretty cage, but a cage all the same. And I know that has to do with how powerless you felt about your mum, but I am not letting anybody take away my freedom like that. I'm an adult and I have the right to make my own decisions. I know what it feels like to have no power and I'm not going back to that again.'

They stared at each other, both breathing hard.

She recalled her heartbreak eight years ago and fear clogged her throat. She slashed a hand through the air. 'What on earth has got into you? Yesterday you were a reasonable human being. Today you're acting like some... caveman!'

He dragged a hand down his face.

'I thought it was women who started building pipe dreams and happy-ever-afters after sex, not men.'

He stared back at her stonily. 'You were a virgin.'

She adjusted her stance. 'So?'

'So it has to mean something. You're twenty-five, for heaven's sake. To have waited this long…'

She had to stifle the frustrated scream that rose in her throat, but behind it shivered a twist of fear. 'It doesn't mean anything!'

She stomped down to the water's edge to kick as much water in the air as she could—dreadfully childish but satisfying all the same. She stomped back to where Mitch stood. 'I'll tell you what it means, Mitch. I'm a prude!'

His jaw dropped. 'The hell you are.'

She chafed her arms, turning to stare back out at the water. 'Maybe not anymore.' And that was a relief to know. 'I…' She had to swallow. 'I don't remember my parents ever being nice to one another.' She sure as heck couldn't imagine them making love the way she and Mitch had last night.

*It has to mean something.*

Her scalp prickled. Her throat threatened to close over. 'There weren't really any role models for me to look up to in that way when I was growing up. Rick's mother and grandmother horrified me. I couldn't imagine…' She shuddered and suddenly he was standing beside her. He didn't touch her, but his presence helped unclench something inside her.

'When I was fifteen, a girl at school got pregnant. Her boyfriend dumped her and her mother kicked her out. She received social security benefits but every time I saw her she looked thinner and dirtier. She died of a drug overdose and her baby went into foster care. Another friend from school was sexually abused by her father.'

Mitch let forth with a curse.

'Precisely.'

They both stared at the far horizon. Eventually she turned to look at him. 'In my mind, sex has been associated with an awful lot of sordidness.' Especially when she'd been a teenager. 'When I was prepared to risk my heart—which is when I'd have risked my body—I was... hurt. It seemed a crap shoot, sex and romance, and I decided I didn't want any part of it.'

He swore again but this time it was under his breath.

'Nobody warned me about hormones, though. The last twelve months I've been getting...antsy. But I don't meet too many new guys these days. That's my own fault. I don't go out to places where I can meet them. All the guys who know me don't ask me out any more because I kept turning them down, but these last few days have been...' she reached into the air as if searching for the right word '...a revelation.'

She stared down at her feet, dug her toes in the sand. 'Last night was amazing. I'm glad it happened. But it was just sex.'

*Liar.*

'The fact I was a virgin doesn't mean anything...except as a sign of my arrested development and teenage hang-ups.' She stared up at him and did what she could to make her face hard and businesslike. 'You hearing me?'

He didn't look at her. 'Loud and clear.'

'I'm going to brush my teeth.'

He didn't follow her so he must've caught her subtext that she wanted to be alone.

She brushed her teeth in time to the panic whirling over and over in her head. She rinsed her mouth and then stomped back to the cabin. Everywhere she looked there was evidence of her encounter with Mitch last night—her bra dangling from a shelf of the bookcase and her T-shirt on the sofa, Mitch's polo shirt under the coffee table.

She grabbed her things and threw them into the bedroom. She grabbed Mitch's shirt and tossed it on the haversack sitting at one end of the sofa. She rubbed her hands up and down the sides of her shorts and turned on the spot.

*You just rejected him, you idiot!*

No, she hadn't. She'd just made it clear that she wasn't ready to move in with him yet.

*You said it was just sex!*

She thought back to last night and a dreamy smile built through her. She'd never known that making love could be so…explosive. Or so utterly satisfying.

Or that it could leave her feeling so vulnerable.

She chafed her arms some more and the smile slid off her face. *It was just sex.* She shook her head. It had been a whole lot more than just sex.

But, for heaven's sake, why did Mitch have to go and get all crazy on her and freak her out? Why couldn't he just take things slow—be casual for a bit until she got used to all of this? He'd scared the pants off her and she'd lashed out, said things in a way that… She wrung her hands and searched for something to keep them busy.

Her eyes lit on the backpack abandoned on the floor by the door. She grabbed it, plonked it on the table and proceeded to rinse out and refill the water bottles, set the torch on the bookcase where it was handy for middle-of-the-night calls of nature. She glanced inside to see what else she could tidy up. The phones could stay there. Ditto with the matches and the first aid kit.

A gold wrapper caught her eye. A chocolate bar! Mitch had been holding out on her?

She reached in, seized it—

'What do you think you're doing?'

She swung, her heart in her throat. 'Dammit, Mitch, don't sneak up like that! You trying to give me a heart attack?'

It was good he was here, though. They needed to talk. They needed to get a few things settled.

'I wasn't the one sneaking.' His face darkened. 'That's obviously you.'

She stared at him.

He strode forward and snatched the backpack from the table. 'The minute my back is turned you're on the phone to Rick, right?'

She held up what she had in her hand. 'Chocolate,' she said softly. 'Not a phone.'

He blinked.

'Despite everything I told you, you still believe Rick is guilty, don't you?'

'Jail changes a person.'

A lump of ugliness blocked her throat until she could barely breathe. 'You have a nasty mind sometimes, Mitch, you know that?' She swallowed, forced scorn into her voice. 'Of course I'm going to seduce you, lull you into a false sense of security and then, the moment your guard's down, steal off with my phone and make secret phone calls.'

'Did you try to ring Rick or anyone else?'

'I'm not even going to dignify that with an answer.' She went to swing away, but then swung back. 'But that accusation is very telling. Obviously, if you're worried I'd do that, then Rick can't be out of phone contact like you said.' Her eyes flashed. 'You lied about that.'

'I did.'

He didn't even look remorseful!

'It was easier than telling you that the detectives on the case refused to trust you.'

She folded her arms, her lips twisting as her heart crumpled. 'It's telling on more than one level. After last night, you really think I'd go behind your back like that?'

'What do you mean?' he demanded, his eyes frigid chips of ice. 'Last night was just sex, remember?'

# CHAPTER EIGHT

HER BREATH CHOKED in her throat as if he'd slapped her.

Mitch turned grey. 'Tash, I...'

It took an effort to keep her eyes wide and to concentrate on breathing through her nose, counting the breaths to keep the moisture in her eyes from spilling over. *Had her words lacerated his heart like that?*

'I didn't ring Rick. Not that I expect you to believe me.' A black pit of acid rose in her stomach. 'But then trust has never been a strong point between us, has it? If you trusted me, that question would never have arisen. Whatever else you've said this morning, it's obvious now that last night didn't change a thing.'

'If you trusted me you'd have told me you were a virgin.'

He had her there.

The silence between them stretched. This conversation wasn't over, not by a long shot, but she didn't have the heart to continue it for now. She suspected Mitch didn't either. There were too many hurt feelings on both sides.

'I'm going for a swim.' She seized her swimming costume and a towel. 'While you ring your colleagues and inform them of your suspicions.'

He didn't say anything, didn't try to stop her.

And she didn't look back. Not once.

* * *

Tash swam.

Yesterday the water had slid like silk against her skin. Today salt and sand stung and chafed.

Yesterday the water had buoyed and supported her and made her feel strong. Today it was all she could do not to sink like a dead, deflated weight.

As she moved through the waves, muscles she'd never known she had ached and protested, screaming out a harsh reminder of her innate weakness for Mitch and all that had happened last night...and how much she'd welcomed it.

*Mitch.* She hadn't been able to resist him eight years ago and she hadn't been able to resist him last night. Putty—that was all she was where he was concerned. A terrible sense of déjà vu settled around her shoulders, making her arms heavy, her chest heavy, her head heavy.

That gilded cage he'd just presented her with... She choked back something that felt suspiciously like a sob. It'd make her miserable. She closed her eyes and her arms pimpled with gooseflesh. Did he need to put her into that cage for his own happiness, though? Without it, would he be the miserable one instead? She opened her eyes and it didn't matter how fiercely the sun shone, the warmth leached out of the day.

She slapped a hand down onto the water and saltwater flew up to sting her eyes. Why couldn't she have resisted for just another day or two when this whole farce would be over?

She spun and breaststroked into the middle of the bay. If she'd fought against her desire last night she might never have known how amazing making love with Mitch could be. He'd transported her to a place of such pleasure and delight that even now her toes curled just thinking about it. She floated, staring up at a flawless sky, the water a satin caress against her skin, and recalled the way she'd made him moan and shake. Her skin tingled and her muscles quivered and for a moment she felt strong enough to fly.

And then she remembered the way everything had unravelled this morning and she sank. She kicked her head back above water, coughing. All she could see was the way his face had darkened in suspicion when he'd walked through the door and found her with the backpack.

Last night she'd stared into his eyes and had shared her soul. How could he—?

Fool me once, shame on you. Fool me twice, shame on me. 'Fool me thrice...' She pushed her shoulders back and lifted her chin. 'Not going to happen.'

Mitch was waiting for her when she finally returned to shore. Silently he handed her a towel. Just as silently she took it. She took a few steps away from him and turned her back to dry off. She didn't know if he watched her or not, but her back burned as if he did.

'Are you okay?' he finally asked.

'Hunky-dory,' she snapped, tying the towel sarong-style around her waist. 'You?'

He didn't say anything and finally the suspense grew too much. She turned. She hoped her raised eyebrow hid the raw ache that sawed through her chest.

'I've been better.'

It was something, but nowhere near enough.

'I think I probably owe you an apology.'

She folded her arms and raised both eyebrows.

'I think I've probably misjudged you. If that's the case then I'm sorry.'

*I think? Probably? If?* Her jaw clenched. Maybe she should just take him apart piece by piece now.

He widened his stance. 'You going to say something?'

She unclenched her jaw to bite out, 'I'm afraid I'm just speechless at such a wholehearted, unreserved apology.'

Red streaked his cheekbones, raw and angry.

She shook her head, just the once. 'I have nothing to say.' The pulse at the base of his jaw jumped and jerked. Swallowing, she dragged her gaze away.

'Then I expect you'll be pleased to know that our time here is done.'

Her eyes flew back to his. The muscles in her arms and legs bunched, but whether in readiness for flight or fight or something altogether different she didn't know. 'It wouldn't have been over if I'd accepted your apology?'

For a moment his eyes blazed as bright as opals. Her lips twisted in an effort to hide how her pulse leapt. 'You were hoping for some more nookie with the bad girl?'

'It's not like that, Tash.'

She hammered in the last nail and any chance they might've had. 'You know what? I don't much care any more.' There really wasn't anything left to say, anything left to rescue.

Those red slashes turned white. She ignored that. Ignored the pounding of her heart too, to push her shoulders back, lift her chin and settle an indifferent expression on her face. 'I take it Rick has been taken in for questioning?'

He nodded.

'I'd like to see him.'

His face darkened, a clap of thunder in a perfect summer sky. 'When are you going to stop making a fool of yourself over him?'

'Fool?' Her mouth opened and closed. How could he possibly think she held a torch for Rick after last night?

The same way he could think she'd lie and cheat and sneak his phone this morning, that was how.

She reached down to grasp her towel from where it had

started to slip. 'He knows more about friendship than you ever will. When are you going to realise he'd never hurt me? He'd never hurt any woman.'

'Tell that to Dixie Bennett and Leah Manning.'

'Still blinded by prejudice after all this time? You might come across as some kind of moral upholder of all that's good, but beneath the façade you're nothing but a hypocrite.'

'As I said.' His words were clipped. 'We're done here.'

'Halle-bloody-lujah.'

They didn't speak a single word on the way back to Sydney. Tash was careful to keep her hands smooth and relaxed rather than clenched fists in her lap. Mitch had made it known in no uncertain terms that if she wanted to see Rick she could make her way to the police station under her own steam and not his. Apparently he'd take no part in encouraging her folly.

She'd taken one glance at the grim set of his mouth and had refused to look at him again. She hadn't dignified his dictate with an answer either.

But as they'd driven away from the cabin, with its private beach and memories branded on her brain—and body—her heart burned as it never had before. She would never return to this place and the grief raked away at her, leaving her insides raw and tender, and there was nothing she could do about it.

As they passed from rural tranquillity to the freeway and then the buzz and noise of the city…and finally to her dingy, less-than-salubrious neighbourhood, her thoughts darkened. Mitch didn't even turn the engine off when they reached her house. He leapt out, pulled her suitcase from the boot and set it by her gate. He didn't set so much as a big toe onto her property.

She went to stalk right past him, but he stepped in front of her. 'We are not finished, Tash. I am not going to let you cut me dead the way you have your parents…and probably every other person in your life who has let you down or hurt you. This is not over.'

'That's what you think,' she flung at him to hide her sudden fear and the dread that trickled down her backbone. Her vulnerability to this man scared her senseless. She wanted him gone. *Now.* She stuck out one hip. 'Give my regards to Rick,' she drawled. 'Let him know I'll be there as soon as I can.'

His lips twisted. 'Not going to work.'

What was he talking about?

Snaking his arm around her waist, he pulled her hard up against him. His lips slammed to hers, hard, demanding, insistent. He bit, suckled and laved, and her head spun, her blood sang and all she could do was cling to him and open her mouth to his as and when he demanded it of her. Her breath and her tongue tangled with his until they felt like one. And whole.

And then he released her and she almost fell, except he kept hold of her so she didn't. He swiped his thumb across her swollen bottom lip, a possessive light in his eyes. 'You were a virgin, but that doesn't make you stupid. What we have is amazing and you'll be a fool to walk away from it.'

Her heart pounded. She couldn't think of a single thing to say.

'I didn't fight for you eight years ago, but I'm not walking away without a fight this time, Tash. I'll see you in the morning. Hopefully by then we'll have both had some time to think things through.'

She watched him walk away and, God forgive her, all she could do was wish tomorrow here already.

\* \* \*

It was a full five hours before Detective Glastonbury and his team had finished questioning Rick. But they didn't have enough evidence to hold him and finally Tash was free to take him home.

Before they reached the freedom of the main door, however, Mitch emerged from an office and blocked their way. He stared at her with angry dark eyes that made her swallow and grip her hands in front of her.

Rick folded his arms. 'Well, well, if it isn't Officer King.'

Mitch leaned in close and his scent sparked such a swirl of longing through her it made her dizzy. She had to grip her hands together all the tighter. 'If you harm a single hair on her head, Bradford, I will come after you with everything I've got.'

'If I harm a single hair on her head I'd deserve it,' Rick countered.

Mitch blinked, but his glare didn't abate. 'We're watching you.'

'Message received, loud and clear.'

Tash rolled her eyes and wondered which of them would beat his chest first.

Those devastating eyes turned to her. 'Tomorrow.'

She nodded once. He was right. She couldn't walk away, but she couldn't help thinking this would only end in heartbreak. For both of them. 'Make it mid-morning,' she said to let him know she wasn't wholly against the idea. One way or the other, they needed to clear the air. 'I'll bake a cake.'

'I'm guessing you'd like me to make myself scarce for your big date tomorrow?'

Tash glanced up from the sofa, where she reclined with her brand-spanking-new cookbook. She'd raced out to buy it this afternoon after she and Rick had arrived home, along with a whole load of groceries. She straightened and set her feet on the floor. 'You're more than welcome to stay for cake and coffee if you like.' In fact it would probably be a good idea for Mitch to get to know Rick better. 'But if you found you had some pressing engagement after that I wouldn't mind. Mitch and I have a few things to, uh…' she cleared her throat '…thrash out.'

'I'll be out of here early.'

She bit back a sigh. It'd probably be for the best. 'Thanks, Rick.'

She really wanted to quiz him more about who he thought was behind this spate of violence, who it was that was trying to set him up, but she bit the words back. They'd compared notes already. They'd thrown around ideas, but nothing had stuck.

She knew Rick. She knew how much this would be gnawing away at him. She didn't want to add to that.

He placed his hands behind his head and grinned at her. 'You really going to cook Mitch a cake?'

What on earth had possessed her? She grimaced. 'Yeah.'

He sobered and leaned towards her, elbows on knees. 'Tash, what's going down? What are you hoping for from tomorrow?' He frowned. 'And…'

'And what?'

'What is it you're afraid of?'

She swallowed. He knew her too well, but if she laughed those questions off he'd leave her be. But she didn't want to laugh them off. She wanted to know the answers too. All the same, she did laugh. Not that it held much mirth. 'I can tell you what I'm afraid of. That one's easy. But what I want?' She slammed the cookbook shut and shook her head.

She hadn't been able to pin that one down. 'That's proving tough to work out.'

'Then start with the easy stuff.'

She met his gaze. 'You understand that…stuff…happened when Mitch and I were holed up at the cabin, right?' She thought he might roll his eyes at that so she added, 'I'm not just talking about sex.'

She sucked her bottom lip into her mouth, worried at it with her teeth. 'We connected in ways…' She leapt up off the sofa to pace. 'I don't know what you want to call it—emotional, mental, spiritual.' She fell back down again. 'Whatever it was, I wasn't prepared for it, but I can't deny it. I can't turn my back on it.' She frowned. 'At least, I don't want to turn my back on it. Yet.'

When she glanced at him, he wasn't laughing. He simply stared back in deadly earnest. 'You and Mitch always connected like that, Tash. Why should it surprise you now?'

'But…but that stuff that happened before was *eight years ago*.'

'Doesn't make it any less real.'

'I was just a kid.'

'You were more woman than child.'

Her mouth went dry.

'And it might've happened eight years ago, but as far as I can see it's still alive and kicking today. The heat the two of you gave off at the police station…' he shook his head '…it was smokin'.'

Oh, great. Just great. She leapt to her feet. 'We only spent four days together. It's just nonsense to think that any of it could be real.'

It wasn't possible to feel this deeply about someone in such a short amount of time. She paced back and forth in front of the coffee table. Truly, when you got down to it, how much time had they spent in each other's company—six weeks eight years ago and four days this week? It was ludicrous. It couldn't be enough to turn her whole life upside down. 'Maybe it's just a lust hormone thing?'

'That's certainly a convenient excuse to hide behind.'

She swallowed slowly before lifting her head. 'He betrayed me, Rick. He used me.'

'Eight years ago he thought he was protecting you.' His lips twisted. 'Eight years ago he had trouble keeping his hands off you too. But he did. He's a good guy, Tash.'

She knew that too. She perched on the edge of the sofa. She eased back until she huddled against its arm.

'You haven't said what you're afraid of yet.'

She didn't want to say the words out loud. Not facing facts didn't help in the long run, though. She'd learned that lesson when she'd been eight years old. She hauled in a breath and hoped her voice would remain strong and steady. 'I'm afraid that Mitch and I are going to fall into some kind of hot and heavy relationship and…and that we'll end up tearing each other apart, destroying each other.' Like her mother and father. Like Mitch's mother and father.

'And yet you still don't want to walk away?'

She slumped. 'I have rocks in my head, right?'

'You don't want to walk away because you think there might be something worth exploring, but you don't want to tear out each other's hearts in the process either.' He shook his head. 'That's not crazy.'

He shifted, straightened a little. A rush of warmth filtered through her. Dear Rick. Always searching for the best solution to a problem.

'So what you want, then, is for Mitch to give the two of you a chance to see where things might go, to see how they might develop?'

'Oh, I'm pretty sure he's going to be all for taking things to the next level.'

'But…?'

'I just don't know how that's going to be possible. He doesn't trust me. He sure doesn't trust my judgement.'

'He just wants to keep you safe.'

She thought about his mother and had to close her eyes for a moment. 'He wants to put me in a cage and I couldn't stand it.'

'Then you have to make him see what it is you need to make you happy.'

Very slowly she nodded. That was *exactly* what she needed to do, but…would it make any difference? Would he see why she couldn't live the kind of life he wanted her to? Would he even listen to her?

The sympathy in Rick's eyes made her reach up to scratch between her shoulder blades. 'What?'

'Why are you hiding from the truth? Seems to me that won't help your cause.'

What truth? 'Go on,' she demanded although her voice came out small.

'Tash, you loved the guy eight years ago and you love him now. I'm not sure you ever stopped loving him.'

'But—'

'Even if you've buried it for years beneath a whole truck-load of hurt and anger.'

She stiffened. 'We haven't known each other long enough for love.'

'Says who? Perceived wisdom? Seems to me that love makes up its own rules—doesn't seem to be any logic to it whatsoever.'

Her heart leapt in recognition, the same way it had that day in the sea cave. Unconsciously, she fingered the shell she kept in the pocket of her shorts. Was Rick right? Did she love Mitch?

Her mouth dried. It was a crazy notion.

Rick gave a harsh laugh—a dissonant note in the soft-filtered early evening light that filled the living room. 'You want to know what's ironic about all of this? Even if Mitch decides he can live by your rules and the both of you do declare your undying love for each other, it doesn't guarantee that either one of you will be happy.'

Her heart turned into a lump of lead.

'Your father said he loved your mother but it didn't stop him from smacking her about. My mother claimed she loved my father—even if she wouldn't reveal his identity—but I can't see that brought her any happiness or joy. All throughout this godforsaken neighbourhood are tales of woe and heartbreak and—'

'This isn't helping, Rick!' She cut him off before he could depress her further. 'Love can't be all bleak and horrible.' She glared, hating what he said, even though at one level she knew it was true.

His head came up as if he'd forgotten an important point. 'You're right.' He grinned and it was a good grin. 'Remember the Schmidts?'

Tash grinned back at him. The Schmidts had been an older married couple who'd lived a street over from Tash when she'd been growing up. They'd been childless and she could see now that it had probably been a source of great sadness for them. Maybe that was why they'd encouraged the neighbourhood children to drop in for milk and cookies on a regular basis. 'Mrs Schmidt's Sachertorte was the best.'

'Don't try and make Sachertorte for tomorrow, Tash. Truly. It's complicated.'

Good advice. Though maybe Mitch could show her how to make it one day. If things worked out.

If.

She fiddled with an earring. 'Mrs Schmidt told me once that Mr Schmidt was the only man she'd ever been with. They married when she was eighteen and he was twenty-two. She said she was glad every day of her life that she'd married him. That was on their forty-fifth wedding anniversary.'

Rick stretched a leg out in front of him and stared at his foot. 'Mr Schmidt told me that the best part of his day was walking into his house after a day at work and seeing Mrs Schmidt.'

'*They* loved each other and *they* were happy. It works out for some people.'

So what was their secret? She glanced at Rick. 'Have you ever been in love?'

He shook his head.

'You don't want to, do you?'

'Seems more hassle than it's worth if you ask me.'

There was a lot of truth in that statement. But… She pulled in a breath. 'I think if you can make it work it might just be the biggest and best thing in life.'

'That's a big *if*, Tash.'

Her heart, that had started to lighten, grew heavy again. She nodded. It seemed an especially big *if* for her and Mitch.

He rose. 'I'm heading down to the cricket oval to watch the day-night game. I'm hoping to catch up with some of the guys. Wanna come?'

She shook her head. 'There're a few things I want to do around here. Have fun.'

Rick left and Tash stared around at the quietness of her living room and blew out a breath. She supposed she at least knew what she wanted now. She wanted to find out if she and Mitch could be happy together.

She threw herself full length onto the sofa and rolled her eyes. 'Easy-peasy. Piece of cake.' Heaviness settled over her and she surged upright again and tried to shake it off. She grabbed her recipe book. First things first. She'd choose a cake to bake for tomorrow. Maybe once that was done she'd be up to tackling the harder issues.

In fact, she could make the cake today. She'd bought all sorts of exotic ingredients earlier. She could bake it today and ice it tomorrow.

She closed her eyes and opened the cookery book at a random page—cheating a bit by making sure she opened it at the easier, front part of the book—and stabbed a finger down. She opened her eyes and stared. Orange pound cake with lemon icing.

Fine. She'd make that then.

She collected the ingredients. She preheated the oven and greased her brand-new cake tin. She started creaming caster sugar and butter like there was no tomorrow. Her arm and the spot between her shoulder blades started to ache, but she didn't stop.

And that was when the idea came to her.

She sat, mixing bowl and all.

Mitch wanted to protect her from all evil—from anything that might hurt or harm her. That was impossible. He had to know that. It was just that he considered her lifestyle more dangerous than most. He thought her job put her in harm's way. What if she could show him, convince him, that she didn't need protecting? What if she could prove she was just as safe as the next person? She could *say* all of that until she was blue in the face, but he wouldn't believe her. But if he *saw* it in action…

Would that ease his mind? Would it allay his doubts and fears?

Could he be happy in a relationship with her then?

It was worth a shot, wasn't it?

She stood. She went back to creaming with vigour until the mixture was light and fluffy, until the pulse pounding in her throat and the hammering of her heart eased and she could breathe again.

# CHAPTER NINE

TASH PACED THE length of the living room—back and forth, back and forth—and sent up a silent prayer that Rick, true to his word, had disappeared earlier this morning and wasn't about to emerge from the guest bedroom to witness her agitation. She should've heard him leave, but she hadn't fallen asleep until the birds had started to chirp. Which, of course, meant she'd then overslept.

She wiped her hands down her shorts and adjusted her shirt. Why hadn't she set a designated time for Mitch rather than that open-ended *mid-morning*? She glanced at the clock—ten-twenty-eight. That was mid-morning, wasn't it? Surely eleven o'clock became late morning. Didn't it?

She forced herself to still and glance around. She'd iced the cake. It looked pretty. She'd even put sprinkles on top. She'd washed the dishes. The table was set with plates and napkins. Coffee was brewing in her brand-new coffee machine. Mitch had been right about that—freshly brewed coffee did taste better.

There was nothing left to do but wait.

Waiting had never bothered her before. She went back to pacing.

*You've never fought for your heart's desire before either.*

She twisted her hands together. Good point.

And then she heard his car pull up out the front and her heart tried to dash itself to pieces against her ribs. She patted her chest and talked it down off its ledge. She took a deep breath, and then another one. It brought a modicum of strength back to legs that had started to shake. She set off down the hallway at the same moment Mitch strode across the veranda. They stared at each other through the screen door. Devoured each other more like. When she reached it, she unlatched the door and pushed it open. 'Come in.'

'Thank you.'

He went to kiss her, but she stepped back.

His eyes narrowed. She swallowed. 'I don't want to cloud things by...'

'A kiss is going to cloud things? I'd have thought I'd have made them remarkably clear.'

For a moment she was tempted, seriously tempted, to do it his way—to fall into bed together now and talk later. *Oh, go on!*

But then what else would she give in to? What else would she give up?

She took another step back. 'You said we needed to talk. So, fine, we'll talk. If you only came around here to—'

He pressed a finger to her lips. 'Don't say it,' he warned.

She stared at him and eventually nodded. She had to stop being so prickly if this conversation was going to go anywhere.

He removed his finger. 'I do want to talk.'

'Good.' She wiped her hands down her shorts. 'That's good.'

And then he swept her close and kissed her cheek. His heat hit her and his scent swamped her and just for a moment she forgot which way was up. And then he released her. Hauling in a breath, she shook herself, turned and led the way into the living room.

'I'd like you to ooh and ah appropriately.' She stalked over to the table and whisked the cover off the cake. 'Ta-da.'

He stared and one corner of his mouth twitched. 'You really made a cake?'

The beginning of that smile disappeared when he glanced around. She bit back a sigh. 'Yes, Rick is staying here, but he's out at the moment.'

He swung back and his eyes were too intense. She did what she could to ignore the judgement in them. She had to try and keep control of the conversation or they'd descend into an all-out brawl within seconds. She gestured to the cake. 'I bought a cookbook. It's an orange pound cake with lemon icing.'

Eventually he swallowed and nodded. 'It looks great. Very professional.'

They stared at each other for several long moments before she found the strength to kick herself back into action. She planted the cover back over the cake and moved to pour them both coffee. She set the mugs onto the table. Mercifully, without spilling them. 'I've been flicking through the cookbook and ANZAC biscuits don't look too hard. I might try those next week.'

She was babbling!

'Tash, I—'

'Sit and eat a piece of cake, Mitch!'

The words shot out of her like bullets. She couldn't— wouldn't—give him a chance to say something that would set her off.

He sat.

She cut and served the cake. 'I channelled Mrs Schmidt while I was making this.'

'Mrs…who?'

'Never mind.' She had to stop babbling. 'Can you make Sachertorte?'

'That's beyond my skill set.'

He lifted his piece of cake. She waited until he took a bite. His eyes widened. She took a bite then too and…

She sat back in her chair and grinned. 'It worked!'

He grinned back. 'You doubted it?'

'Sure I did. First I thought I'd accidentally used salt instead of sugar and then I thought I'd beat the mixture too much or not enough, or if I didn't burn it that it'd sink in the middle because I'd mixed up the measurements or something.' She sobered. 'It seems to me that a lot of things can go wrong in making a cake.'

He sobered too and she could see he knew she was referring to more than cake-making.

He pointed to the cake. 'But nothing did go wrong. You did everything perfectly. You are a baker extraordinaire.'

He took another bite, but he didn't smile. He put his cake down. 'Tash—'

'Eat your cake, Mitch!'

He stared at her. She stared back. He picked up his cake and kept eating. Eventually they both wiped their fingers on paper napkins and sipped their coffee.

Tash set her mug down first. 'I know what you came here to say today.'

He opened his mouth, but she held up a hand. 'I know you think we can sort out our problems, Mitch, that we can make *us* work, but I'm not so convinced.' He opened his mouth again. 'But,' she said.

He swallowed. 'But?'

'That doesn't mean I think there's no chance for us at all.'

His lips thinned. He sat back and folded his arms. 'That's big of you.'

Her hands clenched. Did he think this was easy for her? 'Are you deliberately trying to get a rise out of me… to start a fight?'

He dragged a hand down his face. 'No.' Then he pulled his hand away and his eyes blazed at her. 'But I do want you to admit that what we shared was more than just sex.'

Her mouth dried. She couldn't have said why, but it took all of her strength not to hunch her shoulders. 'It was more than sex,' she managed through a tight throat.

Something inside him unhitched—she saw it in the way his shoulders loosened and the way his spine now curved to his chair. And she couldn't have explained why either, but it made her ache.

*Honesty. If you want this to work...*

Her heart contracted to the size of the shell in her pocket. But she touched that shell and lifted her chin. 'I gave my virginity to you. It meant something.'

His head came up. A triumphant light lit his eyes—a possessive light—that made her heart thunder and brought all her fears rushing to the surface. 'But, Mitch, I can't live the way you want me to.'

'We can work that out!'

'Can we?' she shot right back at him. She refused to allow herself to be pacified by trite platitudes. 'My parents couldn't. Your parents couldn't. What makes you think we'll be any different?'

He sat back, pale. 'That was a low blow.'

Her eyes stung. 'It wasn't meant to be,' she whispered. His nostrils flared, but eventually he met her gaze again. She lifted one shoulder. 'I'm just stating facts.'

'Are you all doom and gloom or do you see some solution to all this?' he bit out.

'Testy, aren't you,' she sniped back.

'Too right I'm testy! If you would just let us do what comes naturally it'd do the exact opposite of "clouding things". It'd make them incredibly clear and simple.'

'Oh, really?' She folded her arms. 'Well, I don't happen to agree with you.'

He leaned in close. 'What's more,' he said, his voice low and delicious, 'I think I could convince you to give my approach a go.'

She had an awful feeling he'd be able to convince her all too easily on that head, but...

This was too important for them to screw up!

'What makes you think you know better than me?'

He blinked.

She slapped a hand to her chest. 'What makes you think you know better than me about what's right for me?'

He eased back.

'For argument's sake,' she continued, 'let's say we do make love with each other right here, right now.'

Her heart nearly failed her when he licked his lips.

'But once we're done—'

'And sated.'

She had to close her eyes and count to three. 'Are you then going to be happy for me to continue living in this house and working at the Royal Oak and living my life the way I see fit? Or will you expect me to give all of those things up just to give you peace of mind?'

He stared at her as if he didn't know what to say. And then his face darkened. 'Are you determined to destroy us before we get a chance to develop any kind of relationship at all?'

'I'm not trying to destroy us! It's what I want to prevent!' The words left her at a shout. She leapt out of her chair and wheeled away. 'I'm trying to find out if we can work! I'm trying to figure out if we can be happy together or if we'll end up shredding each other to pieces.' She swung back. 'And all you're interested in is—'

He shot to his feet too. 'Sorry, I—'

He closed his eyes and dragged in a breath. She ached to go to him, to wrap her arms around his waist and rest her head on his shoulder.

'I didn't mean to keep harping on an old theme, but… but I thought you were going to pull the plug on us before we got the first chance. I thought if I could keep reminding you about how amazing we were together…'

It wasn't something she was likely to forget. Ever.

'Tash, I… We're on the same page. I swear.'

She let out a breath she hadn't known that she was holding. 'Okay, then.'

He stared at her a bit longer and eventually nodded. 'You have a plan?'

'Sort of. I was hoping you'd give me today.' She narrowed her eyes. 'But I want you to be open to the things I'm going to show you.'

He adjusted his stance. 'What are you going to show me?'

She was going to show him her life. 'I'm not giving you an itinerary of the day, Mr Control Freak.' She folded her arms. 'You'll find out, and in the meantime you'll just have to trust me.'

He grinned then and her blood chugged. 'Done.'

'Okay, good.' She moistened her lips and then realised the hungry way he surveyed them. A twist of something red and hot slid through her belly. Oh, dear Lord! She clapped her hands. 'Well, c'mon then. Time's a-wasting.' If she was going to keep her sanity and not kiss him they had to leave. Right now.

She all but threw their plates and mugs in the sink before grabbing her handbag and slipping it onto her shoulder. She gestured for him to follow her down the hall and out of the house. She locked the door and led him past their cars and down the street. 'We're walking,' she said somewhat unnecessarily, but it helped to ease the silence between them.

She remembered another time when they'd walked—into the forest surrounding his cabin—and how he'd taken her hand. He didn't take it now.

Then she remembered what had happened when they'd returned from that previous walk and thought it was probably just as well.

She gestured for them to cross at a set of traffic lights to the council park with its cenotaph, jacaranda trees and picnic tables.

'On our way through we're just going to stop for a moment to say hello to the gents playing chess.'

'They still do that?'

'Sure do. Mind you, some faces have changed over the years, but I guess that's to be expected.' It was a tradition for the half a dozen or so retired men in the area to meet in the park daily and play chess or dominoes. 'I think their wives shoo them out to stop them from getting underfoot.'

The men greeted her before she'd had a chance to so much as wave. There were shouts of 'Hello, lovely lady,' and offers of seats, which she declined. Demands were then made as to where she'd been for the last four days.

'Enjoying the sunshine on my holiday.'

'That's what your boss told us,' Mario said, beaming at her. 'We rang him to find out what had happened to you.'

She was aware of Mitch alternately tensing and shifting beside her. She glanced around the group. 'Where's Alfred?'

'Antoinette has him painting the kitchen.'

That made her laugh.

'Who's your young man?' Nigel asked.

She didn't bother trying to correct them. They'd think

what they wanted to think. Besides, she very much hoped it'd prove true. 'This is my friend, Mitch King.'

She drew him forward and he shook hands with the men, deflecting their teasing with such good humour it made her realise all over again how good—on every level—he must be at his job.

Wading in, she took his arm. 'Leave him be, gentlemen. We have to make tracks, but I'll see you all through the week.'

As soon as they'd taken a few paces she dropped his arm. It was too hard keeping a grip on her common sense when temptation and desire bombarded her. 'I hope you didn't mind that. I knew they'd have been wondering about me.' She rolled her eyes. 'Even though I did tell them I was going on holiday over a week ago.'

He glanced down at her. 'So why do I get the feeling our just dropping by wasn't an accident?'

He wasn't stupid; she had to give him that. She sent him a wide-eyed stare. He shook his head and half-grinned. 'Nosy bunch, aren't they?'

'A bunch of mother hens,' she agreed. 'I call them the Neighbourhood Watch.'

'They wouldn't be real handy if a fight broke out or anything.'

'Perhaps not, but if they thought something looked fishy they'd call the cavalry. And sometimes that's enough.'

She could feel the burn of his gaze, but she didn't turn her head to meet it. She didn't want to drive her point home with so much force it set his teeth on edge.

'Next stop,' she announced, pointing.

Mitch glanced at the bland front of the community hall on the opposite side of the park and wondered what on earth Tash had lined up for him to *see* here.

They entered and he pulled off his sunglasses, blinking to adjust to the dim light. Spread out in front of them was multiple groups of twos on mats, taking part in some kind of martial arts exercise.

'Judo,' Tash told him.

Before he could say anything, he found himself bundled out of the way as four teenage girls surrounded her. Someone showed off a red ribbon and there were ear-splitting squeals and it was such a strange environment to see her in he found himself grinning.

Eventually Tash clapped her hands. 'Okay, girls, on your mats. Show me your latest routines.'

He straightened. She was their *trainer*?

With a smile, she pointed to a chair. It was far enough from the action that he wouldn't be in the way, but close enough for a perfect view of the girls…and their trainer.

'Don't take your eyes off your opponent, Lou. Casey, bend your front knee a bit more. Nice! Jo, I want you to show me the throw we practised last time.'

He sat there, amazed. Amazed that Tash had such a rapport with these teenagers. And amazed that she had such a mastery of the discipline herself.

'She's one of my best students. You must be the friend she told me she was going to bring along. I'm Simon Fletcher. Are you interested in learning the art?'

Mitch rose and shook hands with the man who addressed him. 'Mitch King. Is this your place?'

Simon shrugged. 'I run this judo school, but we share the community hall with many other associates.'

Mitch turned back to Tash and nodded. 'She's good.'

'She'd have a real shot at the state title if she wanted.' Simon shrugged. 'But she doesn't want. You should come by and see her in action some time. Tuesday nights when she's not working.'

He made a note of that.

'Are you interested, Mitch?'

Oh, he was interested all right, but less in the sport and more in the woman.

'I might be,' he told the other man. 'I'm just considering my options at the moment.'

He knew what Tash was trying to tell him—that her world was just as safe as his, that she didn't need a protector or a defender. His heart thumped. That was all well and good, but it didn't change the fact that she'd be safer in an office job and living in a nicer suburb. She'd be a whole lot safer if Bradford wasn't staying with her. But not even that thought could make him drag his gaze from her lithe, assured frame. And his heart kept right on thumping.

Tash set a schooner of beer in front of Mitch and set another for herself on the table before climbing up onto the stool beside him. 'I'm a bit peckish so I ordered some potato wedges with sour cream and sweet chilli sauce to share. If you're hungry I can order you a burger or a schnitzel or something.'

He shook his head. He didn't want to talk about food. He wanted to talk about her.

'It's been a long time since I've been in here.'

They were in the Royal Oak Hotel—Tash's pub. He'd stayed away for all these years because he'd known it was what Tash would've preferred. To tell the truth, it wasn't his kind of pub—distinctly blue-collar. Not that he had anything against blue-collar or the working classes, but he wasn't one of the workers from the nearby glass or automotive factories. Which made him a stranger here.

And if the swift covert glances cast his way were anything to go by, the clientele recognised it. Not that he felt threatened, just…on notice. Very interesting.

Tash wasn't a stranger, though. Just about every patron in this lunchtime crowd had greeted her as she'd ambled past them. He lifted his beer to his lips. 'Do you know every single person in here?'

She didn't even glance around, just lifted one shoulder and sipped her beer. 'Just about.'

'How long have you been teaching those girls judo?'

'Those girls in particular or teaching judo in general?'

He gazed at her blankly. There was so much he didn't know about this woman. He'd been treating her like the girl she'd been eight years ago instead of the woman she'd become.

And then he remembered making love to her and his skin grew so tight it almost cut off his blood flow. Mostly, he amended, shifting on his stool. He'd *mostly* been treating her as that young girl.

'Rick talked me into learning judo when I was fifteen.'

His gut clenched at the mention of the other man's name.

'He knew Simon and we came to an arrangement. I couldn't afford to pay for lessons, you see, but I'd come early and set up the mats and then I'd stay back afterwards to pack everything up, sweep the floor so it was clean for the next group to use the hall and that kind of thing.'

Rick might've been a good friend to her once, but Mitch still didn't trust him as far as he could throw him. Not that Rick would be able to do anything to Tash while the police were watching him so closely. It was the only thought that kept Mitch sane.

'Simon taught me how to avoid a blow, how to fall so as to do the least amount of damage to myself and eventually, when I was ready, how to fight.'

He stared at her. 'You don't like to fight?'

'No! Do you?'

Well, no, but…

'I hate violence, but knowing how to fight—not just to defend myself but to be able to disable someone else—that makes me feel powerful and I like that.'

He grinned. 'You're something, you know that?'

'One of the most useful things Simon taught me was to read an opponent's body language. That's been invaluable. Nine times out of ten I can prevent a brawl from happening in here before it starts.'

He didn't like the thought of her having to break up fights in here.

Their wedges arrived, golden and steaming, and Mitch's mouth watered as their scent hit him.

'By the time I was eighteen I'd progressed so far I started taking on classes myself. Those girls you saw today can't afford the full fees for the classes, but I don't charge Simon a fee for training them.'

The wedges and his grumbling tummy were suddenly forgotten. 'You're doing that for free?'

'Free?' She shook her head. 'I may not be earning any money from it, but it's not free. I'm giving back the way Simon gave to me. And, hopefully, down the track those girls will give back too. It's a responsibility, a duty that needs to be fulfilled, but it's not a chore. I enjoy it. I get a lot out of it.'

He could see that, but still… They both reached into the basket of wedges at the same time. He stopped short to let her go first, every atom aching with the need to touch her. He recalled the look on her face when she'd asked him, *What makes you think you know better than me*? and he forced the need down. When they made love again, he wanted her with him wholeheartedly. He didn't want her regretting it afterwards.

Clarke, her boss, came over before she'd had a chance to demolish said wedge. 'Don't even think about it,' she

said before he'd opened his mouth. 'I am not jumping behind the bar for ten minutes while you duck out to do whatever urgent errand has just come up. I'm still on holidays.'

Clarke rolled his eyes at Mitch. 'See what I have to put
up with? Anyone would think she's the boss and not me.
I'm not going to ask you to work—not even for ten minutes—but I have to hire a new part-timer. Long story. I'll
fill you in next week. But I think you know both of the
people I've shortlisted...and as you'll have to work with
whoever I hire I thought you might like some input.'

'Oh.'

'So I came over to ask if you had five minutes to glance
over the applications or whether you're happy to trust my
superior judgement.'

Tash rolled her eyes and then glanced at Mitch. 'Would
you mind...?'

'Go for it.' He stretched one leg out. 'I'm going to order
a burger. I'm starving. Want anything else?'

'No, thanks.' She grabbed another wedge and hopped
down from the stool. 'I won't be long.'

He watched her amble over to the bar with Clarke, his
eyes dwelling on the long length of tanned thigh visible beneath her shorts, and a sigh eased out of him. He snapped
his attention back to the table, though, when he realised
two men were taking the seats either side of him.

'I'm Pete,' said one, 'and this is Mick.'

Pete looked hard and wiry. No doubt from some kind
of trade or labouring work. Mick was built like a rugby
front row forward—gigantic.

Mitch straightened. 'Mitch,' he said. 'Nice to meet you.
Anything I can do for you gentlemen?' He was determined
to keep things pleasant. He didn't want any trouble. He
probably had a good ten years on both of them. But there
were two of them. And this was Tash's pub.

'Tash has never brought a bloke into the pub before,' Pete said. He was obviously the spokesman.

'But she's a great mate of ours,' Mick said.

'And we just want to say that you better treat her real nice and do right by her, if you know what I mean.'

The hand Pete clapped to his shoulder held an edge. Mitch stared at the two men, and then glanced around the pub. Every patron in here was watching them. A grin built inside him and he turned back. 'I take it almost everyone else in here feels the same way about Tash?'

'That's right.'

'I'm glad to hear it.' If anyone ever tried to hurt Tash in here they'd have these guys to deal with. And these guys would tear them apart. The thought cheered him like nothing else. In fact, her workplace suddenly took on a whole new substance. 'Tash is a great girl. The best.'

He stared across at her. She glanced around as if she'd sensed his gaze, and then straightened and raised an eyebrow. He shook his head to let her know he didn't need her intervention. 'I have no intention of doing anything but treating her right.'

Both men relaxed as if sensing his sincerity. And he was sincere. He just wasn't sure what *treating her right* best entailed.

'But I'm curious. Why are you guys so happy to champion her?'

'She's one of us.' Mick raised a shoulder. 'Plus she got my boy a job here at a time when…let's just say at a good time. I'll always be grateful to her for that.'

Teenage girls *and* boys? She obviously had a wealth of hidden talents. Or maybe they weren't so hidden and he just hadn't seen them before.

'She gave me some very good advice once,' Pete said. He jerked his head at Mick. 'Your shout, isn't it, mate?'

Mick ambled off. Once he was out of earshot Pete turned back to Mitch. 'I'd been having a lot of problems with my foreman at the glass factory.' He held his thumb and forefinger up about a centimetre apart. 'I was this close to losing it. Tash talked me down off a ledge and stopped me from doing something real stupid.'

Mitch could tell he meant something jail-time stupid, something that would've cast a shadow over the rest of his life.

'She got me an application form to work at one of the automotive factories instead and stood over me until I'd filled it out.' He leant back. 'They hired me and...' He spread his hands as if that said it all and Mitch thought it probably did.

Tash came back to the table then. 'Are you monstering my friend, Pete?' She slid onto her stool. She had a grace and ease that fascinated him. And a life that was starting to fascinate him just as much.

'Just making his acquaintance, my lovely.' He tipped his beer in their direction. 'I'll bid you adieu.'

Tash watched him leave and then turned back. 'Everything okay?'

For heaven's sake, she was a walking, talking community services advertisement and she didn't even know it. And he'd wanted her to quit this place so she'd be *safe*? Dammit! She did more real good in her job, it seemed, than he did in his. 'Yep.' His voice came out tight.

Her eyes narrowed, but she didn't challenge him. Instead, she said, 'I ordered a burger for you.'

'Thanks.'

And, bizarrely, given all the thoughts racing through his mind, the conversation moved on. They ate lunch, Tash told him funny stories about incidents that had happened at the pub and he found himself telling funny stories about his time in police training. They laughed. A lot. It reminded him of kayaking with her, of their fishing and snorkelling.

And making love.

He did his best not to dwell on that bit.

Eventually, though, the conversation petered out into a silence that started to itch. There were still too many things unsaid between them. Tash glanced at him and she lost the easy, casual grace she had earlier. Her hands twisted together and her face became tight and pinched.

He did that to her.

Him!

His chest started to cramp. *What makes you think you know better than me?*

'I had a talk with Rick yesterday about love.'

His head jerked up. His mouth went dry. She stopped worrying her hands to lean towards him with a frown. 'It seems very strange to me that something that should be so positive—a force for good and all that—can turn out so bad for some people.'

Like her parents. Like his parents.

'It seems that some people who claim to love each other can be happy together while others who claim the same only seem to destroy each other. I've been trying to work out why that happens.'

She paused, staring—glaring—at the table. 'You see, I do care about you, Mitch.'

Everything inside him froze.

'I don't know how much yet, but it's enough for me to not want to walk away from what we could have just because things have got tough. But, whatever this thing is between us, I don't want it to turn destructive. I know you have feelings for me too, but I don't want them becoming destructive either. I don't want us to be like our parents.'

His stomach started to churn.

'I haven't come to any real conclusions about the difference between good and bad relationships, but today I wanted to show you the things that make me happy, the things that I need in my life—my community, teaching judo, my job. Those things are all good for me. If you hate them, if you hold them in contempt or see them as bad influences then you and I are going to run into trouble. Big trouble.'

'I don't, Tash.' He knew enough now to understand that she wasn't trying to blow him off. He tried to force all of his own insecurities to one side. The way she had.

Honesty hadn't played a great part in their past. It was time for that to change. He pulled in a breath and met her gaze. 'Today has shown me what a shallow view I've had of your life. You do amazing work and you have good friends. I…I'm sorry I leapt to conclusions about all of that.'

She sat back and stared. 'Thank you,' she finally said. Except…

He still didn't trust her current houseguest. Bradford mightn't be in jail, but that didn't make him innocent. Mitch didn't say that out loud, though, because he didn't want them to fight again.

Something in the set of her shoulders and the thrust of her chin eased. 'You can live with my way of life?'

'Easily.' As long as he didn't count Bradford in the equation.

She shuffled on her seat. 'So the question remains…'

He stiffened. 'What question?' He wanted all her questions answered so she could focus on them. He was falling for her so hard and fast it made him feel sick. 'I can promise you I will never ask you to change your job or where you live.'

She stared back at him and smiled. 'I believe you. That's not the question.'

It wasn't?

She leaned in towards him. 'Mitch, what do *you* need to be happy?'

Her. The answer came to him in a rush. All he needed was her. Instinct prevented him from saying the words out loud. They'd freak her out. Besides, he had no right to rush her. He swore then and there, though, that he would do everything in his power to make her happy. To make her feel loved and cherished and secure and anything else she needed. Forever.

He wouldn't rush her, but she was still sitting here at the table with him. She'd said she cared for him. He stretched out a leg and grinned at her.

She sat a little straighter, adjusted her shirt, but the telltale pulse at the base of her throat betrayed her. Heat immediately balled in his groin. 'I'd like you to see my house…where I live,' he said.

Her eyes speared to his.

'I want to see your face as you check out my kitchen. I have lots of newfangled appliances perfect for the hobby cook.'

Her lips twitched.

'I want to watch your face as you check out my music collection and my DVDs—to see if you can live with them.' If she couldn't he'd toss the lot.

She moistened her lips and it was all he could do not to reach across and kiss her.

'I really want to cook dinner for you tonight. I want to watch a movie with you afterwards, listen to some music maybe, drink a little brandy.'

She swallowed. She rolled her shoulders. 'That sounds kinda nice.'

And while she was there he'd show her in every way he could that they were meant for each other. He'd convince her to stay the night. Whether in his bed or the spare one would be up to her.

Of course, if she stayed at his place for the night Bradford couldn't touch her. She'd be safe. Safe and loved as she should be.

And, if nothing else, he'd have the undeniable pleasure of waking up to her in the morning. The knot in his stomach loosened.

Tash stretched and sighed, feeling sated and sexy and warm to the very centre of herself. She opened her eyes and turned her head on the pillow to survey Mitch.

Her heart expanded until she thought it impossible for her chest to contain it. Last night had been amazing, incredible. A smile lit her up from the inside out. Maybe she and Mitch weren't doomed after all. Maybe, if they took things slow, they could make things work. She wanted that with everything she was because...

*She loved him.*

She bit her lip and gave a tiny shake of her head. She wasn't even going to think those words yet, let alone say them out loud. It was too soon.

Slow. They'd take things slow.

Mitch's eyes opened and the smile he sent her curled her toes. 'Morning, gorgeous.'

Her heart pounded. 'Right back at you.'

He leaned across and planted a kiss on her nose and pulled her in close against him. She snuggled against his chest, revelling in the feel of powerful male flesh beneath her hands and cheek.

He nibbled her ear. 'What do you have planned for today?'

*Ah...*

She eased back a little to stare down at him. 'I'm still on hols.'

'Excellent.'

She almost succumbed to the smile he sent her. She eased up to rest against the headboard, dragging the sheet with her. He eyed that sheet and a glint lit his eyes. Oh, how she wanted to succumb to that! But…

'But…' she said.

His gaze lifted to hers and she leant down to kiss his cheek to ease the sting her words might bring. 'But,' she repeated, 'I have a house guest I'm not going to neglect.'

He sobered. He eased up beside her and he didn't say anything, but the tight set of his shoulders and mouth told her all she needed to know.

She cleared her throat. 'If you don't have any plans today, I'd like…'

Those blue eyes searched hers. 'Yes?'

She pushed a strand of hair behind her ear. 'We very diligently avoided the topic of Rick yesterday.'

He eyed her carefully. 'I didn't want to fight.'

'Me neither. It's obvious you still don't trust him, though.'

He kept his mouth shut, which, she reflected, might be wise.

She turned to him more fully. 'I'd like you to get to know Rick.'

He blinked.

'So if you don't have other plans…'

'I don't have other plans.'

'Well, then, maybe you'd consider spending the day with him and me?'

He nodded. 'Okay.' But his face had shuttered closed.

Tash huffed out a breath. 'Yesterday surprised you, right?'

He lifted a shoulder. 'Sure it did.'

'Then can't you be open to the fact that Rick could surprise you too?'

His face darkened again. 'I don't doubt that for a moment.'

'Forget it.' She pushed out of bed.

His hand snaked out to capture her wrist. 'I said okay, all right?'

'No, it's not all right! You're determined to think the worst of him.'

'I want you to listen to me for a moment.'

She stilled at his serious tone. 'Go on.'

'I want you to stay away from him until this whole mess has been cleared up.'

She gaped at him. He couldn't be serious?

'After that I'll be happy to get to know him all you want.'

Rick was her best friend. He didn't deserve that from her. 'No!'

Mitch's jaw tightened and she pulled her hand from his. 'I'd trust Rick with my life. And, as you pointed out the other day—I am not an idiot. Why won't you take my word for it when I say Rick is not behind these crimes? Why won't you even consider it?'

'Because, from where I'm standing, Tash, I think your judgement on this subject is clouded.'

'Then that's your problem, not mine! And I take back my earlier invitation. I don't want to spend the day with you snarling and acting like an idiot kind of guard dog.'

She swung out of bed. 'I'm having a shower.'

When she returned to the bedroom, Mitch was still in bed—in exactly the same position as she'd left him. 'Can I see you tonight?' he asked the moment she met his eye.

She tucked her shirt into her shorts. 'I…no.' She

slammed her hands to her hips. 'How on earth do you think this is going to work if you won't trust me…if you won't *listen* to me?'

He stiffened. 'You just need to give us time. We'll work it out.'

Would time really make any difference? The thought of having this same argument in ten years' time made her shoulders sag. She opened her mouth, but the phone rang. She gestured for him to answer it, grateful for the reprieve.

Whatever the caller said to him, though, galvanised him into immediate action. 'Right.' He hung up, leapt out of bed and started hauling on a pair of jeans. Tash did her best not to get distracted by the long, powerful lines of him.

He turned to her once he was dressed. 'Maybe we can finally put this behind us. Rick has just been arrested on assault charges. Assault against a woman.'

# CHAPTER TEN

ASSAULT AGAINST A WOMAN? Rick?

Tash went cold all over. Couldn't Mitch see it? 'Someone is trying to set him up!'

'I don't want to disillusion or hurt you, Tash, but the sooner those scales fall from your eyes the better.'

He wouldn't even consider her position. Her jaw clenched. Doomed, that was what they were, and she couldn't believe she'd thought otherwise.

She didn't bother arguing with him. There wasn't any point. 'You're going to the station?'

'Yes.'

'I'd like to come with you.'

He shook his head. 'I'm dropping you home.'

Fine. She'd drive herself.

They didn't speak during the ten-minute drive to her house. He pulled out the front of it but left the engine running. With a twist of her lips, she pushed out of the car. 'I'll call you,' he said.

She bent down to stare into the car. 'Don't bother. You and me, Mitch, we're done.'

His face darkened.

She pushed up her chin, grateful that the cold anger stirring in the pit of her stomach gave her the strength not to curl up into a ball and cry. 'There's one thing you might like to think about, *Officer* King.'

He stared back at her, his face as hard and blunt as stone.

'Very soon you'll realise Rick isn't guilty of those crimes you've all pinned on him. When you do, will you kindly turn your mind to who might actually be responsible, because until they're caught I'm still in danger.'

He blinked. He opened his mouth. But then cynicism flashed across his face, chasing away anything softer that might've tried to raise its head. 'The sooner I can prove to you what a nasty piece of work Bradford is, the sooner we can put this nonsense behind us.'

Tash slammed the door and swung away. She didn't watch his car as it roared away. She stamped up the front steps and practically kicked the door open instead. Cursing, she flung her handbag into the bedroom, uncaring where it fell. In fact, she cursed all the way through the house. Coffee. She needed coffee—hot and strong. She filled the jug. She reached for a mug.

'Hello, Tash.'

Every hair on Tash's arms stood to rigid attention. Her scalp crawled as if with a thousand bull ants. Very slowly she turned.

Cheryl O'Hara sat in the easy chair opposite, legs crossed neatly and pointing a gun at Tash's chest. 'It's been a while.' She wore a ludicrously pleasant smile on her face.

Tash swallowed and nodded. 'That it has.'

But not long enough as far as Tash was concerned.

Tash suddenly had to fight an awful weariness and terrible sense of inevitability.

Mitch would kick her butt if she went wobbly now. That thought had her mentally shoving her shoulders back, though she was careful to keep her body language as unthreatening as possible. The jug boiled and clicked off. 'Coffee?'

'No, thank you. This isn't really a social call, Tash.'

'I realise that, but I've had a shocker of a morning. Do you mind if I make myself one?'

'Not at all. I expect we need the calm before the storm.'

Cheryl's words chilled her. She made the coffee. All the while she kept Cheryl in the corner of her eye, readying herself to take whatever action necessary if the other woman made a sudden move. Not that she was sure what action she could take. Cheryl had a gun, for heaven's sake.

'So?' Tash sipped coffee and feigned a moment of bliss. 'You're the one who's behind the violence and not Rick then?'

Cheryl's nostrils flared. 'The police are idiots.'

'You won't get any arguments from me on that head.' Oh, but one of them could make love like an angel. *I'm so sorry, Mitch.* Why hadn't she told him she loved him when she had the chance? It all suddenly became crystal-clear. She didn't care if they argued about the same thing every week from here to eternity. It'd be better than never seeing him again. *Idiot!* She'd been an idiot.

She curled her fingers around her mug and leant a hip against the kitchen bench. 'I should've realised earlier that you were responsible for all this.' She shook her head. 'It never occurred to me.'

She'd been too busy thinking about Mitch. And that might finally prove a fatal weakness after all. She pushed the thought away.

'You've been slow on the uptake.'

And now she was going to pay for it. She tried to strangle the fear that rose up to choke her. She had to keep a straight head if she hoped to get out of this unharmed. And alive.

She glanced at the gun balanced carelessly in Cheryl's hands and then frowned. She leaned across the bench to get a better look at it. Obligingly, Cheryl held it up so Tash could see.

'Cheryl, that's a slug gun.'

'Uh-huh.'

She frowned. 'You're going to kill me with a slug gun?' Getting shot with slug gun pellets would hurt like the blazes, but it wouldn't kill her. Not even at close range.

'Oh, no.' Cheryl sent her a beatific smile. 'I'm not going to kill you.'

Tash tried not to sag in relief.

'I'm just going to scar that pretty face of yours so much that no man will ever look at you again.'

And then she aimed the gun right at Tash's face.

Mitch pulled the car to a screeching halt five blocks from Tash's place. He sat, the engine idling, on the side of the road, drumming his fingers against the steering wheel.

*Trust has never been a strong point between us, has it?*

She could say that again.

*Will you kindly turn your mind to who might actually be responsible, because until they're caught I'm still in danger.*

He pushed back the wall of pain that surrounded him, his innate police training coming to the fore. Detective Glastonbury had told him they were ninety-five per cent certain Bradford was responsible for this spate of violence, and there was no denying that the evidence, while currently circumstantial, was compelling, but…

That still left five per cent room for error.

With a curse, Mitch turned the car around. Five per cent was the slimmest of possibilities, but it didn't change the fact that he should've escorted Tash into the house to make sure everything was as it should be instead of roaring off in a jealous rage. A frustrated growl grated out of him. His professionalism had deserted him for the duration of this entire operation.

He pulled up two houses short of Tash's cottage. Nothing looked out of place. He ignored the front door to ease his way down the side of the house. He paused when he heard voices. Was Tash on the phone?

He listened hard and his lips thinned and every muscle he possessed tensed. There were definitely two voices. Of course, it could be a neighbour or a friend.

Five per cent? The probability was slim, but this time he wasn't taking any chances. He continued around to the back.

One glance at the lock on the back door and he bit back a curse. It had been jimmied. Whoever Tash's company might be, it was a fair bet that they weren't a friendly caller.

He glanced at the lock again. *Damn!* She had the flimsiest locks a man ever had the misfortune to lay eyes on. As soon as he had them out of this mess and Tash safe, he'd read her the riot act about those.

He crept through the back door and into a small sunroom at a crouch. He peered around the doorway and his blood ran cold. A woman had a gun pointed on Tash. A woman mostly with her back to him, and he had to quell every instinct to rush in there like an angry bull. It would only make things worse.

He eased back into the sunroom and flattened his back against the wall. He tried to still the pounding of his heart, to clear the red mist that threatened to descend around him.

Tash. Gun.

*No way!* No one was going to hurt Tash. *Breathe. Think!*

The banging of pots and pans interrupted him.

'What do you think you're doing?' the unknown woman screeched. He frowned. He knew that voice.

'I've had the worst day in the history of the world, Cheryl.'

Cheryl?

Cheryl O'Hara?

And a whole host of events suddenly straightened in his mind. *Rick wasn't the drug dealer.* He closed his eyes. The party had been at Cheryl's house. Traces of marijuana had been found on Cheryl. But Rick had said the drugs were his! *He knows more about friendship than you ever will.* Mitch cracked his eyes open again, his lips thinning. Why would Rick take the rap for Cheryl? Why would he want to protect her? What did she have on him and Tash?

'You're not shooting me until I've had breakfast.'

His shoulders tightened and his eyes narrowed. No one was shooting anyone.

He glanced around the door again to see Tash cracking eggs into a frying pan.

'It's barely ten o'clock, doll face. You haven't had time to have had a bad day yet.'

She dropped bread into the toaster. 'What's that—the wit and wisdom of Cheryl O'Hara?'

*Jeez, Tash, don't make her angry!*

But Cheryl only laughed. 'Uh-huh. So whose place did you stay at last night?'

Tash drove a savage spatula through eggs. 'Mitch King's. Remember him? *Officer* Mitchell King?'

The bread popped up in the toaster. Tash was chatting away as if…as if nothing was amiss. He admired her front, but…

But what? She was buying time, pure and simple.

'Girl, you still have a thing for him?'

She slid scrambled eggs onto toast. 'Looks that way.' She held up a plate. 'Want some?'

Nice idea, he applauded, but it didn't work. Cheryl

slashed a hand in the air and the gun swayed dangerously. 'That guy ruined everything back then! I can't believe you!'

He gathered himself in preparation to launch himself at Cheryl. It wouldn't be ideal, but he wasn't giving her a chance to get a clear shot on the woman he loved.

He wished he'd told her that this morning—last night *and* this morning.

*It would've sent Tash running for the hills.*

He shook himself. He couldn't think about that now.

'Did you sleep with him?'

'Yep.'

The gun stopped swaying so erratically, the barrel pointing towards the ground, and he let out a breath. Best-case scenario would be if he could sneak into the room and get behind Cheryl's chair, where it'd be simple for him to disarm and immobilise her.

'You are such a loser. That guy played you like an idiot when we were in high school.'

'At least I wasn't stupid enough to be caught doing drugs.'

'I'm the one with the gun!'

He heard the sound of cutlery and watched in amazement when Tash lifted a mouthful of toast and egg to her mouth and ate. She met his gaze for a moment. He blinked. When had she realised he was there?

'I heard about your dad, Cheryl. I'm real sorry.'

Cheryl tossed her head. 'He was a miserable excuse for a human being.' Her hands shook. 'At least I'll never have to be Daddy's little friend again.'

Everything inside Mitch froze. *That* was why Rick and Tash had done everything in their power to protect Cheryl. Bile burned his throat. The people who should've protected Cheryl hadn't. It'd been left up to her friends to do what they could. And then he'd blundered in with his holier-than-thou attitude and—

*Think about that later!*

'So I take it you still have a thing for Rick?' Tash said.

'We're meant to be together! We're soulmates! And he'd realise that if only other women would leave him alone!'

He wanted to hug Tash for her presence of mind. Instead, he eased himself into the room and slid into the shadow of a bookcase and stood stock-still.

Cheryl started to turn, as if she sensed something. He flattened himself.

'Cheryl, if you hurt me I will make sure Rick never forgives you.'

Cheryl froze before swinging back to Tash.

'If you scar me, blind me, I'll make sure he feels so guilty that he stays here to look after me. If you hurt me in any way, I'll make sure you never have a chance with him. Ever. You hear me?'

Cheryl shot to her feet. 'He loves me, not you!'

Tash gave a surprisingly elegant shrug. 'I think I can convince him otherwise. I can remind him you're poor little Cheryl and that he shouldn't take advantage of you.'

'You bitch!'

'What kind of chance do you think you'll have with him then?'

That was when Mitch saw that Tash was weighing a stainless steel pepper grill in her hand and he remembered the way she could pitch a rock at a tin can on the beach, her deadly aim.

'I've changed my mind.' Cheryl's voice rose and shook.

He glanced at the pepper grill and then at Tash and nodded.

'I'm going to kill you and then I'm—'

*Not going to happen.* 'Now!' he hollered, bursting out from his hiding place.

Tash launched the pepper grill like a rocket and it hit Cheryl, who'd started to swing to face him, squarely in her right shoulder, knocking her off balance. The gun barrel lifted skywards. He leapt forward, snatched it from her hands before she knew what he was about, but not before she had the presence of mind to rake her nails down his face as she frantically fought to find his eyes. With a curse, he spun her around and shoved her face down onto the floor, one knee in the middle of her back. He slid the gun towards the back door and out of harm's way before grabbing one of Cheryl's arms and forcing it up behind her back. She cried out in pain. 'Be still,' he ordered.

Tash touched his shoulder. 'Don't hurt her, Mitch. She's not well.'

He eased his grip on Cheryl, but only a fraction. He snapped on handcuffs and then hauled her upright and sat her back in Tash's easy chair. He wanted to yell at her, tell her she was crazy, but she'd started to cry.

Really cry.

Tash shooed him aside and sat on the arm of the easy chair and wiped Cheryl's face with a tissue. 'Cheryl, why do you have to take things so far?'

Her empathy amazed him. A minute ago this woman had been pointing a gun at her!

'I have to have him,' she hiccupped.

'Even if it turns you into a scary bunny-boiler?'

More hiccups and a nod.

'Even if it makes you like your dad?'

Cheryl's sobs stopped, as if Tash's words had shocked them out of her. Her face pinched up so white Mitch winced.

'I'm not like him,' she whispered.

'What do you call it when you hurt people to get your own way? What do you call it when you try to force someone to love you?'

Cheryl shook her head wildly. 'No. No!'

Tash placed her hands either side of Cheryl's face and forced her to look at her. 'Rick loves you as a friend, but he will never love you more than that. It's time to face the truth and leave him alone, the way your daddy should've left you alone when you asked him to.'

Cheryl's face crumpled.

Mitch's heart clenched and his mind threatened to explode.

Tash touched his arm. 'Are you okay?'

He nodded. *But...*

Things could've ended so differently today. If they had, that would've been his fault. Tash could've been hurt. Or worse. A black darkness shuddered through him, descending over the brightness of the day. He rested his hands on his knees and concentrated on drawing breath into his lungs. 'Tash, your locks are terrible, you know that? You need to improve your home security.'

That didn't change the fact that he'd screwed up. Rick was innocent. Rick had always been innocent. Tash had tried to tell him, but he'd refused to listen.

The darkness pressed more deeply into him. He'd been so sure she was blinded by prejudice and a shared history and background. But that had been him.

He'd been so sure and it could've got her killed. Acid coated his tongue and burned his stomach. Trust. He'd refused to trust her. He'd betrayed her. Again.

Detective Glastonbury's team came and took Cheryl away. Mitch took one look at Tash's pallor and promised that the two of them would be along in a little while to give their statements.

He touched her arm. 'Are you okay?'

She started and glanced around. 'They're gone?'

He nodded.

'I don't know how on earth we're going to sort everything out, Mitch, but I love you.' She threw herself into his arms and clung to him. 'I've been trying to turn love into something rational and logical that I can control, but it's not like that, is it?'

He wrapped his arms about her and buried his face in her hair and breathed her in. 'No,' he agreed. 'Not rational or logical. But powerful.' Overwhelmingly powerful.

He couldn't believe he had her in his arms, and that she was safe.

Her arms tightened about him. 'When I saw Cheryl with that gun the first thought that came into my head was—I wish I'd told you I loved you.'

'I thought exactly the same thing.' He eased back to stare down into her face. 'I wanted to tell you I loved you yesterday…and last night…and this morning, but I was afraid it'd scare you off.'

She nodded. 'Nothing like a real scare to put that into perspective, huh?'

'Jeez, Tash!' He huffed out a breath. 'That's one way of putting it.'

She swallowed. 'It's just…I thought if we took things slow that…that we'd have a better chance of success.'

He eased out of her arms and swung away. 'Success?' He turned back. 'I screwed up, Tash. Big time! You could've been hurt. Or worse.'

'That wasn't your fault. You're not responsible for Cheryl's craziness. You came back to make sure I was safe, didn't you?'

'Yes, but—'

'We saved the day, didn't we?'

He stilled and a glimmer of light lit through him. 'We made a pretty good team.'

She nodded.

He moved back in close to her, touched her face. 'I'm sorry I didn't believe you about Rick. All I could think about was keeping you safe. Because if anything happened to you…'

He couldn't finish that sentence. She reached up and cupped his face in her hands. 'I am safe. Now. Thanks to you.'

He pulled in a breath. 'I promise you that I will personally see to it that Rick is cleared. Not just of these crimes, but the former drug charges too.'

'Thank you.'

'I can't believe I let myself be so blinded by prejudice.'

'I can't believe I let myself be so blinded by fear.'

He met her gaze again and her face grew even more serious. She released him to back up and perch on the sofa. 'I'm still scared,' she said. 'Not about Cheryl,' she added before he could reassure her. 'About us. We love each other, but can we make this work?'

He moved beside her and took her hand. 'I want it to work.'

'Me too.'

Wanting and making it happen, though, were two different things. 'We've both seen too much of the darker side of life to believe in fairy tales, haven't we?'

Tash nodded, but it didn't stop her from wanting that fairy tale with every fibre of her being.

'Okay—' he turned to face her more fully '—let's talk about deal breakers.'

She blinked. And then she saw the wisdom of that.

'Yes.' She nodded. 'We've skirted around the hard issues for too long.'

'You want to start?'

She pulled in a breath. 'That's what yesterday was about. Did you lie when you said you could live with the way I lead my life?'

'No. I had that all wrong. The life you lead is valuable and important. You're right to be proud of it.'

She let out a long breath. 'Okay, your turn.'

He rubbed the back of his neck. 'My job is important to me.'

She already knew that.

'It's a vocation, not a job. Through it I feel as if I'm contributing to something bigger and better than me.'

'I don't have an issue with your job, Mitch.'

'Not even if I were to arrest one of the Royal Oak's regular patrons that you might be fond of?'

She was silent for a moment. 'It's happened before. All of the pub's patrons know the consequences of getting caught breaking the law. I hate it when someone takes that risk, but I can't control other people's actions any more than you can. You have a job to do. I understand it's not personal.'

Some of the tension eased out of his shoulders and she suddenly realised one of his unspoken fears. 'I would never try to use my influence with you to get you to turn a blind eye to something you shouldn't.'

He stared at her for a long moment. She didn't feel the need to fidget or drop her gaze but held his steadily. Finally he nodded. 'I believe you.'

They both let out a breath.

'I know your community here is important to you, Tash, but what if I was transferred interstate?'

*Ooh, okay.* She sat back. She thought hard. 'As long as

I could still work and continue with my judo or some other form of martial arts then I could live somewhere else. I'd want to come back to visit my friends sometimes, though, and I'd like to invite them to visit me.'

He leaned towards her. 'You'd relocate for me?'

She'd never felt more bared in her life. She opened her mouth to add disclaimers like: Not next week, but if we've been going out for twelve months and everything is going well, yada-yada-yada... But that was just obfuscation.

'Yes,' she whispered.

He stared at her as if she was the most amazing thing he had ever seen. And then he slumped back against the sofa. 'What am I talking about? If you didn't want to relocate, I wouldn't move. Full-stop. I...'

He broke off and his hands clenched. Behind the brilliant blue of his eyes she could see his mind racing. Her mouth dried. 'Mitch?'

He turned to her. 'The secret about love that you've been searching for, Tash?' She leaned towards him. 'I think I just worked it out.'

'Spill,' she ordered.

'It's not going to sound all that romantic,' he warned.

'I don't give two hoots about romantic!' She just wanted truth, honesty...him!

'Respect,' he said.

'Respect.' She rolled the word around in her mouth, testing it.

He gave a firm nod. 'Respect.'

They stared at each other for another long moment. She shifted. 'Okay, let me make sure we're on the same page about that word. When you say respect I interpret it to mean taking into account a person's feelings, emotions, thoughts and beliefs and giving them due weight.'

He nodded.

'So…' She hesitated. She wasn't sure she should go there, but she didn't want anything off-limits in this conversation.

'So?' The warmth in his eyes urged her to continue.

'So if you came to me tomorrow and said you needed to take me to a safe place because there was a police investigation currently underway suggesting Rick was out to hurt me…'

He dragged a hand down his face. Her heart alternately ached and pounded.

'And if I said I didn't believe Rick would hurt me, then…' She bit her lip. 'Then we'd go out to your beach cabin.'

His head lifted.

'Because I understand an innocent citizen's safety is of paramount importance, but then—'

'But then I'd work with you to try and determine—at a distance—who might actually be responsible whilst hassling my colleagues endlessly to explore other avenues, which is what I should've done.'

Something hard inside her gave way. 'Which is what you would've done if there hadn't been so many lies and secrets between us. If I'd been completely honest with you about everything from the start you'd have acted differently.' She saw that clearly now.

'I've never been objective around you, Tash. I want to say it's how I'd have acted if I'd known the full story, but I can't guarantee it.'

'I can.' She felt the certainty bone-deep.

He blinked.

'Keeping me safe is important to you. You'd do whatever necessary to ensure that, but we won't make those same mistakes again.'

One side of his mouth finally hooked up and he nodded. 'I think you're right.'

'Respect...' she started slowly '...is me listening when you tell me my home security needs improving.'

'Respect is me fighting my desire to lock you up to keep you safe because I know you're a person who values her independence, makes a valuable contribution to society and has every right to live her life the way she chooses.'

She wanted to slide right onto his lap then and lose herself in kissing him.

Her skin tingled, her fingers ached and every cell in her body reached towards him. She all but threw herself off the sofa and backed up to perch on the breakfast bar away from him.

He frowned. 'Tash?'

Her heart thudded so hard she had to press a hand to her chest. She hadn't allowed herself to hope, but now it all came rushing to the fore. She could do nothing against the gush of hot and cold, the fluttering and freezing or the surging of her blood. 'Are you saying you promise to respect me?'

'Yes!' He glared and slammed to his feet. 'What are you doing all the way over there? Tash, *I love you!*' He bellowed the words and it struck her that the same craziness and pulsing had overtaken him too. 'I know promising to respect you isn't romantic. But it means I will always take your concerns, your welfare, your health and your wants seriously. My parents didn't respect each other. Your father didn't respect your mother. I figure if we respect each other we—'

He broke off. 'Are you crying?'

'No!' A sob broke from her throat. 'And you're wrong. It's the most wonderful and romantic thing I've ever heard.'

In two strides he was there, arms around her and insinuating his way between her thighs. He stared down at her. 'You mean that?'

She nodded.

'I love you and I want to give us a chance, Tash.'

'I love you and I want you to kiss me.'

He did. Thoroughly and in such an achingly sweet way it touched her soul even as it made her toes curl.

Eventually they broke apart, both breathing heavily. 'We'll take things slow,' he said. 'Just like you wanted us to.'

'Okay,' she whispered.

He frowned. 'What exactly does taking it slow mean?'

She smiled. She threw her head back and laughed out loud for the sheer joy of being able to do so. 'It means we're not moving in together for at least six months.'

He pursed his lips. 'Can there be sleepovers?'

'I'm counting on it.'

'Slow? Right. I won't ask you to marry me for twelve months then.'

'And once we're married I'd like to wait a year or so before we have kids.'

He grinned down at her. She grinned back, winding her arms around his neck. 'I want to savour each and every moment of our relationship.' Because she believed in it now—believed in them. Heart and soul. She and Mitch would make things work *because* they loved each other, *because* they wanted the best for each other.

'I want to savour every day I'm lucky enough to be with you.'

She touched his face, awed by how much she loved him…and at the love she saw reflected in his eyes. 'Mitch?'

He pressed a long lazy kiss to the side of her neck and she arched against him like a cat. 'Hmm…?'

She tried to remember how to breathe. 'When you do propose to me, could you do it at the cabin?'

He eased back to grin down at her. 'Whatever you want,' he promised, his lips descending to hers again.

She kissed him back, telling him in a language that needed no words that she already had everything she wanted.

\* \* \* \* \*

*Look for Rick's story in*
*THE REBEL AND THE HEIRESS*
*Coming soon!*

# WHY RESIST A REBEL?

BY
LEAH ASHTON

An unashamed fan of all things happily-ever-after, **Leah Ashton** has been a lifelong reader of romance. Writing came a little bit later—although in hindsight she's been dreaming up stories for as long as she can remember. Sadly, the most popular boy in school never did suddenly fall head over heels in love with her...

Now she lives in Perth, Western Australia, with her own real-life hero, two gorgeous dogs and the world's smartest cat. By day she works in IT-land; by night she considers herself incredibly lucky to be writing the type of books she loves to read, and to have the opportunity to share her own characters' happily-ever-afters with readers.

You can visit Leah at www.leah-ashton.com.

For Annie—

who has always been way cooler than her big sister
and then went and worked in film, just to rub it in.
Thank you for your endless help and patience as
I researched this book. Any mistakes are mine.
You're awesome, Annie.

# CHAPTER ONE

RUBY BELL ESTIMATED her phone rang approximately half a second before her brisk walk was rudely interrupted by an un fortunately located tuft of grass.

More fortunately, she'd had the presence of mind to hold onto said phone during her less than graceful swan-dive onto the dusty paddock floor. A paddock that had once housed a significant number of sheep, but more recently had become the temporary home of a ninety-strong film crew. Thankfully this particular patch of paddock showed no evidence of sheep occupation.

But, at such close range, Ruby had also learnt that the pad-dock floor was: a) lumpy and b) hard.

'Paul,' Ruby said, wincing slightly as she lifted the phone to her ear. Still lying flat on her belly in the dirt, she shifted her weight in an unsuccessful attempt to avoid the patches of grass that prickled through the thin fabric of her T-shirt and the seep-ing warmth that had once been her half-drunk cardboard cup of coffee. Just slightly winded, Ruby's voice was a little breathy, but otherwise she sounded about as efficient as always. Good. She'd built a successful career as a production co-ordinator that took her across the globe—regularly—by being sensible, unflappable, no-nonsense Ruby. Tripping over her own feet couldn't even begin to rattle her.

'I need you back at the office,' Paul said, even more flustered than usual. 'There's been a development.'

And that was it—he'd already hung up. Ruby knew it was

impossible to interpret her producer's urgent tone—it was quite possible the sky *was* falling, but about the same odds that one of the runners had simply screwed up his espresso again. Either way, Ruby needed to get her butt into gear.

'You okay, Rubes?'

Ruby glanced up at the worried voice, squinting a little against the early afternoon sun. But, even mostly in shadow—or maybe because of it—the very broad and very solid frame of Bruno, the key grip, was unmistakeable. Beside him stood a couple of the younger grips, looking about as awkward as they always did when they weren't busily carting heavy objects around—plus about half the hair and make-up department. Which made sense, given she'd managed to come crashing to the ground right outside their trailers.

'Of course,' she said, pressing her outflung hands into the soil and levering herself up onto her knees. She waved away Bruno's helpful hand as she plucked at her T-shirt, pulling the coffee-soaked fabric away from her chest. The parts of her not damp and clinging were decorated with a mix of grass stains and a remarkable number of dirt smudges.

*Awesome.*

But she didn't have time to worry about the state of her outfit just now. Or her hair—running her fingers through her short blonde pixie-cut confirmed only that it was somehow dusty, too.

A moment later she was back on her feet and her day carried on exactly as before—grass stains and the uncomfortable sensation she was covered in a head-to-toe sticky coating of dirt notwithstanding.

'Ruby!' A yell from somewhere to her left. 'Weather tomorrow?'

'Fine. No chance of rain,' she called out, not even slowing her pace. Paul, as always, would've preferred if she'd gained the power of teleportation. In its absence, she just needed to walk even faster than normal.

The cottage that temporarily housed the film's production office was only a few minutes away—tucked to the left beyond the final cluster of shiny black or white trailers and the slightly askew tent city that was catering.

She kept her focus on her path—already well worn into the grass in the two days since they'd set up camp—mentally crossing her fingers for nothing more serious than a coffee-related emergency. So far she'd already dealt with an unexpected script change, a sudden decision to relocate a scene, and an entitled young actress who'd gone temporarily AWOL. And it was only day one of filming.

'Got a minute?' asked Sarah, a slight redhead in charge of the extensive list of extras required for *The Land*—an 'epic historical romance played out in the heart of the outback'—from the top stair of a shiny black trailer.

'No,' Ruby said, but slowed anyway. 'Paul,' she said, as way of explanation.

'Ah,' Sarah replied, then skipped down from the trailer to fall into step with Ruby as she passed. 'Just a quick one. I've got a call from a concerned parent. They're worried about how we're going to get Samuel to cry in tomorrow's scene.'

By the time she'd reached the last of the row of trailers a minute later, Sarah was on her way with a solution, and Ruby had fielded another phone call on her mobile. Arizona Smith's assistant wanted to know if there were Ashtanga Yoga classes in Lucyville, the small north-west New South Wales country town in which they were filming.

Given the remote town's population was just under two thousand people, Ruby considered this unlikely—but still, with a silent sigh, promised to get back to their female lead's assistant asap.

Ruby broke into a jog as she turned the corner, her gaze trained downward—she wasn't about to hit the dirt again today—and her brain chock-full of potential 'developments' and their hypothetical impact on her already tight schedule.

Consequently, the first she knew of the very large man walking around the corner in the opposite direction was when she slammed straight into him.

'Ooomph!' The slightly strangled sound burst from her throat at the impact of her body hitting solid muscle. She barely registered her hands sliding up sun-warmed arms to grip T-shirt clad shoulders for balance, or the way her legs tangled with his.

What she *did* notice, however, were his hands, strong and firm at her waist, the fingers of one hand hot against bare skin where her T-shirt had ridden an inch or two upwards.

And the scent of his skin, even through the thin layer of cotton, where her face was pressed hard against his chest.

Fresh, clean. *Delicious.*

*Oh, my.*

'Hey,' he said, his voice deep and a little rough beside her ear. 'You okay?'

Slowly, slowly, embarrassment began to trickle through her body.

No, not embarrassment—the realisation that she *should* be embarrassed, that she *should* be extricating herself from this... clinch...as soon as possible.

'Mmm-hmm', she said indistinctly, and didn't move at all.

His fingers flexed slightly, and she registered that now she was moving. Then her back pressed against the cool metal of the shaded wall of a trailer, and she was sliding downwards. He'd been holding her—her feet dangling. Somehow she'd had no idea of this fact until her ballet flats were again responsible for holding her upright.

Had anyone ever held her so effortlessly?

She was medium height, far from tiny—and yet this man had been holding her in his arms as if she weighed as much as the average lollypop-thin Hollywood lead actress.

*Nice.*

Again his hands squeezed at her waist.

'Hey,' he repeated. 'You're worrying me here. Are you hurt?'

She blinked and finally lifted her head from his chest. She tried to look at him, to figure out who he was—but his face was mostly in shadow, the sunlight a white glare behind him.

But something about the angle of his jaw was familiar.

Who was he? He was fit, but he wasn't one of the grips. Some of the guys in Props were pretty tall, but Ruby honestly couldn't imagine enjoying being held in the arms of any of them. Which she was, undeniably, doing right now. Enjoying this.

She shook her head, trying to focus. 'Just a bit dazed, I think,' she managed. Belatedly, she acknowledged that was true. With every second, the fog was dissipating. But it was a gradual transition.

Right now, she found herself perfectly happy where she was. Standing right where she was.

'Are *you* okay?' she asked.

She could barely make out the slightest curve to his lips, but it was there. 'I'll survive.'

His grip on her softened a little as he seemed to realise she wasn't in any imminent danger. But he didn't let her go. Her hands still rested on his shoulders, but removing them wasn't even a consideration.

A cloud shifted or something, and the shadows lightened. Now she could make out the square line of his jaw, covered liberally in stubble; the sculpted straightness of his nose, and the almost horizontal slashes of his eyebrows. But even this close—close enough that the action of breathing almost brought her chest up against his—she couldn't quite make out the colour of his gaze.

A gaze that she knew was trained on her, exploring her face—her eyes, her lips…

Ruby closed her eyes tight shut, trying to assemble her thoughts. Trying to assemble herself, actually.

The fog had cleared. Reality was re-entering—*her* reality. Straightforward, straight-talking Ruby Bell. Who was *not* taken to romantic notions or embracing total strangers.

He wasn't crew. He must be an extra, some random guy minding his own business before she'd literally thrown herself into his arms.

Inwardly, she cringed. Too late, mortification hit. Hard.

Rational, no-nonsense words were right on the tip of her tongue as she opened her eyes.

But instead of speaking, she sucked in a sharp breath.

He'd moved closer. So, *so* close.

The man didn't look worried now. He looked almost…predatory. In a very, very good way.

She swallowed. Once, twice.

He smiled.

Beneath traitorous fingers that had crept along his shoulders to his nape, his overlong hair was coarse beneath her fingertips.

'You,' he said, his breath fanning against her cheek, 'are quite the welcoming party.'

Ruby felt overwhelmed by him. His size, his devastating looks, his nearness. She barely made out what he'd said. 'Pardon?'

He didn't repeat himself, he just watched her, his gaze locked onto hers.

Whatever she'd been going to say—the words had evaporated.

All she seemed capable of was staring at him. Into those eyes, those amazing, piercing…*familiar* blue eyes.

Finally it clicked into place.

'Has anyone ever told you, you look *just* like Devlin Cooper?' she said. Babbled, maybe. *God.* She didn't know what was going on.

One of his hands had released her waist, and he ran a finger down her cheek and along her jaw. She shivered.

'A couple of times,' he said, the words as dry as the grass they stood upon.

No, not quite like the famous Devlin Cooper. This man had dark circles beneath his eyes, and his darkest blond hair was far too long. He was too tall, surely, as well—she'd met enough leading men to know the average Hollywood star was far shorter than they looked on screen. And, she acknowledged, there was a sparseness to his width—he was muscled, but he didn't have the bulk of the movie star. He looked like Devlin Cooper might look if turned into one of those method actors who lost bucket-loads of weight for a role. Not that Ruby could imagine that ever happening—Devlin Cooper was more generic-action-blockbuster-star than the Oscar-worthy-art-house type.

But as the man's fingers tipped her chin upwards any thought of Devlin Cooper was obliterated. Once again it was just her, and this man, and this amazing, crazy tension that crackled between them. She'd never felt anything like it.

She was sure she'd never wanted anything more than to discover what was going to happen next.

He leant forward, closing the gap between their lips until it was almost non existent...

Something—a voice nearby maybe—made Ruby jump, and the sound of her shoulders bouncing against the trailer was loud in the silence. A silence she was suddenly terribly aware of.

That rapidly forgotten wave of mortification crashed back over her, this time impossible to ignore. With it, other—less pleasant—sensations than his touch shoved their way to the fore. The fact she was covered in dirt and drying coffee. The fact her whole body suddenly appeared capable of a head to toe, hot, appalled blush.

She was still hanging off the man like a monkey, and she snatched her hands away from his neck.

'Hey. You're not going to catch anything,' he said, a lightness in his tone as he watched her unconsciously wipe her hands almost desperately against her thighs.

She stilled the movement and met his gaze. His eyes had an unreadable glint to them, and for the first time she noticed their thin spidery lines of bloodshot red.

*'Who are you?'* she asked in a sharp whisper.

His lips curled again, but he didn't say a word. He just watched her, steadily, calmly.

He was infuriating.

She ducked to her left, and the hand that had remained on her waist fell away. Ridiculously, she missed the warmth and weight of his touch immediately, and so she shook her head, desperate to refocus.

She put a few steps between them, taking deep, what-the-heck-just-happened breaths as she glanced to her left and right.

They were alone. No one else stood in this path amongst the trailer metropolis.

No one had seen them.

Relief swamped her. *What on earth had she been thinking?*

But then approaching footsteps made her freeze, as if whoever walked around the corner would immediately know what had just happened.

Of course, it was Paul.

'Ruby!' her producer exclaimed loudly. 'There you are.'

'Ruby,' the man repeated, slowly and softly, behind her. 'Nice name.'

She shot him a glare. Couldn't he just *disappear?* Her mind raced as she tried to determine exactly how long it had been since she'd barrelled into the man. Surely not more than a few minutes?

It wasn't like Paul to come looking for her. Fume alone in his office if she were late, yes—but come find her? Definitely not.

It *must* be a real emergency.

'I'm sorry,' Ruby managed, finally, and meant it. But how to explain? She ran a hand through her hair; the movement dislodged a few forgotten blades of grass. 'I fell over,' she said, more confidently, then nodded in the man's direction. 'He was just helping me up.'

She smoothed her hands down her shirt and its collection of dust, coffee and grass stains for further effect.

There. All sorted, the perfect explanation for why she wasn't in Paul's office five minutes ago.

Out of the corner of her eye, the man grinned. He'd propped himself up against the trailer, ankles crossed—as casual as you like. A normal person would surely size up the situation, realise something was up and—she didn't know—do anything *but* act as if all he were missing were a box of popcorn and a choc-top.

'Thanks for your help,' she said, vaguely in his direction. For the first time she noticed the matching coffee-coloured marks all over the man's grey T-shirt, but she couldn't make herself apologise. He was just too frustratingly calm and oblivious. He could keep his smug smile and newly stained T-shirt.

She walked up to Paul, assuming they'd now go back to his office. 'So, what do you need me to do?'

Paul blinked, his gaze flicking over her shoulder to the man that *still* stood so nonchalantly behind her.

'You left in a hurry,' he said—not to Ruby, but to the man.

Ruby turned on her heel, looking from Paul to the man and back again—completely confused.

The man shrugged. 'I had things to do.'

Paul's eyes narrowed and his lips thinned, as if he was on the verge of one of his explosions.

But then—instead—he cleared his throat, and turned to Ruby. A horrible sense of foreboding settled in her stomach.

'So you've met our new leading man.'

She spoke without thinking. 'Who?'

There was a barely muffled laugh behind her.

The man. His knowing smile. The charisma that oozed from every pore.

Finally, *finally,* she connected the dots.

*This* was Paul's latest drama. *This* was why she'd been rushing back to the office.

They had a new leading man.

She'd just met him.

She'd just covered him in dirt and coffee.

Worst of all—she'd just nearly *kissed* him.

And he didn't just have a passing resemblance to Devlin Cooper. A passing resemblance to a man who commanded double-digit multimillion-dollar salaries and provided continuous tabloid fodder to the world's magazines and salacious television entertainment reports. A man who'd long ago left Australia and now was mentioned in the same breath as Brad, and George, and Leo...

'You can call me Dev,' he said, his voice deep and oh-so intimate.

*Oh.*

*My.*

*God.*

Dev Cooper smiled as the slender blonde raked her fingers desperately through her short-cropped hair.

*Ruby.*

It suited her. She was striking: with big, velvety brown eyes beneath dark blonde brows, sharp-edged cheekbones and a lush mouth. Maybe her elegant nose was a little too long, and her chin a little too stubborn—if she were a model his agent had picked out for him to be photographed with at some premiere or opening or whatever.

But, thankfully, she wasn't. It would seem she was a member of the crew of this film he was stuck working on for the next six weeks. And—if the way she'd been looking at him a few minutes earlier was anything to go by—she was going to make the next few days, maybe longer, a heck of a lot more interesting.

Ruby crossed her arms as she spoke to the producer—Phil? No, *Paul.* The man who'd owed his agent Veronica a favour. A really *big* favour, it turned out, given his agent had bundled him onto the plane to Sydney *before* she'd sorted out the pesky little detail of whether or not he had the role.

Dev guessed, knowing Veronica, that Paul had discovered he was replacing his leading man just before Dev had turned up in his shiny black hire car. Chauffeur driven, of course—his agent was taking no chances this time.

He shifted his weight a little, easing the pressure on his left leg, which throbbed steadily. Had it really only been a week?

The pancake-flat countryside where he now stood couldn't be further away from his driveway in Beverly Hills—the site of 'the last straw' as his agent had put it. Even Dev had to admit that forgetting to put his car into reverse wasn't his best moment. Ditto to driving into his living room, and writing off his Jag.

On the plus side, he hadn't been injured, beyond some temporary muscle damage, and, thanks to the fortress-style wall that surrounded his house, no one beyond his agent and long-suffering housekeeper even knew it had happened.

And, despite what Veronica believed, he hadn't been drunk.

Exhausted after not sleeping for four nights—yes. But driving, or attempting to drive, drunk? No, he hadn't slid that low.

*Yet?*

Dev scrubbed at his eyes, uninterested in pursuing the direction his thoughts had taken him. Instead, he refocused on Ruby and Paul, who had stopped talking and were now looking at him.

Ruby's gaze was direct, despite the hint of colour at her cheeks. She was embarrassed, no doubt. But she was brazening it out.

He liked that.

'I'm Ruby Bell,' she said, 'Production Co-ordinator for *The Land.*'

Her arm moved slightly, as though she was going to shake his hand before thinking better of it.

A shame. He was impatient to touch her again.

Maybe she saw some of what he was thinking, as her eyes narrowed. But her tone revealed nothing. 'Paul will give me your details, and I'll send through tomorrow's call sheet once I've spoken to the assistant director.'

He nodded.

Then Paul started talking, putting lots of emphasis on *tight timelines* and *stop dates* and *getting up to speed as quickly as possible*—all things he'd said in their abruptly truncated meeting earlier.

*Lord,* anyone would think he made a habit of missing his call...

He smiled tightly at his private joke, eliciting a glare from Paul.

Dev tensed. This film might have a decent budget for an Australian production, but it was no Hollywood blockbuster. He was replacing a *soapie star* as the lead, for heaven's sake.

No way was he going to take a thinly veiled lecture from some nobody producer.

'I get it,' he said, cutting him off mid-stream, the action not dissimilar to what had happened in Paul's office when he'd had enough of his blustering. 'I'll see you both,' he said, pausing to catch Ruby's gaze, 'tomorrow.'

And with that, he was off.

Six weeks of filming. Six weeks to placate his agent.

Six weeks working in a town out beyond the middle of no-where. Where—he knew his agent hoped—even Dev Cooper couldn't get into any trouble.

A heated memory of chocolate eyes that sparkled and urgent fingers threaded through his hair made him smile.

Well, he hadn't made any promises.

# CHAPTER TWO

It took all of Ruby's strength to follow Paul up the small flight of brick steps to the production office. She literally had to remind herself to place one foot in front of the other, as her body really, *really* wanted to carry her in the opposite direction. *Away* from the scene of unquestionably one of the most humiliating moments of her career. Her life, even.

*How could she not have recognised him?*

Only the possibility that any attempted escape could lead her back to Devlin Cooper stopped her. Oh—and the fact she kind of loved her career.

As they walked down the narrow hallway of the dilapidated cottage/temporary production office, Paul explained in twenty-five words or less that Mr Cooper was replacing Todd, effective immediately. That was it—no further explanation.

By now they'd made it to Paul's makeshift kitchen-cum-office at the rear of the cottage. Inside stood Sal, the line producer, and Andy, the production manager. They both wore matching, serious expressions

It was enough to force Ruby to pull herself together. She needed to focus on the job at hand—i.e. coordinating this movie with a completely new star.

'I have to ask,' asked Andy, his fingers hooked in the belt loops of his jeans. 'How the hell did you get Devlin Cooper to take this role?'

Ruby thought Paul might have rolled his eyes, but couldn't be sure. 'Let's just say that the opportunity arose. So I took it.'

Despite the catastrophic impact on their immovable filming schedule, Ruby could hardly blame him. With Devlin's star
power, *The Land* would reach a whole new audience. Why Devlin *took* the role was another question entirely—did he want to
spend time back in Australia? Did he feel a need to give back
to the Australian film industry? A chance to take on a role well
outside his vanilla action-hero stereotype?

It didn't really matter.

Filming had started, and Dev's character Seth was in nearly
every scene. Tomorrow's call sheet had Todd's name all over
it—the guy who Dev had replaced. Unquestionably, they'd lost
tomorrow. Which was not good, as Arizona had to be at Pine-
wood Studios in London for her next film in just six weeks
and one day's time. They didn't have *any* time up their sleeves.

'Does Dev know the script?'

Paul just looked at her. *What do you think?*

Okay. So they'd lost more than just tomorrow. Dev would
need to rehearse. Ruby's mind scrambled about trying to figure out how the first assistant director could possibly rearrange
the filming schedule that she'd so painstakingly put together...
and she'd need to organise to get Dev's costumes sorted. And
his hair cut. And...

'Should I sort out a medical appointment?' she asked. A
doctor's report for each actor was required for the film's insur-
ance—everything from a propensity for cold sores through to
a rampant base-jumping hobby had an impact on how much
it cost.

'No,' Paul said, very quickly.

Ruby tilted her head, studying him. But before she could ask
the obvious question, Paul explained. 'He saw a doctor in Sydney when he landed. It's all sorted.'

Okay. She supposed that made sense.

'Accommodation?'

God knew where she'd put him. The cast and crew had already overrun every bed and breakfast plus the local—rather
cosy—motel.

'He's taking over Todd's place.'

*Ouch.* Poor Todd. He must be devastated—this role was widely considered his big break. He was being touted as the *next big thing.*

Only to be trumped by the current big thing.

She felt for him, but, unfortunately, the brutality of this industry never failed to surprise her.

This was not a career for the faint-hearted, or anyone who needed the reassurance of a job associated with words like *stable,* or *reliable.*

Fortunately, that was exactly why Ruby loved it.

Ten minutes later, the four of them had a plan of sorts for the next few days, and she was closing Paul's office door behind her as Sal and Andy rushed back to their desks.

For a moment she stood, alone, in the cottage's narrow old hallway. Noise spilled from the two rooms that flanked it: music, clattering keyboards, multiple conversations and the occasional burst of laughter. A familiar hum peppered with familiar voices.

To her left was Sal and Andy's office. Ruby didn't need to glance through their open doorway to know they'd already be busily working away on the trestle-tables that served as their temporary desks. The office would also be perfectly organised—notepads and pens all lined up, that kind of thing—because it always was. They were in charge of the film's budget—so such meticulous organisation was definitely a plus.

In theory, given her own role, she should be just as meticulous.

Instead, to her right was the room that, amongst other things, housed her own trestle-table desk, many huge prone-to-collapsing mountains of paper and only the vaguest sense of order. Or so it appeared, anyway. She had to be ruthlessly organised—but she didn't need to be tidy to be effective.

The room was also the home of the three members of the production crew who reported to her—Cath, Rohan and Selena. Unsurprisingly, it was this room where the majority of noise was coming from, as this was the happening part of the production office where all day every day they managed actors and scripts and agents and vendors and anything or anyone else needed to keep the film going. It was crazy, demanding, noisy work—and with a deep breath, she walked straight into it.

As expected, three heads popped up as she stepped through the door.

'I guess you all heard the news?'

As one, they nodded.

'Was kind of awesome when he walked out on Paul,' said Rohan, leaning back in his chair. 'Paul came in here and ranted for a bit before charging out the door in pursuit. Guess he couldn't find him.'

Ruby didn't bother to correct him.

Instead, she spent a few minutes further explaining the situation, and assigning them all additional tasks. No one complained—quite the opposite, actually. No one saw the unexpected addition of a major star to *The Land* as anything but a very good thing. It meant they were all instantly working on a film far bigger than they'd signed up for. It was a fantastic opportunity.

She needed to remember that.

Ruby settled herself calmly into her chair, dropping her phone onto her desk—fortunately no worse for wear after hitting the dirt for the second time today. She tapped the mouse track pad on her laptop, and it instantly came to life, displaying the twenty-odd new emails that had arrived since she'd last had a chance to check her phone. Not too bad given it seemed like a lifetime since she'd been busily redistributing those last-minute script revisions to the actors.

She had a million and one things to do, and she really needed to get straight back to it. Instead, her attention skidded about the room—away from her glowing laptop screen and out of the window. There wasn't much of a view—just bare, flat countryside all the way to the ridge of mountains—but she wasn't really looking at it. Instead, her brain was still desperately trying to process the events of the past half-hour.

It didn't seem possible that she'd so recently been wrapped around one of the sexiest men in the world.

While covered in dirt.

And had had absolutely no idea.

Inwardly, she cringed for about the thousandth time.

*Work.* She reminded herself. She just needed to focus on work. Who cared if she'd accidentally flung herself into Devlin Cooper's arms? It was an accident, and it would never happen again—after all, she wasn't exactly anywhere near Dev Cooper's percentile on the drop-dead-gorgeousness spectrum. And he'd hardly had the opportunity to be attracted to her sparkling personality.

Despite everything, that thought made her smile.

No. This wasn't funny. This was serious. What if someone had seen them?

She stood up, as sitting still had become impossible. On the window sill sat the antenna of their oversized wireless Internet router, and she fiddled with it, just so it looked as if she were doing something constructive. On a location this remote, they'd had to bring their own broadband. And their own electricity, actually—provided by a large truck that's sole purpose was to power Unit Base, the name of this collection of trucks and people that were the beating heart of any feature film.

Her job was everything to her, and a spotless professional reputation was non-negotiable. She didn't get each job by circling ads in the paper, or subscribing to some online jobs database. In film, it was *all* about word of mouth.

And getting it on with an actor on set… Yeah. Not a good look.

On the plus side, Dev would have forgotten all about the slightly mussed-up, damp and dusty woman who'd gang-tackled him by now.

Now she just needed to forget about how he'd made her feel.

*I think some time away would do you good. Help you…move on.*

Well. Dev guessed this place was exactly what Veronica had

been hoping for. A painstakingly restored century-old cottage, complete with tasteful rear extension, was where he'd be calling home for the immediate future. It offered uninterrupted views to the surrounding mountains and everything!

It was also a kilometre or so out of town, had no immediate neighbours, and, thanks to his agent, a live-in minder.

*Security.* Officially.

Right.

He needed a drink. He'd walked off a trans-Pacific flight less than eight hours ago. Even travelling first class couldn't make a flight from LA to Sydney pleasant. Add a four-hour road trip with Graeme-the-security-guy and was it surprising he'd had a short fuse today?

*Please play nice with Paul.*

This in his latest email from his agent.

He shouldn't have been surprised that the producer had already started updating Veronica on his behaviour. He'd even learnt exactly what she'd held over the prickly producer—knowledge of an on-set indiscretion with an aspiring actress ten years previously.

What a cliché.

And how like his agent to file that little titbit away for future use.

Good for her. Although he didn't let himself consider how exactly he'd got to this point—to where landing roles depended on tactics and calling in favours.

Dev had dragged an overstuffed armchair onto the rear decking. On his lap was the script for *The Land,* not that he could read it now the sun had long set.

Beside him, on one of the chairs from the wooden outdoor setting he'd decided looked too uncomfortable, was his dinner. Cold, barely touched salmon with fancy-looking vegetables. God knew where Veronica had sourced his fridge and freezer full of food from—he'd long ago got used to her magic touch.

Although the lack of alcohol hadn't gone unnoticed. *Subtle, Veronica.*

But she was wrong. Booze wasn't his problem.

He'd have to send good old Graeme down to the local bottle shop tomorrow or something.

But for now, he needed a drink.

Leaving the script on the chair, he walked through the house, and then straight out of the front door. Graeme was staying in a separate, smaller worker's cottage closer to the road, but Dev didn't bother to stop and let him know where he was going.

He'd been micro-managed quite enough. He could damn well walk into town and get a drink without having to ask anyone's approval.

So he did.

Walking felt good. For once he wasn't on the lookout for the paparazzi, as, for now, no one knew he was here. His unexpected arrival in Australia would have been noticed, of course, and it wouldn't take long before the photographers descended. But they hadn't, not just yet.

He had no idea what time it was, just that it was dark. Really dark—there were certainly no streetlights, and the moon was little more than a sliver.

His boots were loud on the bitumen, loud enough to disturb a group of sheep that scattered abruptly behind their barbed-wire fence. Further from the road nestled the occasional house, their windows glowing squares of bright amid the darkness.

Soon he'd hit the main street, a short stretch of shops, a petrol station, a library. He hadn't paid much attention when he'd arrived—a mix of jet lag and general lack of interest—but now he took the time to look, slowing his walk down to something approaching an amble.

Most of the town was silent—blinds were drawn, shops were certainly closed this late. But the one obvious exception was the pub, which, like much of the town, was old and stately—perched two storeys high on a corner, complete with a wide wooden balcony overlooking the street. Tonight the balcony was empty, but noise and music spilled from the open double doors. He quickened his pace, suddenly over all this peace and quiet.

It was packed. Completely—people were crammed at the bar, around the scattered tall tables and also the lower coffee tables with their surrounding couches and ottomans. It was the cast and crew, obviously, who'd taken the pub over. He'd seen for himself that Lucyville didn't exactly have a happening restaurant strip. This was the only place to drink—and eat—so here they all were.

The pub didn't go quiet or anything at his arrival, but he noticed that he'd been noticed.

It was a sensation that had once been a novelty, had later annoyed him to the verge of anger—and now that he just accepted. He could hardly complain…he was living his dream and all that. *Right.*

He found a narrow gap at the bar, resting an arm on the polished surface. The local bartender caught his eye and did a double take, but played it cool. In his experience, most people did, with the occasional crazy person the exception rather than the rule. The paparazzi were far more an issue than Joe Public—no question.

He ordered his drink, although he wasn't quick to raise the glass to his lips once it was placed in front of him. Maybe it wasn't the drink he'd needed, but the walk, the bite of the crisp night air in his lungs?

Mentally he shook his head. Veronica would love that, be all smug and sure she was right to send him to Australia—while Dev wasn't so certain.

What was that saying? Same crap—different bucket.

His lips tightened into a humourless smile.

He turned, propping his weight against the bar. As he took a sip of his beer he surveyed the large room. It was a surprisingly eclectic place, with funky modern furniture managing to blend with the polished ancient floorboards and what—he was pretty sure—was the original bar. Not quite the backwater pub he'd been imagining.

The lighting was soft and the atmosphere relaxed, with the dress code more jeans than cocktail.

One particular pair of jeans caught his eye. Dark blue denim, moulded over elegantly crossed legs—right in the corner of the pub, the one farthest from him.

Yet his attention had still been drawn to her, to Ruby.

Only when he saw her did he realise he'd been looking for her—searching her out in the crowd.

He watched her as she talked to her friends, wine glass in hand. To all appearances she was focused completely on the conversation taking place around her. She was quick to smile, and quick to interject and trigger a laugh from others. But despite all that, there was the slightest hint of tension to her body.

She knew he was watching her.

Beside her, another woman leant over and whispered in her ear, throwing glances in his direction as she did.

Ruby shook her head emphatically—and Dev was no lip-reader, but he'd put money on the fact she'd just said: *No, he's not.*

Accordingly, he straightened, pushing himself away from the bar.

He liked nothing more than to prove someone wrong.

*'He's coming over!'*

Every single cell in Ruby's body—already tingling at what she'd told herself was Dev's imagined attention—careened up to high alert.

'It's no big deal. We met before.' She shrugged deliberately. 'Maybe he doesn't know anyone else yet.'

'*When* did you meet him?' Selena asked, wide-eyed. 'And how am I not aware of this?'

Ruby's words were carefully cool. 'When I was walking back to the office. We barely said two words.'

That, at least, was completely true.

Her friend had lost interest, anyway, her eyes trained on Dev's tall frame as he approached.

'Mind if I join you?'

Dev's voice was as gorgeously deep and perfect as in every

one of his movies. Not for the first time, Ruby questioned her intelligence—how on *earth* had she not recognised him?

With a deep breath, she lifted her gaze to meet his. He stood on the other side of the table before them: Ruby, Selena and a couple of girls from the art department. They'd been having an after-dinner drink, all comfy on one big plush purple L-shaped couch—now the other three were alternating between carefully feigned disinterest and slack-jawed adoration. Unheard of for professionals in the film industry who dealt with stars every day.

But, she supposed, this *was* Devlin Cooper.

Everyone else appeared struck dumb and incapable of answering his question—but Dev was looking at her, anyway.

To say *yes, she did mind,* was tempting—but more trouble than it was worth. So, reluctantly, she shook her head. 'Not at all.'

Dev stepped past the table and sat next to Ruby.

With great effort, she resisted the temptation to scoot away. Unlike the three other women at the table, she was *not* going to treat Dev any differently from anyone else on the cast and crew.

No adoring gaze. No swooning.

So, although he was close—and the couch definitely no longer felt *big*—she didn't move. Didn't betray one iota of the unexpected heat that had flooded her body.

'You shouldn't be embarrassed,' he said, low enough that only she could hear.

'Why would you think I am?'

Casually, she brought her glass to her lips.

Did he notice the slightest trembling of her fingers?

She risked a glance out of the corner of her eye.

He watched her with a familiar expression. Confident. Knowing.

*Arrogant.*

She sighed. 'Fine. I *was* embarrassed. Let me think: running into one of the world's most famous men, while covered in dirt and looking like crap—*and* then not even recognising said star…' Ruby tilted her head, as if considering her words.

'Yes, I think that pretty much sums it up. I reckon a good nine out of ten on my embarrassment scale.'

He didn't even blink. If anything he looked amused.

A different type of tension stiffened her body. Yes, her stupid, apparently one-track body was all a-flutter with Mr Hot Movie Star so near. But now she could add affronted frustration into the mix.

She didn't know what she wanted—an apology? Sympathy? A *yeah, I can see how that might've sucked for you,* even?

'But you only gave it a nine,' he said, placing his beer on one of the discarded coasters on the table.

'A what?' she asked, confused.

'On your *embarrassment scale,*' he said. 'Only a nine...' He looked contemplative for a moment, then leant closer, close enough that it was impossible for her to look anywhere but straight into his eyes. 'So I was wondering—what would've made it a ten?'

Immediately, and most definitely without her volition, her gaze dropped from his piercing blue eyes to his lips.

Lips that immediately quirked into a grin the second she realised what she'd done. What she'd just revealed.

He leant even closer again. The touch of his breath on the sensitive skin beneath her ear made her shiver.

Logically she knew she should pull away, that she should laugh loudly, or say something—*do something*—to stop this way too intimate moment. A moment she knew was being watched—and if people were watching, then people would gossip.

And there were few things Ruby hated more than gossip: being the subject of *or* the proliferation of it.

For she had far too much experience in the former. Enough to last a lifetime.

'You know,' he said, his words somehow vibrating through her body—her stupidly frozen body, 'I don't think anyone's ever been embarrassed when I've kissed them. In fact, I'm quite sure I've never received a complaint.'

*Oh, she was so sure he hadn't...*

'I was working,' she said, each word stiff and awkward.

So he had been going to kiss her—and she realised it was no surprise. Some part of her had known, had known there was no other way to interpret those few minutes, even though her rational self had had so much difficulty believing it.

But knowing she hadn't imagined it and *wanting* it to have happened were entirely different things.

'I kiss people all the time at work,' he replied, with a spark of humour in his eyes that was new, and unexpected.

Ruby found herself forcing back a grin, surprised at the shift in atmosphere. 'It's a bit different when you're following a script.'

'Ah,' he said, his lips quirking up. 'Not always.'

Now she laughed out loud, shaking her head. 'I bet.'

Their laughter should've diluted the tension, but if anything the air between them thickened.

With great effort, Ruby turned away slightly, taking a long, long sip of her wine—not that she tasted a thing. Her brain whirred at a million miles an hour—or maybe it wasn't whirring at all, considering all it seemed to be able to do was wonder how Dev's lips would feel against hers...

*No.*

'Well,' she said, finally, her gaze swinging back to meet his. Firmly. 'Script or otherwise, I don't kiss anyone at work.' She paused, then added in a tone that was perfectly matter-of-fact and perfectly polite, 'It's late. I need to go. It was nice to talk to you when I wasn't covered in dirt. And I'm sorry about your T-shirt.'

Ruby stood up and placed her wine glass on the table with movements she hoped looked casual. She glanced at her friends, who all stared at her wide-eyed.

She'd need to set them all straight tomorrow. Dev Cooper was so not her type it was ridiculous.

She managed some goodbyes, hooked her handbag over her shoulder, and then headed for the door. The entire time she risked barely a glance at Dev, but thankfully he didn't move.

Not that she expected him to follow her. She wasn't an idiot. He could have any woman in this bar. Pretty much any woman in the *world*.

For some reason she'd piqued his interest, but she had no doubt it was fleeting— the novelty of the crazy dusty coffee lady or something.

Outside, the early October evening was cool, and so Ruby hugged herself, rubbing her goose-pimpling arms. She was staying at the town motel, not even a hundred-metre walk down the main street.

Only a few steps in that direction, she heard someone else leave the bar behind her, their boots loud on the wooden steps.

It was difficult, but as it turned out not impossible, to keep her eyes pointed forward. It could be anyone.

'Ruby.'

Or it could be Dev.

She should've sighed—and been annoyed or disappointed. But instead her tummy lightened and she realised she was smiling.

*Ugh.*

She kept on walking.

In moments, following the thud of loping strides on bitumen, he was beside her, keeping pace with her no-nonsense walk. For long seconds, they walked in silence.

*Really* uncomfortable, charged silence.

'So—' he began.

'This isn't an act, you know,' Ruby interrupted. 'I'm not playing hard to get. I'm not interested.'

He gave a surprised bark of laughter. 'Right.'

Ruby slowed to a stop, her whole body stiff with annoyance. She stood beneath a street lamp that illuminated the gate to the *Lucyville Motel* and its chipped and faded sign.

'You sound so sure,' she said. 'That's incredibly presumptuous.'

'Am I wrong?'

Ruby sighed. 'Does every woman you meet *really* collapse into a pathetic puddle of lust at your feet?'

'You did,' he pointed out.

Her cheeks went hot, but Ruby hoped her blush was hidden in the shadows.

'I was light-headed. Confused. Definitely not myself.' She paused for emphasis. 'Trust me. You're wasting your time. *I'm not interested.*'

A little, nagging voice at the back of her mind kept trying to distract her: *Oh, my God, it's Devlin Cooper! The movie star!*

Maybe that was why she didn't turn and walk away immediately.

'You're serious?'

His genuine confusion was rather endearing. Unbelievably conceited, but endearing.

'Uh-huh,' she said, nodding. 'Is that so hard to believe?'

She knew he was about to say *yes,* when he seemed to realise what he was about to say. Instead, his grin, revealed by the streetlight, was bemused.

He shifted his weight to one leg, and crossed his arms. He still wore the same sexy ancient-looking jeans from before, but he'd traded his ruined T-shirt for its twin in navy blue. The action of crossing his arms only further defined the muscles of his forearms and biceps.

It also defined the unexpectedly sharp angles of his elbows and the lack of flesh beyond his lean musculature.

She knew she was not the only person to notice. The film set's grapevine was, as always, efficient, creating all sorts of theories for his unexpected weight loss.

*Did you hear? His girlfriend left him—you know? That model.*

*I heard it's drugs. Ice. He's been photographed at every club in Hollywood.*

*He's sick. I know! That's why he's come back to Australia. To spend time with his family.*

Not that Ruby believed a word of it. Gossip, in her experience, was about as accurate and true to life as the typical air-brushed movie poster.

*What happened to you?*

But of course the question remained unsaid. It was none of her business.

Dev studied Ruby in the limited moonlight. His gaze traced the angles of her cheekbones, the straightness of her nose and the firm set of her determined mouth.

*Lord, she was...pretty?*

*Yes. Hot?*

*Yes.*

But that, in itself, wasn't *it*...

*And different. Very, very, different.*

That was why he was standing out in the deserted, frankly cold, street. That was why he'd done something he couldn't remember doing in a very long time: he'd chased after a woman.

It was an unexpected novelty.

He liked it.

For the first time in months something—*someone*—had caught his interest. Ruby Bell—the cute little production co-ordinator on a dinky little Aussie film—intrigued him.

'So what is it, exactly, that you find so repulsive about me?' he asked.

She shrugged, dismissing his question. 'I don't know you well enough to form an opinion—repulsive or otherwise.'

'But isn't that why you're not interested?' he asked. Not that he believed her statement to be true. 'Because you think you know me?'

From his movies, from his interviews, from the rubbish they published in glossy magazines and newspapers that should know better. Devlin Cooper the star—the persona. Not the person.

She shook her head. 'This is the longest conversation we've ever had. How could I possibly know you?'

He blinked. She'd just surprised him—for the second time tonight. The first time had been walking out of that pub just as he'd been imagining how good she'd look in that big wrought-iron bed back in his cottage.

'Ah. So, it's not me, it's *you,*' he said, playing with that clichéd line. Then, for the first time, the blindingly obvious occurred to him. She wore no ring, but… 'You have a boyfriend?'

'Oh *no,*' she said, her voice higher pitched and definitely firmer than before. 'Absolutely not.' She shook her head for emphasis.

Okay, now he was completely confused. And surprised, yet again.

Ruby wasn't following any script he'd heard before. How many women had he flirted with in his life? Some fawned, but most were clever, witty and/or sarcastic. But, he realised, normally he already sort of knew what was going to be said next—where the conversation, or the evening, was heading. In itself, that was part of the fun. The dance of words before the inevitable.

But this was undeniably fun, too.

'You think *I* want a relationship?' he asked, heavy with irony. 'Scared I'm going to want to settle down, get married…'

She laughed. 'No.'

'So what, exactly, is the problem? From where I stand this all seems pretty perfect. We obviously both like each other…' he held up his hand when she went to disagree '…we're both single *and* we're both stuck in an isolated country town for the next month or so. Is that not a match made in heaven?'

Ruby rolled her eyes. 'Weren't you listening back at the pub? I don't do relationships at work. *Especially* with actors. I'm not interested in becoming known as Dev Cooper's next conquest. *Très* professional, no?'

'I wasn't suggesting we make out on set, you know,' he said dryly. Ruby raised an eyebrow. 'I promise.'

She shook her head. 'Film sets are full of gossip. And my professional reputation is everything to me.' She paused, then repeated her words, almost to herself. '*Everything* to me.'

Commitment to your job—sure, Dev got that. Until very

recently, he'd practically been the poster child for the concept. But—really? Liaisons between crew and actors were not a crime, and far from uncommon. The world would not end.

But apparently, according to Ruby, it would. It was clear in every tense line of her expression.

They stood in silence for a while. Dev wasn't entirely sure what would happen now.

He was out of his element: he'd just been rejected. Inarguably so.

But rather than shrugging, comfortable in the knowledge that he had many other options, he found himself...disappointed.

And reluctant to walk away.

'Anyway,' Ruby said in a different, crisper, tone. 'You have an early call tomorrow morning, and I need to be at the office an hour earlier. So, goodnight.'

With that, she turned on her heel and walked away. Out on the street he watched as she walked down the motel driveway to an apartment on the bottom floor of the two-storey building. Then he waited until she located her key in her oversized handbag, unlocked the door, and disappeared inside.

Then he waited, alone on the street, some more.

It was odd. All he knew about this woman was that she was blonde, and cute, and felt pretty amazing in his arms.

What was the attraction? Why did he care?

How was she different from the many other women who he'd met in the past few, dark, blurry months? Months where no one had stood out. Where *nothing* had stood out.

Where when, a few weeks after Estelle had left, he'd attempt to chat to a woman—but his mind would drift. Where he'd find himself with suddenly no idea what had been said in the preceding conversation.

And didn't care at all.

*That* was why she was different.

Ruby pushed his buttons. Triggered reactions that had been lying dormant. Attraction. Laughter. Surprise.

So simple.

# CHAPTER THREE

A LOUD BANG jolted Dev out of his dream.

He blinked, his eyes attempting to adjust to the darkness.

*What time is it?*

He lay on his back in the centre of his bed. Naked but for his boxer shorts, the sheets and quilt long ago kicked off and onto the floor.

He remembered feeling restless. As if he needed to get up and go for a run. Or for a drive. Or just *out*. Somewhere. Away.

*Where?*

It wasn't the first morning he'd asked that question.

Another bang. Even louder than before. Or maybe just now he was more awake?

The thick cloak of sleep was slowly lifting, and his eyes were adjusting.

It wasn't completely dark in here. Light was managing to push through the heavy curtains that he'd checked and double checked were fully closed the night before.

He shivered, and only then did he register it was cold. He had a vague recollection of turning off the heater on the wall. Why? The nights were still cool.

Obviously it had made sense at the time.

Another bang.

The door. Someone was knocking on the door.

*What time is it?*

He rolled onto his side, reaching across the bed, knocking aside a small cardboard box and a blister pack so he could see the glowing green numbers of the clock on the bedside table. There were none. He didn't remember turning it off, but it didn't surprise him that he had.

He had set that alarm last night, though. And the alarm on his phone. He had an early call today. He'd been going to get up early to read through today's rehearsal scenes.

*Bang, bang, bang.*

Dev swung his legs over the side of the bed in slow motion, then shoved himself to his feet. Three sluggish steps later, he discovered his mobile phone when he kicked it in the gloom, and it clattered against his closed bedroom door.

By feel he found the light switch on the wall, then rubbed his eyes against the sudden brightness.

His phone located, he picked it up to check the time. He pressed the button to illuminate the screen, but it took a while for his eyes to focus.

*How long ago had he taken the sleepers?*

He still felt drugged, still shrouded in the sleep that the tablets had finally delivered.

Seven thirty-two a.m. *Why hadn't his alarm gone off?*

*Bang, bang, BANG, BANG, BANG!*

'Mr Cooper? Are you awake?'

*Graeme.* Of course.

He twisted the old brass doorknob to his room, then padded up the wide hallway. Morning light streamed through the stained-glass panels of the front door around the over-inflated shape that was Dev's warden.

He took his time, his gaze trained on his phone as he checked that his alarm had been set. It had. So it had gone off.

Presumably he'd then thrown it across the room, given where he'd found it.

It shouldn't surprise him, but that wasn't what he'd meant to do today. Last night he'd felt…different. Today was supposed to be different. Different from the past ninety-seven days.

*How specific.*

He smiled a humourless smile. Who knew his subconscious kept such meticulous records?

The thing was, today wasn't the first day that was supposed to be different. But then, they never were.

Graeme was still hammering away at the door, but Dev didn't bother to call out, to reassure him that his charge was in fact awake and not passed out in an alcoholic stupor or worse—whatever it was that Veronica was so sure that Dev was doing.

In some ways Dev wished he could apply a label to himself. *Alcoholic. Drug addict.*

But he was neither of those things.

*What about his sleepers?*

He dismissed the idea instantly. No. They were prescribed, and temporary.

Definitely temporary.

Hollywood wasn't the shiny happy place people imagined. It was full of egos fuelled by intense insecurity. Stars that shone while simultaneously harbouring the intense fear that their light could be extinguished at any moment: at the mercy of their next role, of public opinion, of the whims of studio executives…always others.

So little control. It was no surprise that so many teetered over the edge. Fell into…*something*. It was just the label that changed.

But Dev had no label.

He just had…nothing.

He opened the door while Graeme was mid-knock. The other man started, then took a step back, clearing his throat.

'We need to leave in five minutes, Mr Cooper.'

Dev scratched his belly and nodded. He left the door open as he turned and headed for the bathroom. Four minutes later he was showered and had dragged on a T-shirt, hoodie and jeans. He pulled the front door shut and locked it as Graeme hovered nearby—impatiently.

When he was growing up, his mum had done the same thing—although not as silently. She'd tap her foot as she waited for her youngest and most disorganised son. The other two boys generally already in the family Mercedes, all perfect and consistently smug. *Hurry up, Dev! You're making us late!*

And just because he'd been that kind of kid, he'd taken his own sweet time.

This was why he didn't like having drivers. Why he insisted on driving himself to and from set for every single one of his many movies. He was a grown adult with a driver's licence—why the hell did he need a chauffeur? He was far from a child any more; he didn't need to be directed and herded and hurried. He was a professional—always on time. Always reliable.

Until now.

Today was not the first time he'd slept through his alarm. Or, of more concern: he'd heard it, switched it off, and deliberately rolled over and gone back to sleep. More than once the action of even setting his alarm had felt impossible. Weirdly overwhelming.

Other nights sleep had never come. Where his thoughts had echoed so loudly in his skull that even drugs had no impact. And those days he'd watched time tick by, watched his call time slip by, and switched his phone to silent as his agent, or the producer, or even the director would call, and call and call...

That had got him fired from his last film. The contract was pulled on his next after whispers had begun to spread.

So here he was.

And although he hadn't meant to—because of course he never *meant to*—it was happening again.

Without Graeme, he'd still be in bed, time passing. He hated that.

He sat in the back of the black four-wheel drive, staring unseeing out of the darkly tinted windows. Beside him was an insulated bag that Graeme said contained his breakfast, but he wasn't hungry.

*You're not welcome here.*

Closer to Unit Base, the bitumen road ended, and the car bounced amongst potholes on the wide gravel track. The irregular movements did nothing to jolt that memory. How long ago had it been? Ten years? No, longer. Fourteen. He'd been nine-teen, home late—really late—after a night out with his mates.

He hadn't been drunk, but alcohol had still buzzed through his bloodstream.

*'Where the hell have you been?'*

*His father stood at the very top of the staircase that rose majestically from the lobby of the Coopers' sprawling Sydney upper-north-shore residence. His mum had left a lamp on for him, and the soft light threw shadows onto his dad's pyjamas.*

*'Out,' he said. Grunted, really.*

*'You have an exam tomorrow.'*

*Dev shrugged. He'd had no intention of turning up. He dumped his keys on a sideboard, and began to head past the stairs to the hallway that led to his bedroom, tossing his reply over his shoulder. 'I'm not going to be an accountant, Dad.'*

*Patrick Cooper's slippered feet were still heavy as they thumped down each carpeted step. Dev didn't pause. He'd heard it all before.*

*He'd gone to uni to please his mum, only. But three semesters in, and he'd had it. He knew where his life was leading, and it didn't involve a calculator and a navy-blue suit.*

*His father picked up his pace behind him, but Dev remained deliberately slow. Unworried. Casual.*

*He was unsurprised to feel the weight of his father's hand on his shoulder. But when Dev kept walking, the way Patrick wrenched at his shoulder, spinning him around...yes, that shocked him.*

*His arm came up, his fingers forming into a fist. It was automatic, the result of the crowd he'd been hanging with, the occasional push and shove at a pub. He wouldn't have hit his dad—he knew that. Knew that.*

*But his dad thought he would. He could see it in his eyes, that belief of what Dev was capable of. Or rather, the lack of belief.*

*Dev saw the fist coming. Maybe he didn't have enough time to move, maybe he did—either way he stood stock still.*

*His father's knuckles connected with his jaw with enough*

*force to twist his body and push him back into the wall. And for it to hurt. A lot. He tasted blood, felt it coating his teeth.*

*But he remained standing, half expecting more.*

*But that wasn't going to happen. Instead, his dad fell to his knees, holding his fist in his other hand.*

*For long moments, it was perfectly silent. It was as if neither of them could breathe.*

*Then a clatter on the stairs heralded his mum's arrival. She gasped as she came into view, then ran to Patrick, kneeling beside him and wrapping her arm around his shoulder.*

*She looked up at Dev, her gaze beseeching. 'What happened here?'*

*'I'm quitting uni, Mum,' he said. 'I'm an actor.' His whole face ached as he spoke, but the words were strong and clear.*

*'That's a dream, not a career.' His dad didn't say the words, he spat them out.*

*'It's what I want.' What he needed to do.*

*'I won't support you, Devlin. I won't stand by and watch you fail—'*

*'I know that,' he interrupted. How well he knew that.*

*That his family wouldn't support him. That not one of them believed he'd succeed.*

*'Good,' his dad said. 'Then leave. You're not welcome here.'*

*It didn't surprise him. It had been coming for so long. His mum, the only reason he'd stayed, looked stricken.*

*He nodded. Then walked back up the hall the way he'd come.*

*He didn't say a word. No dramatic farewell. No parting words.*

*But he knew he'd never be back.*

Graeme slowed to a stop at a paddock gate before a security guard waved them through. A dirt track wound its way over the smallest of hills, and then they were amongst the trailers that sprawled across Unit Base. The set was vast—yesterday the producer had told him it was the corner of a working sheep and canola farm. It spread across the almost perfectly flat countryside, overlooked by an irregular ridge of mountains. Yesterday, Dev's gaze had explored a landscape dotted with eucalyptus, rectangular fields of lurid yellow canola and paddocks desperately trying to hold onto winter hints of green. Today it was just a blur.

But something caught his eye as Graeme parked beside his trailer. Through the car window he followed that splash of colour with his eyes.

A woman in a bright blue dress, more like an oversized jumper, really, was barrelling rapidly along the path towards him. She was unmistakeable, her mop of choppy blonde hair shining like pale gold in the sun.

Ruby Bell.

She'd slipped his mind as soon as his nightly battle for sleep had begun, but now she'd sprung right back to the front, in full Technicolor.

He knew what she was: a distraction. A temporary focus.

But one he needed.

He was here. And thanks to Graeme—via Veronica—he'd be here on set each day, right on time. But right now he couldn't make himself care about the film, about his role.

Oh, he'd perform, right on cue, and to the best of his ability—as much as he was capable of, anyway.

But he wouldn't care. Couldn't care. Any more.

How was that for irony?

With his death, his father had—finally—got his way.

He was on time—just.

Ruby watched as he got out of the car, all loose-limbed and casual.

In contrast, she felt as stiff as a board. She kept making herself take deep, supposedly calming breaths as she gripped the papers in her hand, and reminding herself that she could do this—that this was her job.

It was just incredibly unfortunate it was *her* job. She shouldn't have been surprised, really, when Paul had taken her aside this morning and made her task clear: keep Dev on time and on schedule.

All the Dev-related rumours—a new one this morning hinting at a lot more than tardiness—should've made Paul's request a no-brainer.

Yet, she'd actually *gasped* when Paul had told her, and then had to make up some unfortunate lie about swallowing a fly, accompanied with much poorly acted faux coughing.

Once *again* Dev had managed to short-circuit her brain.

Because the task of babysitting talent was a perfectly typical request for the production co-ordinator, who, amongst other things, was responsible for organising actors' lives while on location.

Actors were notoriously unreliable. Putting together the call sheet was one thing—having anyone actually stick to it was something else entirely.

As she watched Dev watch her, a hip propped against his car, it was suddenly clear that getting him to do anything—at all—that she wanted could prove difficult.

This was not the man who'd smiled at her in the Lucyville pub last night, or who'd teased her on the street. Neither was he the man with the smug expression and the coffee stains on his shirt.

This man was completely unreadable.

'Good morning!' she managed, quite well, she thought.

He nodded sharply.

She thrust the portion of the script he'd be rehearsing today in his direction. 'Here are today's sides,' she said.

He took them from her with barely a glance. It was as if he was waiting for something—to figure something out.

'And?' he asked.

'I'll be taking you to be fitted by Costume, first,' she said. 'Then Hair and Make-up would like to see you prior to your rehearsal.'

'And you'll be escorting me?'

Ruby swallowed. 'Yes. I'll be looking after you today.'

It was immediately obvious that was the wrong thing to say. Something flickered in his gaze.

'I have my call sheet. I know where I need to be. I don't require hand-holding.'

'Paul asked that I…'

His glare told her that was another mistake, so she let the words drift off.

Then tried again. 'Mr Cooper, I'm here to help you.'

Somehow, those words changed everything, as if she'd flicked a switch. From defensive, and shuttered, his expression was suddenly…*considering?*

But Ruby didn't think for a moment that he'd simply accepted she was just doing her job. This was different—more calculating.

'Here to help,' he said to himself, as if he was turning the words over in his head.

Then he smiled, a blinding, movie-star smile.

And Ruby had absolutely no idea what had just happened.

It was dumb—really dumb—that he was surprised.

Heck—if *he* were the producer on this film, he'd have done the same thing.

It didn't mean he had to be happy about it.

He'd never been this kind of actor before; he'd never needed to be led around on some imaginary leash. Lord—he'd thought Graeme was bad enough.

And, of course, it had to be Ruby in charge of him.

It was a total waste of her time, of course. On set, he *was* fine, and not the fine he told himself he was whenever he was convincing himself to fall asleep.

He followed just slightly behind her. She was talking, quite rapidly, but he really wasn't paying much attention.

She was nervous, for sure. He *did* like that.

And he *did* like how the tables had turned. Last night she'd called the shots. Today—it was him.

Juvenile? Yes.

Fun? He thought so.

So Paul thought he needed looking after? No problem.

He'd be that actor, then. The ridiculous type who wanted everything in their trailer periwinkle blue, or who would only drink a particular brand of mineral water—not available locally, of course.

He'd prove Paul right—and irritate the self-important producer in the process.

A small win.

And it would push Ruby's buttons too—trigger that flare of response he'd already witnessed a handful of times, and was eager to experience again.

Dev smiled, just as Ruby stopped before a hulking white trailer and turned to face him.

Her forehead wrinkled as she studied him, as if she knew something was up.

He just smiled even more broadly.

Yes, this was an *excellent* idea.

Completely focused on the email she was reading—Arizona's agent, confirming that his client was available to attend an opening in Sydney the following week—Ruby picked up her loudly ringing phone from her overflowing desk without glancing at the screen.

'Ruby Bell.'

*'Ruby.'* A pause. 'Good afternoon.'

There was no point pretending she didn't recognise that voice. Her disloyal body practically shivered in recognition.

'How can I help, Mr Cooper?' she asked with determined brightness, her eyes not wavering from her laptop screen, although the email's words and sentences had somehow become an indecipherable alphabet jumble.

Even so, she tapped randomly on her keyboard. For her benefit, mostly, a reminder that she was a busy film professional who received phone calls from famous actors All The Time. She was working. This was her job.

No need for her mouth to go dry or for her cheeks to warm.

'Well,' he said, 'I have a problem.'

'Yes?' she prompted, with some trepidation.

He'd been scrupulously polite this morning. Allowed her to take him from appointment to appointment. He'd chatted inanely about the weather, and charmed every person she introduced him to.

But...

Occasionally he'd slant a glance in her direction that meant... she had absolutely no idea.

It wasn't about last night any more. She was sure. No question he'd long lost interest in perfectly average Ruby Bell by now.

Definitely.

'I can't figure out how to use the wireless Internet in my cottage.'

Oh. Her skin went hotter. Of course his phone call had nothing to do with her. *Of course it didn't.*

Hadn't she told him—what, three hours ago?—to call her any time?

Ruby took a deep breath. She really needed to pull herself together.

'I'm sorry to hear that, Mr Cooper,' she replied. 'I'll get that sorted for you straight away.'

'Appreciate it,' he said, and then the phone went silent.

Carefully, she placed her phone back onto her desk, darting her gaze about the room. She half expected everyone to be staring at her, to *know* exactly how flustered she was, despite all her efforts to not be. To somehow *know* that Dev had all but propositioned her outside the salubrious Lucyville Motel, even though she'd told her intrigued friends she hadn't seen Dev after she'd left the pub last night.

To *know* that chaperoning Dev around set this morning was stupidly difficult, despite her constant mental reminders that it was *so not a big deal,* and that she *was a professional* and *they were both adults* who could work together professionally despite the running-into-him thing, or the not-recognising-him thing, or saying-no-to-the-most-eligible-bachelor-in-the-world thing.

But no. Rohan worked quietly at his desk. Cath stood in front of the large whiteboard calendar, studying it with fierce concentration and a marker in her hand. Selena wasn't even in the room—she was out, busily signing in extras.

Ruby bit back a sigh. She was being ridiculous.

So she tilted her head left to right, rolled her shoulders a few times, wriggled her toes—and told herself she was cool, and calm and collected. *She was!*

And then she got back to work.

Less than an hour later, Dev stepped out onto the deck at the back of his cottage, sliding shut the glass door firmly behind him. Inside, one of the more junior members of the production office was busily fixing his 'broken' Internet.

He pressed his phone to his ear.

'Ruby Bell,' she said when she answered, sounding as brisk and polite as she had earlier.

'Ms Bell,' he said, ever so politely, 'thank you. I now have Internet.'

Well, he would once the guy inside realised the router had been unplugged.

'Oh, good,' she said. There was a beat or two of silence, and then she added, 'Can I help you with anything else?'

Dev's lips curled upwards.

'Yes, actually. I need a new hire car.'

'Is something wrong with your current car?' she asked.

*No.* Assuming you disregarded the fact that he had Graeme-the-warden driving him everywhere. Dev's suggestion he drive himself to set from now on was not warmly received. If Dev had access to the keys he never would've asked at all.

*That* would've made Veronica happy. About as happy as she'd been in her email this morning, and her many missed calls on his phone.

Turned out Graeme had passed on his trip to the pub.

*Security—my arse.*

'My current car is too…' he paused, as if in deep contemplation '…*feminine.*'

'Pardon me?'

'Too *feminine,*' he repeated.

The line remained silent. Was Ruby smiling? Frowning?

'I see,' she said, after a while. 'I'm sorry you find your *black four-wheel drive* so unsuitable. Can you explain to me what it is that you dislike about the car?'

There was nothing overtly discourteous in her tone—quite the opposite, in fact. Yet Dev heard the subtlest of subtle bites. He liked it.

'It's the upholstery,' he said. 'It has pink thread in it.'

'Ah,' she said, as if this were actually a valid complaint. 'Fair enough. Don't worry, I'll have a new car to you by tonight.'

'At the latest,' he said, just like one of the many delusionally self-important actors he knew who made these types of requests.

'Not a problem, Mr Cooper.'

'Appreciated, Ms Bell.'

Then he hung up with a smile on his face.

Ruby sat alone in her office, the Top 40 show on the radio her only company. It was late—really late, and she'd sent everyone else home fifteen minutes earlier.

But she had to get everything done—well, an hour ago, really—but Dev had really screwed up her day.

Losing Rohan for an hour to fix Dev's wireless had meant she'd had to run the call sheet alone; and unfortunately the runner she'd assigned to sort out the new hire car was young, and new, and seemed to ask Ruby a question every five minutes. Then, of course, there'd been Dev's email, asking for directions to every amenity in Lucyville. After she'd gritted her teeth and carefully replied to it—and therefore losing another thirty minutes—he'd blithely replied with one word: *Thanks.*

Thanks!

She'd silently screamed.

She'd had no idea Dev was like this—normally talent of the high-maintenance variety came with clear advance warning via the industry grapevine. Put two people who worked in film together, and guaranteed that stuff like 'Dev-Cooper-thought-his-car-was-too-girly' got talked about.

But—until the last twenty-four hours—she'd never heard a negative word about Devlin Cooper.

Oohing and ahhing about how he was *just* as gorgeous in real life—which she now knew to be true—yes, she'd heard that. But unreasonable, prima-donna carryings-on? Not a whisper.

Her phone rang, vibrating against the pile of sides—the scenes being filmed the next day—it rested upon

Of course it was Dev, and reluctantly Ruby swiped her finger across the screen to answer the call.

'Mr Cooper,' Ruby said, setting the phone to loudspeaker so she could continue to work on the latest updates to a transport schedule. She was *not* going to let Dev distract her. 'How can I help you?'

'I was wondering,' he said, not sounding at all apologetic for calling so late, 'if you could recommend anywhere good to eat in Sydney.'

Ruby's jaw clenched. *Really?*

'Was it for a particular occasion?'

'A date,' he said. 'This weekend.'

Ruby determinedly ignored that irrational, disappointed kick she felt in her belly.

'Sure,' she managed to squeeze out. 'I'll get someone onto that for you tomorrow.'

'But I was hoping you could offer some personal recommendations.'

Had his voice become slightly deeper? More intimate?

*Don't be an idiot!* She typed the words on screen for good measure; maybe *then* it would sink in.

'Well,' she said, 'if you were thinking fine dining, then you probably can't go wrong with *Tetsuya's,* on Kent Street. Or *Quay,* at The Rocks.'

'Personal favourites?'

'No. I've heard the food is amazing, but I generally prefer somewhere a little less formal. Where people talk and laugh loudly and you don't need to book months in advance. You know?' Immediately she realised what she'd said. 'Although I'd imagine you don't have too many problems with getting a table.'

'Not usually,' he said, a smile in his voice. 'So where would *you* go for dinner this Saturday night in Sydney?'

She'd grown up in the outer suburbs of Sydney, but as an adult she'd spent little time there—aside from when she was working. And with twelve-to-fourteen-hour days typical on a film set, dining out—fine or otherwise—wasn't exactly a reg-ular occurrence. Although, she'd crashed in the spare room of a set dresser between jobs last year...

'Some friends took me to a French Bistro right in the CBD when I was last in Sydney. It's a little fancy, but still relaxed. Plus, the Bombe Alaska is to die for.'

'Perfect. Would you be able to book me a table?'

Ruby gritted her teeth. *So not my job!*

'Sure!' she said, instead, with determined enthusiasm.

'Appreciate it,' he said, and the words were just as annoying the third time she'd heard them that day.

Then he hung up.

Ruby told herself she'd imagined the beginnings of a laugh before the phone went silent. As otherwise she'd need to drive to his place right now. And strangle him.

The next day was overcast, with rain forecast for the early af-ternoon.

Consequently, Asha, the second assistant director, was rather frantic when she rushed into Ruby's office just after eleven a.m.

'I need your help,' she said, running a hand through her shiny black bob. 'We have a situation in Hair and Make-up. Dev won't let anyone cut his hair, and we need him on set like *now*. We need to get this scene before the weather hits.'

Ruby sighed. She'd left him with hair and make-up not even

twenty minutes ago…but still—she really shouldn't be surprised.

A minute later, both women were striding across Unit Base.

'Dev isn't at all like what I expected,' Ruby said. She wrapped her arms tightly around herself as she walked, the breeze sharp through the thin cotton of her cardigan.

'You mean the whole "haven't slept or eaten in a month" thing?' Asha asked. 'Thank God Make-up and Wardrobe can work miracles is all I can say.' Then a long pause, and a conspiratorial whisper: 'I hear that he's nursing a broken heart. That Estelle van der something? She's already hooked up with someone new. Poor guy.'

*Poor guy?* Right.

'Yeah, that, I guess,' Ruby said. 'But I meant all of his demands? It's driving me nuts.'

Asha shot her a surprised glance. 'Really? Honestly, up until just now he's been a model actor. It's amazing how quickly he's learnt his scenes and he just nailed our rehearsals yesterday. His professionalism is the only reason we can shoot anything today.'

Ruby slowed her pace slightly. 'No complaints about his costume? Requests for a box of chocolates with all the soft-centred ones removed?'

Both were the type of requests that the Dev she'd been dealing with over the past day and a half would *definitely* have asked. Just this morning he'd asked to have new curtains installed in his trailer, as the current set let in too much light when closed. *Apparently.* Then he'd asked for a very specific selection of organic fruit. Rohan was wasting his time on that, right now. Ugh!

'No,' Asha said, coming to a halt outside the hair and make-up trailer. 'This random hair thing is it. But, it's only been a couple of days. Maybe he'll reveal his true self to all of us on set soon.'

'Hmm,' was all that Ruby could say to that. A niggling suspicion that she'd dismissed as ridiculous, impossible, was now niggling, well…louder.

But surely he wouldn't…?

She opened the door to the trailer, taking in the frustrated-looking hair stylist and his assistant—and of course Dev, sprawled ever-so-casually in front of a mirror, complete with two days' worth of—she had to admit—sexy stubble. As she stepped inside he met her gaze in the glass.

And winked.

Ruby dug her fingernails into her palms, then took a deep, calming breath. The action was not soothing in the slightest, but it did help her speak in a fair facsimile of an I've-got-everything-under-control production co-ordinator.

'Could I have a few minutes with Mr Cooper?'

It was a perfectly reasonable request—it was her job to fix exactly these types of hiccups—and so with quick nods and hopeful expressions aimed in Ruby's direction everyone filed out.

Ever so slowly—and Ruby now *knew* he was enjoying this—Dev spun his chair around to face her. His assessing gaze travelled over her, from her flat, knee-high leather boots, up to her fitted navy jeans, cream tank top and oversized, over-long wool cardigan. Then to her face—touching on her lips, her eyes, her hair.

Ruby wanted to kick herself for being pleased she'd made an effort with her make-up today. She'd done so yesterday too, not letting herself acknowledge until just now that it had—of course—been for Devlin Cooper.

God, she frustrated herself. She'd been sure she'd long ago got past this—this pathetic need for male attention. The need for anyone else to provide her with validation, other than herself.

*No.* That hadn't changed.

He opened his mouth, guaranteed to say something teasing and clever. He had that look in his eyes—she'd seen it in his movies, and definitely in person.

She didn't give him the chance.

'Who the *hell* do you think you are?'

Ruby had the satisfaction of watching his eyes widen in surprise. But he recovered quickly, as smooth as silk. 'I believe I'm Devlin Cooper.' He shrugged. 'You know, the actor?'

She shook her head. 'No way. Don't be smart. I'm onto you.'

'*Onto* me?' he asked, raising an eyebrow. 'What exactly are you *onto?*'

Ruby bit her lip, trying to hold onto the barest thread of control. Could he be any more deliberately oblivious? Any more *arrogant?*

'This,' she said, throwing her arms up to encompass the trailer. 'And the phone calls, the emails, the hire car, the chocolates, the fruit, the curtains…' Ruby started to count them off on her fingers. 'What next? What next trivial, unreasonable task are you going to lob in my direction?'

'You don't feel my requests are legitimate?' he asked. If he was at all bothered by her rapidly rising voice, his expression revealed nothing.

'I know they're not.' She glared at him when he tried to speak again. 'And I don't care why you've been doing it: I don't care if you're so shocked by the concept of a woman saying no to you that you need to be as irritating as possible in revenge, but—*please*—just stop.'

Dev blinked. 'Is that what you think I'm doing?' In contrast to even a moment before, now he looked dumbfounded—his forehead wrinkled in consternation. 'That's not it at all.'

But she was barely listening now.

'In case you're not aware, when you pull stunts like this, Paul—you know, my boss?—expects me to sort it all immediately. If I don't—if filming is held up, if we can't shoot a scene because of you, or if I need to ask Paul to call your agent to kick your butt into gear—it isn't *you* who looks like a massive, unprofessional loser. *It's me.*'

Dev pushed himself to his feet. He was in costume: dark brown trousers, a soft tan shirt with the sleeves rolled up, a heavy leather belt and holster, plus chunky work boots—he was playing an early nineteen hundreds Australian drover after all. Temporarily, her tirade was clogged in her throat as she digested the sight of him approaching her. He was so tall, so broad—and suddenly the trailer felt so small.

But then her frustration bubbled over again. Hot, famous movie star or not—*nobody* got away with treating Ruby Bell this way.

'You might have forgotten what it's like to rely on a regular salary, but trust me—I haven't. And I'm not having some entitled, full-of-himself actor think it's okay to stomp all over my reputation, my professionalism, my…'

With every word her voice became higher and less steady.

Dev had stopped in front of her. Not close enough to crowd her, not at all, and yet she found that words began to escape her as he studied her, his gaze constant, searching and…what? Not arrogant. Not angry. Not even shocked…

Sad? No, not that either. But it wasn't what she expected.

It had been silent for long seconds, and Ruby swallowed, trying to pull herself together.

'If you don't stop,' she began, 'I'll…'

And here her tirade came to its pathetic—and now clearly obvious—end.

What exactly would she do? What could she do? She'd just told him that she'd get blamed for any problems he caused, and that was pretty much true. And it wasn't as if she could get him fired.

*Hmm. Let me think: Easily replaceable production co-ordinator versus the man who's starred in the world's highest grossing spy franchise?*

She tangled her fingers into the fabric of her cardigan, suddenly needing to hold onto something.

*Oh, God. What had she done?* All he had to do was complain to Paul and…

Dev was still watching her.

'You'll what, Ruby?'

She made herself meet his gaze. 'I—' she started. She should apologise, she knew. Grovel, even—do anything to patch up the past few minutes as if they had never, ever happened.

But she couldn't do it—it would be like time-travelling ten years into her past.

'I'd *appreciate it*,' she said, deliberately mimicking him, 'if you could carefully consider your future requests, or issues, before contacting myself, or my office. We're all very busy at the moment.'

Even that was far from an appropriate request to make of a film's biggest star, but she just *couldn't* concede any less.

In response, Dev smiled. The sudden lightness in his gaze made Ruby's heart skip a beat. Alone in a room with Dev Cooper, Ruby would challenge any woman not to do the same—irritated beyond belief or not.

'It wasn't revenge,' he said, simply.

'But it was something,' Ruby prompted. What was all this about?

'I'm sorry that you thought I was trying to make you look bad in front of your boss and colleagues. I can assure you I wasn't.'

Even knowing he was a very good actor, Ruby believed him. Those eyes, in real life, were *nothing at all* like what you saw on celluloid. They revealed so much more—more than Ruby could even begin to interpret.

'It's much simpler than that. Much less exciting than some dastardly vengeful plan.'

Ruby crossed her arms, watching him stonily.

He sighed. 'Okay, bad joke. Look...' He looked down at the trailer floor for just a moment. 'It's simple, really. I don't need "looking after".'

Ruby narrowed her eyes. 'And the fact I'm the brunt of this behaviour is an unfortunate coincidence?'

'No,' he conceded. 'I just like...' He studied her face, then focused on her eyes, as if he was trying to work something out. 'I like seeing you react.'

She was not deluded enough to think that she stood out amongst all the other women she *knew* he surrounded himself with. She'd seen the photos of him with Estelle—a *supermodel*, for crying out loud. This juvenile game had *nothing* to do with her. Not really.

This was about his ego, his sense of the way things should be.

She didn't come into it at all.

Ruby spoke very politely. 'Please carefully consider your future requests, or issues, before contacting myself, or my office,' she repeated.

He nodded, and for the first time in long minutes Ruby felt as if she was breathing normally.

'I'll do my best,' he said.

Every muscle in her body that had begun to relax re-tightened, ready for battle. Had he not heard a word she'd said? How could he possibly think—?

'No more stunts like this—I get it. I won't impact the filming schedule.'

*But...*

He grinned, but that brightness she'd seen—just for that moment—had long disappeared. Now there was a heaviness to his gaze, and the lines around his mouth were tight.

'I think I'm having too much fun with you.'

'I'm not interested,' she said, quick as a flash. But they both heard that she didn't really believe that.

Since when had she been this transparent?

He was so sure he knew where this was headed it made her want to scream. And simultaneously made her question her sanity. There was just something about the man, and the way he looked at her, that had her questioning herself. Had her questioning the rules she'd laid down for herself long ago...

She shook her head firmly.

'I'm going to tell Hair and Make-up that it was a misunderstanding and you're happy to go with the haircut as planned.'

He nodded sharply.

She turned to go, but paused at the trailer door.

'You do realise that the kid who threw sticks at the girl he liked in primary school never did get the girl?'

He laughed, the deep sound making her shiver. 'Not in my experience.'

Ruby slammed the door behind her as she left.

# CHAPTER FOUR

'RUBY, CAN I HAVE a minute?'

Paul spoke from the hallway, barely poking his head into the busy office. He didn't bother waiting for an answer—as of course it wasn't a question—and so half a minute later Ruby was closing the door behind her as she stepped into the producer's office.

'Yes?'

Paul was rubbing his forehead, which wasn't a good sign.

'Are the drivers organised for tomorrow night?' he asked.

Paul was attending the premiere of his latest film in Sydney. Both Dev and Arizona would also be walking the red carpet—a bit of extra attention for that film, plus some early promo for *The Land.* 'Of course. All three cars are sorted.'

As was contractually necessary. *Must travel in own car* was a pretty standard condition for most actors. Quite the contrast to Ruby, who had driven up to Lucyville with her hire car packed full with everything she owned, Rohan *and* one of the girls from Accounts. Plus some miscellaneous lighting equipment.

Paul nodded sharply. 'Good, good.'

Then he went silent, allowing Ruby to start dreaming up all the potential reasons why he'd *really* needed to talk to her.

Right at the top of that list was Dev.

'So. I hear you had some luck talking Dev around, yesterday.'

*Got it in one.*

'Yes,' she said, far more calmly than she felt. 'He just needed a little time to understand what was required.'

'Excellent,' Paul said. 'As unfortunately neither his agent or I are having much luck making him *understand* that he signed a contract that specified he walk the red carpet at this premiere. He's refusing to go.'

Of course he was.

Ruby bit back a sigh. 'I don't think I'd have any more chance of talking him around than you would.'

'I have faith in you.'

Which meant: *Go fix this, Ruby.*

Paul had already reached for his phone, casually moving on to his next production crisis, now that—in his mind at least—this particular issue was sorted.

So Ruby walked out of his office, down the hallway, outside onto the dusty grass, then all the way across Unit Base to where the opulent, shiny black actors' trailers that housed Arizona and Dev were situated.

And knocked, very loudly, on Dev's door.

He was, Dev decided, becoming quite accustomed to people being annoyed with him.

There was Veronica, of course, all but breathing fire across the cellular network whenever she called. Her multiple-times-a-day tirades were exclusively for the benefit of his voicemail, however, as Dev considered Graeme a sufficient conduit for anything that Veronica really needed to know. He figured his agent could hardly complain. She'd planted her security guy/minder/driver/spy—she might as well get her money's worth.

Or, more accurately, *his* money's worth. As of course that was what all this was about—Veronica's much-stated concern for him was all about the money. He was her biggest star, and now she was panicking.

But he felt no guilt. He'd made Veronica very, very rich. He owed her nothing.

Then there was Graeme. The director. The producer. The rest of the crew. He gave them all just exactly what was needed—

whether it be his acting skills, the answer to a question, or simple conversation. But not one skerrick more.

Then his mother had started calling. In her first voice message, she explained she'd heard on the news that he was in Australia, and was hoping they could catch up.

He'd meant to call her, but then didn't. Couldn't.

And she'd kept calling, kept leaving polite, friendly messages, that always ended with a soft *love you*.

Each call made him feel like something you'd scrape off your boot, but, as he'd been doing lately, he just shoved that problem aside. To worry about later. Eventually...

Most likely at three in the morning, when he was so overwhelmed with exhaustion that he could no longer ignore the thoughts that caused him pain.

He clenched his jaw. *No.*

The woman on the other side of his trailer door, *she* was who he needed to be thinking about. Somehow, randomly, she'd grabbed his attention. With her, he forgot all the other rubbish that was cluttering up his head.

And she was, unquestionably, very, very annoyed with him.

He smiled, and walked to the door.

He opened the door mid-knock, triggering a surprised, 'Oh!' and she stumbled a step inside.

He didn't step back himself, forcing her to squeeze past him. Not quite close enough for their bodies to touch, but close enough that her clothes brushed against his.

Yes, he was being far from a gentleman, but no—he didn't care.

He found himself craving that flare in Ruby's gaze, that look she worked so hard to disguise.

But it was there—this heat between them. He knew it, she knew it—she just needed to get over whatever ridiculous imagined rules she'd created in her head and let the inevitable happen.

He let the trailer door swing shut behind him and turned to face her. She walked right into the middle of his trailer, in the 'living' section of the luxury motorhome. The trailer was practically soundproof, so now they both stood, looking at each other, in silence.

That didn't last long.

'I thought I made myself clear,' she said, frustration flooding her voice, 'how important my career is to me, and how you have *no right* to mess with it. To mess with my life.'

'But I haven't.'

She blinked. 'What would you call this? Refusing to attend a premiere that's in your contract?'

'Have I held up filming? Have I embarrassed you professionally?'

'You will if you don't go,' she said simply.

He smiled. 'Then you just need to get me to go.'

Her eyes narrowed. 'How?'

'Dinner.'

He hadn't planned this. Hadn't planned anything beyond saying no to Paul and seeing what happened next.

With Ruby there wasn't a script—things just happened.

But dinner, suddenly, was the perfectly obvious solution.

'That's blackmail,' she said, with bite.

He shrugged. 'Yes.'

No, he most definitely was *not* a gentleman.

She sighed loudly and rubbed her hands up and down her arms. 'So if I agree to dinner, you'll attend the premiere.' It wasn't a question.

'And make you look like a miracle-worker in front of your producer.'

She rolled her eyes. 'I'd rather you'd just gone to the premiere and never brought me into this at all.' She paused, meeting his gaze.

Her expression was sharp and assessing. 'Dinner at that French bistro on Saturday night—you booked that for…whatever *this* is.'

Maybe he had? At the time it'd been about riling her up, teasing her, irritating her with the idea he had a date with another woman. Childish, but he hadn't had a plan. Not consciously, anyway.

'Yes,' he said, because he knew she'd hate that answer.

'God, you're so, so sure of yourself, aren't you?'

He didn't bother replying. Instead he walked past her, then settled himself onto one of the small navy-blue couches. 'Why don't you take a seat? We can work out the details of our date.'

'No, thank you,' she said, very crisply. 'I need to get back to the office. I don't have time during my workday to waste on this. Call me later. Or even better, email me. More efficient.'

Lord, he liked her. So direct. So to the point.

She spun on her booted heel, then paused mid-spin.

'So this is your way of maintaining your one-hundred-per-cent never-rejected perfect score or something?'

'You can think of it that way if you like.'

She groaned. 'You think you're very clever, don't you?'

Considering he'd just achieved exactly what he wanted, he didn't consider it necessary to reply to this question either.

She continued her exit, but at the door she, just as he expected, had to deliver a final parting shot. Just as she had yesterday.

'You know what, Mr Cooper? Everything I'd heard about you before this week was good. Glowing even. Everyone likes you. Everyone loves to work with you. So, I reckon you must *really* be a great actor. Because, quite frankly, I don't think you're a very nice person.'

This time he had no pithy retort, so he just let her go.

After all, she was partly right. Right now he didn't feel like the Dev that everyone liked, as she said. The Dev that loved his job and that was beloved of many a film crew. The Dev with a million friends and a lifestyle that most could only dream of.

Right now he didn't know what type of person he was at all.

Ruby had laid out every single item of clothing she owned on her motel-room bed. Not just the clothing she'd brought with her for this film—everything she owned.

Years ago she'd got into the routine of selling her clothes before departing for a job overseas—eBay was brilliant for that purpose—rather than lugging it with her across the world.

She'd always thought it rather a flawless plan. She had a keen eye for an online shopping bargain, so she was rarely out of pocket, and, more importantly, she had the perfect excuse to buy an entirely new, season-appropriate wardrobe every six months or so.

The rare occasions she did date, it was always between films, so having a favourite, guaranteed-to-feel-awesome-in outfit was not really all that essential. She knew well in advance if she had a premiere to attend, so she could plan ahead—and besides, the full-length formal gowns were really only for the talent at those events, not the crew.

So. Consequently here she was, hands on hips—and not far from putting her head in her hands—with absolutely nothing to wear on her date with Dev.

It was tempting, really, *really* tempting, to rock up for her date in jeans and a ratty old T-shirt. So her clothing choice would make a very obvious statement about how she felt about the whole situation.

But, unfortunately, she just couldn't.

Turned out she was—much to her despair—incapable of being truly cool, and strong, and defiant. In this way, at least. Nope. Just as she'd been agonising over her clothing choices for work each day, she wanted to look her best on Saturday night.

Yes, it was pathetic. Yes, it didn't say a lot for her that, despite Dev's ridiculous manipulating of her and their situation, she still felt her body react at even the *thought* of him. And when they were together...well.

But then, he *was* basically the sexiest man on earth. She shouldn't be too hard on herself. Surely she wouldn't be human if she didn't wonder...

It was just a little galling to realise that she—who did know better—could still be distracted by looks over personality. As, really, there wasn't a whole lot about Devlin Cooper for her to like right now.

A long time ago, the Devlin Coopers of the world had been her type. Not that she had a life populated with movie stars, but at high school she'd gone for the captain of the footy team. And the captain of the tennis team. And the very charismatic head boy who every girl had been in love with. Then once she left school, it was the sexy bartender. Or the hot lawyer who ordered a latte every morning at the café where she worked. Or the son of the owner of the café. And...*and, and, and...*

She'd search out the hottest guy, the most popular guy, the guy who was the absolute least attainable for a girl like her—the rebellious foster child, abandoned by her teenage mother, with a reputation a mile long.

And then she would make it her mission to get him.

It was all about her goal, her goal to get the guy, to have him want her—*her*—Ruby Bell, who was *nobody*. Not popular, not unpopular. Not the prettiest, not the least attractive. And when she got him—and she nearly always did—she had that night, or nights, or maybe only a few hours, where she got to feel beautiful and desirable and valued and *wanted*.

But of course that feeling didn't last. She—and her temporary value—was inevitably dropped. She'd hurt and cry and feel just as worthless as she had before that perfect, gorgeous guy had kissed her.

Then the cycle would start again.

Ruby's eyes stung, and she realised she was on the verge of tears. Another memory—one that came later—was threatening, right at the edges of her subconscious.

But she wasn't going there—not tonight, and not because of Dev.

What was important was that she'd turned her life around. Never again would she need a man to make her feel alive—to feel worthy. Never again would she be sweet, and obliging and void of any opinion purely for the attention and approval of another person.

And never again would she be the girl that was whispered about. Who walked into a room only to have the men study her with questions in their eyes—and the women with daggers in theirs.

She'd grown up in a swirl of gossip and speculation, and her adult life had begun that way too—and way too early.

The sad thing was, at first she'd actually liked the attention. She wasn't the shy girl at the back of the classroom, she was a girl who people talked about, who people noticed. Suddenly *everyone* knew her name.

Maybe at first she'd fuelled the gossip. She'd been increasingly outrageous, telling herself she was in control, inwardly laughing at the people who looked at her with such disdain.

But at some point the power had shifted.

Or maybe she'd just never had any power at all.

Now she was all grown up. She was twenty-nine years old. She no longer needed anyone to validate her. She no longer harboured a fear it had taken her years to acknowledge—that if her mother hadn't wanted her, then maybe no one ever would. In men and their fleeting attention she'd received the attention and the *wanting* she'd so badly craved.

But now she knew she didn't need a man. She had her career, and her friends, and a lifestyle that she adored. If she dated, she chose men who were the opposite to the high-school football stars and Devlin Coopers of the world. And it was never for very long.

She was always in control. Everything was perfect.

And another beautiful man was not going to change any of that. She would not slide into habits long severed, or let their date impact her professional reputation: she had never been, and would never be, the subject of gossip at work. Gossip would never colour her decisions—would never control her—ever again.

She didn't hide her past from anyone—but it was the *past*. She couldn't let herself head down that path again. To lose herself while wanting something a man could never give her.

Ruby needed only herself. Could rely, *only,* on herself.

She turned, and flopped onto her back on her bed, uncaring of the clothing she squashed and creased beneath her.

Hmm. That was all well and good—and *right*.

But.

She still had a date with Devlin Cooper in two days' time.

An emergency shopping expedition was—most definitely—required.

Ruby had to spend a few hours in the office on Saturday morning, and so by the time she'd driven the four hours into the city, she was cutting it extremely fine.

Fortunately, one of her good friends was between films at the moment. So she was meeting Gwen, an exceedingly glamorous costume designer, at a boutique in Paddington, rather than hitting the department stores in a fit of mad desperation.

As she stepped into the store, complete with its crystal chandeliers, chunky red leather armchairs and modern, smooth-edged white shelving, Gwen squealed and trotted towards her on towering platform heels.

'Ruby! It's been for ever!' she announced as she wrapped her into a hug.

She'd considered sharing the identity of her date with Gwen, but had decided, on balance, that it was best if she didn't. Yes, she trusted her friend, but…it really was better if no one knew. It was only one date, after all.

In the same vein, she'd taken steps to ensure—as much as was possible—that their date remained firmly under the radar. When Dev had called her—she'd known he wouldn't email—she'd made it very clear that the gorgeous French bistro she'd booked was no longer suitable. It was not the type of place where privacy—and a lack of photography—could be assured. The last thing she needed was some grainy photo snapped on someone's mobile phone making it onto Twitter and, eventually, to the film set.

Yes, she was likely paranoid, and such a liaison with a film's star would not signal the end of her career. She *knew* that film sets could be the home to all sorts of flings and the more than occasional affair. It was natural in an industry where the majority of the crew were well under forty—the transient lifestyle was not ideal for anyone with a family, and roots.

She just didn't want to be that woman Dev had a fling with. She'd been *that woman* enough times in her life. Thank you very much.

So this was, she realised as Gwen unhooked a dress from a shiny chrome rack to display to her, more about how she perceived herself than about how anyone else would perceive her.

Which really was just as important. No. More important than her professional reputation.

But she'd fiercely protect that, too.

'What do you think?' Gwen asked, giving the coat hanger a little shake so that the dress's delicate beading shimmered beneath the down lights.

It was a cocktail-length dress, in shades of green. On the hanger it looked like nothing but pretty fabric, but of course she tried it on.

Ruby was bigger than the average tiny actress that Gwen was used to dressing, but still—her friend certainly had an eye for what suited her body.

As she stepped out of the change room and in front of the mirror Ruby couldn't help but suck in a breath of surprise.

She looked...

'Beautiful!' Gwen declared happily. 'It's perfect.'

Ruby twisted from side to side, studying herself. The dress was gorgeous, with heavily beaded and embroidered cap sleeves and a sweetheart neckline that flattered her average-sized curves. The silk followed the curve of her waist and hips, ending well above her knee. The beading continued throughout the fabric, becoming sparser at her waist before ending in a shimmer of green and flecks of gold at the hem. It was simple—but not. Striking—but not glitzy.

She loved it.

Twenty minutes later she'd parted with a not insignificant portion of her savings, and headed with Gwen to find the perfect matching heels and a short, sexy, swingy jacket.

And an hour after that she was alone in the hotel room she'd booked, only a short walk from the crazily exclusive restaurant where she would be meeting Dev. Really soon.

The dress sparkled prettily on her bed. She had her make-up and the perfect shade of nail polish raring to go in the bathroom.

But she paused, rather than walking to the shower. She looked at herself reflected in the mirrored hotel wardrobe.

There she was, in jeans and hair that had transitioned from deliberately choppy to plain old messy at some point in the day.

She wouldn't say she lacked confidence in herself or her looks. She didn't think she was hideously *un*attractive, but… *really?* When Dev could have anyone, why her?

It must be the challenge. It could be nothing else. And maybe he felt that he should be the one doing the rejecting, not her?

She nodded, and she watched the movement reshuffle her hair just a little.

Yes. That was it.

And after tonight—that would be that. He'd have achieved his goal, and in a week's time she'd be very, very old news.

Which suited her just fine.

Didn't it?

# CHAPTER FIVE

Dev was late. Only a few minutes, but late, just the same.

He'd meant to be later, actually, having liked the idea of Ruby sitting alone at the restaurant, getting increasingly frustrated with him.

Simply because he enjoyed the flash of anger in her eyes almost as much as the heat of the attraction she was so determinedly—and continually—ignoring.

But, after a while, he began to feel like a bit of an idiot sitting alone in his penthouse suite, mindlessly watching the Saturday night rugby, when the alternative was spending time with a beautiful…

No, not beautiful. At least not on the standards that Hollywood judged beauty. But a compelling…intriguing woman. Yes, she was that.

Unarguably more interesting than his own company.

But when he was ushered into the private dining area of the exclusive restaurant by an impeccably well-mannered maître d', he was met by a table exquisitely set for two—but no Ruby.

His lips quirked as he settled into his seat. *Interesting.*

The restaurant sat right on the edge of Circular Quay, its floor-to-ceiling windows forming a subtly curved wall that provided a spectacular view of the harbour. To the right were the dramatic sails of the opera house. Straight ahead was the incomparable harbour bridge. Lights illuminated the mammoth structure, highlighting its huge metal beams.

He'd eaten at this restaurant before, and had certainly dined against a backdrop of the world's most beautiful skylines many, many times—but he wouldn't be human if he wasn't impressed by sparkling Sydney by night.

It was like nowhere else in the world.

However. Sitting alone in a dining room that could seat thirty—and which he'd had organised for tonight to seat only two—even a remarkable view could quickly become boring.

Which it did.

A waiter came and offered him a taste of the wine he'd selected, then after pouring Dev's glass he merged once again, silently, into the background.

Minutes passed. Slowly, he assumed, as he refused to succumb and check his watch.

He considered—then dismissed—the possibility that she wasn't coming at all.

No, she'd be here.

Almost on cue, the door to the private room opened on whisper-smooth hinges. He looked up to watch Ruby being ushered inside. And then kept on looking.

She wore a dress in greens and gold that caught and reflected every bit of light in the room. Her legs were long beneath a skirt that hit at mid thigh, and shown off to perfection by strappy, criss-crossed heels. When his gaze—eventually—met hers, he connected with eyes that were defiant and bold beneath a fringe that was smoother and more perfect than usual: not a golden strand out of place.

Her lips curved in greeting, but he wouldn't call it a smile.

He stood as she approached the table, and she blinked a couple of times as he did so, her gaze flicking over him for the briefest of instants.

The maître d' received a genuine smile as he offered Ruby her seat, and he then launched into his spiel, speaking—Dev assumed—of wine and food, but he really wasn't paying any attention. Instead he took the opportunity to just look at Ruby as she tilted her chin upwards and listened attentively.

This was, after all, about the first time she'd been perfectly still, and silent, in his presence, since their original *interlude* beside the costume trailer.

Then, she'd been veering towards adorable, while tonight she was polished and perfect. Different, for sure—but equally appealing.

After a short conversation, the maître d' repeated his vanishing act, and Ruby turned her gaze onto him.

'You're late,' he pointed out.

She nodded. 'So were you.'

He smiled, surprised. 'How did you know?'

'I didn't. But it seemed the kind of stunt you would pull. You've been very consistent in your quest to irritate me.' Calmly, she reached for her water glass. 'Not very chivalrous of you, however.' Another pause. 'Personally, I am never—intentionally—less than punctual. Time is everything in my job, and I see no reason why it shouldn't be in the rest of my life.'

*Time is everything.*

How true. Often, Dev had only recently discovered, you had a lot less time than you thought.

'So chivalry is important to you, Ruby?'

She took a sip from her water glass, then studied him over the rim. 'Actually, no,' she replied, surprising him. She looked out towards the opera house, her forehead wrinkling slightly. 'I mean, of course being courteous and honourable or gallant—or whatever a chivalrous man is supposed to be—is important.' She gave him a look that underlined the fact she clearly considered him to be none of those things. 'But it has to be genuine. Standing up when I approach the table, for example—' her words were razor sharp '—is meaningless. It has to mean something—have a basis in respect—otherwise I'd really rather you didn't bother.'

'I respect you,' he said.

She laughed with not a trace of pretention. 'I find that very hard to believe.'

'It's the truth,' he said. He wasn't going to bother explaining himself, but then somehow found himself doing so anyway. 'I was late because I like seeing you react, not because I don't value you and your time. I apologise if you feel that way.'

'I'm sure you agree that distinction is impossible to make from my point of view.'

Dev almost, almost, felt bad about it—but not quite. He was enjoying this—enjoying her—too much.

'You like pushing my buttons,' she said. 'You're very good at it.'

He shrugged, studying her. 'So is that what you're looking for? An honourable, perfectly chivalrous specimen of a man?'

Dev knew he was not that man.

Immediately, she shook her head. 'Absolutely not. I'm looking for no man at all.'

'You're focusing on your career?'

Almost silently the maître d' reappeared and filled her wine glass.

'Yes, but that's not the reason. I don't need a man. At all.'

'Need, or want?'

She rolled her eyes dismissively. 'Neither.'

He considered this unexpected announcement as their entrées arrived, but he wasn't about to question her further. Tonight was not for detailed analysis of their respective relationship goals.

For the record, his was—and had always been—to have no relationship at all. Estelle had been an unexpected exception, a relationship that had evolved, at times—it seemed—almost without his participation. Yes, he'd liked her. Enjoyed his time with her. Maybe considered the idea that he loved her.

But that night she'd left, she'd made it crystal clear that what he felt wasn't love. How had she put it?

*Love is when you share yourself—reveal yourself. Your thoughts, your feelings, your fears. Something. Everything! Not nothing. Not absolutely nothing.*

At the time he hadn't questioned her. But later, when he'd asked himself that question—if that *was* what he'd done, and who he was—he couldn't disagree.

They ate their salmon for a while in silence, their knives scraping loudly on the fine bone china.

'Is this really what you wanted?' she asked. She was still focused on her meal, her eyes on her plate, not on him.

She meant this date, this time alone with her.

'Yes.'

Now she glanced up. The harder edge to her gaze from before was gone; now she just looked confused. 'Seriously? Why on earth would you want to spend an evening with a woman who doesn't particularly like you?'

'I thought you said you didn't know me well enough to dislike me.'

She raised an eyebrow. 'I've begun to revise that opinion.'

He smiled. Maybe something resembling his *famous Dev Cooper smile,* as he didn't miss the way her cheeks went pink, or how eager she was to look away.

'You like me.'

Instantly, she met his gaze. 'Here we go again. It's getting tedious. Why on earth should I like you?'

'I'm charming,' he said.

She snorted. 'What exactly is your definition of the word? Blackmailing a woman into dating you? Really?'

'No. I must admit this is not my standard dating procedure.'

'For the sake of the thousands of women you've ever dated, I'm relieved to hear that.'

'Not thousands,' he said.

She waved her wine glass in a gesture of dismissal. 'Hundreds, then.'

No, not that many either. In hindsight, maybe Estelle was not the first to observe his relationship failings. Or, more likely, she was the only one he'd allowed close enough to notice.

A mistake, clearly.

'I'm not—' he began, then stopped.

*I'm not myself at the moment.*

No, there was no need to say that to Ruby. That was the whole point, wasn't it? For Ruby to be his distraction?

'You're not what?' she asked.

He gave a little shake of his head. 'It doesn't matter. All that matters is that we're here now.' He leant back in his chair a little, studying her. 'We're here, in this amazing city, at this amazing restaurant. And you, Ruby Bell, are wearing one amazing dress.'

The pink to her cheeks escalated to a blush, but otherwise she gave no indication of being affected by his words.

'Thank you,' she said, just a little stiffly.

'Here's an idea,' he said. 'How about we call a truce? For tonight. For argument's sake, let's pretend you don't hate my guts, or the way we both came to be sitting together at this table.'

She grinned, then looked surprised that she had. 'I don't hate you,' she said. 'You just haven't given me a heck of a lot to like.'

'I'll try harder,' he promised.

She held his gaze for a long, long while. Considering his words.

'Okay,' she finally conceded. 'But just for tonight.'

Belatedly, Ruby acknowledged that her dessert plate was completely empty—excluding some melted remnants of sorbet. She could barely remember what it tasted like—she'd been so focused on their conversation.

How had this happened?

A couple of hours ago she'd been dreading this date…

No. That was clearly a lie. Anxiously anticipating was far more on the mark.

But now, she found herself in the midst of a really fantastic evening. *Date*. A date with a movie star.

Although, oddly, she found she needed to remind herself of that fact every now and again. A little mental pinch of her arm, so to speak.

He was different tonight. Only for a moment earlier, and even then she was unsure whether she'd imagined it, had his gaze darkened. She realised that up until tonight there had been a kind of shadow to Dev. A…burden, maybe?

But tonight he was different. There was more of an openness to his expression. Oddly, as they chatted—initially about the industry but then, thankfully, about basically everything but—Ruby had the sense that the shadow was gradually lifting. She found herself wanting to find opportunities to make him smile again, to laugh.

It was as if he was out of practice.

Ruby gave herself a mental shake.

Oh, no. Now *that* was wishful thinking. She was putting way too much thought into this.

She needed to keep this simple: it was a date. One date. Only.

They'd just finished trading stories of their varied travel disasters. She'd noticed that Dev hadn't spoken of *that time I was mobbed by fans in Paris* or *this one time I was invited for afternoon tea with the Queen*—it was as if he was distancing himself from what made him so, so different from her. Somehow, he was making himself relatable. A real person.

Was he doing it deliberately?

Yes, for sure. He'd been right before—he *was* charming, and smart.

But also…it was working. She found herself questioning her opinion of him. She'd certainly relaxed. Something she knew was unwise, but the wine, the food, the lighting, and Dev… yeah, Dev… It was…he was…pretty much an irresistible force.

But not quite.

'Why film production?' he asked, changing the direction of their conversation yet again.

Ruby swirled her Shiraz in its oversized glass. 'Would you believe I'm a failed actor?' she asked.

'Yes,' he said, immediately.

She raised her eyebrows. 'Is it that obvious?'

He nodded, assessing her. 'Acting requires a certain…artifice. You—you tell it how it is. You're not pretending, not hiding what you think.'

She shifted a little in her seat, uncomfortable. 'You're saying I'm tactless?' she said, attempting a teasing tone but failing.

'Honest,' he said, disagreeing with her.

His gaze had shifted a little, become more serious. He was watching her closely, and it left her feeling exposed. She didn't like it.

'But,' he said, 'sometimes you try to hide what you're not saying: frustration, dismissal…attraction.'

Ruby had a feeling she wasn't being as successful in that goal as she'd like tonight. What could he see in her expression?

She decided it best not to consider that at all.

'You're partly right,' she said. 'At school I loved to act, but really I was only playing variations of myself. I wasn't any good at stepping into another character.' She laughed. 'But I still wanted to work in film—you know, delusions of glamour—and I couldn't wait to travel the world—so, I went to uni, then started at the bottom and worked my way up.'

'You were good at school?'

She shook her head, laughing. 'Not at all. I went to uni when I was twenty, after going back to finish Year Twelve. I had a… rebellious phase, I'd guess you'd call it.'

Dev's eyebrows rose. 'Really?'

She smiled, pleased she'd surprised him. 'Most definitely. A combination of a few things, but mostly I think I was just a pretty unhappy teenager.' She paused, not sure how much to share. But then, it was no secret. 'I was a foster child, and ended up going through a few different families as a teenager. For some reason I just couldn't stay away from trouble.'

He just nodded as he absorbed her words—he didn't look shocked, or pitying or anything like that. Which she appreciated. Her childhood at times had been difficult, but it could have been a lot worse.

'You were looking for attention,' he said, and now it was Ruby's turn to be surprised.

'Yeah,' she said. 'I figured that out, eventually.'

Although that really was too simplistic. It had been more than that.

She'd wanted to be wanted. To be needed. Even if it was painfully temporary.

'Don't look so surprised,' he said. 'I'm no expert in psycho-analysis or whatever—I can just relate. It's why I started to act. My family is overflowing with academic over-achievers. But I hated school—hated sitting still. But acting…acting I could do. It was the one thing I was actually pretty good at.'

He'd grown up to be a lot more than a pretty good actor.

'Your family must be really proud of you.'

The little pang of jealousy she felt, imagining Dev's proud family, was unexpected. That was a very old dream—one based on stability, and comfort and permanence. She'd dreamt up castles in the sky, with her own prince and toothpaste-advertisement-perfect family. But she'd traded it in long ago; for a life that was dynamic, exciting and unencumbered. *Free.*

'Not particularly,' he said, his tone perfectly flat.

His words jolted her out of the little fairy tale she'd been imagining.

'Your family isn't proud of their world-famous son? I find that hard to believe.'

He shrugged. 'I don't know. Maybe they are. I don't have that much to do with them.'

She was going to ask more, but he suddenly pushed his chair back, scraping it on the wooden floorboards.

'You ready to go?'

He didn't bother waiting for her to reply; he'd already stood up.

'I thought we'd agreed to leave separately?' she asked. All in aid of not being photographed together.

Dev shoved a hand through his hair, then, without a word, walked out of the dining room.

Ruby didn't have enough time to wonder if he'd just left, kind of balancing out being, well, *nice,* for the past few hours—when he returned.

'The staff assure me there's been no sign of paparazzi, so I reckon we can risk it.'

She nodded. Really, there was no reason to leave together at all. But still—they did.

As they left she was hyperaware of him walking closely behind her—down the stairs, then to a private exit that avoided the busy main restaurant. His proximity made her skin prickle, but in the nicest possible way.

It was probably the wine, but she felt a little fuzzy-headed as she shrugged on her coat, so she was careful not to look at him. All of a sudden the reasons why she'd refused the date felt just out of reach.

He held the door open for her, and he caught her gaze as she stepped outside.

Something of her thoughts must have been evident in her expression.

'What are you thinking?' he asked.

They'd taken a few steps down the near-deserted back street before she replied. 'You confuse me,' she said. 'I had you pegged as an arrogant bastard, but tonight you've—*almost*—been nice.'

The warmth of his hand on her froze her mid-stride. He turned to face her, his fingers brushing down the outside of her arm, touching skin when the three-quarter sleeves ended. His fingers tangled with hers, tugging her a half-step forward.

She had to look up to meet his gaze. They were between streetlights, so his face was a combination of shadows, the darkest beneath his eyes.

'No, Ruby,' he said. Quiet but firm. 'I think you had it right the other day, in my trailer.'

She racked her brain, trying to remember what she'd said—her forgetfulness a combination of being so red-hot angry at the time she'd barely known what she'd been saying, but more so just being so, so close to Dev. It was a miracle she could think at all.

'I'm not a very nice person.'

Then he'd dropped her hand, and was somehow instantly three steps away.

Her instinct was to disagree, to reassure him with meaningless words. But she couldn't, because he wasn't talking about blackmailing her for a date, or being deliberately late to dinner—he wasn't talking about her at all.

And because she didn't understand, and because in that moment there was something in him she recognised, she didn't say a word.

Instead she moved to his side, and together, silently, they started walking.

# CHAPTER SIX

DEV WASN'T REALLY thinking about where they were going. He just needed to walk.

But soon the rapidly increasing light and numbers of people that surrounded them heralded the direction he'd taken—and he looked up to the many, many steps that led to the opera house. He came to a stop, and took a deep breath.

He didn't know what to make of what had just happened.

Mostly, he would've preferred it hadn't.

Tonight—and this thing with Ruby—wasn't supposed to be about any of that.

'So,' he said, sounding absolutely normal. He *was* a good actor. 'Where to now?'

This area was well lit, a flat, paved expanse between the string of restaurants edging the quay and the massive sails of the opera house. Even though it was late, it *was* Sydney on a Saturday night, so there were many people around: most near the water, although some sat in pairs or strings on the steps. But right now, where they stood, they were alone.

She lifted her chin and smiled brightly—but unconvincingly.

She really wasn't a very good actor.

'How about we just wander for a bit?'

'Perfect,' he said—and it was. He'd half expected sparky, fiery Ruby to reappear, to announce that their date was over, their deal was done, and to disappear into the distance.

At the back of his mind he was bothered that he was so relieved, but, as he'd been doing so often lately, he filed that thought away. For later—and there was always a later.

In unspoken agreement they walked slowly towards the city—the wrought-iron railing that edged the quay to their right, and a line of old-fashioned sphere-topped lamp posts to their left. The breeze was cool off the water, but he welcomed its touch, his body over-warm beneath his open-collar shirt and suit jacket.

Ruby was talking, about *The Land,* about a play she'd seen at the opera house one time, about the rumours of some action-blockbuster sequel being possibly filmed in Sydney next year, and how she hoped to work on it. At first she seemed comfortable with his contribution of nods and murmurs, but eventually she started to draw him into the conversation. Asking questions about Friday's premiere, about whether it was really as bad as the papers had written today—that kind of thing.

'It wasn't my type of film,' Dev said. 'Maybe it was brilliant, just not for me.'

'So you thought it was boring?' she asked. He glanced at her, noting the sparkle in her eyes.

'Pretty much.'

She laughed. 'So weepy family sagas aren't for you.'

'No. I'm more an action/thriller kind of guy.'

'What a surprise,' she said, teasing him. 'Although, I had been wondering about that. Why *The Land?* Did you want a change of direction?'

'No,' he said, automatically, and harshly enough that Ruby slowed her pace a little, and looked at him curiously. 'I mean,' he tried again, 'yes, that was it exactly.'

'You don't sound all that sure.'

He wasn't. Right now he should be shooting a role he'd jumped at the opportunity to play. A negotiator in a smart, fast-paced hostage drama, a twist on the action-hero-type roles he was known for. But instead the role had been urgently recast, and his contract for his next film, with the now-burnt producer, had been torn to pieces. So here he was.

Only his previously stellar work ethic had prevented the story gaining traction. For now, the people involved had been relatively discreet, and Veronica had so far been able to mostly extinguish the—accurate—rumours.

But Ruby must have heard them—at least a hint of the truth. She watched him with curiosity in her gaze, but not the steeliness of someone determined to ferret out all the dirty details. She'd had all night to ask those questions—to push—but she hadn't.

He appreciated that.

'My agent had to twist my arm,' he said. That was the truth, at least.

He'd agreed only because he couldn't face another sleepless, pointless night in Hollywood. But he'd only traded it in for more of the same in north-west New South Wales.

*Ruby* was the only difference.

'You live in Sydney, right?' he asked, changing the subject.

They were walking amongst many people now—couples on dates, families, tourists with massive camera bags. If anyone recognised him, he hadn't noticed.

'Not any more,' she said.

'Melbourne?'

She shook her head. 'Not there either.' There was a smile in her voice.

Before tonight he hadn't been all that interested in getting to know the woman beside him. His interest in her had not been based around shared interests and the potential for meaningful conversation.

But at dinner, he'd found himself asking about *her,* and unsurprisingly that had led to him talking about elements of *himself* that he didn't share with his dates.

Maybe he was just rusty—it had been months since he'd gone out with a woman. Normally he had charming deflections of personal questions down to an art. He certainly didn't make a habit of welcoming them.

'If I name every city in the world until you say yes, we could be here a while.'

'And then you still wouldn't have an answer.'

They'd reached the end of the walk, and stood between the train station and ferry terminal.

Ruby was looking up at him, grinning—and waiting for him to do something with that non-response.

But he just left her waiting as he looked at her. Leisurely exploring the shape of her eyes, her nose, her lips. Beneath the CBD lights, he could see flecks of green and gold in her eyes he hadn't noticed before.

'You're beautiful,' he said, very softly, realising it was true.

Ruby took a rapid step backwards, and wobbled a little on her heels. He reached out automatically, wrapping his fingers around her upper arms to steady her.

For a moment her expression was soft. Inviting...

But then it hardened, and she shook his hands away.

'Nice try.'

'It's the truth,' he said, but immediately realised he was doing this all wrong as she glared at him. He didn't know how to handle this, why a compliment had caused this reaction.

'Look, it's getting late. Thanks for the lovely dinner. I'm going to head back to my hotel.'

She said all that, but didn't actually make a move to leave. If she had, he would've let her go, but that pause—he decided—was telling.

'If not Sydney, or Melbourne, or any other city in the world—where *do* you live?'

Ruby blinked as he deftly rewound their conversation. He could see her thinking, could see all sorts of things taking place behind those eyes.

'Wherever I feel like,' she said, slowly and eventually. 'I might stay where I've been working for a while. Or fly to stay with a friend for a few weeks. Or maybe just pick somewhere new I haven't been before, and live there.'

'But where's your base? Where you keep all your stuff?'

She shrugged. 'What stuff?'

'You don't own anything?'

'Nothing I can't keep in a suitcase.'

He took a moment to process this. 'Why?'

She smiled. 'I get asked that a lot. But the way I look at it, it makes sense. I've lived in some amazing places, seen incredible things. I'm not tied down—when I get a call offering me a job I can be on set, almost anywhere in the world, basically the very next day.'

'But don't you want a house one day?'

She wrinkled her nose. 'What? The great Australian dream of a quarter-acre block with a back pergola and a barbecue?' She shook her head. 'No, thanks.'

She spoke with the confidence of someone absolutely sure of their decision. He admired that—her assuredness. But he found it near impossible to believe. Could you really live your life the way she described?

'Most women your age are thinking marriage and babies. Putting roots down.'

'You're older than me,' she pointed out. 'Are you putting down roots? Is that what you're doing at your place in Beverly Hills?'

'Absolutely not,' he said. That was the last thing he wanted.

'Well, there you go.'

He must have looked confused, as she then tried to further explain.

'Is it so hard to believe? I told you before I'm a foster child, so my only "family" are the various sets of foster carers I called Aunty and Uncle. Nice people—great people—but, trust me, they couldn't wait to see the back of me, and I don't blame them. And nearly all my friends work in film, or did work in film, so they are scattered all over the place.'

He assumed he still looked less than convinced, as she rolled her eyes as if completely exasperated with him.

'No,' he said, before she tried again. 'I do get it.'

Didn't he, after all, live his life in kind of the same way?

Yes, he owned his home, but that was a financial decision, not one based on long-term planning—it wasn't a life goal or anything. He hadn't extrapolated that purchase into plans for the future: a wife, kids. Anything like that. In fact, he'd only ever had one goal: to act.

And now he wasn't even sure he had that.

'Do you want to get a drink somewhere?' he asked.

Ruby let the invitation bounce about in her brain for a moment.

'I should go,' she said. 'Like I said before. It's late, I—'

'But you didn't go.'

*I know.* She wasn't sure why. It had been the right thing to do—the right time to go. When he'd called her beautiful, she'd been momentarily lost. Lost in the moment and the pull of his warmth, and the appreciation she'd seen in his gaze. So, so tempting...

But then she'd remembered where she was—*who* he was—and why this was all a very, very bad idea.

'I should go,' she repeated. She'd meant to be more firm this time, but she wasn't—not at all.

'Probably,' he agreed. 'Based on what you've told me before—you should.'

He'd moved a little closer. *God.* He was good. He knew what he did to her when he was close. She could see it in everything he did—that arrogance, that confidence.

But unexpectedly, right now, it wasn't pushing her away.

Maybe because tonight she'd seen that confidence contrasted with moments of...not quite vulnerability, but *exposure.* He'd been raw, as if she was seeing Dev Cooper the man, not the actor.

And she'd found herself interested in that man. Oh, she'd always been *attracted* to Dev, by his looks, his charisma, by the persona his career had created. But that type of attraction was—with difficulty—possible to push aside. To be logical about. To walk away from, with the strict rules she lived by providing the impetus.

But *this* Dev. This Dev she couldn't so easily define. This Dev she wanted to know.

This Dev she wanted to understand.

*No, thank you. But thank you for dinner...*

It was suddenly impossible to say anything. She couldn't agree, but there was no other option.

So she was a coward and did nothing at all. But her expression must have portrayed her acquiescence, as he smiled—then grabbed her hand and tugged her after him.

They left Circular Quay, then headed a short way up Macquarie Street.

'Where are we going?' Ruby asked, belatedly.

He came to a stop. 'We're here,' he said. 'My hotel.'

They stood beneath a curved red awning—on red carpet, no less. A suited doorman stood only metres away, but when she glanced at him, he was carefully paying them no attention.

'This isn't cool, Dev, you said—'

'There's a bar on the ground floor, and the staff will guarantee we won't be disturbed—and certainly that no photos will be taken.' His lips quirked upwards—wickedly. 'I'm not inviting you to share a bottle of champagne as we roll about on my bed, Ruby.'

She knew she'd gone as red as the carpet. 'Oh,' she said. 'Of course not.'

'Shall we?' he said, gesturing at the brass-handled doors.

She nodded, and soon they'd made their way through the marble-floored foyer with its sumptuous oriental carpets to the hotel bar—a classic, traditional space. Full of heavy, antique wooden furniture, stunning silk wallpaper and chandeliers dangling with crystals, it was softly lit. A handful of people perched on bar stools, and a couple shared a drink at one table. Along one wall stretched a bench seat, upholstered in delicately patterned black and cream fabric. After Dev asked what she'd like to drink, she made a beeline in that direction, sinking gratefully into the soft cushioning, right in the corner of the room.

She watched Dev as he walked across the bar with their

drinks. He wore a dark suit, but no tie, and a crisp white shirt that was slightly unbuttoned. Somehow he made his outfit look casual and effortless, not formal at all. As if he'd happily wear the same outfit to do his grocery shopping, without a trace of self-consciousness.

The bar definitely was lit for mood, Ruby decided, but even so she was struck again by his unexpected gauntness. He didn't look unwell—just lean. But then, he'd eaten every bite of food in every course tonight…maybe he *had* been sick just like that rumour said? And now he was still putting weight back on. Or something.

She considered asking him, then immediately dismissed the possibility. Whatever had happened outside the restaurant—that moment—told her whatever was going on with Dev, whatever his private pain was, he would not discuss it tonight.

Besides—why would he? She was some random woman he'd even more randomly invited out for dinner.

She would never ask him those questions. They had this one night only.

He sat down, right next to her on the bench seat, rather than across the other side of the table as she'd expected.

*Really?* No. She hadn't honestly believed he'd do that. Of course he sat next to her, not quite touching—but touching was a very, very near thing.

He handed Ruby her wine glass, catching her gaze as he did so.

It was rather dark in this corner of the bar, she realised. Dark and…private.

His fingers brushed against hers and she jumped a little, making her wine splash about in its glass.

'Whoops!' she said, all nervous and breathy, and placed her glass firmly on the table, as if to somehow stabilise her thoughts.

The action was totally ineffective. She took a deep breath, but when she looked up—back into Dev's eyes—her mind went blank.

About all she was capable of at this moment, it appeared, was looking at Dev. And it *was* at Dev she was looking—not

Dev the movie star, but the Dev she'd just had dinner with. This Dev was an enigma—and this Dev, she liked.

He leapt from light to dark, revealing depth—maybe even pain?—that she never would have expected. And then he could slide so easily from teasing to darkly, insistently seductive.

As he was right now. Had he moved closer?

Maybe she had.

He knew she didn't want this, but in this way, at least, he was no gentleman.

He said he wasn't a nice person. Was this what he meant? This determined pursuit of a woman—of her—of what he wanted?

No, she decided. Not entirely. There'd been more, much more...

Ruby was losing herself in his eyes, his gorgeous, piercing blue eyes—but dragging her gaze away proved pointless, as she found herself staring at his lips.

It seemed the most natural, obvious thing in the world to lick her own lips in response.

Okay—now he *had* moved. When had he laid his arm across the back of the bench? She hadn't noticed at the time, but now it seemed a genius move, as it was so easy for his fingers to skim along the delicate, shivery skin of her neck.

Then up, up to her nape, his strong fingers threading through her hair, cupping her skull. But he didn't pull her towards him. Instead, he held her steady—but it really wasn't necessary.

As if she were going to duck her head, or look away now?

Then he was closer again, close enough that even in the dim light she could just see the red that was still in his eyes. For a moment she wondered what was wrong, felt a flash of concern for him...

But then that moment was gone, because she'd let her own eyes flutter shut, and all she could concentrate on was the feel of him breathing against her lips. So close, so close...

And then, finally, he kissed her.

For a crazy, silly moment her mind filled with images of Devlin Cooper kissing other women in movies. Of famous, romantic clinches, and of sexy, twisted sheets and picture-perfect lighting.

But then all that evaporated—as it was all make-believe. All utter Hollywood fantasy. This—this kiss—was real.

She was kissing a very real man. A man who had just teased her lower lip with his tongue. She leant into him, wanting more, needing more.

She needed to touch him, and she reached out blindly, her hand landing somewhere on his chest, then creeping up to his shoulders. His other hand was suddenly touching her, too, beginning at her waist, then creeping around to her back, beneath the little jacket she still wore. His hand splayed across her skin, not that she needed any encouragement to move closer.

He tasted like the wine they'd been sharing, like that crisp sorbet. Fresh. Delectable.

His kisses started off practised, but as she kissed him back, letting herself kiss him in the way he was making her feel, his kisses changed. They were less controlled, more desperate.

Ruby leant into him, matching him kiss for kiss, revelling in the feel and taste of his gorgeous, sexy, sinful mouth.

She felt incredible: beautiful, wanted.

She could sit here for ever, kiss him for ever…

But then his lips were away from her mouth, and trailing kisses along her jaw, up to her ear.

His breath was hot against her skin. So hot.

'Should we go to my room?'

Was that where this night had always been headed? Where they'd been headed since that dusty afternoon they'd first met?

Possibly? Definitely? Ruby didn't know    didn't care.

She just knew that standing now—on legs that would wobble—and leaving this bar for his room was the only imaginable option.

And so when he stood, and held out his hand for her, with that question still shining in his eyes, she knew what she was going to—what she had to—say.

'Yes.'

# CHAPTER SEVEN

DEV LAY FLAT on his back on the sofa, staring up, in the dark, at the ceiling.

He was restless. Completely exhausted, but unable to sleep.

He'd tried pacing the considerable length of the penthouse's living areas, but it hadn't helped—from his experience pacing never did.

If anything his brain's wheels and cogs took the opportunity to whir ever faster, cramming his brain with all sorts of thoughts and ideas—leaving nowhere near enough room for sleep to descend.

He rubbed at his forehead, the action near violent. But as if he could simply erase all this crap away.

And it was crap. Useless, pointless, far-too-late-to-do-anything-about crap.

And so *random*. The stuff his subconscious was coming up with, that was building and festering inside him.

Snatches of time from his childhood.

Rare moments alone with his father.

Rarer words of praise—praise well and truly cancelled out with years and years of frustration and disappointment. At his failures—the straight As he never received, the sports he never mastered, the good behaviour he could never maintain.

And then memories of his brothers, so different from him, and yet who he'd admired so hard it hurt. Almost as much as he'd idolised his father—once.

Okay. Maybe not so random.

Of course he knew what this was about, it was as obvious as the watches his father had worn, the ones that had cost more than the average person's yearly wage, and that his father had made sure everyone noticed. But then, who could blame him? He'd worked *damn hard* for his money…

*I worked damn hard, Devlin, and not so you could throw it all away. You know nothing about sacrifices—about what I would do for my family. Nothing.*

He heard something—footsteps. Soft on the deep carpet.

He turned his head, and watched Ruby as she crept past. He couldn't see much in the almost pitch blackness, but she was most definitely creeping—her shoes dangling from one hand, each step slow and deliberate.

'Ruby,' he whispered. Then watched as she just about jumped out of her skin.

'Dev!'

He sat up and switched on a lamp, making Ruby blink at him in the sudden light.

She stood stock still, in her fancy dress and jacket—although her hair and make-up were somewhat worse for wear.

The reason for her déshabillé made him smile.

Although when he'd left his bedroom she'd been wearing only a sheet and a half-smile as she'd slept. *That,* he thought, was probably his favourite look for the evening. Or morning? Lord. Who knew what time it was any more?

'I thought you were asleep,' she said.

'Otherwise you would've said goodbye?' His voice was unexpectedly rough, rather than teasing as he'd intended.

'Yes—' she said. Then, the words getting increasingly faster, 'Actually, no. I mean, of course I would've said goodbye if you were awake, but I figured it was better if you were asleep. I didn't particularly want an audience for my walk of shame.'

His mouth quirked at her honesty. 'Shame, huh?'

She went pink. 'It's a turn of phrase. Of course I'm not ashamed. Just…' Her gaze flicked to the ceiling. 'This wasn't how I'd planned for the night to end.'

He didn't say 'me, either', because that wouldn't have been true.

It was just other elements of the night that had been unexpected, the moments where he'd looked at Ruby and felt...

He scratched absently at his bare chest.

He had no idea what he felt.

Her eyebrows rose, seemingly reading his mind. 'You are, at the very least, consistent in your arrogance.'

But there was a smile in her voice.

He shrugged unapologetically. 'I was right.'

She sighed, then readjusted the small gold handbag she had hooked over her shoulder. 'I should go.'

He nodded.

Dev went to stand, deciding he should at least be *chivalrous* enough to walk her to the door.

Maybe it was exhaustion. Maybe it was the way his legs had been bent on the too-short sofa, his left leg still weak from his accident—but either way, the result was that rather than ending up vertical, instead, he staggered.

Somehow Ruby was beside him, her arm wrapped tightly around his waist, just above the low-slung waistband of his boxer shorts.

'Careful!' she said, on a gasp.

Not that her slight weight would've made any difference if he'd been about to fall—which he wasn't. He'd tripped over his own feet—he was clumsy. That was all.

He went to shrug her off, annoyed at himself, and annoyed she'd thought he'd needed help.

'I'm fine,' he said. Short and sharp.

But she didn't let go, not completely. Her grip had loosened, but now her other hand traced over his skin, dipping into the slight hollows above and below his left hip.

'I didn't really notice before,' she said, very softly. 'It was dark and we were so caught up in the moment I didn't have much of a chance to look...'

Her fingertips trailed shivery trails across his belly, then up to the corrugation of his abdominal muscles—more defined than ever before. His trainer would be proud.

He meant to push her hand away, but didn't.

She looked up, straight into his eyes, and he was sure—absolutely positive—she was going to ask him what was wrong.

But at the last minute she didn't, and instead glanced away. Of all things, there was a grand piano in the corner of the room, and her attention appeared focused on its glossy black surface.

'I had a tummy bug a few weeks back,' he said, for some stupid reason feeling the need to provide an explanation. 'Lost some weight, and it's taking a while to put back on.' He shrugged. 'I have a fast metabolism.'

She looked up at him, and nodded, but didn't hold his gaze.

Her hand was still exploring, and she'd shifted slightly, so the arm around his waist was now more an embrace as she stood directly in front of him. Her fingers crept up one side of his body, tracing his pectoral muscle, over his flat nipple, then inwards to his breastbone. Then up, up, to the hollow at the base of his throat, across his collarbone, then curling, curling around to his neck.

But now her touch wasn't so gentle. She slid her fingers along his jaw, tilting his head back to her. His gaze connected with hers, darkest brown and startlingly direct.

'Is that why you can't sleep tonight?' she said, her words laced with scepticism.

'That's really none of your business.'

She closed her eyes for a long moment, then shook her head a little. 'No, of course not.'

He felt her begin to withdraw from him, her heat moving away.

His arms, that up to now hadn't moved from his sides, were suddenly around her, tugging her against him.

Her gaze fluttered up, her eyes widening. 'Dev?'

He didn't bother to explain—didn't even know how he would.

All he knew was that he wasn't ready for her to go yet.

So he leant towards her, and covered her lips with a kiss to silence her questions.

A crack between the heavy brocade curtains allowed the smallest slither of early morning light into Dev's bedroom.

Ruby lay on her side, her head propped up on one arm, staring at Dev's back as he slept facing away from her. Where the light hit his skin glowed a delicious olive: from the point of his shoulder it edged the side of his body, tapering gradually down from broad chest to narrow hips. There a sheet was bunched up, tangled around and over his legs.

He slept soundly, his breathing deep and regular.

Given their conversation of a few hours ago, she'd tried to wake him—to say goodbye. But he'd barely stirred when she'd gently touched—and later pushed—his shoulder, so she'd given up. Besides, given the shadows beneath his eyes that Hair and Make-up were spending so much effort covering up, he needed his sleep.

But she'd found getting out of his bed more difficult than she'd expected.

Before, when she'd woken alone, it had been easy. She'd basically leapt out of bed as her eyes had opened in the unfamiliar room—and reality had smacked her, hard.

*What had she done?*

No longer did a gaze she'd practically fallen into, or a touch that had made her whole body zap and tingle with electricity— let alone a kiss that was nothing like anything she'd ever experienced—cloud her judgment.

Now she could see the night for what it was. Not romantic, and surprising, and unexpected.

But a mistake.

Escaping had been the only option. Shoving the whole night somewhere right, right at the back of her mind where *one* day she might look back fondly and remember her date with a movie star.

Ha! More likely she'd remember what an idiot she was for falling for it.

Hadn't she gone beyond this? Beyond being impressed by looks, and a smile, and strength? Beyond decisions that were based on daydreams and chemical attraction—not sense and logic?

Apparently not—as she hadn't moved.

Dev moved though, and rolled onto his back.

In a flash Ruby was out of the bed, backing away until her heels hit the carpeted half-dozen steps that led to the penthouse's sunken bedroom.

But Dev slept on.

As she watched his chest rise up and down, Ruby felt like a complete idiot. So she didn't want him to wake up to see her still here but she *also* didn't want to leave?

She ran both hands through her hair in despair.

This was typical—there was *something* about Dev that had her thinking and acting in contradictions.

*Maybe that* something *is how he looked at me last night? The way he kissed me?*

Ugh! No, she wasn't going to do this to herself.

She was pretty sure she knew what she was doing—she was superimposing the heroes Dev had portrayed in his movies onto the man himself. Giving him traits that his characters—but not Dev—possessed. *Considerate, kind...or even brave, and mysterious...*

Naked, his leanness was blatantly obvious—with every breath each rib was brought into sharp relief. But maybe it was just what he said? A brief illness?

But none of the rumours rang true to Ruby. She didn't believe that he'd been sick, and if he pined for his supermodel ex, he was hiding it remarkably well. And party drugs? It just didn't fit.

She was sure there was something more—something darker. That there were layers to Devlin Cooper.

Or—maybe she should look at this more objectively.

He'd pursued her relentlessly, had arrogantly assumed he'd

get her into bed on the first night—and then promptly had, by being the perfect, charming date. In order to get just what he'd wanted, he'd become her ideal leading man.

He'd done what he was good at—act.

Yes. That was what had happened.

Here was no tortured soul—but simply an arrogant movie star.

So, silently, Ruby dressed, and, again in bare feet, made her escape.

She appreciated the lady at the concierge desk who raised not an eyebrow at her attire, and called her a taxi. Minutes later she was at her hotel, lying flat on her unslept-on bed.

She expected to be full of regret. She certainly should be.

She expected to be berating herself. Furious with herself.

And, she was—that was exactly what her brain was repeating in her head: that she'd made a mistake, that she'd been an idiot, what had she been thinking?

But instead all she could *feel* were memories of that moment she'd stared up into his eyes after he'd nearly fallen. Or out in the street outside the restaurant. Or the way he'd looked at her just before he'd kissed her in the bar.

Pain, passion. And lust, yes…but it had still been…special. In her heart—no matter what her brain was saying—she believed that she was different, that last night was special.

'And how stupid is that?' she said, aloud, and headed for a long, hot, shower.

# CHAPTER EIGHT

WITH A LESS THAN elegant—but effective—movement, Ruby slammed the car door closed with her hip. She considered attempting to push the lock button on her key ring, but after thinking about how she would do that without putting down the pile of papers in her arms—and potentially seeing them fly off over the horizon in the stiff breeze—she decided her hire car was safe enough in a paddock in the middle of nowhere.

In her arms she balanced a reprint of this afternoon's sides, in blue to indicate they were the corrected versions. Today they were filming at the old farmhouse, a couple of kilometres from Unit Base. Really a farming family's actual home, they'd had to repaint the exterior to a less modern hue, and redecorate a handful of rooms—all of which would be returned back to their exact original state once filming was over. So, when she jogged up the wooden steps and through the propped-open front door, she walked into a home without a trace of the twenty-first century—at least not the parts that the cameras would see.

It was an aspect of filming Ruby had always enjoyed—this game of smoke and mirrors. When watching a finished film it never failed to amaze her that it made no difference she knew a staircase led to nowhere, or that a two-hundred-year-old stone cottage had really been built inside a sound studio. In the world of the film it was all real—and so she believed it, too.

Inside she stepped carefully over thick cables that crisscrossed the floor, the bright lights providing welcome warmth after the chill of the breeze outside. She squeezed between the crowds of crew until she found the on-set production assistant, who took the sides gratefully, and quickly filled Ruby in on the latest on-set dramas.

Of course Dev was there; she knew exactly which actors were filming today, so it wasn't a surprise to see him.

She'd been ready to see him this morning. To meet him at his car as had become customary. She'd practised talking him through his day, her standard nothing statements about being available to help him with anything—et cetera, et cetera. She'd been prepared, and totally fine about it—or at least had told herself that—but then she'd arrived at his car and he hadn't been there. And not in his trailer, either.

Graeme had been waiting, instead. To explain that Dev had arrived early, and would no longer require her assistance on set. Given his week of perfect punctuality—but mostly because *not* having to see Dev multiple times a day had massive appeal— she'd conceded.

So really, she should still be totally prepared to see him now. Yet, when she did—carefully only in her peripheral vision— she felt herself react, despite her best intentions. She wouldn't say her heart leapt—or anything so ridiculous—but there was definitely a lightness to her belly, and her skin went warm. She was unquestionably *aware* of him.

He sat at a rough-hewn kitchen table, his legs outstretched and his booted-feet crossed. He held a cardboard cup of coffee as he chatted to the director, that man's trademark baseball cap pulled down low.

If Dev was aware of her, there was absolutely no evidence of it. In his soft cream shirt, pushed up to his elbows and open at his throat, he looked the very epitome of relaxed. Not at all bothered that the woman he'd slept with not even forty-eight hours ago was five metres away.

Had he even noticed she was there?

*Who cared if he did?*

She was loitering—she'd done what she was here to do. She should leave.

So she did, circumventing the gaffer and the director of photography and their vigorous discussion about the room's lighting as she stepped out into the farmhouse hallway. The whole time—and it really bothered her she'd noticed this—Dev didn't as much as glance in her direction.

She made herself walk briskly to her car, as she really did need to get back to Unit Base, after all. She slid into her seat and slammed the door firmly behind her.

But instead of putting the key in the ignition, she found herself just sitting there for a moment, staring at the house.

What was she waiting for? For Dev to come charging out of the house, to wrench open the white hire car door and pull her into his arms?

Certainly not. That was the last thing she wanted. No one could know what had happened between them. Ever.

It was good he'd ignored her. Perfect. Exactly what she wanted. She'd been relieved this morning when he'd cancelled her babysitting services—so what was different now?

Maybe because she was so much better at logical thought without Devlin Cooper in the vicinity.

She started the car, and drove carefully over a paddock rife with dips and potholes, her lips curving into a smile that was sadder than she would've liked.

Because really, this was laughable—that she cared that he'd so blatantly ignored her. That she'd created depth and layers and a *connection* with Devlin Cooper.

When of course, absolutely none of it—just like that early-nineteen-hundreds kitchen he'd been sitting in—had been real.

The unexpected creak of the cottage's front door opening had Ruby nearly leaping out of her chair. She glanced up at the loudly ticking clock on the production office wall: seven minutes past nine.

It was late. Very late. Even Paul had left twenty minutes ago.

It must be one of the security guards, checking up on her.

As she came to that logical conclusion she let out a breath she hadn't even realised she'd been holding, and smiled.

Who else would it be? The boogie monster?

'It's just me, Craig!' she called out to the slowly approaching footsteps. 'I'll just be a few more minutes.'

Her laptop made its little 'new email' pinging sound, and so her gaze was drawn in that direction as a man stepped into the doorway.

'Craig's having a beer with my driver, but I'll be sure to let him know.'

Ruby's gaze darted up—not that she needed the visual to confirm who that unmistakeable voice belonged to.

He'd propped himself up against the door's chipped architraving, as casual as you liked, in jeans and a black zip-up jumper.

For a moment her body reacted just as it had that afternoon in the farmhouse—every cell, every single part of her, suddenly on high alert. And for the same amount of time she was irrationally pleased to see him—long enough for her lips to form into the beginnings of a smile.

And then reality hit. The smile dropped, and Ruby stood up—abruptly enough that her chair skittered backwards on the floorboards.

'What are you doing here?'

He raised an eyebrow. 'Visiting you.'

'Why?'

Dev crossed his arms. 'Because I wanted to.'

Ruby realised she was wringing her hands and so pressed her palms down hard against the outside of her thighs. 'But today—' she began, then cut her words off as she realised where she was going.

He shrugged. 'I assumed the rules still applied—that you wanted no one on set to know.'

She shook her head. 'It doesn't matter. I mean, of course I don't want anyone to know, but I don't care that you ignored me. It was good, actually.'

Her words were all rambling and jumbled, and she sighed, resisting the urge to run her hands through her hair.

What was it about Dev?

Now Dev pushed away from the doorway. 'I wasn't ignoring you, Ruby,' he said, his voice low as he walked towards her. 'In fact, I don't think it would be possible for me to ignore you.'

He stood on the other side of her desk, watching her. He was so close, close enough that too many memories of Saturday night rushed right back to the surface, despite many hours of determinedly burying them all.

Most clear was the feel of his hands on her. Skimming across her skin, pressed against her back, gentle as they traced her curves.

She shivered, and that unwanted response snapped her back to the present.

'You should go,' she said. Very calmly.

He blinked, obviously surprised. 'Why?'

She laughed. 'Come on, we both know what Saturday was. You don't need to spell it out to me. I get it.'

'Get what?' he said, his forehead forming into furrows.

She sighed loudly. 'That it was a one-off.'

'You think I came here tonight to tell you that?'

'Why else would you be here?'

'I don't know,' he said, his gaze flicking to her lips. 'Maybe I was hoping for another kiss.'

It was so unexpected that Ruby was momentarily shocked silent. *Another kiss.*

It was…almost romantic. Somehow he'd taken what they had: a one-night stand—something you'd never associate with anything sweet or innocent, or meaningful—and ended up with that. A request for a kiss.

'That would be taking a couple of steps backwards, wouldn't it?' She spoke harshly, deliberately implying a tawdriness that the night they'd shared deserved.

He took a step back, as if she'd shoved him away with actions, and not only words.

His eyes were wide, and he went to speak—but then stopped.
His gaze sharpened. Darkened.

'Don't work too late,' he said.

Then turned on his heel, and left.

All week, his mum kept calling.

And every time, he let it ring out. She left messages, but after a while he didn't bother listening to those, either.

Couldn't listen, maybe?

It didn't matter.

He knew what she was calling about. The funeral. It had been more than three months now.

That first call, the worst one, hadn't been from his mum, but from his eldest brother, Jared. He was a doctor, a surgeon, actually, and he'd been using his doctor voice when Dev had answered his phone. As always, Dev had been on edge, used to his brother's patronising calls, his regular requests to visit home more often. That his mum missed him.

Never his dad.

But this call had been different. The doctor-voice had been the thinnest of veneers, and it had taken no time at all for Jared to crack. And that was when Dev had finally understood that something was very, very wrong.

A heart attack. No warning. Nothing that could be done.

*Dad's dead. The funeral's next week. You can stay with Mum. It would be good for her, she's...lost.*

Except he wasn't going to the funeral. And he didn't.

He was pathetic not to answer her calls, or to listen to her messages. Pathetic and weak and useless.

But he just couldn't do it—he just couldn't deal with it. Not yet.

It was ringing now, as it had every day since he'd arrived in Australia. Dev couldn't stand it, so he pushed away from his dining-room table to where his phone sat on the kitchen bench, and declined the call.

Gutless.

That was what he was.

Eventually he walked to his bedroom, around his bed and straight to the en suite. The tray of sleeping tablets was looking bare. He knew he shouldn't be taking them every night, his doctor had warned him of the dangers, of the side effects—but he couldn't risk what happened on his last film again. Back then, each night, he'd had every intention of making it to set the next morning. He'd had his alarm set well before his call, he'd re-read his script—everything. Then sleep wouldn't come at all, or he'd wait too late to take the tablet that would lead to oblivion. And by the time he woke up it was too late. Or—worse—he did wake up in time, but in the raw of the morning, before he'd had a chance to wake up, to remind himself who he was, how hard he'd worked, what he'd achieved…he honestly didn't care. He didn't care enough to get out of bed, to get to set. He didn't care about anything.

But this film was different. The mornings hadn't changed, not really—more often than not he slept through his alarm, or threw it across the room—but when Graeme knocked on the door he'd drag himself out of bed, and with every step he'd get a tighter grip of what he was doing, where he had to be, what he was doing that day.

He had his pride. He was a professional, and a damned good actor. A whole film crew was waiting for him.

Or at least it had been different. These last few days when Graeme had knocked, getting out of bed had been harder. He'd needed even more coffee once he'd hit Unit Base—enough that his own coffee machine had materialised in his trailer.

He swallowed the tablet, then cupped his hands under the running tap to collect enough water to wash it down. Water trickled down his neck, then down his bare chest, forming damp, dark spots along the waistband of his tracksuit pants.

He leant forward, staring into his eyes. Under the harsh lights, his eyes were red despite all the drops that Hair and Make-up were giving him. His face was a jumble of sharp angles and shadows, his skin dull…

This had to end.

He was over this. Over it, over it, over it, over it…

Tomorrow would be different.

He switched off the lights and flopped onto his bed, his skin too hot and his legs too restless to cover himself with even a sheet.

Tomorrow would be different.

If he kept saying it, one day it would actually be true.

Ruby hammered on Dev's front door. It was a really lovely door, with panels of stained glass, and part of her worried that she'd damage it. Only a very small part, though. A much bigger part of her wanted Dev to get his backside to Unit Base. Pronto.

'Don't worry,' said Graeme beside her. 'It won't break.'

He stepped forward with an air of much experience and put her hammering to shame, rattling the door with his heavy-fisted knocks.

The delicate glass held. The noise was deafening. But there was still no sign of Dev.

'Do you have a key?' she asked, trying to peer through the multicoloured glass.

'No,' he said.

Ruby took a step back and put her hands on her hips as she surveyed the house.

Paul had called her to his office barely thirty minutes ago, and she'd shot out of her office and to Dev's cottage in record time. Unfortunately, Dev's call had been ten minutes prior to Paul's *'Where the hell is Devlin Cooper?'* rant, and with every minute that passed—and with a twenty-minute drive back to Unit Base…

Basically she needed Dev out of his house and into his car *now*.

There were only two windows on the front of the sandstone cottage, edged in dark red brick. Both were closed, and a quick test proved they weren't going to open easily. The white-painted veranda wrapped around the side of the house, and Ruby followed it, stopping at each window to check for an entry point. So far—no luck.

The back of the house was a modern extension, with the veranda opening out into a deck with views to the mountains—not that Ruby paid any attention to it. Instead she zeroed into a flash of pale colour—curtains that were flapping through a small gap in the sliding doors. It was only a small gap—did that mean Dev hadn't closed it properly when he'd left? Or when he'd returned?

Ruby hoped like heck it was the latter, because he certainly wasn't on set—her phone had remained silent—so if he wasn't in the house she had no idea where on earth to look for him next.

She had to push the door open to create a space large enough to walk through. She stepped through the curtain, pausing a moment to untangle herself from the heavy fabric. Inside it was dark—gloomy despite the sunny day outside. And silent—completely silent.

For the first time it occurred to Ruby that maybe Dev hadn't simply slept in. She'd immediately assumed he was lounging about, deciding he had more important things to do than—you know—his job.

'Dev?' she called out. Or meant to. Instead she managed little more than a whisper.

She cleared her throat, and tried again. 'Dev?'

Again—silence. This shouldn't be surprising given the noise she and Graeme had been making was infinitely louder, and had certainly elicited no response.

But still, only now did Ruby worry.

What if the rumours were true?

She knew many celebrities kept their addictions well hidden—many more did not—but Dev… She just couldn't believe it. She'd spent a night with him—surely she would've guessed?

She stood in the lounge room, and it was clearly empty. The hallway beckoned, and she broke into a run, throwing open doors as she went.

Bedroom—empty.

Study—empty

What would she know, or could she know, really, about Dev?

She thought of his gaunt frame, the sometimes emptiness in his gaze. Not all the time, and certainly not when he'd been looking straight at her—but there'd been moments when there'd been depth and flickers of so much…

No. She needed to stop that, needed to stop imagining things that weren't there. Romanticising no more than a forgettable collection of moments in time.

And she would forget them, eventually.

Right now she needed to focus—on her job, why she was here. She needed to find Dev and get him on set.

Her phone trilled its message notification, but she didn't bother to check. She knew what it was—Paul. Wanting to know where she was, and why she wasn't on set with Dev already. Five minutes ago, even.

Another room—a larger space, a sitting room. Also empty.

The next—a bedroom.

Occupied.

The door creaked on old hinges as she flung it all the way open, and rattled a vase on a side table when it smacked against the wall.

Then she was at the bed, kneeling on the soft mattress as she reached across the wide expanse to grab onto a bare male shoulder. And shake it—hard.

'Dev! Wake up.'

A sheet was twisted around his legs, and his skin was covered in goose pimples in the freezing room, the air-conditioning unit on the wall bizarrely turned on high.

She shook him again. 'Damn it, Dev!'

Her heart raced, her breath caught in her throat.

Then all of a sudden he moved, rolling effortlessly onto his back, his eyes opening slowly.

Ruby let out her breath in a huge sigh of relief, dropping her hands onto her knees. For a minute or so she just took deep breaths, staring down at her own hands as they gripped her jeans.

'You scared me half to death,' she eventually managed.

He reached up, rubbing at his eyes, his movements deliberate and heavy. He turned his head on the pillow to look at her, his lips tipping up into a smile.

'Good morning,' he said, all husky and unbelievably sexy.

'Oh, no,' she said. 'It is *not* a good morning, Mr Cooper. You're late.'

He blinked, obviously confused. Rather than reply, he reached for her, his fingers grazing along the denim covering her thigh.

'Come here,' he said.

She scooted back, but probably not as fast as she should. He grabbed her hand before she slid off the bed, tugging her towards him with a strength she hadn't expected. Or maybe it was just that she didn't resist.

Somehow she was right up beside him, leaning over him, her legs pressed up against the bare skin of his waist, and his hip where his tracksuit bottoms had slid down just a little.

She looked down at him, at his incredibly handsome face—even in the gloom and with pillow creases on one cheek—and forgot what she'd been about to say.

He still held her hand, clasped on top of her legs, and a finger traced hypnotic patterns across the delicate bones beneath her knuckles.

His other hand reached across his body, to touch her other arm where it hung uselessly beside her—neither touching him nor pushing him away. His touch slid upwards, feather light, following the shape of her wrist, her forearm, her elbow, then jumping across, and around her, to her back. And then—he pulled her against him.

She gasped as she fell, landing across his chest. He was warm now, hot, in fact, and her body was fast catching up as his hands travelled across her back.

Ruby looked directly into his eyes, eyes that were anything

but empty. A gaze that she found compelled her, questioned her, wanted her.

So she leant towards him, towards all that, then closer, closer, their kiss mere millimetres, mere milliseconds away...

And then she was gone—off the bed and metres away, her back to him as she took deep, deep, what-the-hell-am-I-doing? breaths.

She shouldn't be doing this. No. She *couldn't.*

Then behind her, he laughed. A low, unexpected sound that reverberated all the way down to her toes.

She spun around, her nails digging into her palms as her hands formed into furious fists. 'What's so funny?'

He'd sat up, his shoulders propped against the wrought-iron bed head. His gaze flicked over her, from her long boots and jeans up to her layers of vests and thin wool jumpers to keep her warm in the cool spring air.

'You,' he said. 'This. What *is* your problem?'

'*My* problem?' Ruby said, and then swallowed, trying to relocate her brain—and, while she was at it, any sense of professionalism she still possessed. 'The only problem I have is that you were required on set—' she pulled her phone out of her pocket to check the time '—over an hour ago.'

For the shortest of moments his eyes flickered, and his expression shifted. He looked—surprised? Disappointed? Angry?

Then it had all disappeared to be replaced by a look she was all too familiar with—arrogance.

He tilted his head back, so it rested against the wall. Then slowly and deliberately, he turned his head towards her, every pore of his body oozing exactly how little he cared.

It was all very...*practised.*

Ruby's eyes narrowed as she met his, trying to see past this hastily erected façade, trying to figure out...*Dev,* really.

No. She didn't have time for this.

'I need you to get a move on, Mr Cooper. So we don't lose the whole morning.'

He nodded. 'Yes,' he said. 'I can see how you would need that.'

Dev didn't move.

Ruby stepped forward, and Dev's gaze dipped to her still-fisted fingers. 'Exactly what do you think you're going to do with those?'

Instantly her fingers were flat against her thighs.

'Are you unwell, Mr Cooper?'

He shook his head. 'I think you're quite aware how healthy I am.'

Ruby's cheeks went hot, but she pushed on, now right beside the edge of the bed. 'Then I really need you to get out of bed immediately. A lot of people are waiting for you.'

He shrugged. Then he looked pointedly at her hands—again fisted. But this time she made no move to relax them. Much more of this and she might well *actually* hit him.

'Mr Cooper. I'm sure you're aware of your contractual obligations.'

'Of course,' he said, with a nod. But then did not elaborate further.

Ruby swallowed a sigh. He knew the deal—this far into filming and with Arizona due to leave the country, there was *no way* that Paul could replace Dev. Besides, it wasn't as if there were a bevy of other A-list actors banging down the producer's door.

'Fine,' she said. 'Let's get to the point. I want you on set as soon as possible. You—for reasons unknown—have chosen to stay in bed today. And—inexplicably—despite the dozens of people relying on the success of this film, wish to stay here.'

'I'd agree with that assessment.' His voice was as dry as dust, his expression patently unmoved.

'So tell me,' she said, making absolutely no attempt to sound professional any more, 'what exactly do I need to do to get you out of this room?'

At this, he smiled. A real smile—a delicious smile. A smile that moved the heat still in her cheeks to somewhere low in her belly. It was a visceral reaction she couldn't have prevented if she tried.

And Ruby had the sudden realisation that this was where Dev had been heading the whole time. To this question.

'A favour,' he said.

He'd locked his gaze to hers. A gaze she didn't have a hope of interpreting.

Why did she even bother? Hadn't she decided he was just an actor, portraying whatever emotion or personality that would get what he wanted out of a situation?

'What type of favour exactly?'

Another shrug. 'I haven't decided yet.'

She gaped at him. 'You don't seriously expect me to agree to that?'

He didn't say a word, just looked at her. Then, after a while, slid down along the mattress until his head hit the pillow. Then, as calmly as you liked, turned onto his side. His back to her.

Ruby's mind raced, considering her options.

Could she go and find Graeme? Get him to somehow strong-arm Dev out to the car?

A quick glance at Dev, and his muscled physique and sheer size nixed that idea. No, that wouldn't work.

She could call Paul?

And…what? Her job was to solve problems. Paul expected her to solve things—once he gave her a problem, quite simply it ceased to be his. It was *her* problem.

'It can't be illegal,' she said, finally.

He casually turned over, to smile that devastating smile at her yet again, his chin propped on one hand.

My God. She was helpless to prevent the rapid acceleration of her heat—even at completely inappropriate moments, her body reacted to him.

'It won't be.'

'And it can't be a…' Ruby had to look away, staring at the elaborate cornicing above the curtains '…a kiss,' she said. Then faster, 'Or anything else like that.'

In seconds he was up, out of bed, standing right in front of her, forcing her to look at him. The emptiness had gone, but what he'd exposed was impossible to interpret.

'Is that how little you—?' he started. Then stopped.

Then in a different, heavier tone, the shutters firmly up again, he spoke. 'No.'

Ruby backed away, needing to put space between them.

'So you'll come now? Right this instant?'

He nodded.

'Okay,' she said. 'Fine. A favour. Done.'

She thought she'd get that smile again—but didn't. He just kept looking at her, revealing not a thing.

So she backed away even further, right outside the room and into the hallway.

'You've got two minutes to meet me out the front,' she said, briskly. Like Production Co-ordinator Ruby, not the Ruby who'd very nearly kissed Devlin Cooper again.

She didn't wait around for him to respond, she was just out of there. Away from him, away from the mass of confusion and attraction and questions and heat that was every encounter with Dev.

Outside, on the decking, she stared up at the cloudless sky. Just stared and stared and stared.

And wondered what on earth she'd just agreed to.

What on earth she'd just done.

# CHAPTER NINE

DAYS PASSED. A week.

Nothing.

Ruby barely saw Dev at Unit Base, and the few times she did get out to set he didn't even notice she was there—or at least certainly gave the impression he didn't.

When she ate dinner at the pub a few times after work, she deliberately kept her back to the door and talked and laughed with her friends as normal—because it wasn't as if she cared if Dev arrived or anything.

And then she hated herself for looking over her shoulder whenever a footfall was somehow heavier or different or whatever. Just in case.

Occasionally she'd kid herself that he'd forgotten about their deal. That he was half asleep and didn't remember, or that he'd never meant it anyway.

But she didn't, truly, believe that.

So late on a Saturday afternoon, after a six-day work week and with every cell in her body desperate to crawl into bed and sleep straight through until Monday, it didn't really surprise her to see Dev sitting on the jarrah bench seat outside her apartment.

Equally, it didn't surprise her when her heart did a little somersault. Didn't surprise her—but she wasn't exactly happy about it either.

He wore jeans, T-shirt and a black jacket. A rugby team's baseball cap was pulled down low over his forehead, and dark sunglasses covered his eyes. He pushed himself to his feet as she slid out of her car.

Ruby locked the doors, and walked towards him as nonchalantly as possible, fumbling only slightly as she located her key.

'Is this your version of going incognito?' she asked as she stepped onto the small porch. 'As I don't think you're fooling anyone.'

'You'd be surprised how many people don't recognise me,' he drawled, catching her gaze with a pointed look.

For what felt like the hundredth time since they'd met, Ruby blushed, and she turned her head to give the task of opening the door her complete attention.

'You'd better come inside before the whole town starts talking,' she said as the door swung open. 'Apparently my motel manager tops even the local hairdresser in knowing all the Lucyville gossip.'

'That's a real issue for you, isn't it?' he asked, following her inside. 'People talking about you?'

Inside her apartment Ruby wasn't exactly sure what to do. After all, she had no idea why Dev was actually here.

'I would've thought you'd understand that,' she said, throwing her handbag onto the tiny kitchen bench. 'Given how much the world gossips about you.'

*Tea,* she decided. She'd make them both a cup of tea.

'For me, gossip's a necessary evil. I can't expect all the perks of fame without some of the crap.'

Ruby flicked the switch on the kettle, then found two coffee mugs that she placed onto the laminate counter. One had a chip on the handle.

Somehow, making tea for Dev in this simple little apartment seemed more surreal than anything else that had happened between them. She rubbed her thumb over the chip a few times, trying to pull her thoughts together.

Why was he here? What favour was he going to ask of her?

Dev was resting both his hands on the other side of the counter, watching her. 'Ruby?'

What were they talking about again?

'Gossip,' she said, reminding herself. 'Well. I'm not famous, obviously. So there's no real positive out of people spreading rumours about me, is there? Wouldn't it be more strange if it *didn't* bother me?'

'But you seem slightly more…obsessed with maintaining a lily-white reputation. Not one whisper of scandal is allowed when it comes to Ruby Bell. No hint of the slightest moment of unprofessionalism.'

Ruby snorted most inelegantly. 'My reputation is not lily white, I can assure you.'

Dev raised his eyebrows, but Ruby just shrugged as she flipped open a box of teabags and dropped one into each mug.

'I told you the other night that I had a bit of a wild youth. Well, unsurprisingly, that type of behaviour generates gossip. A lot of gossip. Some of it accurate, a lot of it not. According to the local grapevine, it's quite frightening the number of people I slept with as a seventeen-year-old.'

Ruby smiled as she reached for the boiled kettle and saw Dev's expression. 'Don't look so shocked. I wasn't as bad as people made out, but I did enough to deserve a good chunk of my reputation. I'm not proud of myself—but it's done now. I was very young, very naïve. But I've learnt, moved on—I'm not the same person any more.'

'You're not the type of person who gets gossiped about.'

Dunking the teabags, she looked up, pleased he'd understood. 'Yes, exactly. I had enough to deal with back then without the speculating glances, the whispers and the innuendo. In fact, gossip made my behaviour worse—I confused people talking about me with people actually giving a crap about me. Although, for a while, just being noticed was enough.' Ruby paused, and laughed without humour. 'And you know what? I was the one who figured out I needed to change, that I needed to grow up, and not one judgmental comment by some know-it-all busybody made one iota of difference.'

Too late she realised she'd raised her voice, and tea was now splashed in tiny droplets across the counter.

'Oh,' she said, in a small voice. Then stepped away, snatching up a tea towel and blotting ineffectually at the hot liquid.

Dev was now in the kitchen with her, and he reached out, taking the towel from her.

'What happened?' he asked.

She looked down at her feet, and wiggled her toes in her ballet flats.

'I didn't say anything happened,' she said.

'But it did.'

She looked up abruptly, her lips beginning to form the words and sentences to explain...

Then she realised she was standing in a two-and-a-half-star holiday apartment with peeling vinyl flooring with one of the most famous men in the world.

No, he really didn't need to know about any of what happened.

So she remained silent.

For a long minute she was sure he was going to push—but he didn't.

Instead he calmly picked up the coffee mugs and tipped their remaining contents down the sink.

'We don't really have any time for a drink, anyway,' he said, his back still to her.

'Why's that?' she replied, for a moment, confused. Then, in a flash, she remembered—the only possible reason why he was here. She swallowed. 'The favour.'

He turned slowly, then leant his hips against the cabinets. Belatedly, he nodded.

'Our plane leaves in just over an hour.'

Ruby knew her mouth was gaping open, but was helpless to do anything about it.

Dev smiled. A devilish smile that was becoming so, so familiar.

'We have a party to attend. In Sydney. No time to drive so I chartered a plane.'

As you did.

'A party?' Ruby asked, when her jaw had begun functioning again.

'It's just casual, at a private home. A birthday party of a—friend.'

He said it as if that was all the information she could possibly need. When she stood, just staring at him, his eyes narrowed impatiently.

'You really need to go pack.'

'What if I have plans tonight?' she asked.

He shrugged. 'You agreed to the deal.'

'I didn't agree to put my life on hold at your whim.'

He grinned. 'Lord, Ruby, I do like you.'

She shook her head, dismissing what he said. 'I have plans tonight.'

Plans involving instant noodles and a small pile of romantic comedy DVDs, but still—plans.

'Well, you should've thought of that at the time. Negotiated appropriate methods of notification of the favour or something—but, you didn't. So—here we are. And I'd like to cash in my favour. Tonight.'

Ruby considered continuing her argument. Or just flat out refusing to go. He wouldn't, after all, drag her out of her apartment against her will.

Maybe he saw what she was thinking in her eyes.

'It's just a party, Ruby. Nothing sinister, I promise. You might even have fun.'

But still, she hesitated. He was so brash, so sure of getting his way...

'I really don't want to go on my own.'

That sentence was said much more harshly than what had come before. But oddly, without the same self-assurance. Quite the opposite, in fact.

And so, somehow, she found herself packing her little red carry-on suitcase.

Then minutes later she was sitting beside him in the back seat of Dev's four-wheel drive, zipping along as Graeme drove them to the airport. And to the mysterious party beyond.

The luxurious Cessna took less than an hour to cover the four hundred and fifty kilometres between the single-runway Lucyville airport—the home of the local aero-club and certainly no commercial airlines or chartered jets—and the private terminal adjacent to Sydney International airport.

Unsurprisingly, Ruby had asked a lot of questions in the drive to the Lucyville airport. Dev had responded carefully with as few words as possible:

Whose party is it? *Ros.*

And she was? *A friend.* He'd managed to say this more confidently this time—regardless, Ruby had still raised an eyebrow.

How many people could be there? *Fifty?* He had no idea.

Where was it? *Her house.*

Why don't you want to go alone?

To this, he'd simply shrugged, and by then they'd arrived at the small strip of tarmac amongst the patchwork paddocks—and there was no more time for questions.

Take-off was taken up with a safety demonstration by their stewardess, plus a bit of oohing and aahing by Ruby over their plush leather seats that faced each other and the glossy cabinetry in the little food and beverage galley behind the cockpit.

'This is completely awesome,' she'd said at the time. Dev agreed—money made life a lot easier and, at times like this, a lot more fun.

Fortunately, in this instance, it also distracted Ruby from her quest to discover exactly where they were going.

During the short flight she was ensconced in the jet's tiny bathroom, courtesy of his explanation that they would need to drive direct from the airport to the party. This had earned him yet another glare, and then later another—from freshly made-up eyes—as she'd buckled up next to him for landing, plucking at the fabric of her jeans.

'I really didn't have anything suitable to wear.'

'You look fantastic,' he'd said—sincerely—running his gaze over her brown leather heeled boots, dark blue jeans, creamish camisole and navy blue velvet blazer.

She'd just rolled her eyes. Which—again—she'd repeated when he'd quickly changed on arrival in Sydney.

'Two minutes to look like *that*? Really?'

But she'd smiled, and he'd been stupidly pleased that she'd approved of how he looked.

Now they sat in the back seat of another black four-wheel drive, this time with a new driver, Graeme having been left a little flabbergasted back in Lucyville. But then, he couldn't do much given Dev hadn't booked him onto the flight.

Which hadn't been a difficult decision. No doubt he'd hear all about it from Veronica—sooner rather than later. But right now, it was all about tonight.

Ruby made a few attempts at conversation, but all fell flat. Instead Dev found himself staring at nothing out of the window, Sydney passing him by in a multicoloured blur of lights. As their destination became closer, even the lights failed to register as his eyes completely unfocused.

Then he didn't know what he was looking at, or thinking about. *Nothing* he told himself, but of course he wasn't.

Snatches of voices, bursts of laughter, moments of anger, conspiratorial giggles. Memories. None fully formed, more a collage, a show-reel of moments in time. All set in one place, at one house—at one home.

When the driver pulled into the familiar ornate gates, Dev waited for the crunch of flawlessly raked gravel—but there was none. The tyres rolled across a driveway that had been paved perfectly smooth some time in the past fourteen years.

The driver expertly negotiated the cars parked along the semi-circular curve, pulling to a stop directly before the tiered garden steps that led to the front door.

Ruby opened her own door, stepping out of the car almost the moment the car rolled to a stop. Hands on hips, she stood, surveying the house, the gardens—and the guests who flowed around them, walking up from the street in couples and groups.

Dev sent the driver on his way and joined Ruby, watching her watch what was happening around her.

Up until this moment she'd displayed not one hint of nervousness about the evening. Yes, she'd been a little bothered about the lack of time to prepare, and had sighed loudly at his halfway answers to her questions. That she was frustrated with *him,* there was no doubt.

But otherwise she'd been typically no-nonsense Ruby. Just as she was on set, she'd been calm, and focused. He'd almost been able to read her thoughts: *It's just a party. No big deal.*

Now they were here, however, he could see sudden tension in her posture.

She turned towards him, tiny lines etching her forehead.

'Who am I?' she asked.

It took him a moment to figure out what that meant.

'You mean if anyone asks?'

Her answering nod was terribly stiff.

Lord. He didn't know. He barely knew why *he* was here, let alone how he should describe his unexpected guest.

'My—'

He was going to say *date,* for the reward of that flash to her eyes—that delicious reaction of heat tinged with anger.

But tonight he found riling her was not on the top of his list of things to do.

So no—he wouldn't push, he wouldn't call this a date when he knew in her head she'd so stubbornly decreed that they would never, ever date again.

'—friend,' he finished.

It sounded lame—and like a lie. As much of a lie as calling *Ros* a friend.

And somehow it was also the wrong thing to say, as Ruby took a big step back, then looked away, staring up at the moon.

'How about we just go with work colleague?' she said, with a razor-sharp edge.

He didn't have a chance to respond, or to even begin to figure out what he'd done wrong, when she began to stride towards the house.

He caught up with her well before they reached the door, where a smartly dressed man—but still obviously a security guard—widened his eyes as he recognised him.

He opened the door for them without a word, and inside, in a redecorated but still familiar foyer, a small crowd of guests mingled.

Ruby looked at him curiously, and he knew what she was thinking. The guests were all older than them, by a good twenty or thirty years.

But then the enthusiastic chatter stilled, and one by one people turned to face him, replacing their cacophony with whispered speculation.

Then, from amongst it all, out stepped a women with silver-blonde hair styled in the sleekest of bobs, and an elegant dress that flattered a figure still fit and trim at—as of today—sixty.

Her eyes, so similar to his, were wide, and coated in a sheen he didn't want to think about too much.

As dignified as always, she approached them politely. Although her smile went well beyond that—it was broad. Thrilled.

Dev felt his own mouth form into a smile in response—not as wide, not as open, yet he still had the sense he'd been holding his breath for hours.

He reached for Ruby, wrapping his hand around hers in an instinctive movement.

'Ruby, this is Ros,' he said, 'my—'

'Mother,' she finished.

Ruby didn't look at him, she simply smoothly accepted the hand that his mum offered, and wished his mother a happy birthday.

'I'm Ruby,' she added, 'a colleague of Dev's.'

His mother glanced to their joined hands, then back to Dev, questions dancing in her eyes.

But no, he wasn't about to explain.

A long moment passed, and Dev realised he'd made a mistake. He should've hugged his mum, or something...but he'd felt frozen. Out of practice.

Then it was too late, and his mum said something that was terribly polite, and trilled her lovely, cultured laugh, and disappeared back into the crowd. A crowd now full of disapproving expressions, all aimed in his direction.

Yes, he knew who he was—the son who'd blown off his father's funeral.

*This is a mistake.*

He still held Ruby's hand, and he would've tugged her outside, straight back to their car, if more guests hadn't filled the space behind them. Instead, he pulled her into one of the front rooms—'the library', his mum called it, with its walls of multicoloured books and oriental carpets.

Or at least he thought he'd drawn Ruby into the room—belatedly he realised it was more Ruby doing the directing. Inside, she dropped his hand, and pushed the door shut behind them, hard enough that it verged towards a slam.

'This is your *mother's* birthday party, Dev?' she said. Then on a slightly higher pitch, 'You invited me to your *mother's* birthday party?'

He nodded, because there was nothing else he could do.

Her hands were back on her hips again, and she took a long, deep breath. 'Okay. So, do you want to hurry up about telling me *what on earth* is going on?'

Ruby was doing her absolute best to hold herself together. What she wanted to do—desperately—was throw something in Dev's direction. Something hard, preferably.

What the hell was he playing at? Just who did he think he was?

A floor lamp glowed in the corner, and flames flickered in

the fireplace, throwing soft light across the room and making the dark leather of the button-backed chesterfield lounge suite shine.

Into that shininess, Dev sank, stretching his legs out long before him. He tilted his head backwards, resting it along the back of the sofa, and stared upwards, as if the delicate ceiling rose suddenly required his full attention.

'We can go in a minute,' he said, just before she was about to speak again.

The low words—quiet and so unexpected—had her swallowing the outburst she'd had ready.

All of a sudden the fight went out of her—and all she could remember was the reason she'd agreed to come here in the first place: *I really don't want to go on my own.*

'Go?'

He looked at her. 'Yeah. There's a restaurant I like, at Darling Harbour. I won't have any trouble getting us in.'

Ruby had been standing near the door, but now she crossed the room, perching on the edge of the single chesterfield armchair directly across from Dev, her booted feet only inches from his distressed leather loafers.

'Why would you want to leave your mother's birthday party? I bet it's a milestone, too, given all these people.'

'Her sixtieth.'

Ruby nodded. 'So why leave?' she repeated.

He stood up abruptly, and shoved both hands into his pockets. 'It was a dumb idea to come. I don't know what I was thinking.'

'How was it a dumb idea to come to your own mother's birthday party?'

Dev's gaze was trained on the fire, and he stood perfectly still.

'It just was. Is.'

Now he looked at her, but in the uneven light she couldn't read a thing. 'I'm confused,' she said.

He shook his head dismissively. 'You don't need to understand. Let's go.'

His fingers wrapped around the door handle, but before he had a chance to twist it open Ruby was on her feet.

'I don't need to understand?' she asked, far from politely, stepping closer so they were almost toe to toe. 'You're telling me I'm supposed to just accept that you whisked me across the state *and* deliberately concealed our exact destination—and ask no questions?'

'Yes,' he said. 'That would be ideal.'

Dev rubbed his forehead, not looking at her. In the flickering shadows, the darkness beneath his eyes was suddenly even more pronounced.

Without thinking, Ruby reached out, running a finger whisper-soft along the top edge of his cheekbone.

At her touch, his hand dropped to his side, but otherwise he didn't move a muscle.

'Does tonight have something to do with *this?*' she asked, her fingertips tracing across to the smudges of black beneath his eyes.

For long moments, their gazes met, his momentarily open and revealing above her exploratory touch.

That his unspoken answer was *Yes,* was obvious—but there was more. A lot more.

His eyes revealed a depth of emotion she'd only seen before in glimpses. But now, right this second, he'd set it all free— for her to see.

But what was she seeing? Sadness, she knew. She recognised. And loss. Guilt?

But then it was all gone, gone as quickly as he gently but firmly took her wrist and pushed it away.

'Let's go,' he said. Again, he reached for the door.

Ruby touched him again, covering his much larger hand partially with hers.

'I think we should stay.'

He was staring at their hands. Ruby could feel the tension beneath her palm, the rigid shape of his knuckles.

'Why?'

'Because you want to stay.'

He looked up, his eyebrows raised. 'And how, exactly, do you know that?'

She had no idea. But she did.

She shrugged, deciding it best to say nothing at all. She stepped away, lifting her hand away from his, conscious that she really had no idea what was going on here. That she was the last person in the world who should be advising anyone on their own family issues.

Dev was right, really—there was no reason she needed to understand any of this. Not why Dev brought her here, not why he wanted to leave—and certainly not why Dev's beautiful mother would look at her son with such a mix of instantaneous joy and pain.

She shouldn't *want* to understand. There was no point.

She was no one to him. *A friend,* he'd said, for the evening. That wasn't even true, and yet still she'd felt a stupid, stupid kick to her guts when he'd said those words.

*Work colleague* was the accurate term. The only term to describe them.

She stepped away, suddenly terribly uncomfortable. As she knew all that, believed all that—and yet all she could think about was Dev, and those dark eyes, and that sorrow behind them.

'I think we should stay.'

Ruby's head jerked up at the deep, firmly spoken words. As she watched, Dev opened the door, holding it open for her.

He looked relaxed and utterly unbothered. As if he'd always been the one who'd wanted to stay the whole time, in fact.

He motioned towards the door. 'Ready?'

Ruby just nodded in response, and then he followed her out into the hallway.

The party spread from the three-storey home's expansive entertaining areas through concertinaed bi-fold doors to the garden. Tall stainless-steel patio heaters dotted the grass, and fairy lights wound their way through the ornamental hedges and carefully

pruned gardenias. The thirty-metre high Ironbarks and Turpen-
tines of the adjacent Sheldon Forest—imposing even at night—
formed a towering backdrop to the evening.

It was—clearly—yet another fabulous party hosted by Ros
Cooper.

For about the twentieth time in the two minutes since he'd
walked out of the library, Dev changed his mind.

He'd been right. He should go.

'Devlin!'

Dev bit back a groan, but turned to face that familiar voice.

'Jared!' he said, as forced and false as his eldest brother.

He blinked as his gaze took him in. How long had it been?
Two years? Five?

Jared had softened just a little around the middle, and his
temples sported new sprinklings of grey. But his expression—
anger mixed with frustration mixed with judgmental dismissal—that was remarkably unchanged.

Actually, not remarkable at all. Jared, like his father, wasn't
known for his swift changes of opinion.

It took barely a minute for Jared to introduce himself to Ruby,
to make some irrelevant, meaningless, small talk—and then get
straight to the point.

'Mum's pleased you're here.'

Dev nodded. 'You're not.'

'No. You'll just end up upsetting her.' His brother casually
took a long sip of his beer.

'That's not the aim.'

Jared shrugged. Over Dev's shoulder he mouthed *hello!* at
someone behind them. He was always so smooth—always so
perfect. The perfect son—one of two both equally, differently
perfect: at school, at sport, at socialising.

Then along came Dev. Not even close to perfect.

'You shouldn't have come,' he said, as friendly as if they
were discussing a footy match. 'I wish you hadn't.' Now he
bothered to catch his gaze. 'But as you're here, at least try not
to ruin tonight for Mum, okay? It's her first party since...' Jared

swallowed a few times, and the pain of his loss was clear even in the moonlight.

Dev reached out—but he didn't know what to do. So he let his hand flop back uselessly to his side. Jared was oblivious, his stare becoming hard.

'Just don't let her down again.' Jared pushed the words out between clenched teeth—and then wasted no time waiting for a response.

'Lovely to meet you,' he murmured to Ruby, and then Dev found his gaze following his brother's suit-jacketed shoulders as he walked away, across the limestone paving and back inside the house.

A hand brushed his arm. 'Dev?'

Ruby was looking up at him, questions in her eyes. 'You okay?'

He nodded sharply. 'Do you want a drink?'

She raised her eyebrows, but let him go. When he returned a few minutes later, she'd found a small bench nestled in the garden. A man he didn't recognise sat beside her, and something he said made her laugh. A beautiful, genuine, honest, Ruby laugh.

'She's with me,' he said, sounding about as caveman as he intended as he came to a stop before them.

The guy looked up and Dev could see the exact millisecond he realised who he was. And that was all it took—the man stood up without a word, and left.

Ruby looked at him disapprovingly as he sat. 'That was rude—and inaccurate.'

He handed her her champagne. 'It's what they all expect of me. And, also, it was technically correct. You did come with me.'

She smiled, just a little. 'That's not what you meant.'

He shrugged. 'I've got other things to worry about than some guy who doesn't have the guts to stand his ground.'

She took a sip of her drink, looking out across the garden. 'Yeah, I'm getting that feeling.' Another sip. 'Are you going to tell me about it?'

'No.'

She shifted on the wooden bench, and recrossed her long legs so they were angled towards him. 'Then why, exactly, did you bring me here tonight?'

'I don't think I know,' he said, deciding she deserved honesty—even if he couldn't provide answers.

*I really don't want to go on my own.*

*That* particular moment of honesty in Ruby's apartment had definitely been unplanned. Until that moment, even he hadn't known it was true. He'd told himself that she'd make the night more fun, that she'd be—his favourite word when it came to her, it seemed—a distraction.

Looking at her now, at her eyes that were wide with concern for him, *distraction* didn't really cut it.

Because Veronica could've organised him a distraction, a stunning accessory for his arm who wouldn't have asked a single question.

But he hadn't wanted that; he'd wanted Ruby. He'd used that stupid *favour*—something he'd dreamt up in some desperate attempt to gain control of a humiliating situation, a favour he'd never thought he'd use—to get her here.

He'd manipulated her—for the second time.

And once again, he just couldn't feel bad about it.

He was glad she was here. *Ruby.* Not anyone else.

'I heard that your father died,' she said, very softly. 'Someone mentioned it, on set.' A pause. 'I'm really sorry.'

'We weren't close,' he said, dismissive. 'The opposite, in fact.'

'I'm sorry,' she repeated.

'I didn't go to the funeral,' he said, suddenly. Unexpectedly.

'You couldn't make it?' she asked, and he liked that she'd jumped to that conclusion, as erroneous as it was.

'He wouldn't have wanted me there. You could say we didn't agree on a lot of things.'

An understatement.

Dev waited for her to judge him on that decision. To tell him he'd made a mistake.

'Is that why your brother is so angry with you?'

Dev managed a tight smile. 'Brothers. And yes, that's partly why. The rest has been a lifetime in the making.'

'You're the odd one out.'

A small, harsh laugh. 'Yeah.'

'Are you close to your mum?'

He nodded.

'But you haven't seen her much recently.' He must have looked at her curiously. 'She was shocked to see you tonight, I could tell. So I guessed you hadn't popped by for dinner in a while.'

'I haven't been here in years. Ten years or more. When I saw Mum, it was somewhere else. A restaurant or something.'

'Because of your dad?'

Another nod.

For a while they were both silent, and little snippets of unintelligible conversation drifted across the breeze to them.

'That really sucks, you know,' she said, finally. 'That you have siblings, parents—and you're estranged from them all.'

He knew what she meant. That she'd had none of that. No family to be estranged from.

'Sometimes I think it would've been better if I didn't have them.'

All he associated his family with were guilt and failure—his. And disappointment—theirs. Except for his mum—but then, she got the consolation prize of worrying about her youngest son all the time.

'Now that,' Ruby said, 'was a very stupid thing to say.'

Her matter-of-fact words made him blink. 'Pardon me?'

She didn't back down—but then, she never did.

'You heard me.'

She spoke without anger, and something—something about how sure she was of his apparent stupidity—made him smile.

'I like you, Ruby Bell.'

'You keep saying that.'

He stood up, holding out a hand for her. 'I think I just figured out the reason I invited you.'

'Invited? Is that what you call it?'

But she was smiling as she wrapped her fingers around his. They were just slightly cool, but where they touched his skin they triggered instant heat.

'I reckon we go enjoy this party.'

Whatever Ruby might think, right now he didn't need to talk. But then, he didn't want a mindless distraction either.

Quite simply, he wanted Ruby.

# CHAPTER TEN

LATER—MUCH LATER—Ruby leant against the mirrored walls of the penthouse's private elevator, and grinned at Dev.

'That was fun,' she said. She felt good, buzzing with a touch of champagne, her toes pleasantly sore from hours of dancing.

'Yeah,' he said, with a slightly bemused smile. 'I know.'

The elevator doors slid open, and Ruby stepped out, her boot heels loud on the foyer's marble floor. A lamp on a spindly-legged side table glowed softly, only partially lighting the room.

But two steps later, she stopped dead.

'Where am I sleeping?'

Dev laughed behind her, and Ruby turned to look at him. He'd propped his shoulders against the wallpaper beside the shiny elevator door, and he looked at her with a sparkle to his eyes.

He pointed at the floor. 'I booked you a suite on the floor below.'

'What's so funny?' she asked. But the narrowing of her eyes was more a habit now. At some point he'd stopped being *quite* so irritating.

Come to think of it, for at least half the night—more if she disregarded the whole favour debacle—he'd been quite the opposite.

'This is a private elevator. You'll need to go all the way back to the lobby. When we arrived I didn't think.'

'Oh,' she said, nodding.

Dev didn't move. His jacket was thrown haphazardly over

his arm, and part of his shirt had untucked itself. He should look like a mess. Instead he looked…rather appealing.

*Dishevelled.* Yes. That was the word for it.

Ruby blinked, and attempted to refocus. She needed to go to her room.

As she walked to the elevator Dev didn't move. He just stayed where he was, looking at her with an unreadable expression.

She pushed the down button—the only button on the shiny brass panel.

And waited.

Not for the elevator door to open—as it did that immediately—but for…*something.*

The doors had opened fully now, and Ruby could see herself reflected in its walls. She looked into her own eyes, trying to determine what was going on here. Why she was still outside the elevator.

Her gaze wasn't so unsure though. Her gaze was…

The doors shut again, and now all she could see of herself was the blurriest of silhouettes.

'You're still here,' Dev said.

Out of the corner of her eye she knew he hadn't moved. But he was watching her. Waiting.

Now all she could hear was the sound of her own breathing—definitely faster than was normal.

She turned, a slow, deliberate movement.

And then Dev was there, standing right in front of her. *So close.*

She tilted her chin upwards to catch his gaze.

'I'm still here.' There was a long pause. 'You're very difficult to resist, you know that?'

His gaze, already warm, flickered hotter.

She reached out, her fingers toying with the untucked hem of his shirt, then travelling upwards, tracing his buttons in slow, irregular movements. 'Maybe it's the whole world-famous-movie-star thing.'

She felt him tense beneath her fingertips. 'Maybe,' he said. But his tone was flat.

Her exploration had reached his collar, skimming across its sharp, starched edge. Then she was touching skin: the cords of his neck. His jaw. Hot beneath her touch.

'Or maybe not,' she said. Then she looked up again, looked up into those blue, blue eyes.

Who was she looking at? At Devlin Cooper, Hollywood star? Or Dev, the man who made her heart flip, and who managed to make her smile just as regularly as he pushed her buttons? Who made her breath catch when he allowed her a glimpse of his true self? The man who'd calmly cleaned up her kitchen and who'd reached for her hand in his mother's front hall?

Could he tell that for her there really was no question?

*Yes,* she thought as he leant towards her, and as she stood on impatient tiptoes.

*Yes,* she thought as their lips finally met, and as he pulled her tight against him—and before the incredible touch of his mouth obliterated the possibility of any further thinking at all.

Dev woke, gradually. It was dark—very much night still.

As his eyes adjusted in the blackness, Ruby's shape materialised before him. She slept on her side, facing him. He liked the way the sheet followed her shape, up along the long length of her legs, over the roundness of her hips, then down to the dip of her waist.

She was asleep, her breathing slow and regular.

How long had he been asleep for?

He turned over, reaching for his phone on the bedside table. Pressing the button to make the screen illuminate simply confirmed what he'd suspected: it was two in the morning. He'd slept for less than an hour.

He bit back a groan. What had he expected? One visit to see his mum and suddenly life would be back to normal? He'd finally be able to sleep?

Well—yes. That was exactly it.

It was exactly why after all these weeks he'd finally sat down about twenty-four hours ago—once again unable to sleep—and listened to every single one of his mother's voicemail messages, no matter how much it hurt.

The decision to charter a flight and attend the party had come much later the next day, out of the blue. He hadn't questioned it at the time, nor his decision to take Ruby with him.

And he didn't regret either decision. Tonight had been…he didn't know. Something good. A step forward maybe.

To where he had no idea, but the sense of moving in any direction was certainly a welcome contrast to the past few months.

Except—he still couldn't sleep.

He wasn't magically cured.

It made him want to hit something.

Instead, he pushed himself off the bed in jerky, frustrated movements, and headed for the en suite. He shut the door carefully behind him before switching on the light, not wanting to wake Ruby.

Someone had ensured his zip-up bag of toiletry supplies had made it into the bathroom, and he barely had to look into it to find the familiar tray of tablets. A moment later he'd pushed a couple out onto his hand, but, rather than transferring them to his mouth, he found himself just staring at them.

He was reluctant to take them with Ruby here. They lasted a good five hours, and if Ruby tried to wake him before then he'd be groggy, a mess.

Last time she stayed with him, he'd lain on the couch, wanting to put distance between himself and Ruby. Then, after her aborted attempt to leave, he hadn't thought twice about his tablets. He'd known she'd be gone in the morning, and told himself he didn't care—that it was exactly what he wanted.

But tonight that option held no appeal. He didn't want to retreat to another room, and he didn't want to be a drugged-out lump beside her.

Was it so much to ask? A night where he got to be normal again? Where he could sleep beside a beautiful woman with only thoughts of *her* in his stupid head, and not useless things he could do nothing about?

He just wanted to sleep beside Ruby. To wake beside her and not feel as if the weight of the world were on his shoulders, or that getting out of bed was an impossible option.

He dropped the tablets into the sink, then twisted the tap so hot water chased them down the drain.

Decision made, he switched off the bathroom light, and climbed back beneath the sheets.

But once there, even the gentle in and out of Ruby's breathing proved no use.

Sleep was as elusive as always. Tonight was no different from the many nights before it.

Finally, hating himself, he surrendered—to the pills, and to the necessary oblivion of sleep.

Dev was still asleep when Ruby stepped out of the bathroom. She wrapped her arms around herself as she watched him, cosy in the thick terry-towelling robe she wore. He slept just as he had that morning—was it really only last week?—when she'd agreed to the silly deal that had landed her here. Which was like a log, basically.

Now what?

Briefly she considered repeating her exit from a fortnight earlier—and simply disappearing.

But this morning, that just didn't seem right. Or, at least not an option she was letting herself think too much about.

She'd get dressed, then figure out what would happen next. After all, that would fit the theme of the last twenty-four hours—making decisions without pretty much any thought of the consequences.

Her clothes were puddled on the floor, and as she bent to gather them in her arms her familiar red carry-on suitcase caught her attention. It lay on its back, right beside Dev's backpack, in front of a wardrobe.

Disappearing was suddenly a *very* viable option, she decided as she stalked on bare feet to their luggage.

*Had he really even booked her another room? How dared he assume—?*

But just before she snatched the bag up, an unevenly folded note drew her attention, balanced atop the red fabric.

She'd barely read the single handwritten sentence, when she heard a sleepy laugh behind her.

'I had the concierge organise for your bag to be brought up here after you fell asleep.'

*Oh.*

'I thought you might want your things.'

She turned to face him. He'd raised himself onto his elbows, the sheet falling low to reveal the delicious strength of his chest.

She glanced down at Dev's note again, his neat all-capitals script.

'Cross my heart,' he added, into her continued silence.

She believed him—that wasn't the issue. It was just taking her a moment to absorb the thoughtfulness of the gesture—firstly that he'd thought to organise for her bag to be delivered, and secondly that he knew her well enough to guess her reaction at the bag's discovery.

It felt…nice.

'Thanks,' she said.

He rubbed at his eyes, his movements slow and heavy-looking. 'How does breakfast in bed sound? Room service here is exceptional.'

And just like that, she'd decided what she was doing next.

They ended up spending the day in Sydney.

With no driver—and Dev in dark glasses and a baseball cap—they headed for Bondi beach.

Ruby had pointed out an advertisement as she'd read the paper, the many Sunday sections spread like giant colourful confetti across the bed. *Sculpture by the Sea.*

Dev couldn't say he was a regular visitor to art exhibitions, but he figured he could do a lot worse than walking from Bondi along the coast down to Tamarama—with Ruby. So yeah, he was sold.

It was a mild October day, and yet keen sunbathers still dotted the beach. They both held their shoes in their hands as they walked, the sand smooth beneath their feet and the ocean as perfect a blue as the sky.

'Where's the art?' Dev asked.

Ruby smiled and pointed vaguely ahead of them, the slight breeze ruffling her hair. 'I think it starts down there somewhere?'

But really, neither of them was too worried about the sculptures.

During the short drive from the city, they'd chatted easily—a continuation of their easy breakfast picnic-of-sorts on his bed. It all stayed very light, which suited him just fine.

No talk about anything serious. No talk about last night, and certainly no talk about tomorrow.

But now, in Bondi, they'd gone quiet.

Not an awkward silence—quite the opposite. But still, Dev didn't like it.

'What's your favourite movie?' Ruby said—all in a rush, as if maybe she didn't like the silence either. 'I mean, of yours. That you've been in.'

As she walked she stared at a spot somewhere on the sand ahead of her.

'*Now You See Her,*' he said, immediately.

She looked up at him, her eyes squinting a little in the glare. 'I've never heard of it.' She paused a second. 'Sorry.'

He smiled. 'Good. It's awful. I had about two lines in it, a straight-to-video effort filmed on the Gold Coast when I was twenty.'

'And so it's your favourite because?'

'I got paid for it. My first paid role in a movie.'

They'd reached the end of the beach and paused to step back into their shoes before walking up a small ramp to the footpath.

'That's interesting,' she said. 'Not your first starring role, or first blockbuster, or first Golden Globe nomination?'

'Nope. It was the money in my bank account—as small amount as it was. Proved it wasn't just a dream—but that it could be my career.'

They walked a little further without speaking, past the famous Bondi Icebergs swimming club. Dev had been here a few times—not to swim in a pool so close to the ocean that the Pacific's waves often broke straight into it, but to the bar. For a few promotional events, the occasional dinner...

Irrationally he imagined coming back here with Ruby, in summer, to swim. For a moment he could almost see it—her hair slicked back just as it had been after her shower this morning, smiling at him across the water...

But he quickly erased that idea—he wouldn't be in Australia in summer, he'd be in Hollywood.

By then, everything would be back to how it was. And Ruby would be off working on her next film, along with all her rules about dating cast and crew, and her refusal to ever settle down in one location.

'Dev?'

Ruby had asked him a question, he realised. 'Sorry, I was...' He ran a hand through his hair. 'What did you say?'

'I was worried I'd offended you,' she said. 'Don't worry, it was a stupid question.'

He slanted her a look. 'You do know you have to ask me it now?'

But they'd reached a little temporary marquee—the start of the sculpture walk. A few minutes later, equipped with a catalogue, they'd descended a series of stairs to reach the first set of sculptures, scattered across the tiers of rocks that lined the cove and spread their way into the ocean.

Ruby stood in front of one—a giant red nail that appeared to have been hammered between the rocks, tall enough to loom above them both.

'What was your question?'

She sighed. 'It was nothing. I was just saying I was surprised that the money meant so much to you.'

'Given my background,' he finished for her.

She shifted her weight awkwardly. 'As I said, a stupid thing to say.'

'I'm not that easily offended,' he said. At least, not with her. But then—if she was someone interviewing him—he never would've answered the original question honestly, anyway.

Actually, he wasn't entirely sure he'd told anyone the truth before.

Not that it meant anything—it was a trivial thing. Meaningless.

'Having a privileged background doesn't mean I don't have an appreciation for hard work, or for money.'

'Of course not,' she said, very quickly.

He knew he could've left it at that, but as they walked further along the path he found himself explaining. 'My dad was a self-made man,' he said.

Ruby didn't say anything, but her pace slowed.

'He started with absolutely nothing—as a labourer, actually. Mum met him back then. He worked his way up, he became a builder. Then began his own construction business, and started to buy and sell property. Sometimes to renovate and sell, other times to hold, or to rent.'

They'd walked straight past the next sculpture, Dev realised. But he didn't want to stop; if he did, the words would, too.

'All he wanted for us boys was security. A secure career. A good income. A good family.'

'So he didn't want you to be an actor,' she said.

He lips quirked, but it wasn't a smile. 'No.'

Ruby didn't even glance at the next sculpture. Stairs rose above them, leading out of the cove, and they walked up side by side, Ruby's fingers brushing against the hand rail.

'I was supposed to be an accountant.'

'No!' Ruby said, and it was such an exclamation that Dev had to grin.

'That's what I thought, too. I wasn't as good at school as my brothers—Dad said it was because I didn't apply myself, and he was probably right. I just didn't like sitting still, I didn't like being quiet and studying in my room.'

'I believe that,' Ruby murmured. 'I bet you were a trouble-maker, too.'

'Yeah,' he said, smiling fondly at a million memories. 'Dad didn't like that, either.'

To their right, greenery and grass reached up to the road above them. Tiny painted totem poles decorated the slope—but Dev wasn't really paying any attention.

'So, yeah, earning my first pay cheque meant something. A lot.'

She nodded. 'Your dad must have been pleased.'

'I doubt it. I'd moved out by then.'

She looked at him, with questions in her eyes—and as they walked he found himself telling her everything. About that night when his dad had been waiting for him; when he'd been drunk—and arrogant; when he'd felt the crunch of his father's fist against his cheek.

How he'd never gone back.

Ruby just listened, letting him talk.

'You were right the first time,' he said, after a while. 'About your surprise that a wealthy kid would appreciate a pay cheque so much. Six months earlier, I wouldn't have. I *was* spoilt. I did take my life for granted. I'd never have admitted it—maybe because I didn't even realise it—but deep down I *knew* I had a safety net. I'd subconsciously given myself the option to fail.'

The footpath ended, and grassy flat parkland spread before them. Large pieces of abstract art—some whimsical, some just bizarre—attracted groups of people. A pride of lions made out of what looked like straw; a delicately balanced collection of chairs topped with two metallic acrobats, and even an over-sized mixer tap.

'But you didn't fail,' she said.

'I couldn't,' he said.

No way would he let his dad be right.

'So you did achieve what your father wanted for you: a career, financial security.'

'Not the way he wanted.'

They'd left the park, the footpath leading them to another cove, the blue-green waves splashing across tiers of huge, smooth rocks.

'Did that matter?'

He didn't know. That was the problem, *his* problem.

And now it was too late.

So he didn't answer the question. They just walked, and Ruby didn't ask again. They followed the edge of the ocean, in silence, until they hit the white sand of Tamarama beach. Ruby quickened her pace a little, and led him between sculptures— finally flopping cross-legged beside a giant turtle constructed of tyre rubber.

He sat beside her, his legs stretched out, the sand warm beneath his skin.

'A miscarriage,' she said, out of the blue.

'Pardon me?'

She was looking at the ocean. Surfers bobbed just beyond the cresting waves.

'Yesterday you asked what happened. And that's it. What made me take my life in a less scandalous direction.'

There was a deliberate lightness to her words that she didn't come close to pulling off.

'I'm sorry, Ruby.'

She nodded. 'Thank you. I'd been seeing this guy—a nice guy. From a good family, very smart, very handsome. He had his choice of anyone. I wouldn't say he chose me, though. Or at least, he didn't mean to.'

Dev held his tongue, although it was near impossible.

'It was an accident, me getting pregnant. I hadn't meant it to happen, although of course that isn't what people said.'

*People.* People gossiping about Ruby, judging her.

She shifted a little on the sand, so she faced him. 'But I

was *so* happy. I didn't expect it, but it was like—' she bit her lip, looking down for a moment '—like finally I'd have a family. I didn't care if it was just me and my baby, but then the father surprised everyone and decided to stay with me. He was a good guy.'

She was tracing a hand through the sand, drawing illegible scribbles that instantly faded away.

'So I had everything: my baby, a guy. It was perfect. Finally I felt like I had a purpose. That I belonged. I wasn't the girl who people whispered about, I was going to be a *mother,* and I had a boyfriend who said he'd stand by me. A *family.*'

Her hand moved from the sand, to her stomach. Somehow Dev knew she was unaware of what she was doing, the way her fingers lay across the perfectly flat line of her T-shirt.

'I was stupid, and I told people as soon as I knew. I was showing off, I guess. Over-excited—proving them all wrong. I never considered the possibility of miscarrying, and I certainly didn't understand how common it was so early in a pregancy. And then one day I started bleeding, and when I went to the hospital they told me I'd lost my baby. I felt like my world had ended.'

He couldn't just sit still any more. He reached for her, wrapping his arm around her waist and pulling her close against him. She pressed her cheek against his chest.

'That's when I figured it out—figured out that I had it all wrong. I dumped the guy—a relief for him I'm sure—and quit my dead-end job to go back to school. I decided I was all I needed in my life—that I didn't need some guy, or a family, or *anyone,* to be happy. I just needed me.'

She was so sure, her voice so firm.

But her body shook, just a little.

She tilted her chin up, to look at him, finally.

He didn't know what to say. Or maybe he knew that there wasn't anything he could say, anything that would make a difference.

Besides, that wasn't what she wanted. It wasn't what he'd wanted, either, when he'd told her about his dad.

So he did the only thing that did make sense—and kissed her.

But it was different from their kisses of before—this wasn't flirty, although it was certainly passionate. It was…beautiful, and sad, and he was suddenly *sure* there was something different between them, some connection, something special. And he was the last guy to think anything as fluffy and romantic as that.

But with Ruby, on the beach, beneath the sun and beside the giant friendly tortoise, it was unlike anything he'd ever experienced.

'Oh, my *God,* it's *Dev Cooper!*'

The shriek tore them apart. Immediately Ruby retreated, shrugging off his arm in a brutal motion, and jumping to her feet.

He glanced up to see a group of teenage girls approaching him, all pointing and chattering loudly. Across the beach people were twisting on their towels to have a look, to see what all the fuss was about.

Earlier today he'd seen a few curious, wondering glances, but he'd been lucky. No one had approached him, no one had burst the little bubble that he and Ruby had so inadvertently created. After a while he'd stopped even noticing, he'd been so wrapped up in Ruby.

But that bubble was gone now—destroyed. Ruby was looking back towards the houses and the road above the beach, as if determining her escape strategy.

Not from the rapidly approaching crowd—but from him.

He was on his feet. 'Ruby—'

She had her phone in her hand. 'I'll sort out a car. You won't be able to walk back to Bondi, now.'

Not *we won't,* but *you.*

She spoke in her work voice, as professional and false as it got.

And as the girls slowed their charge to look at him almost shyly, momentarily lost for words, his pasted-on smile was equally plastic.

But then he *was* a good actor, so he submitted to the autographs, and the photos, and the screaming—while the whole time all he wanted to do was to yell and shout and tell them all to go away. To leave him alone.

Although even if they did it would be too late. Ruby was only metres away, her arms wrapped around herself, watching.

But that moment had passed. Their moment.

He told himself it was for the best, that it wasn't something he wanted, or needed.

Just like Ruby, he'd long ago made his own path.

And he walked it alone.

# CHAPTER ELEVEN

On Monday evening, Ruby nosed her hire car up the long gravel driveway to Dev's cottage. Even as she pulled to a stop she wasn't entirely sure what she was doing.

She'd been driving home from another long day, already planning what she was going to order at the pub for dinner. And then—unexpectedly—she was here.

No. That wasn't completely true.

It wasn't at all unexpected. Given the amount of time her subconscious had allocated to Dev today, her arrival here could even be considered foreseeable.

That fact didn't make it any less a bad idea.

She held the car key in her hand, and made a half-hearted attempt to reach for the ignition before stopping herself.

She was here now. She might as well go talk to him—clear the air.

Yesterday's flight home had been awkward. There was no other word for it. It was obvious neither of them had intended what had happened at the beach.

She should regret it, she knew. Why would she share something so personal with a man she barely knew?

A few times, during that long hour in the jet, she'd meant to say something. To somehow laugh off what had happened.

But it was impossible. She couldn't very well tell him: *Look, I've never told anyone else—ever—what I told you today. Just forget it, okay?*

Right.

Last night she'd lain in bed, telling herself she'd made the sensible decision to back away. That her immediate reaction to that dose of reality—as shocking as if someone had dumped a bucket of salt water on top of her—was appropriate.

He was *Devlin Cooper*. She needed to remember that. It was so easy to be seduced into reading something more into the situation, imagining so much more than there was between them, or would ever be.

He wasn't looking for for ever, and she certainly didn't want it.

So today, her mind had wandered for the hundredth time to little flashbacks of how Dev had looked as he'd leant against the wall beside the elevator; or the way he'd looked at her, that moment before he'd kissed her, down at Tamarama...

She shoved open her door, stepping out into the cool evening.

Belatedly she realised the front door was now open. Dev stood, propped against the doorframe, watching her.

Waiting for her.

'Looked like you were doing some serious thinking there,' he said as she stepped onto the veranda.

'No,' she lied, quickly. 'Quite the opposite. I was thinking we've been spending way too much time being serious.'

His lips quirked. 'How so?' he asked, a little gruffly.

Where he stood, half in the shadows and half illuminated by the hallway light, she couldn't read his gaze.

She stepped closer, attempting what she hoped was a flirtatious, happy-go-lucky, I'm-totally-cool-about-all-this smile.

He took a step backwards, gesturing for her to come in.

But she didn't. She needed to get this sorted first. They needed to both understand what this was.

'Maybe you were right,' she said. Dev raised his eyebrows. 'A few weeks ago, outside the pub. When you said we were just two single people stuck in a country town. How did you put it? A match made in heaven.'

He nodded. 'You said you didn't date anyone you worked with.'

'Too late now,' she said, with a bit of a laugh. 'Besides, some-how we've flown under the radar. No gossip.'

'Except for Graeme. Graeme thinks you're great, by the way. You should hear him on our drives into set.'

Ruby smiled. 'Well, then, Graeme is very discreet. I'll have to thank him.'

They both fell into silence.

'So what you're saying is?' Dev prompted.

Ruby narrowed her eyes. 'Isn't it obvious?'

'Not at all,' he said. But was that a sparkle in his eyes?

She gave a little huff of frustration. 'Fine.' And she closed the gap between them, and before she had the chance to lose her nerve—and just because she wanted to—she kissed him.

Not tentatively, not questioning.

When, after an age, they broke apart, she needed to take a few long breaths to pull herself together.

'That's what I want,' she said.

He was reaching for her again. 'I like this plan.'

'Just until the film is over,' she clarified as he almost carried her inside, slamming the front door behind them.

Maybe it was the sound of the door, or the distraction of Dev kissing her neck, and the shiver it triggered through her body—but her words weren't as firm, or as clear, as she'd like.

But she didn't have a chance to repeat them, as now Dev had swept her up into his arms and was carrying her to his room.

And really, now wasn't the time for talking.

Ruby had dinner with him every night, and they took advan-tage of all the food in his fridge—which magically doubled in volume, thanks to Graeme.

It was easy, and fun. He continued to pay her no special at-tention on set, although it was difficult. Especially when Ruby broke her own rules—just once—when delivering an updated copy of the day's script.

It had been a genuine, work-related visit—but the kiss behind his very firmly closed trailer door was far from professional.

The memory made him smile as he stretched out along his couch. Ruby walked back from the kitchen, a glass of red wine in her hand.

'Now don't you look comfortable?'

He smiled, and tapped the space in front of him on the striped fabric. Her eyes sparkled as she sipped her wine, then placed the glass carefully on the coffee table.

She came into his arms easily. How long had it been now—a week? A week since she'd turned up at his front door, still with her rules, but with him, and this film, a temporary exception.

But he could live with this, especially when she kissed him. When Ruby was kissing him, *that* was all he thought about, all that filled his mind.

But when she left—and she always did—then he would think.

She'd leave around midnight. Ruby said it was because sometimes she gave members of the crew lifts to set—which sounded plausible.

But it wasn't the real reason. She was keeping this light, and simple. Waking up together, or breakfast in bed, or conversations where they bared their souls—no. They were not things they wanted, not what this thing they had was about.

They both knew that.

Did she guess he still wasn't sleeping? Sometimes he thought so. She'd look at him with concern in her eyes, and occasionally he'd be sure she was going to start asking questions.

But she never did.

On set, the rumours had dissipated. Dev had done nothing to perpetuate them—excluding that one morning, he'd never missed his call, had never been anything but prompt and professional. Everyone seemed to love Dev Cooper.

And, thank goodness, there were no *new* rumours. This was Ruby's nightmare, the niggling fear at the back of her mind that suddenly All Would Be Revealed somehow, or that the paparazzi that occasionally bothered to make the trip out to Lucyville would snap a photo of her and Dev together.

Which would be difficult—given their relationship existed entirely within the walls of his cottage. Graeme got rid of any loitering cars anywhere near the property, and so far it was proving remarkably effective.

But still—Ruby worried.

And not just about becoming the subject of gossip once again, but about Dev.

She needed to go. She lay curled on his couch, her back to Dev's chest, a warm blanket covering them both. Earlier they'd been watching a nineteen-fifties Danny Kaye musical they both loved—but not enough to be rather easily distracted. It had long ago ended, the TV screen now black.

Dev was breathing steadily behind her, but she knew he wasn't asleep. She seemed to have a talent for dozing off, but not Dev. Except for that morning in the penthouse, she'd never seen him sleep. Not once.

He mustn't be sleeping. Not well, anyway. She knew that whenever she saw the red in his eyes and his skin after he washed off his day's stage make-up. She'd seen a packet of sleeping tablets in his bathroom, but she had no idea if he took them. She'd never asked.

She'd never asked about anything.

She could guess what was wrong. Extrapolate from what he'd told her at the beach that day. All the rumours had been way off. Her guess was that Dev was still processing his father's death, and his own grief. That was the cause of his weight loss, his problems sleeping, the sadness in his gaze.

But that was all it was—a guess. So many times she was tempted to ask him about it. Like right now, in this darkened room, and in this intimacy they shared.

Did he want to talk to her about it? Did he want to share something so personal with her?

Did she want him to share something so personal?

*No.*

On the beach, it had all been too intense. Too much, too over-whelming. He'd felt the same way, too.

She didn't want that. She couldn't want that—not when they had only weeks together.

What would be the point?

So she turned in his arms and kissed him goodbye. And, as she did every other night, drove home to her own, lonely bed.

And she told herself she was doing the right thing.

Ruby woke up with a start, blinking in the unfamiliar room.

*Dev's place.*

She'd fallen asleep. Her handbag was still out in the lounge room, so she turned over, planning to reach across Dev to where she knew he left his phone on his beside table, so she could check the time.

But Dev wasn't there.

She crawled across the bed, wrapping herself with a sheet before she checked his phone. Three-twelve a.m.

Far too late to drive back to her place.

She realised she didn't mind.

A thin crack of light glowed beneath the en-suite door. 'Dev?'

No response. She stood, arranging the sheet like a towel. She felt faintly ridiculous for her sudden modesty—Dev had, after all, seen her naked.

But still, just walking about his house in the nude felt like a step too far—a dose of reality in their perfect little world.

She knocked on the door, but the slight touch pushed it open.

Dev sat on the closed toilet lid, in boxer shorts only. His head had been in his hands, and as he looked up at her he raked his fingers through his hair, making one side stand up on end.

He looked—awful. Worse than she'd ever seen him, despite the much-needed weight she'd noticed he'd put on in the past few weeks.

The shadows beneath his eyes were verging on black, and his eyes were rimmed red.

He looked exhausted. Broken. Ruined.

Of course it wasn't a surprise.

But she'd made herself ignore it. She hadn't wanted to know.

It didn't fit with what she'd decided was allowable between them. This was far, far too serious.

'Oh, Dev...'

She went to his side, automatically wrapping her arm around his shoulder. She crouched awkwardly beside the cistern but didn't care. She had to do something.

But he shrugged her off.

'I'm fine,' he said, angrily. Much louder than she expected. It made her want to back away, but she didn't let herself.

'No,' she said, 'you're not.'

He looked away—at the towel rail. At nothing.

'I'm just having trouble sleeping,' he said, all dismissive. 'That's all.'

She glanced at the sink. A tray of tablets lay almost empty on the counter top.

'It's not good for you to use those for too long,' she began.

He stood up abruptly, crossing the room. 'I *know* that,' he said. He was looking at himself in the mirror, as if he hated what he saw.

Ruby straightened, but didn't go to him.

'Without them I just don't sleep. I can't.'

'Okay.'

He looked at her, his gaze unbelievably intense. 'If I don't take them, I don't sleep. And if I don't sleep, I can't—'

*Act.*

He snatched at something. Two tablets, she realised, sitting on the ceramic counter.

Right in her line of sight. As if he'd been staring at them.

For how long?

He tossed them at his mouth, then wrenched the tap on, gathering water in his cupped hands that he tipped haphazardly down his throat.

Everything inside her screamed at her to leave.

She'd decided she didn't want this. This was supposed to be fun, and flirty, and temporary.

Nothing that was happening right now was *any* of those things.

'Can you please leave?' he said, meeting her gaze in the mirror.

Because he asked, she nodded.

But she didn't go very far. Not to her car, and certainly not back home to her apartment.

Instead, she shut the bathroom door behind her, and crawled straight back into Dev's bed.

She didn't know what she was doing, or what she could offer him.

But tonight, she was not walking away.

After Ruby left, Dev spent long minutes in the bathroom, waiting for his whirring brain to slow.

He'd known she hadn't meant to stay, but when she had, he'd been glad.

*Really* glad.

Stupid, really.

Because what did it matter? Filming ended in two weeks, and then he'd fly back to LA. And Ruby would... He didn't even know. *That* was how transient this relationship was.

But even so, he'd tried again. Tried to sleep like a normal person. To fall asleep beside Ruby.

Predictably, just like last week in that fancy penthouse, sleep hadn't come. But tonight he'd really resisted the tablets.

Tonight he'd thought it might be different.

Why?

Just like how the mornings hadn't been any different? The one single variation from the murky fog that was his mornings was last Sunday, when he'd woken beside Ruby. And even that had only worked because he'd been fortunate she'd slept in so late. He'd been nearly normal.

He'd hoped that would become the norm, but it hadn't. Nights were hard. Mornings even worse. It was a constant, awful cycle of frustration—and in between he managed to be to all appearances a fully functional human being.

A miracle, probably, that on this film at least he could hide whatever the hell was wrong with him. He could hide it from Ruby.

Until tonight. Tonight he'd done a really crap job of hiding it.

He didn't think Ruby would be coming back tomorrow night. This wasn't what she'd signed up for.

He pushed the door open, not bothering to switch off the light. The bathroom light flooded the room, and the obvious feminine shape on the bed.

For a minute or more he just stood there, then gave his increasingly blurry head a shake, and switched off the light.

In the gloom he slid onto his side of the bed, and without letting himself think too much—and quite frankly with the drugs unable to do much thinking anyway—he reached for her.

She wasn't asleep, he realised, and she turned to face him in his arms.

'I'm fine,' he whispered into her hair.

'I want you to be,' she said, her breath tickling his chest.

And then his eyes slid shut, but a moment before the thick blackness of drugged sleep enveloped him he made a decision.

Tomorrow things would change. Not because he'd crossed his fingers or shouted into his brain that it would, but because he'd just lied to Ruby.

And he didn't want to do that again.

*I want you to be.*

Finally, he slept.

# CHAPTER TWELVE

LATE ON WEDNESDAY afternoon—two days later—Dev knocked on his mother's front door. He shoved his hands in the pockets of his jeans to stop himself fidgeting, but it was a pretty useless gesture.

He was nervous.

He'd chartered another jet, and the entire flight he'd bounced his legs, or tapped his toes or *something*. Now he turned around on the spot, looking out onto the manicured front garden and his nondescript hire car, taking deep, relaxing breaths.

This really wasn't a big deal. It was his mum, and—despite everything—he knew she loved him.

Behind him the door rattled—the sound of the brass chain lock being undone, the click of the deadbolt, the twist of the door handle.

By the time the door opened, he was staring at it, waiting.

'Devlin!' his mum exclaimed, once again with a smile broader than he deserved. Then she paused. 'Is everything okay?'

She looked momentarily stricken, and he wanted to kick himself. Was a disaster the only reason she could imagine him visiting her unannounced?

Well, given the past fourteen years—probably.

'Everything's fine. Everyone's fine, as far as I know.'

She nodded, then opened the door wide. 'Well, come in! I was just going through the photos from my party. It was so wonderful to have you there.'

He nodded automatically, then reached out, grabbing his mum's hand and holding it tight.

'Mum, I'd like to talk to you about Dad.'

Instantly he saw the pain in her eyes, but she squeezed his fingers tighter.

'Good,' she said. 'Because I've got something I want to show you.'

Dev had cancelled dinner last night, and as Ruby walked to his front door late on Wednesday evening she wasn't sure what to expect.

Tuesday morning had been…eye-opening. When his alarm went off Dev just kept on sleeping, and it wasn't until she'd given him a decent shake that he'd finally woken.

He'd looked unhappy to see her, though. As if he'd wished the night had never happened, that she'd never seen him like that.

She'd felt like such an idiot, as the final pieces of the puzzle had fallen into place. That morning a few weeks back when she and Graeme had nearly bashed the front door down, Dev hadn't been sleeping in. He hadn't been so arrogant to believe his needs were more important than the rest of the cast and crew.

Something serious was going on with Dev, and she'd been at first oblivious—and then later deliberately dismissive—of the signs.

She'd been scared by how close she'd felt herself get to him, so she'd kept her distance.

Yeah, that was the word: scared.

But now what was she to do? All she could offer him was two more weeks. That was all she had. And she desperately wanted to help.

Now wasn't that a contradiction? So worried for Dev her heart ached, but so sure she had to leave.

He'd left the front door ajar, so she pushed it open, her heeled boots loud on the hallway's floorboards.

'Dev?'

He called out from the kitchen, and so that was where she

headed. He sat at the rustic dining table, cutlery, a bottle of wine
and two glasses set out neatly. On his placemat only, however,
lay a battered-looking notebook. He stood as she walked into
the room.

'What's all this for?' she asked, taking in the soft lighting,
and the scent of something delicious bubbling on the stove.

'I cooked,' he said, then added when she must have displayed
her scepticism, 'Really. I make a mean puttanesca.'

She smiled, his enthusiasm completely infectious. 'Lucky
me.'

He bent to kiss her, his lips firm. It was more than a quick
hello kiss, and when they broke apart Ruby's heart was racing.
Without thinking she brought her hand to her chest, and his lips
quirked at the gesture.

'Me, too,' he said.

Dev wouldn't let her help as he confidently moved about the
kitchen, so she propped a hip against the bench, and watched
him as she sipped her wine.

They chatted about the day on set—about the temporary
disaster of Arizona falling off the horse she was riding, the director's latest tantrum, and even the glorious cool but sunny
weather.

But not the little notebook on the table.

Ruby would glance at it every so often, and after a while Dev
grinned. 'I was going to explain while we ate—but you can go
grab it if you like.'

She didn't need to be asked twice.

She sat at the dining table, facing Dev. But he'd slowed right
down, his gaze regularly flicking in her direction.

The notebook had a brown leather cover, with Dev's sur-
name embossed in a corner. Ruby ran a finger over it, already
sure she knew who it once belonged to.

'It's your dad's, right?'

Dev nodded, but he kept his eyes focused on the pot he
stirred.

Ruby opened the book. The first page was covered in numbers and dollar symbols. As was the next. A quick flick through the entire book showed it was nearly full with almost identical pages—dollar amounts. Some huge. Tens of millions of dollars. Hundreds of millions.

'What is this?'

Dev was carrying two plates piled high with pasta to the table. He placed them down carefully, then waited until he was in his seat before looking at Ruby—straight into her eyes, his gaze crystal clear.

'All I wanted, growing up, was for my dad to be proud of me.'

His voice cracked a little, and Ruby wanted to reach for him, but knew, instinctively, that now wasn't the time.

Dev swallowed. 'A cliché, I know. When I failed at that as a kid, I told myself I'd stopped caring what he thought. I used to tell myself that I wanted to become an actor because Dad would hate it, not because, deep down, I knew I was good at it. And that maybe, eventually, he'd see that.'

He kept twirling his fork, the same strands of pasta wrapping tighter and tighter.

'But he didn't. Then I left, and that was that. No more caring what Dad thought about me, no more looking to him for praise and approval. Except, then he went and died. And I realised that was all absolute crap. I've been waiting fourteen years to speak to my dad.'

'You still cared what he thought.'

Dev nodded, but then shook his head. 'Kind of. Of course I still wanted the slap on the back, the *good job, son,* all that stuff. But most of all, I just wanted to hear his voice. He worked so hard to achieve his goals, and he reached every single one. I should've swallowed my pride.'

His tone was so different from that afternoon on the beach. Now he spoke with near reverence—it was such a contrast. 'He could've called you, too,' Ruby pointed out. 'You're his son just as much as he's your father.'

Dev smiled. 'Of course he should've. But he was a stubborn old guy. Mum said he never even considered calling me.

Or coming with her when I visited. But then, I was exactly the same. As stubborn as him.'

He reached across the table, and took the notebook that was still in Ruby's hands. 'You know what this is? It's the takings at the box office for each of my movies. Every single one, right from that stupid one up at the Gold Coast that bombed. If he could find how much I was paid, that's there, too.'

He flipped through the pages, running his fingers over the print.

'Isn't that a little…?' Ruby struggled to find the right word.

'Harsh? Brutal? Mercenary? Yes. But that's Dad. That's what he understood: cold, hard cash. He could relate to that in a way he couldn't relate to my career.'

'Doesn't it bother you that this is what he focused on?'

Dev handed her back the book. Ruby opened it on a new page, now understanding the scribbled letters and numbers. It was meticulous: the box office takings across the world, DVD sales—everything.

This wasn't something thrown together in minutes—it was hours of work. Hours of research over months—years even. Crossing out numbers, updating them, adding them together.

'No,' she said, answering her own question.

'No,' he repeated.

'I went to a doctor today,' Dev said, later, in bed.

Ruby's back was to him, his body wrapped around hers.

She was silent, long enough that he thought she might have fallen asleep.

'Yes?' she said, eventually.

Her head was tucked beneath his chin, and her blonde hair smelt like cake, or cookies. *Vanilla-scented shampoo,* she'd told him, when he'd asked.

He hadn't been going to tell her this. Stupid, really, when he'd told her all that other stuff.

He hadn't even told his mum. He'd driven straight from his doctor's appointment in the city to the house where he'd grown up. Not on the advice of the GP, but because he'd planned on doing it anyway.

He'd made his decision the night before. Things had to change—*he* had to change—and no one but Devlin Cooper could do it.

'He thinks I could be depressed,' he said. Then he said the rest much more quickly, before he second-guessed himself silent. Ruby deserved to know. 'The trouble sleeping, the loss of appetite, the horrible mornings, it's all textbook, apparently.'

Had she tensed in his arms?

'I thought depression was…I don't know. When people lock themselves in their house all day. Can't work, can't function, can't…feel.' Her words were very soft, almost muffled in the sheets.

'It can be, I guess. My doctor explained the different types to me, and their symptoms. It just all fits, and the cause is pretty damn obvious. To be honest, I'm not all that surprised.'

She turned, pulling herself up a bit in the bed so her head rested on her pillow and she faced him. It was late, but enough moonlight filtered through the curtains for Dev to make out her expression; for once it was completely unreadable.

His palm felt cool against the fitted sheet, no longer touching her.

'I knew something was wrong, right from when I first met you.'

She reached for him, tracing the line of his jaw, across to his lips.

'I should've asked more questions, I should've pushed harder.'

Dev blinked, confused. 'I wouldn't have said anything. Not until now.'

She shook her head against the pillow, and carried on as if he'd never spoken. Her touch reached the fragile skin beneath his eyes, just as she had in his mother's library. 'I ignored this. I went back to my place each night *knowing* something was wrong.'

'You didn't do anything wrong,' he said. 'You *did* ask, but it wasn't the right time for me to say anything. No time was right.'

Her fingers fluttered away from his skin, and she twisted her hands awkwardly together in front of herself.

'I'm sorry,' she said.

He smiled, but she was too busy staring at her hands to notice. 'Don't be. I used to call you my distraction. I did feel when I was with you.'

In different ways. To start with it was very simple, very basic: lust. The thrill of the chase. His competitive nature to win the girl who rejected him.

But it was still heady, still an abrupt contrast to the beigeness of the rest of his days—and certainly the blackness of his nights.

And even her presence hadn't been enough to take him away from that.

But later, maybe even the first time she'd been in this room—when she'd been willing to do *anything* to get her job done, to get him to set—what he *felt* had shifted.

Oh, the lust was still there. There was something about Ruby, something about her smile, her laugh, her eyes…

But now there was more. Now there were moments of quiet that were the opposite of awkward. Times he looked at her and felt more connected to her than he could ever remember being with anyone. More comfortable but simultaneously completely off balance by his lack of familiarity with the emotions he felt around her.

'A distraction,' Ruby said, very, very softly.

Automatically he reached for her, but she moved, and his hand slid from her hip. 'In the very best possible way.'

Her lips curved into somewhat of a smile, and he knew he'd made a mistake.

'You're more than that, you're—'

But she cut him off.

'So what happens next?'

He needed a moment to refocus. 'With my depression?'

Her gaze flicked towards the ceiling. So she didn't like that word. He was the opposite—the label, in its own way, was powerful.

'The doctor gave me some pamphlets to read, and told me to have a think about it, and we'll meet again in a few weeks' time.'

'When *The Land* wraps.'

'Yeah,' he said.

'That sounds…'

'Anti-climactic?' Dev said, and she nodded. 'Kind of. We talked for a while, and even though I'd already decided to visit my mum, what he said just made it even more obvious. Depression is the symptom—I needed to resolve the cause.'

'And you think you have?'

Dev shifted his weight a little. 'Maybe. I hope so.'

Would he sleep tonight? He had no idea.

He expected Ruby to ask more questions, but she didn't. Instead they just lay there together, not touching.

More than anything he wanted to touch her, to pull her close against him again.

But if he did, she'd leave. He could as good as hear her excuses in his head.

It made no sense, none at all.

But Dev wanted her here, even at arm's length—so he didn't reach for her, and he didn't say a word.

And, eventually, he slept.

Ruby didn't sleep. She might've dozed, just a little, but mostly she just lay there, watching him.

Could it really be that easy? One visit to his mum, one battered leather notebook—and Dev was all better?

She didn't believe it.

Something had changed, though. A switch flipped, a corner turned…something like that. Not once tonight had she glimpsed a bleakness in Dev. No more little moments where he'd leave her, leave whatever they'd been doing, and retreat to wherever it was where his sadness, his regret, his guilt and his doubts lay. A weight had lifted.

She *was* happy for him. Thrilled. For him. Watching him sleep like this—*really* sleep, a true, natural sleep—was kind of wonderful.

No, just straight wonderful. Now she knew what she'd seen before, that drugged nothingness masquerading as restfulness—and the difference was undeniable.

What confused her was how *she* felt.

She felt restless, and she fidgeted as she attempted to sleep, her legs tangling in the quilt.

Finally she gave in to the compulsion to move, and climbed out of bed, walking on silent feet out of the room to avoid disturbing Dev. In the kitchen she automatically poured herself a glass of water, but she didn't drink it—just set it down on the granite bench top and walked away.

Her laptop sat on the dining-room table, from when she'd needed to make some changes to the script for Paul. She settled in front of it, flipping it open and blinking at the sudden brightness of the screen in the darkened room. She'd barely noticed the darkness, the moonlight flooding through the open kitchen blinds more than enough illumination for her to find her way.

She reopened an email that had arrived yesterday. A contact in London, who'd recommended her for a role. A great role, on a huge movie—big budget, already one confirmed big-name star.

She had to smile as she realised she was excited at the prospect of working with such a famous actress, given she had an even more famous star sleeping no more than ten metres from her right now.

Funny how quickly his job became irrelevant. At least—when they were together.

Other times, it seemed it was *all* he was. A movie star.

On set, or at Unit Base, that was who he was. Devlin Cooper, Hollywood star. Heartthrob. Sexiest man on earth. All those things.

But alone, particularly tonight, but at other times too—he was just Dev. Just a normal person. Far from perfect. The opposite of perfect, maybe.

That should be a good thing, right? That he was as normal as everybody else. As normal as her.

She sat back in her chair, stretching her legs out in front of her. It was cool, and her skin had goose pimpled where it wasn't covered by the oversized T-shirt she wore. She should really go back to bed.

She let her eyes blur, so she couldn't read the actual words of the email. But she knew them all, almost off by heart.

A request to send her CV. Such a simple thing. In this case, it was little more than going through the motions—if she wanted this job, it was hers.

And yet yesterday she hadn't sent it. Not today yet either.

Her eyes flicked to the time on the microwave. Well. Now it was tomorrow, and still she'd done nothing.

Pre-production began in three weeks, after *The Land* wrapped. The perfect amount of time to get herself sorted, maybe book herself into a hotel room for a week somewhere fun in Europe—France maybe, or Croatia—before she needed to get to London. She even knew where she'd stay—a tiny shoe-box of a room at a friend's place that she rented whenever work took her to London.

It was beyond easy. Exactly what she wanted.

She drew her legs up to her chest, wrapping her arms around herself, her chin propped where her knees touched. And just sat like that, thinking.

There was a noise, the sound of a tree branch scraping against the tin roof. It was loud in the silence, and her body jolted.

She was being ridiculous. What was she waiting for? For Dev?

Now *there* was a waste of time. He left in two weeks too, back to LA, a place where the unions could make it tricky for a foreigner to work—even if she was silly enough to daydream about things that would never happen. And that she didn't want to happen anyway.

She loved her life; it was perfect as it was. Dev just didn't fit. And as if Dev would want her to fit into his life either.

If that thought rang a little hollow she ignored it.

Instead, she leant forward in her chair, and made the few clicks necessary to reply to the email and attach her CV. Then another to press send.

She walked back to Dev's bedroom. He still slept, flat on his back now, his chest rising and falling steadily.

She'd wanted to leave, before. She wanted to leave, now.

She should, she knew.

Dev didn't need her. He had his life back on track—there was no more need for her. No more need for her to be his distraction.

Had she ever thought she was anything more?

*Yes.*

That was the problem. That was why she'd tried, and failed, to keep her distance.

But she wasn't about to disappear in the middle of the night. Tonight she'd sleep in his arms—just this once.

Because, she didn't really want to leave. That was the problem.

# CHAPTER THIRTEEN

THE FLASH OF blonde hair was unmistakeable.

Dev tripped, the toe of his boot catching in the uneven dirt, and he took a moment to steady himself.

'You right, mate?'

Dev nodded. A moment ago he'd been in the middle of a conversation with the young actor as they led their horses in readiness for their next scene. Now he had no idea what they'd been talking about.

He smiled. This was crazy.

He watched as Ruby flitted amongst the crew, as busy and efficient as always.

And, as always, not as much as one glance was thrown in his direction.

His smile dropped. Up until today it hadn't bothered him, her obsession with keeping their relationship private. Of course he understood.

But after last night, it just didn't sit right.

This wasn't just some fling; he knew it.

So what was it, then?

His horse shoved his head against Dev's side, rubbing his ears against his shoulder.

It yanked his attention back to what he should be doing—running through his lines.

Right now he needed to focus. Tonight, he'd talk to Ruby.

He ended up talking to her a lot earlier than that.

Dev opened his trailer door in response to angry hammering, and Ruby flew into the tiny space. She stalked straight past him, and then kept on pacing, not even catching his gaze.

'I thought we were past this?' she asked, agitation oozing from every pore.

He held up his hands in surrender. 'I have absolutely no idea what you're talking about.'

She spun about, getting right up close to him. He knew she was frustrated, but his reaction to her closeness, to the fire in her eyes, was obviously not what she'd intended.

She shoved one of his shoulders. 'This isn't funny!'

'I have no idea if it's funny or not,' he pointed out.

Ruby took a deep breath, then one big step back.

'The Australian Film Association Awards'? Does that ring a bell?'

He nodded. 'Sure. Paul spoke to me about them about an hour ago.'

'And?'

'I said I'd get back to him.'

She put her hands on her hips, and just stared at him—as if that explained everything.

Ruby sighed. 'Do I seriously need to remind you about your contract? You walking the red carpet at the awards is all about generating early buzz for *The Land*.'

She then muttered something about arrogant overpaid actors under her breath.

He reached out, wrapping his hand around Ruby's. 'I said I'd get back to him. And I will—once I speak to you.'

She blinked, then glanced down at their joined hands. 'What do I have to do with it?'

He squeezed her palm, but she didn't respond. Her gaze was now wary, and he watched as she shifted her weight from foot to foot.

He grinned. 'Normally I'd hope for more enthusiasm when I'm inviting a woman to a red-carpet event.'

Her eyes narrowed. 'Is that what you're doing?'

He nodded.

'Why?'

This wasn't the reaction he'd expected when he'd had the spur-of-the-moment idea. He'd forgotten all about the awards night, but once Paul mentioned it it seemed perfect.

'Because I want you to come with me.' Then, he added, before she could say what he knew was on the tip of her tongue, 'I *want* people to know we're together.'

She tugged on his hand. Hard. He let her go, but he didn't understand why she was doing this. *He* wanted to wrap his arms around her, to kiss her. To tell her how amazing it was to realise what he had right in front of him—what he had with *her*.

But she didn't want to hear it.

Ruby wrapped her arms around herself, rubbing her fingers up and down the woollen fabric of her oversized cardigan.

'What if I don't?'

'Why wouldn't you?' he asked, slowly. Confused.

She rolled her eyes. 'I don't know, maybe because I don't want people to know about…' she threw her hands out in front of her, vaguely encompassing them both '…whatever this is.'

'What do you think this is?'

She shrugged. 'Something fun. Temporary. *Private.*'

He shook his head. 'How can you believe that? I've spent more time with you in the past few weeks than I've spent with another woman *ever.*'

He ignored yet another eye roll, his blood starting to simmer in anger. Why was she doing this? Why would she deny what they had?

'I've told you more than I've told anyone. I've revealed more of myself to you—*given* more of myself to you—than I thought I was capable of.'

More than Estelle—or anyone—had thought him capable of.

She was staring out of the window, through a tiny crack in the curtains.

'You've gone through a tough time,' she said, as if she was choosing her words carefully. 'I was just the girl who happened to be here. The distraction.'

'That's just a *word*,' he said. 'It's meaningless, and it isn't true when it comes to you—not any more. Not since that morning you came into my room prepared to bodily drag me onto set.'

She wasn't listening. 'When you go through really emotional events, it's natural to attach yourself to someone—'

'You're just making this up as you go along,' he said. 'You don't know what you're talking about.'

She crossed the trailer, putting more space between them. 'No,' she said, 'I think I do. This was never supposed to be anything serious. And it isn't.'

'Is that the issue, Ruby? *You* don't want serious, so you're ignoring what's happening right in front of you? I didn't think I wanted it either, but I can't pretend this isn't happening. I won't.'

Ruby just shook her head, still avoiding his gaze.

'You told me on the beach the other week that you learnt you didn't need anyone, years ago. I get that. I definitely get that. But I'm not like the men from your past. I won't let you down.'

Now she turned to him, her gaze suddenly sad. 'How, exactly, will you manage that?'

'To not let you down?' he repeated.

She give a sharp nod. 'Yes. What exactly have you planned for us beyond this film, and beyond this awards night?'

He was silent. Honestly, he hadn't thought beyond that. He just knew he wanted Ruby.

She smiled, very slowly. Dangerously. 'Let me guess—we'd go back to Beverly Hills.'

'I guess—' he began. It made sense, he supposed.

'And I would work where?'

He knew this wasn't leading anywhere good, but found himself helpless to change the direction of the conversation. 'I don't know. I live in Hollywood. So—'

'So that's where I'd work.'

He ran a hand through his hair. 'Damn it, Ruby—I was just inviting you to the AFAs. That's it. We don't need to plan out every second of our future together.'

'That wasn't what I was asking you to do,' Ruby said. 'Not at all.'

She walked towards him—past him—to the trailer door.

He couldn't let her leave, not like this, and in two strides he was in front of her, blocking her exit.

'Ruby, I'm new to this, too. I don't know what I'm doing.' He managed a dry laugh. 'Obviously. But—I just know that things feel *right* with you. Different right, special right. I haven't felt this good in for ever. And don't you dare attribute that to my dad.' She snapped her mouth shut. 'I can't describe it, Ruby, but I'm not ready to let it go. I can't let you walk away from this.'

She caught his gaze, her eyes a richer brown than he'd ever seen them. 'Try and describe it,' she said, so softly he leant closer to catch the words.

'Describe it?' he repeated, then, gradually—he understood what she was asking.

'Yeah,' she said. 'Describe what we have, what it is that you expect me to give up so much for—my privacy, my independence, the career I love, a lifestyle that suits me perfectly.'

*Love.*

That was what she was asking. Was this love?

His mind raced, whipping about in circles but coming to no meaningful conclusion. It was a word he rarely used, that he'd never said to anyone but a blood relative.

Was it even possible to love someone after so little time?

Little vignettes of their time together mish-mashed in his brain. At the beach, in bed, alone together on set, talking, laughing, loving.

He cleared his throat. 'I never said I wanted you to give up anything for me.'

She twisted the door handle, and it clicked open loudly in the heavy silence.

Then, without a word, she left.

And Dev was powerless to say the words that might bring her back.

* * *

Ruby walked briskly back to the production office, deftly handling the standard peppering of questions and minor dramas that always accompanied her progress across Unit Base.

She sounded totally normal. Totally like herself.

And why wouldn't she?

She'd known they'd reached the end of their thing. Their fling.

*Fling.* Yeah, that was the perfect word. Disposable.

*Love.*

Ruby dug her fingernails into her palms as she jogged up the steps to her office.

No, it wasn't love.

But still, it was the word she'd been waiting for him to say.

How silly, how delusional.

Besides, she should be angry with him. Angry with him for not understanding how far she'd come, and how important—how *essential*—her independence was to her. She could never give up her career, or her nomadic lifestyle. Not for anything, and certainly not for anyone.

At the doorway to her office she paused. Inside, her team were working busily away. They didn't even look up, all so used to the frantic comings and goings of the office.

Everything was just as she'd left it. As if Paul had never called her into his office, as if she'd never stormed over to Dev's trailer, and as if she'd never so vehemently refused his invitation.

And yet everything had changed. Right in the middle of all that, right in the middle of doing what she knew she'd had to do, what she'd known had been inevitable, she'd paused. For that one moment she'd reconsidered, she'd tossed everything up in the air that she'd worked so hard for, waiting on bated breath for Dev to say the words that would...

What?

Mean that she and Dev would live happily ever after?

No way. Ruby had long ago thrown away her dreams of a knight in shining armour, of the one man that would wake up

in the morning and still want her—and then again the next day
and for ever.

Love was for fools, for the foolish girl she'd once been.

It wasn't for her.

Dev brought the hire car to a stop in the familiar driveway.

There weren't nearly as many cars as his mum's birthday
party, but there were enough to let him know he was the last to
arrive. Typical—his older brothers were *always* early.

The front door was unlocked, so he followed the buzz of conversation and squeals of children to the back of the house. In
the kitchen both his brothers stood at the granite bench, beers
in hand, talking to his mum as she busily chopped something.
Beside Brad stood a woman he didn't recognise—a girlfriend
perhaps. Outside was Jared's wife who he *did* recognise from
the wedding photos his mum had emailed him years ago. Two
children raced across the paving on tricycles, shrieking with
exuberant laughter that made him smile. But the smile fell as
the adults' conversations stalled—his presence had undeniably been noted.

He strode with determined confidence to his mum and kissed
her on the cheek.

Once again she looked thrilled at his appearance, as if she'd
expected a no-show, or a last-minute cancellation.

Neither of which were unprecedented.

He was ashamed of his behaviour. The worst had been most
recently—skipping the funeral, avoiding her calls. He'd been
incapable of processing his own emotions, telling himself he'd
be no use to his mum, that he'd just cause more tension, more
trouble, more hassle. That his dad wouldn't have wanted him
around, anyway.

Which was all total rubbish, of course.

But well before that—the decade before that—he'd neglected
his mum. His visits home to Australia were limited, and always
due to work, never specifically to see her. Now he suspected
it was because he'd wanted to completely box away and forget

his family, a family he considered unsupportive and just completely different and disassociated from him. In his family he had always felt like a square peg in a round hole.

Not that he'd done anything at all to test that theory since he was nineteen.

Or at least, not until now.

A Sunday afternoon barbecue—a simple thing, and, he hoped, a step in the right direction.

His brothers were not exactly effusive in their hellos, but they were cordial enough. Samantha, Jared's wife, and Tracey, Brad's girlfriend, were much more welcoming—if not a little star-struck, despite doing their best to hide it. It made him smile. In this kitchen, where he'd been forced to eat his vegetables and load the dishwasher, he didn't feel even the slightest bit like a movie star.

They ate lunch outside, the table piled high with barbecued everything—prawn skewers, sausages, steak, fish. Dev didn't say much, allowing the conversation to happen around him.

'I heard you're filming in New South Wales,' Samantha asked, catching his eye from across the table. Beside her, Jared eyed Dev warily.

He nodded. 'Yeah, a romantic drama, something a bit different for me.' Dev then spent a few minutes describing Lucyville, some of his co-stars, and making generic comments about how much he was enjoying working again in Australia—which, he realised as he said it, was actually true.

Beside Sam, Jared slowly relaxed before Dev's eyes.

What had Jared honestly expected him to do? Say something inappropriate? Grunt a response? Throw food across the table?

He realised he'd tensed his jaw, and that his back had become stiff and unyielding.

As Sam chatted away, asking questions about the film industry and about LA, Dev forced himself to relax.

He couldn't get angry with Jared. Or Brad.

They were just protecting his mum, and had absolutely no

reason to believe that today was the start of something new. That he wouldn't let her down—let them all down—again.

If this was a movie, the script would probably call for him to dramatically jump to his feet—to declare his grief for the loss of his father and for the loss of more than a decade of time with his family. For never meeting his niece and nephew before today. He'd use words and phrases like *a tragedy* and *regret* and *I can only hope you can forgive me* and that type of thing, and then all *would* be forgiven, and the camera would pan back, and they'd all be one big happy family. The End.

But life didn't work like that, at least not in the Cooper household.

Today was not the day for dramatic declarations, and it was not the day to expect a magic wand to be waved and for everything to be okay.

It was, and remained, simply a step in the right direction.

He needed to earn a conversation without tense undertones. And he intended to.

Ruby was the first person to tell him he was being stupid to wish the family he had away. The words had resonated more than he'd realised—when he'd been unable to sleep, when the words had been piled on top of all the other snatches of memory and guilt that filled his subconscious to the brim. Even now they still resonated, even when sleep came—mostly—much more easily.

*That was a very stupid thing to say.*

So to the point, so straightforward. So Ruby.

It was why he was here. She was why he was here.

'How is Ruby?' his mum asked from the head of the table, reading his mind.

'The blonde from Mum's party?' asked Brad, and Ros nodded.

'I liked her,' she said.

'Me, too,' Dev said, without thinking. Then he cleared his throat. 'She's well, I think. I don't really know—we're just colleagues. She's the Production Co-ordinator.'

As of three days ago, it was all true, but still the words felt just like a lie.

Three days since whatever had happened in his trailer. Even now he wasn't sure what had really taken place—or what he could've done to ensure a different ending. Sometimes he was angry at her, and frustrated at the crazy assumptions she'd leapt to; how unfair it had been of her to put words into his mouth, to assume the worst of him—and to fast-forward their relationship to a point where they needed to consider anything beyond the next night, or next week.

But other times he was furious with himself. Furious for letting her walk away, for not running across Unit Base—screw what anyone thought—and saying whatever he needed to say to get her to stay. Furious for not considering how she'd react, not considering what a public relationship with him might mean to her—a woman still scarred by the gossipmongering of her past. Of course she didn't want to open her life up to the world for a fleeting fling.

But would she do it for something more?

Because what they had couldn't be on her terms any more—no more secrets, no more end dates.

And she hadn't wanted to hear that, hadn't wanted to consider it.

Until *love* had come into it. Out of nowhere. And love just wasn't something he was familiar with. That he knew how to do.

The conversations around him had moved on, but he barely heard a word.

*Had* it been out of nowhere? *Had* it been so shocking, so unexpected?

Yes, he'd told himself.

But now—it was a no. An honest, raw, no.

Everything he'd told her in that trailer, about what he'd shared with her, what he'd revealed—that came from a place of trust, of intimacy, of connection.

A place he'd never gone before—that he hadn't been capable of going to before.

A place of *love*.

In his mother's back yard he was surrounded by his family, and he was here because of love. Love he'd tossed away, not appreciated, and now was hoping to win back, slowly and with absolutely no assumptions. It was going to take time.

And he was doing this because in his darkest moments, when the darkness had sucked the world away from him so that he was left isolated and so, so alone, *love* was what he had craved. Love from his father, but also from his family. Love and respect were all that he'd ever wanted.

In his rejection of his father, he'd tossed away a family who loved him. And they must love him, to allow him to sit here after so long.

He'd let himself believe he'd failed his father, and his family, with his chosen career.

But he'd been wrong.

His failure was in being as stubborn as his dad. For closing himself off from the possibility of love—from his family, or from anyone. He'd rejected love, because he'd been too scared to risk it—to risk failing in the eyes of someone he loved again.

Now he wanted love back in his life, regardless of the risks.

He'd wasted a huge chunk of life alone, even if he had been surrounded by people and the glitz and glamour of his career.

But enough was enough.

He wasn't letting Ruby go without a fight.

# CHAPTER FOURTEEN

RUBY PADDED TO her front door in bright pink fuzzy bed socks and floral printed pyjamas, a mug of instant noodles warming her hands.

It wasn't late, not even nine p.m., but it had been a long day and the lure of her couch had been far stronger than that of the pub and the rest of the crew.

Whoever was at the door knocked again as she opened the door just a crack, and the insistent pressure pushed the door to the limits of the short security chain.

'Settle down!' she said, 'I'm here.'

'You're not really in a position to complain, you know.' The all too familiar deep voice froze Ruby to the spot. 'I've learnt my door-knocking technique from you. Loud and...demanding.'

She ignored that.

'Why are you here?' she said, trying to sound calm. She considered, and dismissed, pretending to assume this was work-related. Or simply closing the door and walking away.

Option two had the most merit, but...well...

It was Dev. He just didn't do good things to the logical, sensible, decision-making part of her brain.

'We need to talk,' he said.

He'd stepped up right close to her door, so he could peer through the opening at Ruby. A dim globe above the door shone weak light over him, throwing his face into angular sections of darkness and light.

He met her gaze, and his was...too hard to make out.

She told herself that was why she mechanically reached upwards to close the door temporarily to unhook the chain, and then to swing it wide open and gesture him inside.

He paused for a moment, as if gathering his thoughts or taking a deep breath, and then strode into her tiny living area. He stared at her couch and its piles of blankets and magazines, and the small collection of DVDs she'd hired from the motel's surprisingly extensive supply.

Ruby swallowed her automatic apology and the compulsion to fuss and tidy. He'd just turned up uninvited—he could stand.

'So?' she asked, crossing her arms across her chest. 'Talk.'

If he was ruffled by her abruptness he revealed none of it.

'You don't have to live in Beverly Hills,' he said. 'Or work in Hollywood. I wouldn't expect you to.'

Ruby walked back to the door. 'I think you should go.'

He raised an eyebrow. 'Why did you let me in? What else did you think I was here to talk about? The film?' He laughed. 'No. You knew this was about us.'

She shook her head, but he didn't move. He just looked at her.

Now she could interpret his gaze. It was…just Dev. Honest, with not a shred of the actor's artifice that had fallen away as their time together had lengthened.

But right now, she didn't want to deal with that. She wanted to deal with the arrogant actor she'd originally thought him to be, the man who always got his way, who manipulated people—manipulated her—to get what he wanted.

As hard as she tried, she couldn't now believe any of that was true.

She didn't know what to say, but she did walk away from the door. She remained standing, more than an arm's length away from Dev, too far away to touch.

'Ruby?'

She picked a spot on the wall to stare at—a crack in the plaster beyond Dev's shoulder. 'There is no us,' she pointed out.

'There could be,' he said. 'I want there to be.'

'I don't do relationships,' she said.

'Neither do I—don't you remember?'

That night out on the main street, under the street lamp.

'We'd need to figure out the details—find a way for our careers to work together—but they can. I don't care where I live, and I don't need to cram a million films into each year.'

Ruby sniffed dismissively. 'So you'll just hang around whatever place I end up, waiting for me to come home each day from work? Right.'

He shrugged. 'Why not? I could do with a break. I've been filming back to back my whole career. And who knows? I've always been interested in production. Maybe I could look into funding a few projects, having a go at being an executive producer or something.'

Ruby tried hard to hate him for having enough money to have these choices. But couldn't.

Besides, logistics weren't the real issue. Not at all.

'No,' she said. 'This isn't what I want.'

Now she met his gaze, so he knew she wasn't talking about career decisions.

'Isn't it?' he said. He took a few steps forward. Now touching would be really easy—all she had to do was...

She curled her nails into her palms, hoping the tiny bite of pain would bring her back to her senses.

'No. I like my life. I'm happy just as I am.'

His lips quirked, and the small movement shocked her. 'Now you're just being stubborn.'

Her eyes narrowed. 'I am not. I—'

Then he was closer, really close. Still not touching, but crowding her, as he had the day they'd met.

This wasn't fair. He *knew* what he did to her, how his nearness loosened her hold on lucidity.

She felt herself faltering, felt herself tilt her chin upwards, her fingers itch to reach out and touch him, regardless of the contradictory indignation that rushed through her veins.

*No.* She couldn't let this happen—she couldn't let her hormones have so much control over her. She was right. She'd

made the right decision to walk away. This could never end
well; this was all wrong; she didn't need this; she didn't need
Dev; she didn't…

'Love.'

The single world stopped the tumult in her brain. It stopped
everything, actually. Ruby's whole world went perfectly still.

Automatically she opened her mouth. To what? Question?
Deny?

But Dev was too quick for her.

'I figured it out today,' he said, really softly. 'That you were
right. That is the word to describe this, to describe us. *Love*.'

'I never mentioned love. I don't do love.'

She sounded just as stubborn as Dev had accused her of
being. She squeezed her eyes shut, trying to regroup.

She didn't know how to deal with this. How to deal with
any of this.

She was tempted to repeat what she'd said before, something
about the stress that Dev had experienced, about his depression,
about how it was natural for him to read more into his feelings
for her at such a vulnerable time.

But she couldn't say that. Firstly because she didn't believe
any of it, but secondly because that neat little explanation didn't
explain *her*.

It didn't explain why she'd so haphazardly and unwisely spoken in his trailer. Words she hadn't planned and a concept she
didn't even know she was capable of considering.

It also didn't explain the rest. Sharing her past with Dev—
not just the version she rolled out to everyone just to get it over
with: her foster child upbringing, a hint of her rebellious past.
But the real stuff—the stuff that mattered. The stuff that had
hurt, that had changed everything—and continued to hurt.

And it didn't explain why, despite her fear of what was happening with Dev and her ingrained habit of distancing herself
from men, she hadn't run away from him. Not when it counted.

So did that mean she loved him? That she was in love
with Dev?

Ruby opened her eyes, incredibly slowly. She looked up at Dev, catching his gaze and holding on tight.

Did he love her? The way he was looking at her right now, it was tempting to believe it.

To imagine that finally it was actually real.

That he was her fairy-tale prince, about to carry her away into the sunset.

Away from her life as she knew it.

To her happy ever after.

*That was a fantasy.*

Ruby took a deep breath, and straightened her shoulders.

With great difficulty she took a step backwards, the action suddenly the hardest thing she'd ever done.

'I don't do love,' she repeated. 'This isn't love.'

Eventually, he nodded. A sharp movement.

The next thing she knew he was gone, and she was standing alone in her tiny apartment. So she walked to her kitchen, and turned on her kettle. Then, with fingers that shook only slightly, she found a new mug, and tore open a packet of noodles.

And the night continued on exactly as she'd planned.

It had to.

*The Riva, Split, Croatia—two weeks later*

Ruby strolled across the wide, smooth tiles that paved Split's Riva, a line of towering palm trees to her right, the Adriatic Sea to her left.

Beside her was—*Tom?* Maybe. Some guy who'd been on the walking tour of Diocletian's Palace that she'd just completed. She'd paid little attention to the tour, to be honest, and hadn't even noticed the tall, blond thirty-something guy who now walked beside her.

Accepting his invitation for an ice cream and a walk had been a reflex action. She needed to move on—needed a *distraction,* she supposed. The occasional times she did date, it was always somewhere like this—somewhere exotic and amazing where everything was light and, importantly, temporary. No hopes, no expectations.

She hadn't touched her ice cream, and it had begun to run in rivulets down the waffle cone as it melted, trickling stickily onto her hand.

The breeze whipped off the ocean, and she shivered despite the warm autumn sun.

Tom was talking about what he did back in Canada.

'I'm sorry,' she said, cutting him off mid-sentence. 'I shouldn't have accepted your invitation. I'm…' What? Getting over a break up? That didn't sound right in her head. Too…trivial. So she just finished lamely: '…not interested.'

*Ouch.* Quite rightly, Tom was less than impressed. He plucked her cone from her fingers, and dumped it, along with his, in a bin, before walking away.

Ruby felt a little bad, but mostly relieved. Not her proudest moment, but she just couldn't pretend any more.

This little side trip to Split for a week before pre-production began in London was *not* exactly what she needed. It was *not* the perfect distraction.

It was not helping her relax and gain some perspective and just, well…get over it.

Get over Dev.

She'd been standing looking at nothing out at the ocean, so now she turned away, heading for the small apartment she was staying in, on the second floor of a local family's stone cottage, right at the end of the Riva.

Maybe she should move her flight forward. Choosing to be alone was obviously her mistake. Surely her friend Carly wouldn't mind if she moved in a few days early? And she was fabulous at entertaining her guests. A few nights out with her and then Dev and *The Land* would all be a distant memory…

Right. Kind of like how she'd told herself that working for Dev for another week wouldn't be so bad, even though she'd then spent every hour of her work day preventing herself from throwing herself at him and babbling something ridiculous about having made a terrible mistake…

It had been most frustrating. She had done the right thing. For her.

She didn't need Dev. She'd been absolutely happy before she'd met him. She didn't need Dev to make her life complete, to give her anything in life she wasn't perfectly capable of achieving herself. Her life was full and lovely and gorgeous—and she didn't need a partner, and certainly not a husband, to finish it off.

And she'd hate herself if she ever let herself believe differently.

It wasn't peak tourist season in Croatia, and so around her people dotted the Riva, rather than cramming it full. Some were obviously tourists—couples holding hands, families with small crowds of children. Others not so much. An older couple walking in companionable silence, a group of women chatting enthusiastically away.

*I wish Dev were here.*

The thought came out of the blue, and Ruby walked faster, as if to escape her traitorous subconscious.

The thing was, now wasn't the first time she'd wished such a thing.

Like on the plane to Heathrow, where one of the movies was so awful she'd turned in her seat to list all its flaws before realising that it was a stranger snoring softly beside her, and not Dev.

Or waking up in her gorgeous little Split apartment, the sun flooding through gossamer curtains onto her bed, and she'd turned and reached out for familiar, strong, warm, male skin.

But all she'd touched was emptiness.

She really needed to get over this.

She'd never spent every night with a guy like that—never in her whole life. That had been her mistake. She'd got too used to him, and now he was like a habit. A bad habit.

That theory didn't even begin to convince her.

Ruby undid the latch of the wrought-iron gate that opened to the series of stone steps leading to her apartment.

As she unearthed her keys from her handbag she remembered her sticky ice-creamy fingers, tacky against the smooth metal.

*What a waste of a perfectly delicious ice cream.*

The random thought made her smile, but she noticed that something was blurring her vision.

Not tears, at least, not proper ones. These stayed contained within her lashes. Mostly.

In the bathroom she washed away the remnants of vanilla and caramel, and made the mistake of meeting her own gaze.

She looked pale, and blotchy—but mostly just miserable.

Like a woman who'd just walked away from the love of her life.

And who had absolutely no idea what to do next.

The sleek, low-slung car slid to a stop at the end of the long red carpet.

It was still daylight—late afternoon actually. Dev bit back a sigh—these awards nights started early and went notoriously late. He could think of another billion or so places he'd rather be right now.

Outside, temporary metal fencing kept rows of fans a good distance away, but he could already hear them calling his name. Other cars arrived around him, and women in dresses every colour of the rainbow emerged into the sunlight in front of the glamorous, sprawling Darling Harbour hotel. Their partners in monotonous black provided little more than a neutral backdrop.

Dev watched as each couple walked only a few metres before television cameras and shiny presenters swooped. Dev knew the drill; he'd been here—or at events just like this one—a thousand times. He knew this stuff, knew the name of the designer of his suit, exactly the right thing to say and how to smile enthusiastically for every single fan's photo.

He could do this.

Graeme twisted in his driver's seat to look over his shoulder at Dev. Graeme, Dev had decided, was his new Sydney driver. He was a good guy—and he still hadn't breathed a word of his and Ruby's relationship. In this industry, such loyalty was very nearly unprecedented.

'Ready?' he asked.

Dev shook his head, but Graeme was already climbing out of his seat. 'I'll just be a minute,' he said. Not that another minute would make him look forward to the next handful of hours any more.

Besides, he was perfectly capable of opening his own door.

But—it was too late, and he straightened his shoulders, and brushed imaginary lint off his extremely sharp designer suit.

He could do this, he repeated, looking towards the red carpet, and the many ascending steps it richly covered.

Then the other door opened—the door across from him, facing the street—and he twisted around, surprised.

'Graeme, you may need a bit more practise opening—' he began, but the words stuck in his throat as a woman slid onto the leather seat beside him, and Graeme shut the door firmly behind her.

Ruby.

'Hi,' she said, very softly.

She wore a long dress in red—a deeper red than the carpet—a red that matched her name. It flowed over her body, slinky in all the right places, and with a V neckline that was…remarkable.

Her blonde hair was perfectly sleek, her make-up immaculate, her lips—of course—ruby red. It was Hollywood glamour—red-carpet glamour.

'Hi,' he managed, although it took quite a bit of concentration.

Her lips curved into a smile, but it was only fleeting. She caught his gaze with hers, and didn't look away.

Her gaze might have been rock steady, but uncertainty was obvious in her chocolate eyes, in her shallow breathing, and her fingers that twisted themselves in the delicate fabric of her dress.

'I thought that if I was with you, that if I *needed* you…' she took a deep breath '…that I would lose myself.'

He nodded, knowing now was not the time to speak.

'I used to confuse sex with intimacy, and I've worked really hard not to make that mistake again. And I haven't. But now I've made a different one—I've confused intimacy with just sex. A fling. It's taken me a few weeks to figure that one out.'

He could see the depth of emotion in her eyes, and he desperately wanted to move closer—to reach out—to touch her. But he didn't move. He needed to let her finish.

'I tried to ignore it, even when it was happening. I tried to pretend that I didn't care, that I didn't worry about you more than I can remember worrying about anyone—ever. I kept a distance between us, I closed my eyes and pretended you weren't hurting, because then I wouldn't need to admit that I hurt, too. For you.'

And for herself, too.

'I'm not familiar with love, you know?' Now she looked away, but only for a moment. 'I don't know how to recognise it—how to filter it out from my ancient habits—to distinguish it from misguided infatuation or fantastical daydreams. But when I wasn't with you, when I walked away from you—that didn't make it easier. What I felt didn't go away, not even a little bit. What I was feeling for you ruined *everything*.'

But she was smiling, and he realised he was smiling, too.

'I don't want this, you know?' She nodded out of the door, towards the hordes of people and the observant cameramen who were trying to peer through the black tinted windows. 'But I didn't want this even without the movie-star thing. Even if you worked in Props, or wrote scripts, or didn't even work in film at all.'

'Me either,' he said. 'I thought I was good at going it alone. That I had it all sorted, the best way to live my life.'

'Me too!' she agreed, and laughed briefly. 'And it's risky changing direction.'

'What if I decide this way is better? Then what happens if it doesn't work out?'

Ruby nodded, her eyes widening in surprise. 'Exactly. It's scary.'

Dev shrugged. 'I decided it was worth the risk.'

And it was. Even when she'd said no, it had still been worth it. Even though it had sucked. Really, really sucked.

His life wasn't going to be about regrets any longer. Except—even then, when he'd laid his heart on the line—he hadn't been entirely an open book. He'd still withheld one thing.

'I love you, Ruby Bell.'

Quick as a flash, she replied, 'I love you too, Devlin Cooper.'

Then for long moments they smiled huge, idiotic grins at each other.

Over her shoulder a camera flash momentarily stole his attention, bringing him abruptly back to reality—to *his* reality.

'What about the paparazzi, Ruby? The gossip and the rumours? With me, it's as good as guaranteed.'

She shocked him when she shrugged. 'I used to think that I had to prove something to the gossips—prove them right or prove them wrong. But you know what? I don't care any more. You arrived on set amidst a storm of rumours, and you didn't change one thing—you didn't react, you didn't engage, you didn't deny. You were just you.' She paused, then reached out to grip his hand. 'People can say whatever they like about me, or you, or us—but I know the truth. We do. And I've decided that's all that matters. I'm in control of my life, no one else.'

She was amazing. If he hadn't fallen long ago, just that would've pushed him over the edge.

'Do you want to walk the red carpet with me, Ruby?'

She nodded, and amongst a sea of camera flashes he opened his door, and stepped out, only to turn and offer her his hand.

She slid across the seats, and swung her gold stiletto heels onto the red carpet. He bent closer to whisper in her ear.

'This is serious, you know that? For ever stuff. Happy every after, like in the movies.'

'No,' she said, so firmly he went still. He caught her gaze as she looked up at him from the car's leather interior. 'Not like in the movies,' she said, 'and not like in fairy tales.'

Finally she reached out to take his hand, letting him pull her to her feet.

They stood together, side by side, the red carpet before them, fans screaming, cameras as good as shoved in their faces. But all he was aware of was Ruby, of her hand in his, and the look in her eyes as she looked up at him. With love, and with everything she had to give.

He knew he was looking at her in exactly the same way.

'This is real life,' she said.

* * * * *

# MILLS & BOON®
# By Request

**RELIVE THE ROMANCE WITH THE BEST OF THE BEST**

## A sneak peek at next month's titles...

In stores from 15th June 2017:

- **Powerful & Proud** – Kate Hewitt

- **A Night in His Arms** – Annie West, Cat Schield & Kate Carlisle

In stores from 29th June 2017:

- **Bound by Passion** – Cara Summers, Katherine Garbera & Kate Carlisle

- **Single Mum Seeking...** – Raye Morgan & Teresa Hill

*Just can't wait?*
Buy our books online before they hit the shops!
**www.millsandboon.co.uk**

**Also available as eBooks.**

0617/05

# Join Britain's BIGGEST Romance Book Club

**2 in 1** GREAT VALUE

**50% OFF** your first parcel

MARINELLI
...nt Conquest

- **EXCLUSIVE offers every month**
- **FREE delivery direct to your door**
- **NEVER MISS a title**
- **EARN Bonus Book points**

Call Customer Services
**0844 844 1358***

or visit
**millsandboon.co.uk/subscriptions**

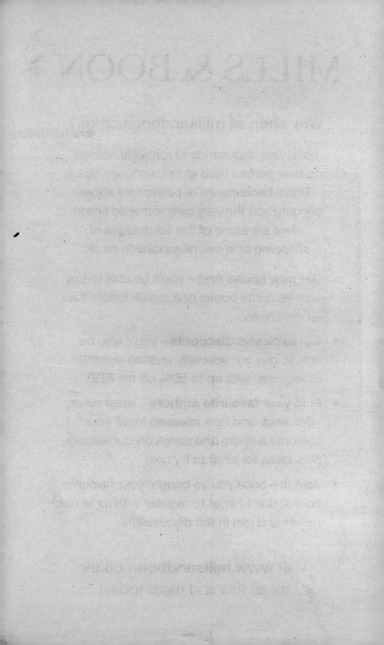